BLAME THE DEAD

FORGE BOOKS BY ED RUGGERO

Blame the Dead

OTHER TITLES BY ED RUGGERO

Nonfiction

Duty First: A Year in the Life of West Point and the Making of American Leaders

Combat Jump: The Young Men Who Led the Assault into Fortress Europe, July 1943

The First Men In: U.S. Paratroopers and the Fight to Save D-Day

Army Leadership (with the Center for Army Leadership)

The Leader's Compass (with Dennis F. Haley)

The Corporate Compass (with Dennis F. Haley)

Fiction

38 North Yankee

The Common Defense

Firefall

Breaking Ranks

The Academy

BLAME THE DEAD

ED RUGGERO

FORGE

A TOM DOHERTY ASSOCIATES BOOK

NEW YORK

This is a work of fiction. All of the characters, organizations, and events portrayed in this novel are either products of the author's imagination or are used fictitiously.

BLAME THE DEAD

A Forge Book
Published by Tom Doherty Associates
120 Broadway
New York, NY 10271

www.tor-forge.com

Forge® is a registered trademark of Macmillan Publishing Group, LLC.

The Library of Congress Cataloging-in-Publication Data is available upon request.

ISBN 978-1-250-31274-7 (hardcover)
ISBN 978-1-250-31273-0 (ebook)

Our books may be purchased in bulk for promotional, educational, or business use. Please contact your local bookseller or the Macmillan Corporate and Premium Sales Department at 1-800-221-7945, extension 5442, or by email at MacmillanSpecialMarkets@macmillan.com.

First Edition: March 2020

Printed in the United States of America

0 9 8 7 6 5 4 3 2 1

To Domenick & Bob

"He ain't heavy . . ."

What like a bullet can undeceive!

—Herman Melville,
"Shiloh"

BLAME THE DEAD

1

2 August 1943
Near Palermo, Sicily
0600 hours

"We got a waver," Lieutenant Eddie Harkins said when he spotted the GI up ahead. A soldier was flagging them with both arms, right near a dirt-road turnoff marked with a hand-lettered sign saying 11TH FIELD HOSP.

"Two hands. Must be more than one bedpan missing."

Harkins directed these comments at his driver, Bobby Ray Thomas, who sat shivering in the passenger seat of their jeep. Malaria. Sweating and shaky, too sick to drive but not wanting to let Harkins down. Harkins had been behind the wheel all night and now, just after dawn and coming off twenty-four hours straight duty, he and Thomas were exhausted bone deep.

Since the invasion began on July 10, over a hundred thousand GIs and British Tommies had poured ashore, engulfing first the southern and then the western end of the island, overwhelming the roads until nothing could move, drinking the wells dry, looting stores of wine, driving up prices of everything from whores to fresh food, leaving the detritus of battle covering the sun-scorched landscape. Every roadside was littered with discarded ration cans and cigarette packs, fire-blackened German and Italian war equipment, bloody bandages, used condoms, splintered furniture, filthy clothing, dead burros, and the occasional unburied enemy soldier, bloated and black and stripped of his shoes.

"We've turned this place into a shithole," Harkins said to Thomas that morning, when first light revealed that they'd parked in a field alongside a dozen dead cows.

"We liberated them from the Germans," Thomas had offered, mock-serious. "And from the Fascists."

"I bet they're overcome with gratitude," Harkins countered. He got his red hair and light blue eyes from his mother, but he'd inherited from his father a mistrust of all landlords and liberators.

For the past six days, Harkins and his platoon of twenty-five military police soldiers, riding in eight jeeps, had been shepherding columns of American war machines—tanks, trucks and wreckers, jeeps and trailers hauling bulldozers, ambulances and big Dodge staff cars, all of it crammed onto the patchwork of dirt trails that passed for roads in western Sicily, all of it headed to Palermo, where Harkins had promised his men a dip in the sea. In the meantime, everyone was struck dumb by the heat.

Harkins' neck was sunburned, raw. There were salt stains on his trousers where the sweat had dried repeatedly; his socks were damp as dishrags inside his GI shoes.

Thomas opened his eyes; his voice was cracked and just loud enough to be heard over the jeep engine.

"We should have invaded Ireland," he said. "I read it's always green and cool there."

"You should write to General Eisenhower," Harkins said.

Thomas dreamed of someplace cool. Harkins, who'd been running on little sleep for what seemed like months, craved rest. Now it looked like they'd be sidetracked; Harkins hoped it wouldn't be for long.

The soldier up ahead had spotted the military police brassards they wore, big armbands with "MP" in white letters. This happened more than Harkins would have expected—GIs coming to them—but it was usually for help with some small, impossible-to-solve crime: someone took my pocketknife, somebody stole my poker winnings, some jackass pissed on my bedroll.

Harkins let the jeep roll to a stop. "Big crime spree here?"

The soldier, whose helmet had the red cross on white circle of a medic, saluted then jumped into the back. He looked shaken, a little bug-eyed.

"Glad you guys were driving by," the medic said. "Straight ahead. You'll see everybody. Look for First Sergeant Drake."

The dirt track into the hospital compound was lined with dozens of U.S. Army tents of various sizes, all of them sun-blasted and coated with dust. Harkins had seen medical units positioned throughout the battle zone, chains of care starting with small aid stations just behind the front. There, medics and perhaps a single doctor treated minor wounds and injuries and, for more serious cases, stabilized a wounded soldier for evacuation to the rear.

Here—Harkins estimated they were some twenty-five to thirty miles behind the front—field hospitals did major surgery. Soldiers who required long-term care were moved to more permanent station hospitals even farther from the fighting. A GI in Harkins' platoon, a Californian named Maretsky, talked endlessly about the "million-dollar wound," one that didn't hurt too much and wouldn't mean permanent disability, but was serious enough to warrant evacuation all the way back along the chain to some cushy stateside hospital, with "fresh orange juice and fresher nurses."

A hundred yards along, Harkins found a small crowd of fifteen or twenty soldiers standing in the wide alley between two large tents. Some of them had their heads pressed together, whispering. A few stood with arms folded, looking worried. The crowd parted a bit and Harkins saw the body, felt the adrenaline jolt he knew from his days as a street cop in Philadelphia. Beside the corpse was a big man wearing the stripes of a first sergeant and a slouch campaign hat that was twenty years old if it was a day. He looked at Harkins, checked the MP brassard, and tipped his chin down in silent greeting.

The dead man lay on his stomach in the dust, left leg straight behind, right leg cocked, arms shoulder high and bent at ninety degrees, like he was demonstrating how to crawl beneath barbed wire. His helmet was a few feet away; his hair on the right side was dark and curly. The top left side of his skull was a tangle of blood and brains. Exit wound.

In his six years as a patrolman, Harkins had worked a couple dozen murder scenes, and five or six times he'd been the first cop to arrive. The exhaustion he'd felt a moment ago faded as his training and the adrenaline kicked in, like someone had flipped his own personal power switch to "on."

Secure the crime scene.

He looked around. Didn't seem much chance the killer was lurking in the crowd, waiting to shoot someone else.

A second man was beside the first sergeant, close to the victim's head, bent over, hands on knees.

"I'm going to ask you to move away from him," Harkins said. "Just move back a few yards. Please."

The man straightened up but didn't move. He had a stethoscope in his front pants pocket, two silver bars of a captain on his collar. A doctor.

"He was right behind me," the doc said. "Running for the shelter right behind me. He said something and I kept going. But he never made it."

Harkins looked in the direction the dead man had been running. About twenty yards along, three rows of sandbags marked the top of a slit-trench air-raid shelter.

The first sergeant put his hand on the doctor's shoulder, gently nudging him back.

"What did he say?" Harkins asked.

"I don't know. I couldn't hear because of the yelling and the sirens and ack-ack."

There'd been a German air raid at first light, one of those surprise last-ditch sorties by whatever shattered remains of the Luftwaffe wanted to test Allied air control of Sicily.

When the first American and British troops came ashore on July 10, most of the Italian units collapsed immediately, surrendering rather than risking death for their cartoonish dictator, Mussolini. But the Germans were proving as formidable here as they had in North Africa, as they no doubt would prove formidable as they backed up all the way to Berlin, if that day ever came.

"Maybe it was—what do you call it, a strafing run." This from a nurse in the crowd.

Harkins looked around for evidence that the German plane had machine-gunned the area, but there was no other damage. The staff just didn't want it to be a shooting at close range. A murder.

"I'm First Sergeant Drake," the big man said. He did not salute or offer a handshake, just gave Harkins a once-over.

"Lieutenant Harkins, military police."

Drake's eyes flicked to the MP brassard.

"I guess you figured that part out," Harkins said. "Anyone touch the body?"

"You mean besides the murderer?" Drake said, a bit smart-ass.

Conscious of the twenty sets of eyes on him, Harkins knelt beside the corpse for a closer look. There was some stippling below the wound, a tattoo of small black dots from the powder, no contact burn from a barrel. The shooter had been behind the man, holding the gun at an upward angle. The entrance wound was large; Harkins guessed a government-issue .45 caliber pistol. Only about fifty thousand of those on the island. The exit wound, left side, top of his head, was massive, pieces of skull mixed with blood-soaked hair.

Harkins saw, from the corner of his eye, someone step into the clearing Drake had created around the body.

"I came as soon as I heard, First Sergeant."

Harkins turned to see a tall full-bird colonel with a narrow face and sharp widow's peak. He wore a clean uniform with a silver eagle on his right lapel point and the caduceus of the Army Medical Corps on the other. Another doctor, probably the hospital commander. Behind him, a nurse wearing captain's bars. She put her hand to her mouth when she saw the body up close.

"Oh, my God," the colonel said. "It's Stephenson, right? Can't we get him moved?"

"I'd rather we didn't move him just yet, sir," Harkins said.

"Who are you?"

Harkins thought about saluting, skipped it since Drake kept his thumbs hooked into his belt, like he was waiting for a bus.

"Lieutenant Harkins, military police."

Harkins wanted to pass this mess off to the provost marshal, the command section that had jurisdiction for crimes committed in the war zone.

"I think we should wait for the provost, sir. And we might want to get some photos."

A couple of spectators sucked in their breath.

"Crime scene photos," Harkins explained, eyes still on the commander. "For the investigators. It'll be helpful in the long run."

The colonel studied Harkins for a moment, then looked at Drake and tilted his head to the crowd.

"You people go back to work now, hear?" Drake said to the circle of onlookers.

The enlisted men moved smartly; the officers—doctors and nurses—either scattered or made a pretense of moving. Clearly the first sergeant was a not a man to trifle with.

"Probably a good idea to wait a bit, Colonel," Drake said, low, so no one else would hear.

"It's just that poor Stephenson is there, with his head blown open," the colonel said. "And it's upsetting the rest of the staff." It was a polite dismissal. "I'd like to see him taken to the morgue, First Sergeant, if you don't mind."

After a beat, Drake managed an unenthusiastic, "Right away, sir."

The colonel walked away without introducing himself to Harkins.

The first sergeant stepped back and pointed at two orderlies, who had appeared with a canvas litter. When the privates moved toward the body, Harkins nodded to Bobby Ray Thomas, who blocked them. The stretcher-bearers stopped, unsure.

"Sorry, First Sergeant," Harkins said. "All due respect, we should wait for the provost, for the investigators. They're going to want to see the scene."

Drake looked a little sad, like he was about to get into something he'd tried to avoid. He was older than most noncoms Harkins knew; in his late thirties, at least, with crow's-feet framing small brown eyes. Probably Regular Army before the war.

"You heard the colonel, Lieutenant," Drake said, stepping closer. He had five inches on Harkins, who was five ten. Thick across the chest and shoulders, with a slight paunch. Big arms and hands. Harkins imagined the enlisted men in the unit avoided pissing him off. Also not a bad strategy for lieutenants.

"This is my hospital, and that's one of our docs," Drake said, calm, maybe a bit menacing. "Go find a traffic jam that needs unscrewing."

Harkins had been chewed out by lots of sergeants when he was a trainee back in the States, but here in the combat zone most noncommissioned officers at least made a show of military courtesy, even for junior officers. Harkins felt his hands tense into fists, forced them to relax. No margin in arguing with the ranking noncom in front of his people.

"It may be your hospital, First Sergeant, but for the moment it's my crime scene," Harkins said, his voice even, almost a whisper. "I'm sure you and the colonel are going to want a thorough investigation. We're not talking about some dumbass being late for formation. Pretty sure we're looking at a murder here."

Behind the first sergeant, the orderlies fidgeted with their stretcher.

"Are you even a real cop?" Drake asked.

"I was a cop in Philadelphia before the war."

"A detective?"

"A patrolman."

The whole truth was that Harkins felt like an accidental solider. He'd enlisted right after Pearl Harbor, only partly because of what everyone called, as if it were one word, the-dirty-Jap-sneak-attack. He'd also joined to get away from a brewing scandal at home: a woman who was someone else's wife, and a husband who was both suspicious and a detective in the same precinct as Harkins.

The army made him a military policeman because he'd been a Philadelphia cop, and he got sent to Officer Candidate School because of good scores on some aptitude tests, and now here he was, battling the Hun, or at least battling sunstroke. He was determined to keep his head down, do what he was told and whatever good work he could, and not get killed.

"Look, I've secured dozens of murder scenes," Harkins continued. "Waiting for detectives. I know what they want to see."

The first sergeant shook his head. "Whole goddamn army full of amateurs. Did you at least send for the provost?"

"Just about to do that. And when he gets here, he's going to make better progress if the crime scene isn't compromised."

"Make it quick," Drake said. "Then let's get him out of here. We got a hospital to run."

It was just at that moment, when Harkins was savoring his little victory, that Bobby Ray Thomas fainted. Passed out cold. Didn't crumple at the knees, but fell like a tree onto his face. A couple of the nurses reached him first.

"He's got malaria," Harkins said. "Fevers, then chills."

Drake pointed at the orderlies with the litter. They rolled the driver, who was barely conscious, onto his side and got him loaded.

"We'll get some fluids in him, see if he should be admitted," one of the nurses said.

When Harkins turned around again, Drake wore an unfriendly smile.

"Crackerjack operation you're running, Lieutenant. The investigation is obviously in good hands."

Then the first sergeant turned on his heel. "OK, back to work," he said to the few people remaining. "This shitshow is over."

This day keeps getting better and better, Harkins thought.

Harkins asked the duty sergeant to send a runner to the provost marshal at corps headquarters. Since everyone was on the move, very few units had static command posts. But the headquarters of the parent unit,

II Corps, was gigantic, with scores of vehicles and hundreds of soldiers—mail clerks and typists, radio operators and mechanics, cooks and translators and photographers—who did everything but fight. Harkins had read somewhere that for every frontline GI firing a weapon, there were seven men behind him keeping the beast fed and in motion.

With so many men moving around, many of them with their own vehicles, it was inevitable that some GIs spent chunks of time doing things other than what they were supposed to be doing; "goldbricking," in Army lingo. And not every soldier spent his time well.

In fact, Harkins thought there was a sense of barely restrained lawlessness behind the battle lines, which were moving steadily, bloodily eastward. Men who might have been upright citizens their entire lives were tempted to petty crime; men who were already criminals picked up where they left off at home: robbery, rape, assault. Harkins had seen it in North Africa, where the local people whose lives were overturned by war were brown and powerless and unable to communicate with the GIs. Sicily was more of the same. As the fighting pushed east, there was a vacuum of authority behind the front, and the zone of chaos expanded; it would take a while for the Allies to reestablish the local police functions and civil authority.

He doubted the provost himself would come, but he'd send a deputy. In the meantime, Harkins asked a soldier to cover the body with a blanket, then approached a few of the nurses who drifted back after Drake had cleared the area. From them Harkins learned the victim was Captain Meyers Stephenson, a surgeon. The doctor who'd been running ahead of Stephenson was a Captain Gallo.

"And that colonel was the hospital commander," one of the women said. "Boone. Colonel Walter Boone."

"And that first sergeant is Drake?"

"Irwin Drake."

"How about that nurse, the captain? She came up with the colonel."

Two of the women exchanged glances but said nothing.

"You do know who I'm talking about, right?"

Finally, one of them spoke up. "Captain Palmer. Phyllis Palmer. She's the head nurse."

Harkins wrote the names in his pocket notebook as the nurses gave him a rundown of the morning. The sirens went off while it was still totally dark. Anyone not on duty headed for the slit-trench shelters; doctors, nurses, and orderlies in the recovery wards stayed with their patients and surgery continued in blacked-out tents. There was an antiaircraft unit, four trucks with quad fifty machine guns, on a small hilltop beside the hospital compound. It would have been impossible to hear anything while those were firing, and none of these women had noticed Stephenson until the all clear sounded.

Harkins was still listening and writing when a jeep pulled up with a captain in the passenger seat—a deputy provost, Harkins hoped—and a private in the back. Time to turn this over to someone else and get some sleep. Harkins thanked the nurses and said someone would get back to them with more questions.

The captain climbed out of the vehicle, waved his hand in front of his face in an effort to clear the dust. He didn't approach Harkins or the body, so Harkins walked toward him. Stuck his notebook in the pocket of his shirt, which was salt-stained, sweat-soaked, and already sticking to him. Ninety degrees at seven in the morning. Fucking August in Sicily. Harkins had been perpetually sunburned in North Africa, where he'd landed back in November as part of Operation Torch, the first big American offensive of the war in Europe. He'd probably stay lobster red until he left this island, too.

"Morning, sir. I'm Lieutenant Harkins."

"Captain Adams, deputy provost."

Adams held an army-issue canvas briefcase in front of him. His face was shiny with sweat, his collar and shirtfront dark. On his left collar point was the insignia of the Judge Advocate General Corps.

"You asked for a photographer, right?" Adams said, punching back the round spectacles that were sliding down his nose.

The man who climbed out of the jeep wore a private's single stripe but looked like he was forty. He had a camera with a flash attachment on a strap around his neck, a cigarette stuck to his lip.

"You a real photographer or an army photographer?" Harkins asked.

"Ten years shooting Chicago crime scenes," the private said, eyes scanning past Harkins to the body beyond. "I guess I know what to do."

"Make sure you get some ground-level shots, OK?"

"Ain't my first rodeo, Lieutenant."

"All right, then."

Harkins turned and walked toward the body, Adams falling in beside him, holding his canvas bag even tighter.

"Captain Meyers Stephenson. Surgeon. Single gunshot to the head, a forty-five, I think. Probably as he was running toward the shelter during the air raid this morning. All that noise." Harkins pointed at the antiaircraft battery. "I haven't found anyone who saw or heard anything."

Harkins knelt beside the draped corpse to remove the blanket for the photographer, and then realized Adams wasn't with him. The captain had stopped several paces away, looking sick.

"You OK, Captain?" Harkins asked.

"I . . . uh . . . I've never been to a crime scene."

"Oh," Harkins said. He lifted the blanket, used it to fan away gathering flies. They buzzed around his face instead, droning like little fighter planes.

"He's gonna get ripe fast in this heat," the photographer said as he started shooting.

"You a criminal lawyer, sir?" Harkins asked.

Adams had a tight grip on the satchel, like he was trying to wring water from it. He removed his helmet. A few thin strands of hair stuck to his sweaty scalp, which he wiped with his shirtsleeve. Some flies attacked, and Adams waved one arm, to no effect.

"What? Uh, no. I was writing contracts for the War Department in Washington when this chance to come overseas opened up."

"You volunteered to ship out?"

Adams, who had been staring wide-eyed at the body, now looked at Harkins, tried a weak smile. "I didn't want to have to tell my grandchildren that throughout the whole of the great World War Two I lived in Maryland, where I was wounded once by a stuck typewriter key."

"OK, then," Harkins said, nodding. "Let me show you what we have. Can you come a little closer, sir?"

Adams took two short steps toward the body. Harkins used his pencil to point to the entrance wound. Adams nodded, his lips pressed together.

"Come around this side," Harkins said, directing Adams so that he could see the top of Stephenson's head. "Exit wound."

"Is that . . . ?"

"Skull fragments," Harkins said.

Adams brought his canvas bag to his mouth and turned away. He made it to a drainage ditch behind the hospital tent before losing his breakfast.

Harkins stood and got out of the way of the photographer, who was unfazed by the scene. Then he followed the captain.

"You all right, sir?"

Adams nodded yes, then leaned over again, choking up a bit more.

Harkins rubbed his eyes, which felt like they had sand beneath the lids. The photographer was shaking his head, probably thinking what Harkins was thinking. No way Captain Adams was going to take over the investigation this morning.

"Are you the provost marshal?"

It was Drake, the hospital first sergeant. When he walked up to Adams, the lawyer wiped his mouth with the back of his hand. Drake did not salute.

"Captain Theodore Adams, Sergeant. Deputy provost."

"That's *first* sergeant, Captain," Drake said.

Harkins had made this mistake before. It took a long time and a lot of work to become a first sergeant, and the job came with massive responsibility. Drake was the top noncommissioned officer in the unit and oversaw the daily operation of the hospital outside of the actual medical work: everything from who set up the tents and where to who pulled guard duty. He had to look out for two hundred enlisted men and thirty-plus officers, all so that the medicos could concentrate on saving lives. First sergeants deserved to be called by their full title. Still, Harkins thought, Drake didn't have to be such a gold-plated ass about everything.

"Right," Adams said, intimidated. "First Sergeant."

"You going to take over this investigation from our patrolman friend here?" Drake asked, tilting his head toward Harkins.

"I'll initiate the paperwork, yes."

"Can we move the body now?"

Harkins looked at the photographer, who gave him a thumbs-up. He had the shots. Harkins met Adams's eyes and nodded.

"Yes, ah, First Sergeant," Adams said. "We can move the body now."

"You got a stomach bug?" Drake asked.

"No, I . . . I've never seen a murder victim before."

Drake looked at Harkins, who could almost read the older man's mind. *Fucking amateurs.*

"Well, Captain, you're going to need a little more grit than that to hunt down a murderer."

Drake motioned Adams closer to the body, then put his arm around the man to keep Adams from turning away. The first sergeant was either teaching him or messing with him. Harkins thought it a toss-up.

"Entrance wound at left occipital bone. Exit at the frontal bone, of course, forward of the coronal structure, I'd say. Left cerebral hemisphere destroyed pretty completely."

As Drake talked and pointed, the flies came back, and that was all Adams could take. He stumbled back to the drainage ditch.

Harkins stepped beside Drake, who said, "So far, looks like neither you or the deputy provost are up to the task."

Harkins looked around. The orderlies Drake had brought along were not close enough to overhear.

"You don't seem all that upset by what happened here this morning, First Sergeant."

Drake looked at Harkins for a long few seconds, looking sad, maybe a tiny bit amused. "Are you that much of a dumbass, Lieutenant? You think the first person you talk to is going to, what? Confess?"

Harkins, who'd been hoping exactly that, didn't answer.

"Now, shall we do what the colonel wanted and get this body out of here?" Drake said.

"Sure."

When Drake walked away, Harkins motioned to the orderlies. "You got a morgue, right?"

One of the men spat a stream of tobacco juice into the dust. "Yeah, but they won't keep him long. In this heat he'll be cooked like a Coney Island dog in two hours. Got a temporary cemetery about a half mile from here."

They unfolded the stretcher, then covered Captain Stephenson with the blanket, gently tucking it in along the sides as if to make him comfortable. When they lifted him, Harkins—acting more out of habit than faith—crossed himself.

He found Adams sitting on a supply crate around the corner of the big tent.

"Well, I made an ass of myself, I guess," Adams said.

"Lots of people lose it at their first crime scene."

"Yeah, but I gave our friend the chance to show he's boss, right?"

"I'm pretty sure he never doubted that he's the boss," Harkins said. The adrenaline rush was fading. He wanted to check on Thomas, then get back to his tent and close his eyes.

Adams stood. "What now?" he said.

"What do you mean?"

"I'm going to start the paperwork saying that there's been a murder here," Adams said. "How are you going to proceed?"

"I'm *proceeding* back to my bivouac," Harkins said. "I'm not an investigator. That's your job."

"I'm not a detective."

"Neither am I. I was a beat cop. You need somebody popped in the head with a nightstick, I'm your guy. But this is serious stuff. Aren't there any detectives or former detectives with the provost marshal?"

"We're stretched thin," Adams said. "This one belongs to you and me."

"Captain, I've been on duty for twenty-four—" Harkins looked at his watch. "Make that twenty-six hours. My driver dropped over with a fever. We were headed back to link up with the rest of my platoon and get some sleep when we got flagged down. Hell, we just happened to be driving by."

"Good thing," Adams said. When Harkins didn't respond, he added, "Well, good thing for me, I guess. Not so great for you."

Harkins pressed the heels of his hands to his eye sockets. He wanted to look up and see a potbellied Philadelphia detective, somebody with a bourbon habit and thirty years' experience. But there was just Adams, with his crumpled briefcase and a string of vomit on his shirt.

"Look, I've done exactly zero investigations, unless you count contract scams," Adams said. "You've at least got some idea of what to do next, right?"

"Kill myself."

"What?"

"I said I guess I do, but I'm going to need help. There's got to be a hundred thousand GIs on this island. Somebody had to have been a detective, or at least a sheriff."

"Absolutely," Adams said. "I'll start looking right away. In the meantime, we both better get to work."

2

2 August 1943
0800 hours

After Adams went back to a desk somewhere, Harkins found Stephenson's tent and looked through the dead man's gear. There was a wooden footlocker stenciled STEPHENSON, MEYERS, CAPTAIN, USA MC.

Harkins used the ax from his jeep's pioneer kit to break the lock. Inside the chest he found some toiletries, two of the new paperback books—mysteries, by the look of them—that were available to every GI, some clean and some dirty clothes, a half-dozen medical journals, seventy-two dollars in cash, a half-empty bottle of Tennessee whiskey, and three pairs of women's panties, different sizes, none of them especially clean. Under the panties Harkins found three dozen condoms, which seemed like a lot for a guy who had a full-time job. No personal letters or even letter-writing materials. There was a pistol belt with a canteen and an empty holster hanging from the central tent pole. The weapon was probably stored with the supply sergeant, since doctors did not routinely carry sidearms.

He looked around the tent, which Stephenson had to himself, though there were two unused cots. He walked outside along a line of five other pyramidal sleeping tents, poked his head in one or two whose inhabitants were elsewhere. Looked like Stephenson was the only doctor who lived alone.

Next Harkins headed for the mess tent, where he found three nurses sitting by themselves, heads close together, whispering. The sidewalls of the tent were rolled up to let the air flow through, but the sun beating on the roof drove the temperature up. Two GIs in stained and sweaty T-shirts hovered over a grill, serving late breakfast to people coming off shift. The place smelled like bacon and burned canvas.

"Mind if I sit down, ask you a few questions?"

A first lieutenant with tight, dark curls said, "You doing the investigation?"

"For now," Harkins said, dropping onto a bench at the rough lumber table. There was one dirty mess kit in front of the three women, three cups of coffee, and the bottom of a shell casing, sawed off for an ashtray and filled with butts.

"Name's Harkins. Eddie Harkins."

"I'm Felton," the first lieutenant said. "This here's Savio. And Melbourne."

Felton held a cigarette between long fingers; the nails on one hand were ringed with a crust of something dark. Dried blood, maybe. The other women were both second lieutenants, one grade below Harkins and Felton. Savio had black hair and almond eyes and could pass for a local in Sicily. She was smoking and fidgeting with a lighter, flipping it open and lighting it; flipping it closed. Her fingernails were chewed to the quick. Melbourne had big shoulders, an athlete; straight hair pulled in a tight bun and a small gap in her front teeth. Even sitting down, she looked tall.

"You a detective?" Melbourne asked. "I mean in real life."

"No. I was a beat cop in Philadelphia."

"The army doesn't draft detectives?"

"None of the ones I knew," Harkins said. "And I wasn't drafted."

"Great," Melbourne said. "So we're all volunteers. Patriots."

Harkins wasn't sure he had the patience this morning for a hostile interview. Maybe Melbourne was as tired as he was. Maybe she'd been a friend of the victim.

"What can you tell me about Captain Stephenson?" Harkins asked.

The three women exchanged looks with each other, said nothing.

"I went to Stephenson's tent," Harkins tried. "Looks like he lived alone. Was the only doc who lived alone. That seemed kind of odd."

"He was one of those guys people either liked or hated as soon as you met him," Felton, the senior nurse, said. "Some of the docs liked him, I guess, or at least thought he was fun to be around. Though apparently not enough to share a tent with him."

"Any idea why?"

Nothing.

Harkins' head swam like he'd just been tagged with a good jab. He wished he'd had a few hours' sleep, even an hour. He wished he'd paid more attention to how detectives back home conducted interviews.

Just behind the nurses and under the rim of the tent, he saw the legs of a stretcher detail, four men carrying a body wound head to toe in a dirty sheet. A pair of filthy boots, possibly the dead man's, stood at the foot of the stretcher.

"Any idea who might want Stephenson dead?"

"I don't know about dead," Felton said. "But he was a train wreck, a disaster. A lot of people who wanted him gone. Transferred out of the hospital."

"Why?"

"Last week a nurse passed out drunk in his tent—this is down near Gela. She choked on her own vomit."

"She make it?"

"No."

"Was it Stephenson's fault?"

Felton let blue smoke drift from her mouth, picked a speck of tobacco from her bottom lip with thumb and forefinger. Harkins waited.

"Who knows?" Felton said. "He said he'd left the tent before it happened, and somebody found him passed out in the latrine the next morning, so he left her at some point. But it could have been after."

"Stephenson gave liquor or tried to give liquor to lots of nurses," Melbourne said. "Whitman accepted. One time."

"How do you know it was only one time?"

"She was like most of us. Tried to avoid Stephenson mostly."

Felton said, "Whitman was a little bit lost, I think."

Savio spoke up for the first time. "I'm not sure it's going to be worth getting in hot water with Palmer," she said to the other two women, her eyes on the table.

Harkins flipped a page in his notebook. "Is that Captain Palmer, the head nurse?"

"Yeah," Felton said.

Felton watched the smoke curl from the end of her cigarette. Melbourne, her hands clenched like she was about to hit someone, watched Harkins. When a cook dropped a metal tray, Savio jumped, fumbling her lighter.

"Are other people in danger?" Harkins asked.

"I don't think anybody anticipated *this,*" Felton said. "Murder. I mean, Jesus."

Harkins said, "Has there been other violence?"

"Depends," Melbourne said. "You consider it violent when a man shoves you up against a cabinet or a table and grabs your tits, grabs your ass? Tries to kiss you on the fucking mouth?"

Harkins hadn't expected the women to talk like every other GI he'd met in nineteen months in the army. He looked down at his notes. "That stuff goes on here?"

"Every goddamned day," Felton said. She glanced at Savio, who was petite and looked twenty, tops. "To some more than others."

The three women traded looks again. Harkins took a breath. As a young patrolman taking witness statements, he'd been swayed several times by what the older detectives called "fucking sob stories."

"Somebody is always going to try to sell you some bullshit story that makes them look better," a twenty-year veteran named Tenneato had warned him. They'd been standing beside a gut-slashed corpse that lay in an icy gutter, stomping their feet and trying to keep warm while they waited for a captain.

"Or they'll see the cops around and think, 'This is when I get back at my prick of a neighbor,' and you'll hear all kinds of stuff that'll get your investigation absolutely nowhere. Stuff that'll just waste your time. Gotta take all that shit with a grain of salt."

Harkins didn't have enough time on the force to become as cynical as Tenneato had been, but he was wary of being led down some side-track that would do nothing but make this case more complicated. He wondered for a moment if Adams would really look for a replacement investigator, or if that was a load of crap, too.

"Stephenson do those things?" Harkins asked.

"Yeah," Melbourne said. "Captain Meyers Stephenson. Talented surgeon; big jock at Cornell; fancy New York family; regimental boxing team, if you can believe that. And a first-class sonofabitch. Thought we were all here, the nurses that is, for his amusement."

"Satisfaction," Felton said.

"Gratification," Savio said.

Harkins had heard stories about what went on between doctors and nurses at these hospitals. The only American women in theater were nurses and Red Cross Donut Dollies. Tens of thousands of GIs fantasizing about a hundred, maybe a hundred and fifty women scattered among a score of medical units and hospitals across the whole island. Most of the GIs would never even see an American woman, much less meet one; the odds were terrible. Unless you were a doctor. It was an unchallenged truism among the sex-starved soldiers that doctors lived hedonistic lives, kept harems dressed in olive drab.

"So Stephenson was the one pushing people, uh, pushing women up against cabinets and stuff?"

"He was one of them," Savio said.

"The worst one," Melbourne said.

"How many women did he do this to?"

"Half a dozen, easy," Felton answered, stabbing her cigarette into the pile of butts.

Harkins looked up from his notes. "How many nurses you have here?"

"Eighteen when we're at full strength."

"Stephenson cut a wide swath, huh?" Harkins said. "He bother Whitman?"

"Don't know. It looked like she went to his tent willingly," Felton said.

"Or was too drunk to resist," Melbourne said. She and Felton looked angry; Savio looked fragile.

"He do it to you?" Harkins asked Felton.

"Once," she said. "I told him that if he did it again or if I heard of him doing it to another nurse, I'd cut off his dick with a dull knife."

"That's what you felt like doing to him?" Harkins asked.

Felton gave a little snort. "Come on, Lieutenant. If you're any kind of investigator you're going to find out I said *exactly* that in front of ten people. I told you to save your skinny Irish ass from getting all excited, thinking you caught the murderer in the first hour."

Harkins rubbed his eyes with thumb and forefinger. Drake had said almost exactly the same thing to him.

Still not a detective, he thought.

Felton leaned forward, jabbed an index finger onto his notebook. Falling ash from her cigarette stuck to the damp page. "I didn't shoot him. Write *that* down."

"Was anyone else angry enough to do this?"

Felton lit another cigarette, one-handing a lighter. She said, "Who knows what people are capable of when they're pushed?"

Harkins was having a hard time getting from what sounded like predictable grab-ass—not pretty, but nothing that struck him as criminal—to motivation to shoot a man in the head at close range.

And then Savio started to cry. Her lips didn't tremble, her breathing didn't change, but fat silver tears rolled from the bottoms of her eyes. Melbourne put an arm around the smaller woman and the two of them got up and walked out of the tent.

Harkins watched them go, realized that he'd been hoping to run into a dead end, or that some clear reason for Stephenson's murder—along with a killer—would just drop into his lap and he could go back to his platoon.

So far, the nurses' story was all he had. He'd never been that cop who cut corners, so he had to follow it.

He stood, pulled his canteen cup from his pistol belt, and walked to a row of big pots sitting atop gas burners. Squinting against the steam, he scooped a helping of coffee and grounds, sat down again.

"Any of the other docs do this kind of stuff to the women, the nurses?" he asked Felton.

"Stephenson was the worst, but there are a couple of others who've behaved badly at some point or other."

"Colonel Boone know about this?"

Felton took a long pull on her cigarette, then exhaled in a slow sigh.

"People complained," she said. "Nurses complained. He knew. Palmer knew."

"And Boone never did anything?"

"Oh, yeah, he did plenty. Lectured us on how we shouldn't wear our uniforms too tight and how we should and shouldn't spend our free time and even whether we walked someplace alone at night. He thought everything that was happening was our fault. He always took the doctors' side, like he was afraid to call them on this shit."

The handful of commanders Harkins had worked for in his time in uniform had various levels of ability—one was a certifiable idiot, he thought—but most of them had taken care of their people, their soldiers. If anything, he thought commanders might be more inclined to look out for women.

"So Boone wouldn't do anything to stop them, even though he's the commander?"

"He probably thought he was only going to be commander for a short time. The hospital commander we had when we landed, guy named Logan, got pretty sick by D-plus-three or -four and had to be evac'd to North Africa. Boone was the senior surgeon on the aux team, so they stuck him with the job."

"What's an aux team?" Harkins asked.

"Auxiliary team," Felton said. She leaned forward and pushed the ashtray to one side. "This is your field hospital, right? That's a couple hundred people. Orderlies, cooks, drivers, all kinds of folks who support the mission." She pushed her pack of cigarettes in front of her. "Then you have these teams—auxiliary teams: surgeons and surgical nurses, anesthetists, specialists—and they're assigned to various hospitals on an as-needed basis."

"Okay," Harkins said.

"The army is still trying to figure out the best way to structure all this, to tell you the truth, and I don't think we got it yet."

She took another pull at the cigarette, one eye winking closed at the drifting smoke.

"Anyway, Boone was in charge of one of the aux teams, but when Logan got sick, the Second Corps surgeon—he's the big boss one level up—he came down and put Boone in charge of the whole field hospital. He's been floundering since day one, especially with the surgeons. He wasn't really in their club. They didn't respect him."

"What do you mean?" Harkins asked. "He's a surgeon, right? The commander and the highest-ranking guy."

"Yeah, but he's from Iowa, Indiana, some cornfield state. The other docs called him 'country boy' behind his back. Shit like that. They weren't openly disrespectful, not all of them, but Boone had to know they thought he was kind of a bumpkin. Stephenson wasn't the only Ivy League asshole around here."

Harkins scribbled in his notebook, then stopped, his pencil poised above the damp page as he tried to remember other questions the detectives typically asked. There was an insistent pain that seemed centered right behind his eyes, like someone was using a sledgehammer to break out of his skull. He needed water, chow, sleep.

"So Captain Stephenson was a problem for Colonel Boone?"

"I know where you're going," Felton said. "Boone cleaning house by getting rid of Stephenson. I don't see it."

"Why not?"

"Boone didn't think Stephenson was the problem. To Boone, to Palmer, to the other docs, the nurses were the problem. When a nurse complained, she got marked as a troublemaker, a Bolshevik. Boone sent one girl to a theater hospital in North Africa; another one got shipped back to the States."

Harkins pictured an assignment stateside. Someplace with shade and cold beer after hours. "That doesn't sound too bad," he said. Immediately regretted it.

Felton narrowed her eyes, snuffed her cigarette in the ashtray, and leaned closer. "This may surprise you, Lieutenant, but we have a pretty important job here. I didn't volunteer because I like the clothes, or because I wanted to see every shithole in Europe."

Two men carrying mess tins and wearing stethoscopes began to sit at the next table but moved when they heard the edge in Felton's voice.

"I'm a *great* surgical nurse. These women are great nurses. We volunteered to do a job that needs doing. We shouldn't have to go through an extra layer of difficulty—a layer of overgrown, oversexed frat boys—just to do our work."

"Right," Harkins said. "Yeah, of course you're right."

Felton leaned back, calming quickly. One corner of her mouth turned up in what might have been a smile.

"Didn't mean to jump on my soapbox, but I am sorely tired of this bullshit. And frankly, that's the only reason I'm talking to you. Hope I'm not wasting my time."

She yawned, which made Harkins yawn, too.

"Did you work last night?"

"Coming off twenty-four hours," Harkins said. "Had to chase down a jeep stolen by some locals, then break up a fight in a whore . . . a brothel."

"I'm not made of porcelain," Felton said. "You can't use a cuss word I haven't heard or said myself."

"What about First Sergeant Drake?"

"What about him?"

"He seemed pretty pissed off this morning. Not very cooperative."

"Oh, he's okay. He just thinks all these new people who've come into the army—excuse me, *his* army—are screwing things up. We're all just civilians playing at being soldiers."

"Actually, that pretty much describes me," Harkins said.

"You and ninety-nine percent of us, I'd say," Felton said. "Anyway, he doesn't hate you or anything. He's just not a friendly guy."

"Maybe he doesn't hate me in particular. Maybe it's all lieutenants. Or all MPs."

"Nah, if he really hated you, he'd adopt this real exaggerated military courtesy. Absolute kiss-ass. 'Yes, SIR! No, SIR!' Like some cheesy movie about fucking West Point. Also, the man had his sense of humor surgically removed."

"Yeah?"

Felton smiled. "One time he came into the admin tent, where the nurses keep the records. This was after our orderlies started visiting the whorehouses. He asked me, 'Lieutenant, where do we stand on VD?' So I said, 'We're against it, First Sergeant.' He didn't even crack a smile."

Harkins laughed. "How do I get him to cooperate?" he asked.

"When he sees that you know what you're doing and that you're trying to do the right thing, he'll be less of a pain in the ass, but that's the best you can hope for."

"Great."

"By the way," Felton said. "You can add him to the list of people who hated—I mean *hated*—Stephenson."

"Really?"

"He had Stephenson figured out from the start. And I'm pretty sure he tried to talk some sense into Boone. Tried to get Boone to transfer Stephenson, or at least rein him in. But for all that Stephenson was a pain in the ass, he was actually a good surgeon, and we need all hands, you know?"

"You think Drake was capable of killing Stephenson?"

Felton thought for a moment. "If you'd have asked me yesterday if he was capable of murder, I'd have said no, because he's a by-the-book guy. Today I'm not so sure."

"What happened to make you reconsider?"

"Well, there was an actual murder. It seems pretty clear that one of our people shot another one of our people. Stephenson's jackass nature aside, it's pretty shocking, don't you think?"

Harkins did not think that at all. He'd seen worse among blood relatives, between people who'd promised to love, honor, and cherish 'til death do us part.

Felton stood, stretched her arms overhead. There was a dark stain on the front of her blouse. More dried blood. "What a morning, huh?"

She leaned over and pointed at Harkins' notebook, which lay open on the mess table. "You're going to want to talk to a doc named Wilkins, one of Stephenson's piggy friends. And Boone, of course. A nurse named Ronan, and her friend, Donnelly."

Harkins stopped scribbling. "Donnelly?" he asked. "Any chance that's Kathleen Donnelly, from Philadelphia?"

"Yeah. You know her from back in the States?"

"I'm hoping it's the same one."

"Ronan's first name is Moira," Felton said. "But she probably won't want to talk to you. She's had a rough time, so you be sweet with her."

Felton patted Harkins on the shoulder as she walked past him and toward the tent flap. "Good luck. You're going to need it."

After Felton pushed through the door, Bobby Ray Thomas stuck his head inside.

"I thought you were dead," Harkins said. "Didn't they admit you?"

"Yeah. Gave me some fluids through a needle in my arm. I feel a lot better, so I checked myself out."

"You checked out? This isn't a hotel."

"Okay, I walked out. I feel fine. Got some sleep."

"You passed out. I'm not sure that counts as sleep."

"Well, I couldn't leave you stranded here."

"I have the jeep; I was going to leave you stranded."

Harkins stepped through the door, blinking in the bright sun. He could see inside a couple of the big tents, their sides rolled up in hopes of a breeze. Wounded men lay on cots, some with limbs wrapped in thick casts and strung to overhead frames.

He was bent over, peering into one of the wards, when he heard Thomas say, "Morning, ma'am."

Harkins turned to see Thomas saluting a captain, the woman who'd been with Boone when he first saw Stephenson's body. Phyllis Palmer was the head nurse; Savio had been afraid of getting into trouble with her by talking to Harkins.

"Morning, ma'am," Harkins said, pulling himself up straight, fingertips touching his eyebrow. It was the first time he'd ever saluted a woman.

"Good morning," Palmer said, returning the salute.

Her uniform and hands were clean, Harkins noticed, and the captain's insignia on her right collar point was crooked. He guessed that she was not, like First Sergeant Drake, Regular Army. She had a prim little mouth, brown hair pinned in place.

Palmer said to Thomas, “Run along, young man.”

“It’s Harkins, isn’t it?” she said when Thomas had gone.

“Yes, ma’am.”

“I’m *sure* you would have gotten around to talking to me,” she said, sarcastic. “But I thought I’d just come and find you. You’ve spoken to some of the nurses already.”

Harkins wondered if she’d been listening in on his conversation in the mess tent. “Yes, ma’am. A few. There are more I want to talk to.”

“Be careful about putting too much faith in what you hear. Everyone is upset, of course, by this awful crime, and some of the nurses were already, well, let’s just say some of these young girls can be a bit hysterical.”

“Hysterical?”

“Just like other soldiers, they spend a lot of time waiting around, and to pass the time they make up stories, or exaggerate things that may have happened, or that they imagine happened.”

Harkins studied the captain, who looked forty, old for her rank. She had a small white scar on her chin, something from childhood. He wondered for a second if Palmer was a Detective Tenneato, who was either, depending on where you stood, too jaded to care or too smart to let people waste his time.

Harkins expected Boone to take care of all his soldiers; Palmer, the head nurse, should be even more rabid about taking care of the women.

“I see,” Harkins said, which was a lie; he was as clueless as he’d been while standing over Stephenson’s body.

“So I should discount, say, stories about doctors grabbing women?”

“Look, Lieutenant, I’m not saying that stuff doesn’t happen. But most of our doctors are terrific, and we’re doing important work here. Saving lives. And while I’m sure some of the nurses were genuinely upset that the doctors could be a bit—let’s say aggressive, other nurses thrive on the drama.”

He supposed it could be true that some nurses actually liked the attention, and others liked the fact that it gave them something to bitch about. But the stuff Felton and Melbourne told him? They had a right to be pissed off about the groping and pawing, if that’s what was happening. But even that—bad as it sounded—was that enough to get a man murdered?

“The real problem is that they talk about it nonstop, and that’s what interferes with their work," Palmer said. "And the more they talk about it, the worse that interference gets."

"So they shouldn't complain?"

Palmer closed her eyes, took a breath, sighed it out, exasperated with Harkins. "Look, there have been a lot of changes because of this war. How many women have you worked with in the past? Worked alongside? And I'm not talking about teachers and secretaries."

"None."

"Exactly. And while our doctors have worked with nurses back in their stateside hospitals—well, there's just a pecking order, that's all I'm saying. Heck, in the last war, women stayed home rolling bandages. There's a price we pay to serve out here, in such close quarters with all these men. Sometimes the girls have to put up with certain kinds of, uh, *attention*. But making a big deal out of it makes it worse for everyone. Better to just ignore it and focus on the work at hand."

Harkins wondered if this was the pep talk Palmer gave arriving nurses.

"Okay," he said. "Anything else you want to share with me, ma'am?"

It came out a bit more dismissively than he intended. Palmer noticed, narrowed her eyes. She was not a big woman, but she suddenly reminded Harkins of a couple of the nuns he'd had in school. He'd had a knack for getting on their nerves, too.

"I just want you to know what you're dealing with here," Palmer said. "And don't ever forget that our primary mission is to care for patients. The quicker you can find the murderer and let us get back to our jobs, the better for everyone. Especially those wounded boys who arrive every day."

"Yes, ma'am."

"You should come to me with any questions," she said. "In fact, I'd like you to keep me informed whenever you talk to any of my nurses."

"I'll do my best, ma'am." Another lie. There was no way he was including her.

He saluted, and Palmer snapped her hand to the brim of her fatigue cap. When she was gone, Thomas sidled up. "That's the head nurse, right?"

"The very one," Harkins said.

"So how're things shaping up?" Thomas asked.

"Great. Really great. I got a dead doc who was probably shot by somebody he worked with. There are at least a handful of nurses who, if they didn't kill him, are at least glad he's dead. I got into a pissing contest with the hospital first sergeant. The deputy provost is a pencil-pushing lawyer who threw up when he saw the body and then practically ran away after telling me that I'm the investigating officer. Me, the army's favorite traffic cop. We got docs who play grab-ass with the nurses, which isn't at all surprising. Also not surprising is that any nurse who complains is labeled a troublemaker, and it looks like the head nurse is one hundred percent on board with that.

"Oh, and one more thing, I got a driver who can't drive. I think that's about it."

"That's a helluva mess, all right," Thomas said as he climbed into the passenger side of their jeep. "And it's only ten in the morning."

"Oh, yeah," Harkins said. "Still plenty of time for things to get worse."

3

2 August 1943
1100 hours

Startled out of a deep sleep, the first thing Harkins did was pull his pistol.

"Whoa, whoa! Don't shoot!"

In the seconds it took Harkins to swim up to consciousness, he thought he heard his brother Patrick.

"It's me, gunslinger."

Sure enough, Patrick came into slow focus, then held out his hand, pulled Harkins up from the ground and the tiny sliver of shade he'd managed to find beside his jeep.

"Damn, I'm glad to see you," Harkins said. His big brother pulled him into a clinch, squeezed his shoulders.

Patrick, a Catholic priest, was a chaplain with the Eighty-Second Airborne Division and one of the three thousand or so American paratroopers who had jumped into Sicily during the early-morning hours just before Allied landing craft hit the beaches on D-Day.

"Geez, you've lost a lot of weight," Harkins said. His brother had been a big man since he was fifteen, with upper arms as thick as some men's legs. They'd both been amateur boxers, Patrick with more wins. When Patrick got an opposing boxer in a clinch, he could squeeze the breath and fight right out of him.

"You're not looking so great yourself," Patrick said, poking Harkins in the chest.

"Fortunately, there ain't too many mirrors out here," Harkins said. "So as far as I know, I'm still the good-looking brother."

Harkins had not seen his brother since a short leave they had together at their parents' home in September of 1942, nearly eleven months earlier. Harkins had already been training in the States for seven months by then, and had shipped out for North Africa in October, landing in Casablanca just a few days behind the first waves of American troops. Harkins and his platoon of MPs spent the next eight months guarding German POWs and shepherding traffic behind the front as the Allies battled the Afrika Korps. He'd nearly died of boredom.

"Why are you here?" Harkins asked, lifting his hand to indicate the hospital.

Harkins had practically dragged Thomas—who was still very sick—back to the nurses, who put the driver on a cot and stuck another needle in his arm. Harkins had stashed his jeep on the edge of the compound to get some sleep before resuming the—make that *his*—investigation.

"We've got a couple of paratroopers here," Patrick said. "Some injured on the jump, some wounded. I came to visit them, see if they need anything."

"Saving souls, huh?" Harkins said. "How was the jump?"

"Mostly confusing. We were scattered all over the place. But our guys pulled together in little groups and started making trouble, cutting roads and telephone lines and setting up ambushes, just like they'd been trained. Our colonel says the Germans and Italians never figured out how many of us there were. We had this one guy, a real Texas cowboy, captured the regimental objective by tricking the enemy into surrendering."

"How's that?"

"The Italians and Germans were all dug in around this intersection. Concrete pillboxes, minefields, a real strongpoint."

"Strongpoint, huh? Listen to you, talking like Georgie Patton."

"You pick up some of the lingo," Patrick said. "Anyway, this captain has collected about eighty of his guys; no way they can assault, right? Now the navy is trying to shell that intersection with those big darn guns they have, but they're missing. All the rounds are going long, and the spotter plane that's supposed to call back to the ship with adjustments has been shot down. Oh, and the army can't talk to the navy 'cause the radios don't connect, so this company commander can't ask the navy to adjust fire."

Patrick was animated now. He'd been proud to become a paratrooper, with their gaudy silver wings and shiny boots, and he was obviously proud of what they'd accomplished in the invasion.

"So what'd he do?" Harkins asked, humoring him.

"He's got this trooper who speaks the lingo—the kid's parents are from Sicily—and he tells the kid to send one of their Italian prisoners down to tell the guys in the pillboxes to give up before he adjusts the navy's fire and blows them all to smithereens."

"But I thought he couldn't do that. Adjust the fire."

"He couldn't, but the guys in the pillboxes don't know that."

"Wow," Harkins said. "A ruse."

"Yep. I heard this captain—his name is Sayre—I heard him tell the story the other night. He sets up the whole thing, talks about watching the prisoner run down the hill. He's got everybody tuned in, and finally the colonel says, 'Then what happened?'

"And Sayre—he's got this great accent—Sayre says, real slow, 'Well, I reckon that prisoner was an eloquent speaker, 'cause they all just give up.'"

Exhausted as he was, Harkins had to laugh.

"The plan called for almost a thousand guys to do what he did with some fast talking," Patrick said.

"They should put him on the phone with Hitler," Harkins said. "Save the rest of us a lot of trouble."

Harkins noticed that his brother's uniform blouse had been torn and repaired.

"How'd you do in the jump?"

"Easy," Patrick said, smiling. "I landed in a huge pile of cow dung."

"And here I thought you had your first-ever tan."

"How about you?" Patrick asked. "You fry in North Africa?"

"Close to it."

"How was it?"

Harkins shrugged. There was too much to say, so he said little. "Well, we learned we could beat them, but it's going to cost. Worst part was, right after the Krauts surrendered, there were all these rumors that we were going home, that we'd done our part," Harkins said. "That was really hard on the guys when we found out it wasn't true."

"Ouch," Patrick said.

"Now I'm just hoping I'm home by 1950 or so."

"I've already heard why you're here at the hospital," Patrick said. "Some orderly couldn't wait to fill me in. It's all the enlisted guys can talk about, how some doctor nobody liked got himself killed and some poor schlub former Philadelphia beat cop is doing the investigating. Is it true you got in a fight with the hospital first sergeant?"

"Hardly, though we're not exactly best of friends. And the commander didn't even speak to me."

"So you're off to a great start."

For a moment, they were kids again, Harkins getting teased by his big brother.

"Don't give me any shit, all right? I'm not in the mood. And I've still got a pistol."

Patrick looked like their father and was a conciliator like the old man, too; a peacemaker who could talk to anyone. Harkins looked like his mother's brothers—red hair, wiry limbs, freckles—and occasionally acted like them too. Whenever Harkins got in trouble in school, his father called him Jimmy Junior. Uncle Jimmy, his mother's youngest brother—and the one with the shortest fuse—thought it a slow week if he didn't get into a couple of fistfights.

"I also heard your driver is sick," Patrick said.

"Malaria. I don't know how he's been functioning, to tell you the truth."

"Well, if he's a patient, I got another man for you. Another driver."

"You got friends in the military police now?"

"Nobody has friends in the MPs. In fact, don't tell anyone that you're my brother, okay?"

"Very funny."

"I got a paratrooper being discharged today who needs a job. He even speaks Italian. Or Sicilian; I guess they're different. Anyway, his parents are from Palermo."

"Doesn't he already have a job? As a paratrooper, I mean?"

Patrick looked like he was about to answer; instead, he said, "Put your shoes on."

Harkins dressed, and the two men drove Harkins' jeep back to the main hospital area, Harkins keeping an eye out for First Sergeant Drake, whom he wanted to avoid.

"He's in here," Patrick said, pointing to a tent with a hand-painted sign that said RECORDS.

When Harkins shut the jeep's engine, they could hear men arguing. Then a crash and what sounded like wood splintering. They stepped into the open door of the tent and a soldier in the shadows shouted, "Ten-shun!"

There were two figures on the dirt floor, rolling on the remains of a smashed wooden field table and a scattering of papers. One man—who was on his back—looked like he'd already absorbed a couple of shots to the face. His lip was bleeding and there was a cut above his eyebrow. The GI on top was holding the other's throat as he pulled his fist back for another blow. With the command, the two men stopped and scrambled to attention. One of them—short, with dark, wavy hair—wore the distinctive uniform of a paratrooper: calf-high brown boots with the trousers tucked into the top, a long blouse that hung outside his pants. On his left shoulder was the double-A patch of the Eighty-Second Airborne Division, the "All Americans." Harkins had a bad feeling that this man was to be his project.

"Colianno," Patrick said. "What's going on here?"

"Just a misunderstanding, sir."

"Don't give me that malarkey," Patrick said. Then, to the other man, "Who are you?"

"Private First Class Weston, sir. I'm the admit-and-discharge clerk."

"What happened here, Weston?"

Weston blinked some sweat out of his eyes, then wiped his swelling lip with the back of his hand.

"You're at attention, Private," Patrick said. The GI immediately put his hands back down along his sides. Harkins was used to Patrick's gentle priest-voice. This officer-voice was something new.

Colianno spoke up. "He called me a dirty fucking dago, Captain. Excuse my French."

"That's not French and I won't excuse it, so watch your tongue. Nor will I excuse your getting into a fight over some schoolyard taunt. Is that clear?"

"Yes, sir," Colianno said.

"And you," Patrick said, turning to the clerk. "Does that seem like a good way to treat your patients? Would you call me a filthy mick?"

Weston, apparently thinking it was a rhetorical question, didn't answer until Patrick said, "Well?"

The soldier looked up—Patrick was a good four inches taller and, even underweight, clearly not a man to mess with. Plus he was a captain and a chaplain.

"No, sir."

"Are you finished with his paperwork?"

"Yes, sir," Weston said.

Patrick turned to Colianno. "Get your gear and meet me outside."

Harkins and Patrick had just walked out of the tent when Harkins heard the clerk say, "Thought all you dagoes had your own dago priests."

He was halfway turned around when Patrick put his hand on Harkins' arm, and a second later they heard a *whump*, an exhalation, something that might have been a body crumpling. Colianno came out palming a small canvas bag.

Harkins told the young trooper, "Wait here," then took his brother by the arm and pulled him several yards away. "What the hell are you doing to me?"

"Look," Patrick said, "the guy was a good soldier, a very good soldier, right up until the invasion. He was in one of those small groups that operated on its own for about thirty-six hours. They were in some fights, some of the troopers got killed. But ever since we pulled out of the line he's been in trouble. Fighting, like you just saw."

"And that's why you think he and I make a good team?"

"No," Patrick said. Then, "Well, maybe. He's got some stuff going on, and I thought maybe you'd understand him. His sergeants tell me he'll take on anybody, big or small, but he seems especially touchy about the whole 'dago' thing."

"The 'dago' thing?"

"The guys are always putting somebody down; it's just how they talk. Everybody's a drunken mick or a stupid pollack, or a cheap kike or a dirty dago. Most of them don't mean anything by it, but Colianno takes it personally."

"Maybe he doesn't like that we're here killing his people," Harkins said. "His parents' people."

"I don't know," Patrick said. "His sergeants and his officers tried to talk to him. No dice. Me? I think something happened to him during those first two days that changed him."

"So what was it? Combat?"

"I'm not sure. I'm looking into it, but I'm having a hard time tracking down the guys who were with that lost patrol, and the ones I have found aren't keen to talk."

"So why dump him on me?"

"We're not taking him along when we go back to North Africa to train for the next operation."

"So?" Harkins asked.

"He'll get assigned as a replacement someplace and will wind up in the stockade. Or dead."

"So why don't you take him on as a project? Chaplain's assistant."

"I argued for that, but I lost. The orders are that he stays behind when we leave Sicily in a few days."

"So now he's my problem? I ain't got enough going on with this murder?"

"I'm asking you as a favor."

Harkins studied his older brother. "And if I say no?"

"I'll excommunicate you. Bring back the Inquisition and the rack."

"I'm screwed here."

"I'll slip you those celibacy pills the church makes us take so you'll never get a hard-on again."

Harkins smiled. Patrick had made up the "celibacy pills" story when he went into seminary and his younger brother asked him about a life without girls.

"Nice talk from a priest," Harkins said.

"Eddie, the kid is going to wind up dead if no one takes an interest in him."

"This is about the old man, isn't it?"

"What do you mean?"

"Dear old Da," Harkins said, using one of the affectations that lingered from their immigrant grandparents. "The poorest lawyer in Philadelphia. Always taking on the charity cases."

Now it was Patrick's turn to smile. "Remember the guy who paid him in bootleg whiskey? Mickey something."

"The car thief?"

"No, Mickey's dopey son was a car thief. Mickey was a bootlegger."

"Oh, that stuff was *baaaaad,*" Harkins said. "Talk about keeping your dick soft."

"Nice talk in front of a priest. And you should talk about Da's influence. He's probably the reason you care about finding whoever killed some guy that everybody hated."

"Got no choice there," Harkins said. "I'm a lawman."

Patrick gave him a smile that could have meant he agreed, he understood, or he thought his brother was a bullshit artist. Harkins looked over to where Colianno was standing, still waiting, another kid getting pushed around by forces beyond his control, maybe beyond his understanding.

"Sometimes maybe you have to choose justice or the law," Patrick said.

"That kind of stuff is for judges and priests to decide," Harkins said. He took off his helmet, mopped his forehead with a kerchief.

"You going to take my guy?" Patrick asked. "I'll take care of the paperwork putting him on temporary duty with you."

"Okay. You owe me, then. Gotta say a couple of prayers, a couple of masses, work my name in there."

Harkins was trying to make a joke—he was the least religious person in the family—but it fell flat. He was sure that Patrick already prayed for him. He wished he still believed it might do some good.

4

2 August 1943
1130 hours

Patrick promised to find Harkins on the hospital grounds in the next day or so to see how Colianno was doing, then the priest and his driver left. Harkins found Colianno where he'd left him, near the registration tent. There was no sign of Weston, who'd apparently had enough.

"My brother talked me into taking you on as my driver," Harkins said. "Against my better judgment."

Colianno came to attention. In ten minutes he'd already demonstrated more military courtesy than Bobby Ray Thomas had in a year. Of course, Thomas didn't get into fights with everyone he met.

"At ease," Harkins said.

Colianno spread his feet and put his hands behind his back. He was about five eight, a couple of inches shorter than Harkins. Skinny—lots of GIs had been fighting dysentery, bad food, nasty water. He had dark hair and delicate, almost feminine features. Not a mark on his face; Weston, the clerk, hadn't touched him.

"Sir, I'd like to go back to my unit."

"And I'd like to get to third base with Betty Grable, but that ain't about to happen either. According to my brother, your unit is going back to North Africa without you, and your choices are me or the repple depple; probably the stockade at some point, the rate you're going."

The "repple depple" was GI slang for the replacement detachment, a pool of GIs where commanders found replacements for their dead and wounded. The army actually set them up as pens, complete with barbed-wire fencing. Harkins thought they looked like stockyards, which was both sad and, he often thought, appropriate.

Something passed over Colianno's eyes. He was hurt, but too proud to show it to Harkins.

"You were in the hospital. Were you wounded or sick?"

"Both. Took some shrapnel in the arm and it got infected. They had to open it up and let it drain. I also got the dysentery in North Africa. Seemed like our whole unit came down with it. It was a mess. Guys lined up at the shitter all day. I got a little better, then got it again after we landed here. Lost a bunch of weight that I really couldn't afford to lose."

"You speak the local language?"

"Yes, sir. My parents were born here. I still got relatives here."

"That why you punch out anybody who says . . . who insults the locals?"

"Part of it, I guess."

"What's the other part?"

Colianno looked at him, considered the question for a moment, then said, "I don't know, sir."

"OK, I guess that makes as much sense as anything else I've seen in the army."

"Sir, you don't mind my asking, what do you do? What outfit you with?"

"Military police. I'm investigating the murder that happened here this morning."

"You're the beat cop they put on this case?"

Even the privates were talking about how he was in over his head.

"Looks like the provost is a little shorthanded, so this fell into my lap. The hospital will probably move toward the front lines in a day or two, which will make the investigation harder. I got a snowball's chance in hell of solving this, and that's only if I get moving right away, *and* if I catch a break."

Colianno was quiet for a moment, studying Harkins. "Maybe I could help you, sir. I mean, if I have to stay behind."

"Yeah? How's that?"

"Officers think that enlisted men don't know what's going on, or that we only know what they tell us. But the GIs see everything. I can talk to guys who might not want to talk to you."

"Go on."

"Permission to speak freely, Lieutenant?"

"Of course."

"The Stephenson guy was a pig, what I heard. Always grabbing the nurses and stuff. Drank, too."

"Here at the hospital?"

"He managed to get into Palermo a couple of times, even though the hospital has only been here a few days, a week at the most. Anyway, he came back drunk and the nurses were afraid he was going to try to operate like that. Shit-faced, I mean."

"Any opinions among the GIs as to who killed him?"

"Not that I heard. I know the first sergeant didn't like him much."

"Drake."

"Right. He's Regular Army, twelve or thirteen years in. Most of the enlisted guys say he's hard but fair."

"You ever dealt with Drake?"

"I stay clear of the guy. I have a reputation, I guess you could say."

"I'll bet. Where were you this morning when the air raid hit?"

"I was packing my stuff in my ward tent, 'cause I knew I was being discharged today."

"Alone?" Harkins asked.

"A few other guys in there."

Harkins pulled out his notebook. "Names?"

"Guy from the First Division named Marshall. Another paratrooper, an H Company guy named Harris."

"What air-raid shelter did you use?"

"We didn't. They've had four or five of these alerts without a single Kraut plane showing up. All false alarms. I think the Luftwaffe is finished, so me and the other guys stayed put."

"What else do you know?"

"Can I get in trouble for talking about officers?"

"Not as much trouble as you can get in for fighting all the time," Harkins said. "Look," he went on. "You're right. The enlisted guys might talk to you more readily than they'll talk to me. Plus you've already been here, what? A few days? If you can find out things that help me in the investigation, you don't have anything to worry about."

"OK, then," Colianno said. "The staff says that Colonel Boone, the commander, likes to gamble, but he isn't very good at it. Some of the other docs wonder how he sends any money home to support his family, given how much he loses at poker."

"OK," Harkins said. "Not sure what the connection might be, but most murders are about money, sex, or power. Any talk among the men about how Colonel Boone and Stephenson got along?"

"Some of the guys didn't like Stephenson, but most of them wished they were the ones scoring with the girls."

"I'll have to talk to more nurses."

"You don't think a girl could have done this, do you? Shot some guy in the head at close range?" His expression said he thought it a ridiculous idea.

"Doesn't seem likely, I'll admit," Harkins said. "Right now I'm just trying to get a complete picture of what was going on at this hospital."

"There was a lot going on, all right," Colianno said.

Harkins heard a commotion in the registration tent. He started walking away and toward his jeep, Colianno following.

"Hold it right there."

First Sergeant Drake barreled out of the tent, following them. When Harkins and Colianno turned, Drake spoke directly to the paratrooper, ignoring Harkins.

"Did you get in a fight with my clerk, you little sonofabitch?"

Colianno had come to parade rest, the appropriate military courtesy when addressed by a senior noncommissioned officer.

Harkins held up a hand just as Colianno started to speak. "There was a disagreement, First Sergeant. But the chaplain and I took care of it."

Drake narrowed his eyes, leaned too close, put his hands on his hips. He clearly wished Harkins wasn't in the way of his chewing out Colianno.

"What chaplain?"

"From this man's unit. He was visiting, and I was there, too. It's all taken care of. In fact, Private Colianno has been discharged, so he's not your problem anymore, First Sergeant. He's working for me now."

"Your boy was trouble from the moment he got here. Now I got a busted-up table in there, Lieutenant. Records and papers all over the place. I got a clerk with a fat lip."

Harkins could play pissed off as well as the next guy. He lowered his voice and said, "Don't know what to tell you, First Sergeant. Maybe you should take care of your guy and I'll take care of mine. How about that?"

Drake looked at Colianno, then back at Harkins. "You two will make a great pair."

"Colianno, go over to the jeep," Harkins said. When the private was gone, Drake turned as if to walk away.

"Just a second, First Sergeant."

Drake stopped but did not turn around. Harkins knew the older man wanted to keep on walking, but all those years of discipline made it hard for him to ignore a direct order from an officer, even a lowly lieutenant he clearly did not like.

Rather than test him by telling him to turn around, Harkins walked to Drake's front. The old noncom had murder in his eyes. Harkins tried a different approach.

"Look, we got off on the wrong foot," Harkins said. "I've only been here a few hours; usually it takes people a day or two to really dislike me."

The humor didn't work. Drake managed to look bored and pissed off at the same time.

Harkins looked around. They were surrounded by tents; no one could see them. Would Drake take a swing at him?

"No one is unhappier than I am about catching this case. But I plan to do my job as best I can and as fast as I can. Then I'll get out of your hair. How does that sound?"

After a few seconds, Drake said, "Anything else?"

"Yes, as a matter of fact. From now on I want you to show me the proper military courtesy, and I'll do the exact same for you."

"You've got to earn respect," Drake said.

"And I may or may not, based on the job I do. That's for a future conversation. But we both know you salute the rank, not the person. The army made me a first lieutenant. If nobody asked your opinion about whether I was a good choice, well, I'm sorry about that. But in this thing, at least, your opinion doesn't really matter, just like my opinion as to whether or not you should be a first sergeant doesn't matter."

There was a long pause. Harkins wondered if, in his weakened condition and nearly asleep on his feet, he could take a punch from someone Drake's size.

"Let me show you something," Drake said. He motioned for Harkins to follow him, turned in to a tent marked with a white sign: SURGICAL 2.

The walls to this tent were down, probably to keep out the dust. It had to be ninety, a hundred, a hundred and ten degrees in there. There were three electric lights hovering above an operating table—the sound of generators was a constant background noise across the compound. Two surgeons were at work, their arms bloody to the elbows. Two nurses stood close by, one handing instruments from a tray, the other using forceps to hold a large triangle of bloody meat out of the doctors' way.

Harkins looked on for a moment, Drake watching him, then the two men stepped outside.

"That's the mission, Lieutenant. Those eight hands trying to save one kid, trying to sew him back together so he leaves here on a stretcher, not in a body bag. Everything else—all the shit I do day to day, all the stuff everyone else does—is to support those eight hands."

Drake, who was already standing close to Harkins, leaned in. "Anybody in this hospital who gets in the way of that performance in there—no, wait—anyone who isn't *contributing* to making that performance better, why, I roll over them like a truck. Crush 'em. And I sleep like a fucking baby."

"Is that what you did to Stephenson? Crush him?"

Drake snorted, a mean laugh. "I'm talking about you and your so-called investigation, which we both know hasn't got a chance of doing anything worthwhile. Stay the fuck out of my way. Stay out of the way of the hospital staff. You slow us down, and I'll deal with you myself. Got it?"

"I hear the GIs in the hospital are afraid of you; the officers, too, for that matter."

Drake wasn't expecting it, but Harkins stepped closer. He had to look up, but the two men were practically nose to nose. Harkins felt what had to be his last reserves of adrenaline kick in.

"Lot of big guys like you never have to fight, because most people back down. But I will beat your ass if I have to. We can do it here, no rank, or in front of as many people as you want to invite. I know I can take a punch. How about you?"

Drake straightened up, unafraid but uninterested in anything more. "You are something else, Lieutenant," he said. "Don't know where they found you, but you are something else."

Then the first sergeant turned and walked away without looking back.

"At least he called me lieutenant," Harkins muttered. "We're practically pals."

5

2 August 1943
1200 hours

Colonel Walter Boone had a headache.

He went back to his sleeping tent, pulled a bottle of aspirin from his bedroll, and shook a couple into his mouth.

Yesterday his problem had been the nurses, with their complaining, and fucking Stephenson, of course. Even though Stephenson was out of the picture, the nurses were still talking, gabbing endlessly about how bad they had it. Now he had some dumb cop and a pathetic deputy provost snooping around.

He went to the door of his tent closest to the orderly room and yelled for his clerk.

"Whitaker!"

The soldier hustled out of the orderly room tent, pushing his glasses back up his nose. Too smart for his own good, this one; always huddled with the first sergeant, clamming up whenever Boone was around.

They didn't respect him. Even Whitaker, a goddamn PFC, probably thought he could do a better job. And Drake, with his Old Army attitudes, always complaining about the influx of amateurs. Boone would like to see Drake try to ride herd on a bunch of egotistical surgeons. He'd like to see Drake scrub in when the casualties were rolling in. Seven hours on his feet with his hands inside some kid's chest, trying to put everything back together. They all thought they knew better.

"Yes, sir?" Whitaker said.

"Any word on when we're moving forward?"

There were more than twenty hospitals and medical units trailing the fighting units as they pushed east across the island. The bigger ones, like Boone's Eleventh Field Hospital, were a traveling circus: three platoons, each with a hundred-bed capacity. Scores of tents and sixty-plus vehicles that leapfrogged forward so that a GI wounded at the front could reach the care he needed as quickly as possible. Speed saved lives.

"No, sir. We haven't heard anything."

Hospital commanders like Boone weren't privy to the Allied attack plans, but they were often given a "warning order," telling them to be prepared to move within twenty-four hours.

"When was the last time you checked?"

Whitaker looked at his wristwatch. "About two hours ago, Colonel."

"Well, go fucking check again!" Boone said.

It came out more harshly than he'd intended, and Whitaker scampered away.

Screw him, Boone thought. The little bastard thought it was a hard day if he had to type a dozen reports.

Boone was banking that a move forward would throw off the investigation; at least delay it a few days. If that wasn't in the cards, then the key to getting rid of Harkins was the provost marshal.

Boone knew there'd be a big stink at headquarters because a surgeon had been murdered, and there'd be command pressure to solve the crime. But the attention would fade quickly. There were murders every day: GIs stabbing GIs, soldiers beating up locals and robbing prostitutes. Two Americans and two Brits had been arrested recently for setting fire to a bank in Santa Croce Camerina; the four drunks thought they'd come up with a novel way to stage a robbery. Then there was the awesome scale of the black market and the thousands of tons of supplies and equipment that were being siphoned off by corrupt GIs and their local cronies. As far as the war effort went, surely that problem demanded more attention than the shooting of one pain-in-the-ass captain. Boone just had to persuade the provost to see it that way.

And he could always get rid of the nurses who talked too much, or intimidate them into shutting the hell up. He doubted any one of them had any idea what kind of questions an inquiry or court-martial would throw at them.

His stomach churned. He held his hands in front of him, the right one shaking a bit. A brisk walk around the compound would help. He set his helmet on his head and stepped into the sunshine, walked to where the engineers had cut a perimeter road for the hospital. He kept looking over his shoulder, suddenly wanting to know where Harkins was, where Drake had gone, where the Bolshevik nurses were.

By the time he looked up, he'd reached the line of pyramidal tents that housed the rest of the officers. With a full complement there would be nine surgeons, a dentist, and three anesthesiologists, along with eighteen nurses. The Eleventh was supposed to have three hundred beds, while the overall Allied invasion plan called for some three thousand beds over multiple facilities, but limited sea and air transport from the staging areas in North Africa meant every medical unit landed in Sicily already short of people and equipment. And in the nearly five weeks since D-Day, they'd continued to lose medical staff to sickness—malaria was rampant—accidents, and transfers to hospitals that were even more short-staffed.

And still the wounded streamed in, day and night, and Boone was somehow supposed to maintain a standard of care. No American mother wanted to hear that her wounded boy had made it to a U.S. Army hospital only to die in a surgery queue.

He'd had a dream the previous week in which he was filling sandbags for an air-raid shelter. He could hear German planes approaching, but he couldn't move quickly enough, and the sand leaked from the bag faster than he could shovel it in, and all the while the nurses and other docs stood around laughing at his efforts.

It made him want to kill someone.

Boone was already sweating through his shirt, but he continued walking fast, hoping the exercise would take the edge off his anxiety. When he reached Stephenson's tent, he looked around and found he was alone on the street.

He went inside.

It took a few seconds for his eyes to adjust to the darkness. The tent was empty of all of Stephenson's personal gear, uniforms, bedding, and footlocker. Drake had probably been through, collecting stuff, sorting government property from personal, then combing through the personal to make sure they weren't sending anything embarrassing back to the family. Sometimes the first sergeant found postcards with photos of naked women. No one wanted to send those home to Mother.

Suddenly the thought of Harkins rooting around in whatever detritus Stephenson had left behind made him anxious all over again. He blotted the sweat on his forehead with a sleeve.

"Help you, Colonel?"

Boone jumped, turned around to see David Wilkins' bear shape blocking the door. Wilkins, another surgeon, might have been close to Stephenson. Boone wasn't sure.

"No. I, uh, no thanks, Captain Wilkins. I was just checking to make sure First Sergeant Drake had removed all of Captain Stephenson's personal belongings."

Wilkins didn't answer, just stared without blinking.

"Shame what happened to him," Boone said.

Wilkins grunted, noncommittal.

Boone had once come up behind Wilkins talking to some of the other docs, thought he heard the beefy captain say something about "Doctor Dirt Farmer." The other men widened their eyes—they could see Boone and were probably warning Wilkins—but the big man was unfazed. He turned, saluted, and said, "We were just talking about you, sir. About how efficiently the hospital jumps when we have to."

Snotty bastard, Boone thought.

"How were your patients today?" Boone asked.

"They'll pull through," Wilkins said without enthusiasm.

"Well, I better get moving," Boone said, stepping closer to the door. Wilkins took his time getting out of the way and Boone had to squeeze by him. The captain made no move to salute, did not offer a greeting.

Boone knew this was one of the reasons they had no respect for him: he couldn't bring himself to enforce standards, at least not equally across the entire hospital. Boone had no trouble intimidating privates, but nurses and his own doctors were another story.

Boone was several steps outside the tent when he turned back.

"Aren't you forgetting something, Captain?" Boone asked.

Wilkins wrinkled his brow, as if thinking about the question hurt him.

"A salute?" Boone said.

Wilkins brought his right hand up, but instead of saluting, he pointed to the side of his head.

"Not wearing headgear, Colonel. Didn't think we were supposed to salute without a hat or helmet."

"Right, well," Boone said, flustered. "Carry on, then."

He turned again, wanted to look back, wanted to scream at Wilkins, at his goddamn smug look. Instead, he stepped back onto the perimeter road and walked away from doctors' row.

Instead of calming him, his walk had upset him. Fucking disrespectful assholes.

Boone stepped through a gate that separated the compound from a few sad buildings that constituted a tiny village. Some of the buildings had been bombed, but Boone didn't know if it had been the retreating Germans or the advancing Americans who inflicted the damage. Probably didn't matter to the locals.

He saw the little storefront where some Sicilian women had set up a laundry. Patting his pockets to see that he had money, he ducked inside. It was too hot for a walk anyway.

"Hello," he said when he entered. There was no front door, and Boone didn't know if it was because of the heat or because some GI had stolen it to make a table in the hospital compound. He could see all the way through the tiny shop and out into a small courtyard in the back, where two iron kettles sat atop a three-sided brick stand. A smoky fire burned below one of the pots.

"Hello," he called again.

Shelves lined the right-hand wall, clean laundry wrapped in newspaper and tied with string. He lifted the edges of the packages, found his name scrawled in crayon, pulled the bundle free. He looked out the back again; neither of the women seemed to be around.

"Anybody here?"

He reached into his pocket and pulled out a few notes, invasion currency printed by the Allies to supplant the Fascist government currency. At first the locals had refused to take the money, but after the Americans got a couple of the banks open and the notes started circulating, the Sicilians came around.

"I'm going to leave the money on the counter here," he called, though he knew that neither woman spoke English.

There was an ancient ledger book on the counter; he tucked a few bills under the edge, used the pencil stuck inside the book to put a small checkmark next to his name, indicating that he'd paid.

That's when he saw Stephenson's name. He looked on the shelves, found a bundle tied with string and marked "s-t-e-f."

Such an ordinary thing. You drop off laundry and expect to be back in a couple of days to pick it up. But you might not get a couple of days.

He was a bit surprised the hyperefficient Drake or the nosy cop hadn't thought to retrieve Stephenson's laundry. They'd gone through everything else belonging to the man.

That's when he thought of the letter.

Boone hurried outside and back to his own sleeping tent, trying to outpace his panic. When he arrived he closed the flap behind him. There was no sign of Whitaker, who sometimes doubled as an orderly. The man had no reason to go through Boone's things; even so, perhaps Boone had not been careful enough.

Stephenson had expected to pick up his own laundry. He certainly didn't anticipate someone—Drake, Harkins—pawing through his stuff, looking for secrets. Everything could change that quickly.

He unlocked his footlocker with a key he kept on his dog-tag chain, pulled out the top tray to reveal some folded clothes and a box of stationery. He'd brought the box with him from the States, but he had not written a single letter in the nine months since leaving New York Harbor. If the mail clerk or the junior officers who censored the outgoing mail ever noticed, they certainly didn't say anything to him.

No outgoing mail, no incoming mail. Inside the box, just one extra envelope, his name and rank in a feminine script on the outside.

He tried to imagine Drake's reaction if he'd found this. Or Harkins'. Surprise, perhaps.

Boone found a pack of C-ration matches in the footlocker tray.

And what, exactly, would have been so surprising? That he'd had a sweetheart? That he wasn't always despised?

He lit a match, held the letter by a corner, and dangled it into the tiny flame.

He hated admitting it, even to himself, but he supposed they would have been surprised that someone once cared for him. Doctor Dirt Farmer.

"Fuck them."

When the flames licked at his fingers, he dropped the letter to the dirt floor, ground the ashes under his boot heel.

6

2 August 1943
1300 hours

It took Harkins and Colianno over an hour to find his MP platoon, bivouacked in the courtyard of a big country house. Colianno drove, with Harkins in the passenger seat and an unhappy Bobby Ray Thomas in the back. Thomas didn't like that he was being replaced.

"Couple of days' rest," Harkins told him. "Light duty. You'll be good as new."

At least half of Harkins' men—the day shift—were out guarding convoys of supplies, which had become targets for bandits who supplied the black market. Harkins' second-in-command, Platoon Sergeant Mike Desmond, was under a jeep when Harkins pulled up.

"Sergeant Desmond," Harkins called.

Desmond crawled out, his hands and chest spotted with motor oil. "Hey, Lieutenant. We been wondering what happened to you."

Harkins explained that he'd been detailed to a murder investigation, and that Thomas would be returning to the platoon for light duty and rest.

Desmond motioned to Colianno, who stood twenty yards away, filling his canteen from a fountain. "Who's that?"

"My driver, for now. My brother convinced me to take him on. Kind of a special project."

"Your brother the chaplain? He's got you saving souls now, too?"

"Why, Sergeant Desmond, sounds like you doubt I can be a good influence on America's fighting men."

Desmond laughed, used a clear spot on one wrist to blot sweat from his chin.

Another jeep pulled into the courtyard; the battalion mail clerk jumped out with a canvas sack. “Got some mail for you, Lieutenant Harkins, Sergeant Desmond.”

Harkins did not look at his platoon sergeant, who hadn’t had a letter from his wife in six months and had stopped lining up for mail call.

“Christmas in August, boys!” Harkins called out. “Mail’s here.”

A dozen of his men shuffled toward him, all filthy hands, grimy faces, and exhaustion.

He reached inside the bag, grabbed a bundle, and yanked off the rubber band. “Monroe!”

Monroe stepped up, hand out, a raccoon stripe across his eyes where his driver’s goggles had covered his face.

“Thomas!”

Thomas was still in the back of Harkins’ jeep, so the lieutenant went to him to hand over two letters, both envelopes typewritten.

“Thanks,” Thomas said.

Thomas had been Harkins’ driver for ten months, the two of them living side by side through the campaign in North Africa and now Sicily, and Harkins was pretty certain Thomas had never called him “sir.” Harkins sometimes wondered if he should care more about military courtesy.

“Pulauskus!”

Sometimes the mail caught up in bunches, and his men got stacks of letters. Sometimes they could go weeks without mail, cut off from family and evidence of some normal world back home.

“Hey, Lieutenant, thought you might like this.”

Harkins looked up to see a solider named Clendening holding out one of the Armed Services Editions paperbacks that were being shipped to GIs in the war zones. Printed on pulp stock, they were clearly not made to last long. GIs got them for free to help stave off the boredom that was every soldier’s lot.

“The guys say you read this kind of stuff.”

The book was *Poems of Carl Sandburg*; the smooth cover told Harkins it had not been opened.

“You don’t want to give it a try?”

“Nah. I was looking for something, you know, something maybe with some dames in it.”

"I know what you mean," Harkins said. "I've been looking for a sleeping bag that came equipped with a woman."

Clendening smiled, showing two broken teeth. Harkins took the book, tossed the volume into the back of his jeep. He had never tried to hide the fact that he read the occasional history and poetry books that came with their morale packages, but he'd never told any of the soldiers that he had a year of college. Figured it would ruin their impression of him, former amateur boxer and tough city cop.

"Thanks, Clendening. You get any more you don't want, I'm happy to take them."

Harkins put his hands back into the mail sack, pulled out the last few envelopes. There were four letters for him, but none for Sergeant Desmond. He walked to where the noncom sat in the passenger seat of his jeep, smoking and looking out over the hood.

Over the garden wall, the road out of town dropped as it headed northeast. Two lines of hills stretched to the horizon like outspread arms, framing a valley dotted with toylike houses and dense groves of fruit and olive trees. At the far end of the valley was Palermo, and beyond that, the Tyrrhenian Sea.

"Pretty," Harkins said.

After a silent moment, Desmond said, "Appreciate you always checking on me, Lieutenant."

Desmond's marriage trouble started before they left the States. Harkins had arranged—had begged their commander for—an emergency leave for Desmond just before they embarked for Africa. Since that last, apparently failed effort, Harkins and Desmond had only spoken once about Desmond's worries. His wife wound up leaving the two-room tarpaper shanty they rented in the scrub pine of Florida's panhandle for a war-industry job and a better life up North someplace. No forwarding address.

"Right," Harkins said, feeling worse than useless. "Well, you know where to find me if you need anything. If you want to talk."

Harkins refilled his canteen at the courtyard's small fountain, then sat under the stingy shade of a tree and spread his letters out in front of him. Usually he sorted them by postmark, reading the oldest ones first, but this time he sorted by writer.

Harkins was the second of six children. Patrick, his chaplain brother, was oldest. He wasn't surprised to see that there was no letter from the priest. Maybe Patrick's mail had caught up, too, and if they managed to get together again in the next day or so they could swap, share a few laughs together.

Nor was there a letter from Michael, the youngest, in the navy somewhere on the other side of the globe.

Michael had tried joining the navy the same day that Harkins enlisted in the army, but was turned down because he was only sixteen. The recruiting sergeant had been surprised at the date on his papers, since Michael looked like a grown man. Michael and Patrick favored their father's side of the family, sharing the same thick, almost black hair and square-jawed good looks that garnered a lot of attention. Eddie was always amazed at how many women were not dissuaded by Patrick's Roman collar or the fact that Michael was a kid.

One of Michael's schoolmates had managed to fool the army recruiter by changing his birth certificate, which Michael pronounced a swell idea. Both Patrick and Eddie tried to convince their brother to wait until he turned seventeen, when he'd be able to enlist with a signature from one parent.

"Mom will never do that," Michael had countered, "and I'll have to wait until I'm eighteen."

"Then you'll have to wait," Patrick said with oldest-brother finality. When Patrick left, Michael started working on Eddie, who felt for the kid.

Eddie reached out to a friend who worked in city records, and twenty bucks later Michael had an official birth certificate that added fifteen months to his age. Michael told his parents that he'd gotten the forgery on his own, though Eddie suspected that his parents knew the truth. His mother had been angry for months; it was still rare to get a letter from her.

Harkins' three little sisters, on the other hand, were faithful correspondents. There was something from each of them, plus a thin envelope from Dad. He'd save that for last.

He got up and washed his hands at the fountain, savoring what was coming, and feeling, as he'd told his men, a bit like it was Christmas. For the first time in days, maybe weeks, he didn't feel completely exhausted. He also knew that a batch of mail came with a built-in letdown.

There was the elation of a connection, however tenuous and artificial, with home. But after he read the letters, the distance, the great void of time and space that separated him from those he loved, weighed on him.

He opened Aileen's letter first. She was nineteen, strawberry blond hair and blue eyes, and apparently in love with Timothy Brady, the Philadelphia patrolman Harkins had introduced her to before he left.

I was going to just hand out punch, she wrote about a USO dance she attended, *since Tim couldn't come. But then I thought it would be more patriotic to dance with some of the soldiers and sailors.* She'd underlined the word "patriotic" twice, added, *Ha ha.*

She told him about the women she worked with at the Frankford Arsenal, where she spent her days making mortar shells, and her breaks learning to smoke cigarettes. *The older, married women are teaching me a great deal,* she wrote. Harkins read the line twice, decided he did not want to think the women talked about sex, at least not with his kid sister.

Aileen closed with a list of boys from the neighborhood who'd joined the service, of the girls who'd gotten married right before their sweethearts shipped out. In the nineteen months she'd been writing to him, she had—out of concern for him, he supposed—never mentioned a single casualty.

"Looks like a big haul," Thomas said as he sat down under the next tree.

"Pays to have a big Catholic family come mail call," Harkins said.

He opened Saoirse's letter, a single sheet of pink stationery, a short one for her.

My dear brother, it began. *I'm so sorry you'll be alone during this tough time.*

Harkins scanned the rest of the short page quickly. The word "guilty" jumped out at him.

I know that as Catholics we feel guilty about everything, and as Irish Catholics we even feel guilty that maybe we don't feel guilty enough, but you know I've never thought much of that philosophy. Don't beat yourself up too badly, big brother. You are a good man, and I love you dearly.

"Shit," Harkins said. His sisters must have found out about Maureen Conner, the woman he'd fallen for the autumn before the war. Maureen was beautiful; Patrick said she turned heads while walking to Holy Communion. She was also married to a detective in Harkins' precinct. They had flirted for a few months, and finally Harkins had kissed her after a Halloween party, both of them tipsy, both of them breathing hard and shying away from the cliff-edge of some disaster.

On the Monday before Pearl Harbor, Detective Conner walked up to Harkins in an otherwise deserted precinct locker room, showed him a photo of three children: two little girls in frilly dresses, a boy with a lazy eye.

"My kids" was all he said, didn't even name them, just walked out, tucking the picture back into his coat pocket. Nine days later Harkins enlisted.

But all that was a year and a half ago. Had something happened to Maureen? If her marriage broke up, did she blame Harkins?

Jesus, he thought. *And I only got to kiss her. Once.*

Harkins looked at the date of Saoirse's letter: May 29, 1943. He picked up Aileen's letter, which was dated May 2. Then the postmarks of the remaining two: Dad's was mailed after Aileen's and before Saoirse's. If the old man had found out about Maureen, that would be another strike against Eddie. Strike two, counting Michael's forged birth certificate.

He started to open the letter from Dad, then decided to postpone the inevitable and distract himself with Mary's letter.

Dear Bee, Mary began. The pet name came from his initials; his given name was Bernard Edward. *I am so sorry and know that you must be heartbroken, as we all are.*

Christ. Did Maureen kill herself? That can't be right. He was pretty sure that once he left she'd just find another cop to flirt with.

I spent a couple of days with Mom—Mr. Hatter at work said take whatever time I need. Nice man. Bee, she is inconsolable, as I would be in her shoes.

"What's wrong?" Thomas asked.

Harkins looked up. "What?"

"You look like you seen a ghost, and you're talking to yourself. More than usual, I mean."

Harkins looked at his driver, afraid to turn his attention back to the paper in his hand. "I . . . I don't know yet. Bad news, I think." He drew breath, looked down again.

I thought about moving the photo, Mary wrote, *the one of you three boys when you were all home on leave, all looking so handsome in your uniforms.*

Harkins stood abruptly, felt a wave of nausea.

He looked at the postmarks again. Mary and Saoirse had each written believing that he'd already gotten whatever bad news was in his father's letter. He turned the last, thin envelope over once, twice. Pinched the corners. Of course the old man would be the one to tell him.

Harkins leaned over and put his forearms on his knees. When he felt a hand on his shoulder, he looked up into Thomas' kind face.

"You need help, Lieutenant?"

Harkins didn't trust his voice. He held the last envelope out to Thomas, who opened it with a dirty finger. He pulled out a single sheet—Harkins could see it was written on the letterhead of his father's law firm—and read it silently. When he finished, he said, "You want me to read it to you?"

Harkins fell back to a sitting position; Thomas squatted beside him, and Harkins nodded. Thomas licked his chapped and sunburned lips, swallowed.

"'My dear son,'" he read. "'We received a telegram yesterday from the War Department.'"

Thomas paused, looked at Harkins, who nodded.

"'Michael's ship was sunk on or about April 19. Michael was not among the forty-two survivors rescued by other vessels.

"'I am so sorry to have to tell you in this way, and sorry that you are so far away from us when we all need one another.'"

Thomas' voice faded into the background, replaced by a low moan, an animal in pain. Harkins pulled his knees in tight, heard the sound coming from his chest, his tightened throat, his breaking heart.

7

2 August 1943
1400 hours

Colianno and Harkins were almost back at the hospital before the paratrooper, driving now, asked, "Something wrong, Lieutenant?"

Harkins thought of a reply: *My kid brother was killed in the Pacific.* But he didn't trust himself to say it out loud, so he nodded. "Uh-huh."

He would have to tell Patrick. Christ, was it just this morning they were together and happily ignorant?

When Harkins offered nothing else, Colianno asked, "Where do you want to go?"

"Why don't you go to the mess tent. Get yourself something to eat."

Colianno parked the jeep in a row of ambulances and trucks. A half-dozen mechanics in greasy overalls crawled over the nearby vehicles.

"You coming, sir?"

"No," Harkins said. He needed to be alone, but alone was hard to come by at a crowded hospital compound, on an island crawling with GIs, when he was supposed to be leading a murder investigation. He'd have to stick his grief somewhere, stow it away like a bad memory he'd relive later.

"I'll stay with the vehicle. You come back and get me when you're finished and I'll figure out who I'll talk to next."

"Can I bring you something? A sandwich?" Colianno asked.

Harkins shook his head, watched the paratrooper walk away, then pulled out his sweaty pocket notebook and tried to focus on the list of names there.

Boone.

Drake.

Gallo.

Palmer.

"Hey, Lieutenant. Lieutenant!"

Harkins looked up. A sergeant was standing in front of his jeep. No telling how long the man had been there, trying to get his attention.

"Sorry, sir. Could you move this thing over there?" The GI pointed to another dusty patch on the edge of the compound.

"I gotta get a tow truck in here and it'll be easier without your jeep in the way, sir."

Harkins moved the vehicle, thought about how the world would keep going, oblivious to one family's heartbreak.

He remembered a young GI in his platoon, a McDuffy from Bethlehem, Pennsylvania, who'd had a brother killed in North Africa in May, just days before the surrender of Axis forces there. Harkins had gotten the message from their chaplain, and it was his duty as platoon leader to tell the soldier.

When Harkins broke the bad news, McDuffy had simply dropped his gaze to the dirt. Then he sat in the shade for a few hours before telling Sergeant Desmond that he wanted to get back to work.

The next day, Harkins' platoon was assigned to guard some German POWs near Bizerte in Tunisia. The prisoners were in a barbed-wire enclosure, nothing more than a corral, really, waiting for a ship that would take them to England. The holding area was crowded, and scores of the defeated men leaned on the wire, filthy, exhausted, thoroughly beaten. Harkins, looking at them, had a hard time thinking of them as "the enemy."

He was making his rounds, checking the guards just before dusk, when he walked up on McDuffy, who was aiming his rifle at the Germans. Not holding it loosely, or pointing it generally in their direction. Had the stock to his cheek, right eye open and trained on the front sight, the muzzle steady.

"McDuffy," Harkins had said. Quietly, not wanting to alarm the kid. "What are you doing?"

Without lowering the weapon, McDuffy said, "Could've been one of those bastards who killed my brother."

Harkins had no idea what to do. Twenty yards away, one of the prisoners saw what was happening. He called out something in German, defiant. Then he opened his shirt, baring his chest to McDuffy's rifle.

"Could have been," Harkins said. "Probably wasn't, though."

McDuffy lowered his weapon, and Harkins told Sergeant Desmond to put him back on traffic duty. Looking back on that strange evening,

Harkins remembered how calm McDuffy had been. He hadn't even seemed angry.

Maybe each person handled this kind of thing differently. Harkins had always thought it strange when the victim of some crime said, "It didn't seem real," or, "It was like it was happening to someone else." But that was what he felt.

He looked at his watch, figured Colianno would return in ten or fifteen minutes. For now, that was all the time he had to grieve, then it was back to work. Deal with it later.

Funny, Harkins thought, he'd been craving sleep for days. Now he was a bit afraid to close his eyes and see what fresh hell his dreams brought.

By the time Colianno came back, Harkins had decided he'd go back to the nurses. The two men were walking near the women's sleeping tent when Harkins was blindsided, rushed by some small person, hit full body and nearly knocked over.

"Eddie!"

Kathleen Donnelly laughed as she held on to him, trying to keep him from stumbling sideways. "I'm so glad to see you!"

Harkins regained his footing and turned in to her hug. She was the first American woman he'd touched in sixteen months.

"Let me look at you," he said, peeling her arms from his shoulders.

Donnelly and Harkins had lived on the same street in Kensington, a neighborhood of narrow row homes north of Philadelphia's city center. She had been a year ahead of him in school, all long curls and flashing eyes and movie-star smile, not a timid bone in her compact frame. They'd been friends, but—in Harkins' mind, at least—she was always out of his league.

The woman who let her arms fall from his shoulders looked nothing like he remembered. Her dark hair was chopped short and threaded with dust, a few lonely grays wiring out from her temples. Like every other GI in Sicily, she was drawn and sickly-thin, dirt ground into crow's-feet beside eyes that did not flash, barely looked blue anymore. She wore a man's fatigue uniform cinched tight at the waist. The legs of her trousers stood clear of her own legs like stovepipes; the uniform was dirty enough to stand up in a corner on its own.

Oh, my God, Harkins thought. *She looks like hell.*

"Oh my God, Eddie," she said, appraising him right back, but not holding her tongue. "You look like shit."

She put her hands on either side of his waist above his belt, squeezed, as if trying to encircle him with her fingers.

"Ha, I'll bet you weigh what I did when I joined up," she said. "I guess army life doesn't agree with either of us."

She turned to Colianno. "I know you."

"Yes, ma'am," the paratrooper said. There was an awkward moment, and Harkins couldn't tell if Colianno was caught off guard by this lively nurse throwing herself at his new boss, or if it was something else.

"You were on the ward for a few days, right?"

"Yes, ma'am," Colianno managed.

Donnelly turned back to Harkins, made a *What can you do?* face.

"I heard you're investigating what happened here this morning. What are the chances that we'd run into each other like this?"

"I wish it didn't involve me playing detective," Harkins said.

Donnelly led Harkins and Colianno to the edge of the hospital compound, to an ancient stone wall surrounding a church. There were four neat, almost perfectly round holes shot through the building's roof, black gaps like missing teeth where the windows used to be. As they waited to cross one of the lanes between rows of tents, a jeep rolled by slowly, an orderly in the driver's seat, a stretcher on the back and another on the hood, each holding a body packed inside a cloth sack of some sort.

"Are those . . . ?"

"Mattress covers," Donnelly said. "When we boarded the ship in North Africa to come here, they gave us each two mattress covers to carry. We joked that we were carrying our own shrouds. Turns out it wasn't much of a joke."

There were three pyramidal tents along the church wall, all of them with their sides rolled up. She pointed to a large thermos in one of the tents and said to Colianno, "That coffee has been there for six hours at least. Maybe since last night, possibly since D-Day. But it'll be strong, and it's free."

With Colianno settled into a patch of scanty shade under a shot-up olive tree, Donnelly took Harkins into one of the tents. There were three field tables, with stacks of papers held down by bricks from the damaged church. No one else was inside.

"This is where the nurses do paperwork," Donnelly said. She grabbed a wooden chair someone had liberated from a house and straddled it like a man.

It was midafternoon now, the hottest part of the day, no breeze stirring. Flies droned lazily near the top of the tent.

Donnelly took off her uniform blouse. She wore a man's T-shirt underneath. It had once been white, he imagined, and it hung in loose folds on her small frame, so big that there was no sign of any curve or bump.

She lifted her arms, sniffed unselfconsciously. "Whew. We could use my armpits as secret weapons. Kill a lot of Germans with that aroma."

"Yeah," Harkins said. "I've gotten used to smelling like the police stables."

She pushed the short sleeves up over bony shoulders.

"How did you wind up here?" Harkins asked.

"It was the Eleanor Roosevelt poster," she said.

"What?"

"Eleanor Roosevelt did an advertisement for army nurses—they were looking for forty thousand volunteer nurses, something like that. And Eleanor was quoted saying, 'I just want my boys'—she's got four sons serving, I think—'I just want my boys to have the best care. Won't you do that for them?'"

"Classic guilt trip," Harkins said.

"I know. And Eleanor—I feel like I can call her that, don't you think?—Eleanor isn't even Catholic."

"So you volunteered?"

"Me and about a dozen other girls from Pennsylvania Hospital. At first it seemed like an adventure. They sent me to Washington, issued me some snazzy uniforms—all skirts and dresses, nothing you'll ever see here. On the ship coming over, a converted liner, we got to stay in first-class cabins. Had meals with the senior officers on board. Colonels and generals."

"I'm sure they were all feeling very fatherly," Harkins said. "Wanted to tuck you in at night."

"Something like that," Donnelly said, arching one eyebrow.

"So it was like a sorority?"

"Absolutely. Of course, it wasn't like that for the gals that went ashore with the first wave in North Africa."

Harkins was surprised. "How's that?"

"Yep. Climbed down those big cargo nets, jumped for the landing craft that was bobbing up and down, just like in the newsreels. Went in under fire. Started treating casualties right away, right on the beach, even though their equipment didn't come in for forty-eight hours."

"I didn't know they sent nurses ashore with the first wave."

"No one knows. I heard Ike got spooked—what would the folks at home say if they found out he was sending nurses, America's daughters, onto an invasion beach? On Sicily, we came ashore at D plus three, though I still had to dig my own foxhole and sleep in it for five nights."

"Probably won't see those photos in *Life* magazine," Harkins said.

"That's for sure. And at the rate I'm going, I'll never willingly get my picture taken again," Donnelly said. "See this?" She pulled at the hair on the sides of her head. "Gray. I'm twenty-six years old."

"The work doing that?" Harkins asked.

Donnelly raked her fingers through her hair, took a breath. "Mostly the work. Also the lies."

Harkins was quiet. Outside he could hear women's voices, a vehicle going by, an inept driver grinding the clutch.

"Some of them ask 'Am I going to die?' And you know they are. Shot up bad or burned so that there's nothing we can do except get some morphine into them, kill some of the pain. And when they ask me that question, I look them right in the eye and I lie to them." Donnelly wiped her nose with the back of her hand. "Jesus," she said.

"I'm sorry, Kathleen."

She smiled, passed her hand over her eyes. "You?"

"Seemed like the thing to do after Pearl Harbor."

"Your brothers joined, too, right?"

"Patrick is here on the island, in fact. Saw him this morning. He's a chaplain with the paratroopers."

"That's great you got to see him!" Donnelly said. "And Michael, that other cutie-pie brother?"

Harkins swallowed, not sure if his voice would hold. He wanted to bury his face in his hands, but he forced himself to hold Kathleen's eyes.

"Michael was lost at sea this spring when his ship went down."

Donnelly's mouth formed a perfect O, like a cartoon character. "Oh, Jesus, Eddie, I'm so sorry."

"Thanks" was all Harkins could say. He wondered if he would ever tell anyone about the forged birth certificate. Could someone keep a secret like that? For life?

Donnelly got up and walked over to him, stood beside him, rubbed his upper back. She didn't smell as bad as he did, and her touch was a blessing.

After a minute or two, she asked, "You want to talk about it?"

"Not really."

She stood beside him for another moment, then squeezed his shoulder. When she sat back down, Harkins managed to say, "I always had a crush on you."

"So why didn't you ever ask me out?"

"Didn't think I had a chance," he said.

Harkins remembered walking behind Donnelly and her girlfriends as they all left a high school dance one autumn night, must have been in '35. He'd hung back, awkward and tongue-tied, secretly hoping that some guy they passed would mouth off at the girls so he could rush up and rescue them.

"You sure you weren't just chicken?"

"Quite possibly. You were one of those girls who didn't even know how many hearts you were breaking."

Donnelly laughed. "Oh, I knew exactly what was going on. But go on two or three dates with the same boy and he's talking to your dad about marriage. I wasn't going to settle for some guy who couldn't pass math without copying my homework."

"*I'm* good at math."

"I'll keep that in mind," she said, holding his eyes. "Anyway, I got plans for when this show is over."

"Oh?"

"I'm going to medical school."

"A girl doctor?"

"Yes," she said. "A girl doctor. I've been watching surgeons up close for a couple of years now. I can do anything that they can do. Hell, I can already run circles around some of them."

"I'll bet you can," Harkins said. "But do medical schools even admit girls? Will patients be OK with it?"

"Nobody admits girls. But some schools admit *women*. I might start by just treating female patients."

Harkins smiled, sang a line from the old World War I song. *"'How you gonna keep 'em down on the farm after they've seen Paree?'"*

"Something like that, I guess. How about you? What do you want after all this glamour?"

After he'd enlisted, all Harkins could think about was getting back to his beat, his precinct, his family. Lately he wondered if he'd fit in. Somebody he once read claimed you can't go home again.

"Not sure," Harkins said.

"Weren't you in college? Villanova?"

"Yeah, I don't let that get around too much. Being labeled a college boy is a big insult in the army."

"Why'd you leave school?"

"Might have had something to do with I beat the crap out of some asshole from the Main Line."

Kathleen chuckled. "Couldn't get along with the rich kids, huh? You can take the boy out of Kensington . . ."

Harkins was surprised to feel a flush of embarrassment for something that happened years ago. Back home he had a reputation as a hothead, a stereotypical Irish street tough, fists up, touchy about any insult. He didn't want Kathleen to think of him that way.

"Did he deserve it, at least?"

"Yeah, I thought so. Still think so. He was some big jock, a rower. Every day in the dining hall he's picking on this little guy. I told him to stop."

"Or?"

"Or what?" Harkins said.

"Story in the neighborhood was that you told him he'd miss the next rowing event, him having a broken arm and everything." Kathleen was smiling, but Harkins still felt a tinge of shame.

"Some people just don't listen," he said. "Anyway, Father Stanford thought I should take my talents elsewhere, so I became a cop."

She studied him for a moment, a smile wiping away some of the exhaustion around her eyes.

"You'll go back," she said. "To school, I mean. You always had your nose in a book. Like your brother Patrick. Like your dad."

Patrick, who could always hold his temper, wound up with the education. Harkins wound up carrying a nightstick, getting into fights with drunks and wife-beaters. Uncle Jimmy with a badge.

"You'll make a great doctor, Kathleen."

"Thanks," she said, still smiling. Harkins tried to think of something else to say that would keep her looking at him that way, but at that moment another nurse pushed into the tent. She looked at Donnelly, then at Harkins.

"Wow, hot in here," she said.

Donnelly smiled, then said, "Alice, this is Eddie Harkins, a friend of mine from back home and the investigator for what happened this morning. Eddie, this is Alice Haus."

Harkins stood, and Haus shook his hand. Her face was pretty, clean, but with a ring of grime starting at the collar of her T-shirt. Firm grip. She squeezed tighter when she said, "We had problems in this hospital before anybody got shot."

She let go of Harkins' hand, stashed some papers under one of the bricks, and retrieved what looked like a bunch of blank forms from a brown paper wrapper.

"Care to elaborate?" Harkins said.

"Stephenson was a pig. You know about the Whitman girl?"

"Some."

"He got that nurse so drunk she choked to death on her own vomit. She was twenty years old."

"I heard he claimed he wasn't there when it happened," Harkins said.

"And that would mean something if he had any credibility," Haus countered. "If he'd told me a patient had two legs I'd look under the sheet anyway."

"Yeah, the picture I'm getting of Stephenson isn't pretty, but it's still a murder investigation."

"Is that all it is? Or are you going to do anything about all the other crap that goes on here?"

"Get the docs to stop bothering the nurses, you mean? Honestly? I doubt it."

"Boys will be boys, huh?"

Harkins wished he had a better answer. "I've got to start by figuring out who killed Stephenson."

"Yeah, justice served, rest in peace, all that happy horseshit, right?" Haus said.

She stepped toward the door, looked at Harkins again as if she wanted to say something more. When that passed, she addressed both of them. "You kids take care now, hear?"

Harkins was quiet. After a few moments, Donnelly said, "So you've already gotten an earful about what a wonderful place this is for nurses?"

"You could say that. I also heard from Nurse Palmer that I shouldn't put too much stock in what some women have to say, since they're hooked on the drama."

"Palmer thinks that if you insist the world is rosy, that makes it so. All the nurses have to do is play along with whatever the doctors want. Her life would be easier if everyone acted like an adult. But she'd rather sweep things under the rug than try to fix what's wrong. I'm sure she's never confronted Boone about any of this. I think she's afraid and in over her head."

"What about this thing with Whitman? Palmer try to hide that, gloss over it?"

"She would like it to go away," Donnelly said. "But there's more to it than Palmer or Alice know. I think only a couple of us knew that Whitman was pregnant."

"Stephenson the father?"

"That's what the other nurses think, and it seems fairly obvious, what with her winding up in his tent. But I'm not sure."

"Why?"

"Two things. Stephenson used to dump his used condoms on the ground behind his tent instead of in the trash, like he wanted everyone to see them. Like those pilots who paint little swastikas on their airplanes for every Kraut fighter they shoot down."

"He had a bunch of condoms in his footlocker," Harkins said. "A month's worth. Maybe more."

"Sounds like him," Kathleen said. "Anyway, I think he was careful about not impregnating his conquests. And whoever the father was offered her an abortion—which means it was probably a doc—but the thing about it was that she was surprised. She really thought that the guy, whoever he was, would take care of her, do the right thing. Not marry her, but at least support her."

"I heard she was naïve."

"A bit, I guess. She was from this real religious family out in Minnesota, and she was worried about how they'd react. Her parents would have been upset, but they wouldn't have kicked her out.

"But I don't think anyone could be so naïve as to think, even for a minute, that Stephenson would do the right thing. About anything. All the shit he pulled? If he'd have done that crap back in the neighborhood with somebody's sister he'd have ended up in the Delaware chained to some car parts."

"So he claimed he wasn't there when she choked," Harkins said. "Suppose that's a lie and he was there. Is there any reason he would have wanted her dead? Would have let her choke? Maybe hide the pregnancy?"

"More likely he'd have bragged about knocking her up."

"Well, it could be that he got what he deserved, but you can't blame the dead guy for getting murdered, and I still have to investigate."

"There's something else, too," Kathleen said.

"What?"

She hesitated a moment, measuring her answer. "I'm not convinced she choked to death," she said.

"Why not?"

"I have my reasons."

"That's not helping me any," Harkins said.

When Kathleen didn't add anything, Harkins asked, "So what killed her then?"

"I wanted to kill somebody around here? Trying to hide it? I'd use morphine."

"Those little injectors the medics carry?"

"Syrettes. Four or five of those would be enough to do somebody in. Truth is, I think the frontline medics do that on the battlefield sometimes, for guys who are never going to make it."

"Mercy killing," Harkins said.

Kathleen nodded, then said, "Trouble is, I don't know who would have wanted to kill her, or why. Unless it had to do with the pregnancy."

"But you're not really sure about any of this?"

"I'm sure that she was pregnant."

"You're sure that she *told* you she was pregnant?" Harkins asked. "Or you're sure that she was actually pregnant?"

"Why would she lie about that?"

"If I find out, I'll let you know," Harkins said.

Kathleen folded her arms. Harkins sensed there was more she wanted to say, but he'd have to be patient.

"And what about the other shit going on?" Kathleen asked. "The fact that Boone ignored all this stuff when we told him about it?"

"I guess if it rises to the level of an actual crime, I'll investigate that, too. Or at least report it to the provost. But I'm way out of my league here. Hell, yesterday at this time I was busting up whorehouse fights. So far all I've heard is that other docs are pushing the limit, too. If they put guys in jail for being assholes, there wouldn't be enough people around to fight the war."

Donnelly smirked. "So you've got your doubts as to whether you're ready to handle a murder investigation," she said. "Much less corral a bunch of doctors acting like horny teenagers, and a commander who won't look after his nurses."

"That's putting it succinctly."

"But you aren't the running-away kind, so how can I help?"

For the next hour Donnelly confirmed what Harkins had already gleaned from his conversations so far. As they talked, other nurses came in and left, and when Donnelly introduced him to her colleagues, their comments ranged from "I can't believe what happened" to "You ask me, that bastard had it coming."

"So Stephenson drank, even here in a combat zone with all the casualties coming in."

"He did, and he always seemed to have a supply," she said. "And he was always willing to share it with the nurses, which is how a lot of the trouble started."

"He'd get them drunk?"

"Some of the girls are really young. Whitman was. Never been away from home before. Then you stick them in a man's uniform and they're dirty all the time and exhausted, they don't feel much like women. Some handsome guy like Stephenson pays them some attention, geez."

"First time today I heard anyone describe him as handsome."

"Handsome on the outside only. I'd say he was a pig, but that would be insulting to pigs everywhere."

"Is it true he went into Palermo to get drunk?"

"Can you believe that? We'd only been here three days, and he went into the city twice and came back pissed. One night we had casualties coming in; he was passed out somewhere. So it's all hands on deck, you know? And he shows up at surgery and starts washing up. He could barely stand up by himself."

"What happened?"

"What else? The nurses took care of the problem. Me and Felton and Melbourne dragged him out of there and shoved him back into his tent."

"Colonel Boone find out?"

"Far as I know. But no one expected anything to happen. Boone always has the boys' backs."

Harkins pushed the heels of his hands into his eye sockets. He was feeling no better for the hour of sleep he got before Patrick woke him.

A sudden thought: If Patrick hadn't heard yet about Michael, would it be better to hear it from a brother or from a letter? Were there any gradations in such terrible news?

Harkins looked up at Kathleen, no idea how long he'd been silent.

"Is that Boone's story?" Harkins asked. "He backs up his docs?"

"Some of the other nurses think he's really a scheming, manipulative bastard. I think he's just an odd duck, certainly a moral coward. He just let this stuff with Stephenson go on and on. Tell you the truth, I think he was afraid of Stephenson. Boone mostly lectured the nurses about what we were doing wrong."

"That's what Felton told me."

"Like we were flouncing around in low-cut party dresses."

Harkins looked at Donnelly, tried to picture her in a party dress, or anything low cut. It had been days, maybe weeks since he'd thought of a woman, thought about sex; the constant state of exhaustion had killed his daydreams. Suddenly, that part of his brain was alive again, or at least had a weak pulse.

"Felton told me there's some people I need to talk to, one nurse in particular." He pulled his sweat-damp notebook from his pocket.

"Moira Ronan," Donnelly said before Harkins found the page.

"Yeah. I understand Stephenson had a thing for her."

"When you have a *thing* for someone you send her flowers, leave her notes. Stephenson *targeted* Moira."

"Will she talk to me?"

"Maybe, if I introduce you as a friend from back home. But if you start playing the obnoxious cop, asking her if she encouraged him, she'll clam up, and I'll poison your canteen."

"Understood."

The two of them went outside; there was no sign of Colianno or the jeep.

"He probably stole it to sell to some of his Sicilian relatives," Harkins said.

"Why do you have a paratrooper as a driver?"

"My brother Patrick. He's in the salvation business. He gave me Colianno as a project."

"Colianno was—is, I guess—sweet on Ronan," Donnelly said. "She helped take care of him while he was sick."

"And?"

Donnelly shrugged. "He's a handsome guy, and this place is kind of a hothouse, and I don't mean the weather. Stuff happens fast here."

"An enlisted guy and an officer?"

Donnelly laughed. "We only have relative rank."

"What's that?"

"Most nurses are second lieutenants. They gave us gold bars so the GIs would have to take orders from us. But we don't rate salutes, we rarely get promoted, and we get paid half of what a male second lieutenant makes."

"That's a lousy deal."

"Yeah, it is. But I'm happy knowing Eleanor Roosevelt can sleep better at night."

They walked about two hundred yards to the nurses' sleeping quarters, which also had its sides rolled up. A large sign tacked to the doorpost said NURSES ONLY. Inside, Harkins could see four or five figures crumpled on cots in various states of undress.

"They just got off thirty-six hours straight duty. They could sleep if it were two hundred degrees. You wait here."

Moments later, Donnelly emerged with another woman.

"Eddie Harkins, Moira Ronan."

Ronan had auburn hair, cut short like Donnelly's. She wore a man's T-shirt and pants rolled up to show chunky GI shoes. Red-rimmed eyes and sunburned cheeks. She was a couple of years younger than Kathleen and marginally cleaner, like she'd just taken a sponge bath from her helmet. With some rest and a bar of soap, Harkins thought, she'd look like Vivien Leigh.

"Eddie is investigating the murder," Donnelly said.

"I don't have anything to tell you," Ronan said, voice flat.

"I just want to ask you a few questions," Harkins said. "It'd be a big help." Then, to Donnelly, "Is there any place we can go?"

"Private? Hardly. I guess we could walk to that bombed-out church. It might be empty."

"I go on duty in a few minutes," Ronan said. "And I don't know how I can help. I don't think I can."

Two nurses emerged from the tent, stepped around Ronan, glanced back at the trio, and whispered to each other. Harkins backed off a few feet to a supply tent that had its sides down, gestured for Donnelly and Ronan to join him.

"I've had people tell me I should talk to you about Stephenson."

"What difference does it make now?" Ronan said. "Whatever he was doing, he won't be doing it anymore."

"Yeah, but I still have to find out who might have wanted him dead."

Ronan pointed at the large tent behind her. "Anybody living in there."

Another woman, wearing a first lieutenant's bar, emerged from the tent. "Let's go, Moira. The others are waiting on us to relieve them."

"Gotta go," Ronan said. Still the flat tone.

When she was gone, Donnelly said, "Cut her a break. She's been through a lot."

"I wouldn't know," Harkins said, "since she won't tell me."

"You're going to have to earn her trust. I'll talk to her and we'll try again in the morning."

"Would you say you guys are friends?"

"She's certainly the best friend I have here, and I think she feels the same way."

"Did she confide in you, like Whitman did? What do you know about what happened to her?"

"I don't know everything," Donnelly said. "Back in North Africa, Stephenson was always trying to get her alone. Followed her around like a dog. Gave her liquor. But I think something else happened here a couple of days ago, maybe a week, and Moira and I haven't been alone since. You can see how hard it is to find a place to talk privately."

Colianno pulled up beside them in Harkins' jeep, stirring clouds of dust.

"Where have you been?" Harkins said.

"I found something; you're going to want to come along."

Harkins looked at the paratrooper. Thomas had been a good driver, taking care of the vehicle and, to some extent, Harkins; but that was it. Colianno, it seemed, already thought of himself as kind of a junior partner in the investigation. Maybe this was some of that initiative the paratroops fostered and Patrick bragged about. Harkins was too tired to think about whether this was a good thing or not. He climbed into the passenger seat, turned to Donnelly.

"See you later, OK?"

She touched her eyebrow with two fingers, a Boy Scout salute.

"Wait!" Another nurse came up behind Donnelly. It was Felton, the lieutenant Harkins met a few hours earlier in the mess tent. Harkins got out of the jeep.

"Harkins, right?" Felton said.

"Yes."

She nodded at Donnelly. "Kathleen."

"Brenda," Donnelly said. "What's with the duffle bag?"

Felton was dragging a GI duffle, packed only half full, by the looks of it.

"That's why I came looking for you," Felton said to Harkins. "Boone's at it again, has started his counterattack."

"What do you mean?"

"I got word to pack my gear and get on a truck for another hospital. I'm getting transferred."

"What happened?"

"I might have had a little run-in with our commander. He came around a couple hours after the murder to ask how we were doing. Big friggin' act, like he's really concerned.

"Anyway, I told him that I hoped we'd get another surgeon here fast to help with the patient load. Then I said, 'I hope you can find one that isn't an asshole.'"

Donnelly looked at Harkins, then turned back to her friend, who was smiling.

"This was in front of the other nurses?" Donnelly asked.

"No! I'm not an idiot. I'm just fed up with Boone and all the shit he lets go on here. Anyway, next thing I know, First Sergeant Drake comes for me and tells me to pack. I'm going on a trip."

"Did we get a replacement?" Donnelly asked. The nursing staff was already shorthanded, she'd told Harkins, and Felton was one of the most experienced hands.

"No," Felton said. "And this also means you're in charge of my section. Ronan, Melbourne, and Savio."

A two-and-a-half-ton truck stopped at an intersection about thirty yards away. There were four enlisted men and two nurses sitting on bench seats in the back. A sergeant in the front passenger seat called out, "Lieutenant Felton!"

"My chariot awaits," Felton said.

Then, turning back to Harkins, "He's going to get rid of anybody who can uncover him as the shitty commander he is." She hefted the duffle bag onto her shoulder, and it pushed her helmet to one side, left it cock-eyed, like a newsboy's cap.

"I think it's your move, Lieutenant."

8

2 August 1943
1600 hours

After Felton left, Kathleen Donnelly watched Harkins and Colianno drive off. She was truly happy to see Harkins, whom she had always liked. She wasn't all that surprised that he didn't want to talk about his brother's death—lots of people handled their grief by throwing themselves into work. She hoped, for his sake, that would be enough for a while. Eventually, she knew, it would all come crashing back down on him.

The question Donnelly had to answer was: Could she trust Eddie Harkins? She didn't doubt his sincerity or integrity; it was his competence as an investigator that she wondered about. Because Kathleen Donnelly had a secret, and if she shared it with Harkins and her cop friend was careless with it, Donnelly would end her brief military career in front of a court-martial.

By the time Donnelly learned that Whitman was dead, the nurses were already talking about how she'd choked on her own vomit while blind drunk. There'd been a couple of nurses who didn't like Whitman, and the story fit their idea of the young woman: naïve, irresponsible in the way she flirted with the doctors.

Then there were the nurses who hated Stephenson, Whitman's drinking partner that night. For this gang, the whole incident was more evidence for what they already believed: that Stephenson was to blame for just about everything that was off-kilter at the Eleventh Field Hospital. He'd gotten her drunk; he'd left her alone when he shouldn't have.

Even Captain Palmer, the head nurse, had latched on to the storyline that Whitman had choked to death. All Palmer wanted was a cautionary tale she could use to berate the other nurses: This is what happens when you don't behave like a lady, when you don't control yourself.

But the story didn't make sense to Kathleen. By the time she got off shift that morning, poor Whitman's remains had already been moved to the morgue. Donnelly walked in just as two orderlies were slipping a mattress cover over the corpse, pulling it up toward her head.

"Hang on, guys," Donnelly had asked.

She recognized one of the men, a corporal named Barton. The two soldiers paused, quiet and respectful.

"Can I have a few minutes with her? She was my friend."

"Sure thing, ma'am," Barton, the older of the GIs, said. The men had plenty of other work, and they left Donnelly alone.

The morgue didn't occupy a big tent. It could hold about a half-dozen litters set on spindly-legged stands. Whitman had been the only occupant that morning. Since army field hospitals did not routinely do autopsies—the cause of death for most of their patients was sadly and sometimes horrifically obvious—the morgue was just a way station, a place to make sure the records were updated before a body was picked up by graves registration soldiers and taken to the big temporary cemetery near Gela, on the southwest coast of Sicily.

Donnelly stood looking at her friend, a slight twenty-year-old with corn-silk hair. Kathleen brushed her fingers across Whitman's forehead, already cool to the touch. Then she put her hand on the dead woman's stomach, imagined the tiny fetus there.

Donnelly didn't buy that Whitman had been so drunk that she couldn't wake up when she vomited. She knew lots of women drank during pregnancy, but attitudes had been changing in the medical community. The most progressive thinkers now held that a mother's drinking was bad for the baby. Whitman, who'd studied nursing in Saint Paul, had been a well-educated and well-informed professional. Was it possible that she had a drink with Stephenson? Donnelly supposed so. Did it seem likely that she guzzled ten or fifteen drinks until she blacked out? That she drank until the alcohol defeated the reflex action that would have saved her from choking? Donnelly had a hard time believing that.

There was a chart hanging from the end of the stretcher, and Donnelly picked it up. Cause of death was listed as *Asphyxiation. Choked on vomitus.*

It was signed by Colonel Boone.

Donnelly stood in the dark and stifling tent, chewing the inside of her lip. The physician's signature was supposed to be the last word, was meant to stay unchallenged. There was a caste system in the medical profession, and ever since she put on her first white cap, Kathleen Donnelly had been reminded where she ranked. If she'd stayed at Pennsylvania Hospital she might never have questioned the status quo. But over the last year she'd been asked to do difficult, frightening things that were far beyond her station, beyond her training. She'd been bombed and strafed and seasick, she'd been hot and tired and dirty, but she had done what was asked of her and more. She had saved lives. She was bigger than she'd been.

And she was sick and goddamned tired of *deferring.*

Something told her there was more to her friend's death. Boone's signature on the chart was a signpost telling her to let it go; that her hunches didn't matter; that smarter, better-qualified people were on top of things and she should go back to whatever duties were entrusted to nurses by the powers that be.

"Screw it," she said.

She left the morgue and walked to a supply tent a few yards away, where she picked up a canvas-wrapped bundle of sterilized instruments no bigger than a woman's clutch. No one paid her any special attention as she walked back to the morgue.

She went back inside, unrolled the instrument package, and took out a scalpel.

"I'm sorry, Whit," she whispered. She put the instrument bundle under Whitman's neck at the base of her skull, so that the dead woman's head was tilted back, her throat exposed despite the onset of rigor mortis. And before she could change her mind or think about the implications of what she was about to do, Donnelly put her thumb and two first two fingers of her left hand on Whitman's throat. She found the thyroid cartilage, moved her hand down just the width of two fingers, then used the scalpel to incise the skin just above the sternal notch. She cut through and pushed aside the thyroid to get at the trachea, which she opened with a single smooth incision, like a fleshy pipe sliced lengthwise. She held it open with two fingers while she fumbled for the small flashlight she kept in a pocket on her left sleeve. She clicked the light on and looked inside.

There was no sign of any vomitus in Whitman's airway. No chunks of food, no excess fluids, just some that she expected to see. She inserted her index finger upward and felt no obstruction of the larynx between the vocal cords.

It didn't look to her that Whitman had choked to death. And Donnelly didn't believe the pregnant woman would have drunk enough alcohol to poison herself, like some ignorant moonshiner.

Something else had killed her.

Donnelly had been standing there, looking at her friend's flayed throat, when the two orderlies came back in.

"You, OK, ma'am?" Barton asked. They stopped just inside the door, courteous enough to give Donnelly time to be with her friend.

"I'm almost done," Donnelly had said. She reached down and tugged the edge of the mattress cover to Whitman's chin, hiding this new violation, the incision that would never be closed.

"Help me, would you?" she asked.

Barton stepped to the other side of the litter and lifted Whitman's shoulders so they could pull the canvas over the top of her head.

"She goes to the cemetery from here, right?" Donnelly asked.

"Yes, ma'am," Barton said. "The graves registration guys are already outside. I had them wait, you know, in case you needed more time."

"Thanks, Barton." She looked at the other soldier, a young private she'd seen around. "Thanks," she said.

Donnelly had almost reached the door to the tent when Barton called her. "Lieutenant Donnelly?"

She turned around and saw him holding the instrument bundle she'd used to prop Whitman's head.

"You leave this here, ma'am?"

She didn't answer, just smiled, took the bundle, and walked out. If Barton wondered what she'd been doing, he didn't say.

Two weeks later, Eddie Harkins shows up and suddenly she's talking about Whitman again. Everyone is talking about Whitman. But only Donnelly knew the truth.

9

2 August 1943
2050 hours

"I spent some time in the motor pool while you were with your old girlfriend," Colianno said.

"I wish. What were you doing?"

"Thought I'd nose around a bit, see what I could learn that might help."

Harkins studied Colianno's profile. He hadn't asked the private to do anything; on the other hand, Harkins believed the kid when he said that the enlisted men know a lot more than officers usually gave them credit for.

"What'd you learn?"

"The name of the driver who took Stephenson into Palermo on at least one of his trips. Pritchard. James Pritchard. I thought you'd want to talk to him."

"Good thinking. So why are we heading into the city?"

"Because that's where his buddies think we'll find him."

"Jesus," Harkins said. "I'm going on forty hours straight duty; everybody else has time to sightsee."

"And visit whorehouses. That's where this guy's supposed to be. And it's where he took Stephenson."

Colianno drove them north out of the hills, the sun rolling behind the ridges to their left. Below them, Palermo's waterfront curved into a blue distance. They dropped down onto a main east-west road that some GIs had renamed with a large hand-painted sign that said SACRAMENTO HIGHWAY. Easier to understand, especially on a radio, than some soldier's attempt at pronouncing "Via Villagrazia."

When they turned a corner, Harkins' copy of Sandburg's poetry slid out from under his seat. He picked it up and opened it to a random page.

Colianno glanced over. "What's that?"

"Poetry book. Carl Sandburg. Ever hear of him?"

"Sure, my family sits around and reads his poems to each other every night after dinner."

Before he could catch himself, Harkins said, "Really?"

Colianno laughed. "No, not really. What the hell kind of family you think I have?" The paratrooper shook his head. "Poetry. Jesus."

Harkins laughed. "Yeah, well, keep your fucking opinions to yourself."

They were almost at the botanical garden when the air-raid sirens began their low whine.

Colianno gripped the steering wheel hard, voice tense, no trace of panic. "Where do you want me to go?"

"Let's get away from the waterfront," Harkins said.

The harbor was thick with Allied ships, mostly small craft hauling supplies ashore. If the Luftwaffe were looking for targets, this would be the place, and Harkins and Colianno were only a few hundred yards from the water's edge.

The paratrooper did a three-point turn, bumping over a median lined with dust-dry, weed-choked flower beds. The jeep was pointed away from the docks when the antiaircraft fire began, long bright bands of tracers arcing up at planes Harkins couldn't see. Something heavy banged off the hood of their vehicle.

"What the hell was that?" Colianno asked.

"Expended rounds. What goes up gotta come down."

Harkins saw a stone arch entrance with a wooden gate fronting the road. There was enough room under the barrel-shaped vault for their vehicle.

"Pull in there."

Colianno tucked the jeep under the stone canopy. Out in the street just a few feet away, another spray of expended antiaircraft rounds slammed to the pavement.

Harkins left the protective cover of the archway and, staying pressed to the wall, inched to the street corner to get a view of the harbor.

"Where the hell are you going?" Colianno called to him. The paratrooper stayed between the jeep and the big wooden door inside the arch.

Harkins could not see the harbor; the trees in the arboretum blocked his view, but the sky above that was scarred with bright outgoing fire.

Harkins called back to Colianno. "You should see this!"

He doubted the driver could hear him. He turned back toward the harbor in time to see a German bomber shudder as it was a hit, flames trailing from its left wing. The Kraut was already low and dipped even more as jagged fragments of the fuselage tore away. Then the whole aircraft flipped upside down, tearing itself apart in the dive.

Harkins was mesmerized.

And just like that, the dying plane was headed for him.

For the longest two seconds of his life, Harkins was unable to move, his feet rooted as if in a nightmare, the aircraft headed straight for his nose. Then he dove to the ground, pressing himself to the foot of the wall.

And it missed him.

The tail of the plane crushed the top of a building behind him, the street flashed white and orange as the wreck set fire to something in the next block.

By the time Harkins found his feet, Colianno had pulled the jeep out from its cover and had raced up to retrieve Harkins. They sped to the waterfront, then Colianno cracked a sharp right, scraping the wall of a house with the jeep's side. Neither man spoke until they had reached a hill about a half mile from the harbor, where Colianno parked on a sidewalk.

"What the fuck was that about back there?" Colianno asked, eyes wide.

"I've never been on the front lines," Harkins said. His breath was shallow; he felt light-headed. "I've heard stuff, artillery—theirs and ours—but the only Germans I've ever seen were already prisoners. I've never seen—you know—live shooting. A real battle."

Colianno, clearly puzzled, just looked at him. "OK," the paratrooper said, nodding slowly. "OK. Well, I hope that satisfied your curiosity, 'cause I've already seen enough shooting to last me a lifetime. I'm sure I'll see more, but I ain't going looking for it."

They rested there for a half hour without talking. A few civilians came out of their homes to look around, but no one approached them. Harkins wanted to ask Colianno about his first fight, his reaction, but he didn't.

Finally, Colianno said, "I gotta take a leak." He left Harkins and the jeep and stepped into an alley.

Harkins felt an urge to laugh, though at what, he wasn't sure. He was smiling when Colianno returned. The young private looked at him, then shook his head.

"And they say I'm the nutcase," he said, starting the engine.

Minutes later they were in the city proper, three- and four-story apartment blocks above shops shuttered for the night.

"Not a lot of love for Il Duce here," Colianno said, pointing at some of the anti-Fascist slogans painted on the walls.

"I wonder how many of those were painted after we showed up?" Harkins said. "Seems to me the smart thing for the locals to do is to get along with whoever's in power."

"So you think they covered up the anti-American stuff right before we got here?" Colianno said. That chip on his shoulder again. Colianno wanted to defend the Sicilians, but he was also an American soldier.

"What do I know?" Harkins said.

Harkins looked at his watch. Nearly nine thirty. Twenty-one thirty in army-speak. Harkins had not eaten all day, meaning his sunstroke headache would not go away at nightfall.

They did not know the exact location of the bordello, but when they pulled over near a church with an elegant blue sign that said SAN CATALDO, they saw three young women in white cotton shifts perched on the sill of a second-floor window in an apartment a few doors away. One woman, who looked to be about twenty, waved at them; Harkins waved back. When she smiled, he could see a black gap where she was missing a tooth.

"My keen detective skills tell me we found the place," Harkins said.

"Hang on," Colianno said, reaching into a cloth sack on the floor of the jeep. He pulled out some cured meat wrapped in brown paper and a small loaf of bread. He broke the loaf, gave half to Harkins, then pulled a wicked fighting knife from a sheath strapped to his boot and cut the meat in two quick strokes. Harkins wondered if he'd had the knife with him at the hospital. Most patients had to give up their weapons.

"I'm starving," Colianno said.

"Hope there's no Kraut blood on your knife," Harkins said. He'd meant it as a joke, but Colianno looked at him without smiling.

Harkins chewed on the salami, which was salty but delicious, and studied Colianno.

Harkins was twenty-six; he figured Colianno for twenty or twenty-one. The paratrooper was along to drive and translate, but he'd also thought to go to the motor pool, had even found them some food. Colianno had been in at least one hard fight, had apparently seen some things that changed him. For all the ugliness Harkins saw as a cop, he doubted it compared to what Colianno had been through.

Harkins was a few big bites into the salami when three GIs strolled off the Via Maqueda and onto the side street where they were parked. The men turned into a small courtyard below the window where the women sat.

"Bun-jerr-no," one of the men called up to the women.

"Let's go," Harkins said, stuffing the uneaten bread into his musette bag. "Before our boy slips out another door."

Colianno got out of the jeep, pulled a carbine out of the back, and slung it on his shoulder.

"Where'd you get the peashooter?"

"It's a war zone, Lieutenant. I don't like to go around naked."

Colianno bent over, dragged a chain and a heavy padlock from under the back bench seat.

"And the chain?" Harkins asked.

"Motor pool," Colianno said. "Same place I got the chow. I figured you'd need me to go into these places with you, and we want the jeep to be here when we come out, right?"

"It'll probably just drive up the cost of bolt cutters on the black market," Harkins said.

Two boys stood nearby watching them. Colianno said something to them, and the boys nodded and smiled, then climbed into the two front seats.

"You hire them as guards?" Harkins asked.

"Nah. Lookouts. There's a fifty percent chance they'll come and get us if someone starts messing with the jeep."

"Good thinking," Harkins said. Colianno did not acknowledge the compliment.

They went into the courtyard, where a teenage boy sat by the door at a small table with several different types of ammunition arrayed before him, the individual bullets standing on end, lined up like shiny soldiers on parade.

"No bullets inside," the boy said in clear English.

Colianno, who had a carbine slung on his shoulder, said, "Keeps the GIs from shooting each other. Pretty standard in these places. Give him your rounds, Lieutenant; hang on to the weapon."

Colianno cleared his carbine, and Harkins pulled the magazine from his pistol, ejected the round in the chamber. The boy held out his hand and Harkins gave him the ammo. Then the boy put out his hand again.

"He wants a tip," Colianno explained.

"Tell him to always wear a rubber," Harkins said, walking by the boy.

Colianno produced a tropical chocolate bar from the pocket of his shirt and handed it to the kid.

"Smart thing to do, Lieutenant, would be to acknowledge that we're on their turf, maybe do things that will make our investigation easier. Don't you think?"

Harkins stopped and faced Colianno. Two more GIs squeezed past them, heading inside. They could hear women chattering behind a curtain.

"I need a translator, not a coach," Harkins said.

"You sure, Lieutenant? 'Cause I'm thinking you need an interpreter. I could just tell you the words people are saying, but maybe you want to know what's really going on."

Harkins thought about it for a moment. "Whatever happened to privates who just shut up and do what they're told?"

When Colianno didn't answer, Harkins said, "OK. Just don't forget that it's my ass hanging out there. I'll decide which way we go, right?"

"You got it, Lieutenant," Colianno said without a trace of sincerity.

The two men turned in to the front room of the bordello. Harkins saw a line of chairs along one wall, with eight women in scarves and tiny slips, some of them smoking, one of them picking her teeth with what looked like a hairpin. Behind them, a threadbare wall hanging showed plump women bathing in a stream. The only other attempt to relieve the dreariness of the space was a table with a red cloth and an elaborate lamp. An older woman, probably the madam, stood beside the table and chatted with the men who had gone in ahead of Harkins and Colianno. Once they agreed on a price, the GIs walked along the line of seated women and made their choices.

After she got her other customers settled, the madam came back to where Harkins and Colianno stood waiting.

"Salutamu, senora," Colianno said. *"Comu si?"*

The woman smiled as Colianno continued in Sicilian, then said something back to him.

"She says she's going to charge you more because you're an officer," Colianno said, grinning.

"Tell her we're looking for this guy, Pritchard," Harkins said. "You have a description?"

"Yeah. Little guy. Blond hair. Looks like he's twelve."

Colianno continued talking to the madam. The woman clucked her disapproval—it was not a good business practice to identify your customers. But Colianno persisted, at one point even reaching out and taking her hand. For a moment, Harkins thought he might kiss her ring. Watching him chat up the madam, Harkins imagined that Colianno could be charming when he wasn't in a fistfight.

The woman turned away from them, and Colianno said, "She's going to bring him out to us when he's finished."

"He'll run out the back," Harkins said. He followed the woman through a curtain and up a narrow staircase. When she reached the top she turned to face Harkins, putting her hands on her hips and unleashing a torrent of Sicilian.

Colianno was right behind Harkins. "I said we'd wait for him downstairs, Lieutenant," he said. "That was the deal I made."

"Tell her to get out of my way," Harkins said as he continued his slow climb. "Tell her I said please. Tell her I don't want the guy running away from us."

Harkins could tell that Colianno was apologizing for him, and he hoped the woman stood aside by the time he reached the landing.

She did not.

Colianno was still talking when Harkins stepped up to the woman. He smiled at her, put his hand on her elbow, and tried one of his few Sicilian phrases.

"Pi fauri."

When she didn't move, Harkins tried English. "Please."

He looked over his shoulder at Colianno, who'd kept up his patter. Finally, she shifted her weight and let Harkins move her aside, though she was still muttering rapid-fire.

Harkins went down a hallway lined with small rooms on either side. He pushed aside a curtain and saw a GI with his back to the door, pants around his knees, bony white hips rising and falling. A woman wearing a look of complete boredom looked at Harkins over her customer's shoulder. The man, who did not match Pritchard's description, did not turn around.

In the second room the GI, another big man, was facing the door when Harkins lifted the curtain. "What the hell?" he said.

"Sorry."

The third curtain opened as Harkins approached; Pritchard stepped out. He was about five six with straw-blond hair and fine features. He looked like a shirtless schoolboy, except for the bite marks on his neck. Behind him stood a large woman, an inch taller than Pritchard and a good thirty pounds heavier. She pulled a thin cotton robe around her ample stomach and breasts, then cooed something into Pritchard's ear. He laughed, reached behind, and patted her rump.

"James Pritchard?" Harkins asked.

"Who wants to know?" Pritchard was drunk, weaving a bit.

"We want to talk to you about Captain Stephenson," Harkins said.

Pritchard's eyes went wide, and Harkins could see that he wanted to run, but he and Colianno were blocking the stairs, and he probably didn't feel quite his athletic best. After a few seconds he gave a resigned sigh.

"OK," he said. "I got it right here."

He went back into the room, which had a slit for a window, a tiny table with an overflowing ashtray, and a lamp. Pritchard pulled his shirt off of a chair, then reached under the narrow bed and pulled out a musette bag. When he came out into the hallway he handed it to Harkins. Beneath the "US" stenciled on the side were hand-inked letters spelling "Stephenson."

"Downstairs," Harkins said. Colianno turned and led the soldier down, Harkins following. When they got to the front room, Colianno had Pritchard sit to put on his shoes and shirt. The women moved out of the way.

Harkins loosed the straps that held the musette bag closed and looked inside. There were a few rolls of American ten- and twenty-dollar bills, maybe five hundred dollars. At the bottom, a metal disk of some sort.

"Where did you get this?" Harkins asked. Colianno stepped up and Harkins showed him the contents of the bag.

Pritchard, still drunk but sobering up rapidly, said, "Well, Stephenson didn't need it anymore, did he?"

"The milk of human kindness," Harkins said. He motioned with his thumb. "Outside."

Colianno led the way again, followed by Pritchard, then Harkins. They collected their ammo, then went into the street, where the two boys still sat in the jeep. One of them, who could not have been more than eight years old, was smoking an American cigarette. Colianno gave them each a pack of Lucky Strikes, threw his gear and weapon in the back, then unlocked the heavy chain. Pritchard leaned against the front of the vehicle, looking sick.

"I don't feel so good, Lieutenant," he said. "Maybe we could do this inside?"

"Tell me about Stephenson. Was this his money?"

Pritchard got an idiot's grin. "I spent a lot of it," he said. "Was planning on working my way through about half them gals in there. The ones with teeth, anyways."

"Just the society girls, huh?"

Pritchard blinked at him, then pitched forward at the waist and threw up. Harkins jumped back, but not before his shoes got splashed with wine-red bile. Colianno, standing by the driver's side of the jeep, smiled.

"This just ain't your day, Lieutenant."

Pritchard straightened up, burped, and said, "Sorry, Lieutenant. Musta ate something didn't agree with me."

"Your drove Stephenson here last night?" Harkins said.

"Yes, sir."

"Was he meeting anybody in particular?"

"Just them wop gals, I guess," Pritchard said.

Colianno stepped around the front of the jeep until he stood beside Pritchard.

"Private Colianno here takes exception to ethnic slurs like 'wop,'" Harkins said.

Pritchard looked to the side and, apparently unimpressed, said, "Fuck should I care?"

Colianno delivered a lightning backhand that split Pritchard's lip. The private yelped like a kicked dog and staggered against the jeep.

"Beats me," Harkins said. "Maybe you'll think of a reason."

"You gave me a bloody lip!" Pritchard complained. "You goddamn MPs!"

"I'm not an MP," Colianno said helpfully. "I'm a paratrooper."

Pritchard looked confused but a bit more eager to cooperate.

"What were Stephenson's instructions when you dropped him off?"

"He told me to go away and come back in two hours."

"Then what?"

"That's it. He was drunk as a coot when I came back; I had to help him into the jeep, then into his tent."

"That's when you saw where he kept the musette bag?"

"Yeah. Yes, sir."

"Go on. Don't make me drag it out of you."

"When I heard somebody shot him, I figured there'd be a lot of confusion, so I went to his tent. Sure enough, the bag was still there. Came here when I finished a run this evening. Figured nobody would miss me for a few hours."

"Jesus, that's cold," Colianno said.

Harkins had heard worse. There were a lot of Pritchards in the world.

Harkins looked into Pritchard's eyes, which were bloodshot. He had vomit on his chin and the front of his shirt and was still pretty drunk.

"I felt bad, you know? I mean, I drove Stephenson a couple of times. He was a bit of a wild man, a fun-times guy. But at least he didn't hate draftees. Not like that bastard Boone."

Pritchard flicked his eyes to Harkins, then Colianno, as if afraid this comment might get him popped again.

"You ever drive Colonel Boone?" Harkins asked.

"Just once or twice. In North Africa. Treats GIs like we're his servants. Him a degenerate gambler and all."

The gambling comment made Harkins think about the contents of the bag in his hand; suddenly he knew what the metal disk was. He opened the bag and fished around inside, finally pulling out a nearly flat metal plate, about seven inches in diameter. It was hard to see in the dim light from the few windows around them, but it looked like gold on one side.

"What's that?" Colianno asked.

"You ever an altar boy?"

"Sure."

Harkins held the dish horizontally, just below his chin.

"A paten," Colianno said. "For Holy Communion."

"What?" Pritchard asked.

"The priest or altar boy holds it under your chin when you receive Holy Communion," Colianno said. "That way, if the host drops, it doesn't hit the floor. The host is sacred, so you won't want it touching somebody's nasty shoes."

"Sounds like some dago Catholic voodoo shit," Pritchard said.

As soon as the words were out of his mouth, he cringed. Colianno didn't move, but said, "Keep it up."

"OK, you need to go back to your unit," Harkins said to Pritchard. "You're AWOL now, but by tomorrow you'll be a deserter, and they shoot deserters."

Pritchard looked sad as he tucked the tails of his blouse into his pants and wiped at the vomit with filthy hands. "Listen, Lieutenant," he said. "I promised them girls I'd be staying for a while, you know. And they sure need the money, what with their families going hungry."

"So?" Harkins asked.

"So can I just get enough of that cash for another round or two? It won't take much."

"Unbelievable," Harkins said. "Get out of here before I shoot you myself."

Pritchard pulled himself up as straight as he could, gave a sloppy-drunk salute, then stepped into the street.

"Make sure you're at your unit where I can find you," Harkins called after him.

Pritchard just waved over his shoulder. Two women appeared at the window on the second floor, and one of them called out something to the blond soldier.

"I'll be back," he told her. "Don't go nowheres. I'll definitely be back."

When Pritchard was out of sight, Colianno said, "You think Stephenson won that money from Boone?"

"Could be," Harkins said. "Could just as easily be from other docs."

"That enough of a reason for somebody to kill him?"

"Maybe. Could be that somebody owed Stephenson more than he could pay."

"So that's, what? A clue, right?"

"Except that Stephenson's poker buddies will just say they didn't owe anything, or any more than this. So unless Stephenson kept an account book, we won't know. I didn't see anything like that in my first pass through his gear. I'm more curious about this paten. What was it doing in this bag, and what was he planning to do with it?"

10

2 August 1943
2200 hours

“What’s with you and Ronan?” Harkins asked as he slipped into the passenger side of the jeep.

“Not sure what you mean, Lieutenant,” Colianno said.

They rolled back into the hills to where the hospital compound was tucked into a shallow valley. The jeep’s blackout drive—tiny slits of headlamps—did nothing to light the road. There was a steady stream of slow, two-way traffic, the GI drivers calling out as they passed within a few feet of one another.

“Kathleen—Lieutenant Donnelly—thought that you two had become close while you were on the ward. She help take care of you?”

“She was one of the nurses, yeah. Yes, sir.”

Colianno slowed as they passed a couple of GIs on the side of the road, picking up crates that had fallen off their truck.

“OK, you don’t want to talk about it. I get that. I’ll bet every GI that passes through that hospital has a crush on her.”

Nothing from Colianno. Harkins felt like a nosy parent, fishing for information. He waited.

“They were the first American women we’d seen in months,” Colianno said at last. “Just like it was for you. That alone makes them pretty special. But at least I can talk to the local women. Most GIs can’t.”

“So it’s not hard for you to find female company?”

“It wouldn’t be hard, I guess, if I wasn’t spending my time chauffeuring you around.”

“Fair enough,” Harkins said, too tired to play any more games. He fell asleep immediately, woke when Colianno grabbed him by the shirt to keep him from spilling out of the vehicle at a corner. In spite of the hard seat, the bumpy road, the sharp turns, he was in a deep slumber when they finally stopped. Harkins came to and recognized the line of three pyramidal tents up against the churchyard wall.

"Time to get out, Lieutenant," Colianno said.

Harkins put his feet on the ground, reached behind his seat for his musette bag, picked up the paperback book from the floorboard.

"Lieutenant Donnelly said you'd be able to find a spot here to stretch out. I'll be back at dawn."

When the jeep pulled away, Harkins stumbled toward the closest tent, asleep on his feet. The sides were down, but his mind was too fuzzy to recall if they'd been down earlier.

In a pleasant dream, Kathleen Donnelly came out of the tent and took him by the hand, led him through the darkened doorway. He stood still in utter blackness, then a match strike, a halo of yellow light as someone lit a kerosene lamp.

"Eddie, you with me?"

Harkins woke to see Donnelly dressed in only a long T-shirt, sidelit by the lamp.

"Hi," Harkins said.

She came toward him, kissed him full on the mouth. She had just brushed her teeth and tasted like something this side of heaven. She took off his helmet, his pistol belt with its holster and canteen, then helped him with his blouse and T-shirt. His boots, belt, and pants.

"I smell really bad," he said.

There were two five-gallon jerrycans stenciled POTABLE WATER, a small pile of sponges, and two clean hospital hand towels. She sat him on a crate, had him lean forward until his head was over a basin on the tent's duckboard floor, then poured water on his hair. She soaped his head, used her fingers to massage his scalp, loosen the sand and dirt, which fell to the basin when she rinsed him. They switched places, and he washed her hair, his fingertips working along the edge of her scalp, her neck, the sides of her head. At that moment he was quite sure he had never felt anything as perfect as her ears.

She stood, lifted the T-shirt over her head, pulled down his shorts, and washed him slowly with the sponge, lathering his neck, his chest and back, his legs. The soap—of course they would have soap at a hospital, he thought—the soap was an incredible luxury. When she knelt he watched the top of her head, the wet hair, her narrow shoulders, the curve of her spine, the ridge of her vertebrae, her careful movements. She nursed him back to someplace closer to civilization, closer to the simple things they missed: chairs and tables, hot coffee and clean sheets, iced drinks, sleep.

He put a hand on the tent's center pole to steady himself as she washed his feet. Then it was her turn.

This was not the body he'd fantasized about endlessly when they were teenagers hanging out on Howard Avenue. That body was as mysterious as a sacrament, and it had moved on to wherever beautiful things are taken by time. The body before him had borne pain. She was thin; he had seen that through her clothes. Her neck and hands, her forearms and face were sunburned. She looked up as he washed her throat, smiled as he washed her small breasts, let the soap run down into the patch of hair below the points of her hips.

He rinsed her using one of the jerrycans, the water and suds sliding off her in a glistening wave. It was the most erotic experience of his life or even his dreams, surpassed immediately when she pulled him, not to the hard folding cot behind her, but to a stack of clean laundry, over which she'd thrown a single white sheet.

"So *that's* a sponge bath," Harkins said when they'd finished.

"That's the *deluxe* sponge bath. Only for special GIs."

Harkins propped up on an elbow, looked at his watch, and calculated they had four hours until dawn.

"Should we be worried about somebody seeing us?" Harkins asked.

"Nah. The nurses have a system worked out. We protect one another's private moments."

"So this happens a lot?"

"Not a lot, but we're adults. And this may surprise you, your not being a medical professional and all, but women have needs, too."

"You can't just say a couple of Hail Marys and get over it, like the priests told us boys?"

"I've been saying Hail Marys for months."

Harkin knew it wasn't the right question to ask, but he asked anyway. "So you . . . ?"

"Use the supply tent? No. This is too small a community. It would be very uncomfortable, I think, to sleep with a colleague. But you're different. I know you, and you're . . . safe."

"Wow, safe, huh? I'll bet that puts me in the running for world's greatest lover."

11

3 August 1943
0530 hours

Donnelly was already fully dressed when she shook him awake before dawn.

"Let's go, sleepyhead, there's a war to be won."

Twenty minutes later they were in the mess tent. Thirty or forty people moved in and out, some of them coming off shift, some on break, some, like Kathleen, getting ready for her day.

On a collapsible table near the door was a bowl full of yellow Atabrine tablets, a malaria preventative that every soldier was supposed to take once a day. A corporal handed a tablet to each person coming in. Donnelly popped hers in her mouth; Harkins stuck his in his shirt pocket.

"No wonder your driver got malaria," she said.

"Yeah, well, I'll take my chances, too. First week on that stuff I threw up for a couple of hours a day until my sides hurt, and that's when I wasn't squatting beside a road somewhere. Hard to say which is worse, malaria or the side effects of the cure."

"First Sergeant Drake looks for GIs who have yellow stains on their shirts. The guys put them in their shirt pocket, like you just did, and the tablets melt in the heat. Stains the shirt yellow. Now the enlisted guys have to take their dose in front of a noncom."

"Like having another mother," Harkins said. "One the army picked out for you."

"A hairy, smelly mother," Donnelly said.

They got in line with their mess kits as sweating cooks ladled out reconstituted eggs, strips of bacon. Two big aluminum pots held boiling coffee.

"It's not a bad idea for some of our guys, though," Donnelly said. "Some of them need a lot of coaching. Before anyone was allowed to go on pass, Drake had a formation with the junior enlisted guys, showed them how to put on a condom."

Harkins wondered if all nurses talked this openly about sex. Or maybe it was all adult women. Not for the first time it occurred to him how little he knew about what the polite writers at *The Saturday Evening Post* called "the fairer sex."

"He *showed them,* showed them?"

Donnelly laughed. "Not like that. He used the end of a broomstick. The guys were all laughing, but it was nervous laughter, you know? You could tell that the younger ones were paying attention."

"The nurses have to go through that?"

"We got a pass. I guess he figured we knew enough about anatomy."

When they got to the front of the line, Harkins put two thick slices of bread on his plate, then had the cook ladle a spoonful of eggs onto one slice so he could make a sandwich. He had his canteen cup hooked to one finger, and he held it out for a ladle full of coffee. The coffee grounds, floating on top, formed a little island.

There were half a dozen wooden tables with benches, banged together by someone who was definitely not a carpenter. Harkins and Donnelly found a space, but before they could sit, Captain Adams, the deputy provost, touched Harkins' sleeve.

"Can I get a minute?" Adams said.

Harkins put his breakfast down next to where Kathleen sat, then the two men stepped to the side.

"Glad I found you," Adams said. "Colonel Boone has already talked to my boss, the provost, complaining about you."

"He's been busy, then," Harkins said. "He's already shipped out one of the nurses who talked to me yesterday. Looks like he doesn't want me to dig very deeply."

"Well, this whole mess certainly looks bad for the kind of command he's running here. Maybe he's starting to clean house—a little late, you ask me."

"Maybe," Harkins said.

"The provost wants to make sure you share everything with Boone. He's to be part of this investigation."

"What if Boone is a suspect?"

"Is he?"

"Not yet, but he could become one."

"Based on what?"

"So far? Boone looked the other way when his docs, some of his docs, acted like assholes with the nurses."

"Like how?"

"Grabbing them, groping them," Harkins said. "Kind of stuff, you did it in my neighborhood, to somebody's sister, you'd get your ass beat. Or worse."

Harkins looked over at Kathleen, who watched him over the rim of her canteen cup. He wondered if Stephenson had tried to force himself on her. And that's when he felt something turn for him. He would not leave Kathleen in this mess any more than he would leave one of his sisters.

"That's not much. Hardly seems enough to kill somebody over."

"I don't know," Harkins said. "Look at Stephenson from the nurses' point of view. How would you feel if some guy—bigger than you, stronger than you, some important job, maybe with a commander willing to look the other way—how would you feel if that guy told you every day that he wanted to stick his dick up your ass?"

"Whoa," Adams said, looking around to see who'd heard.

"Exactly. You wouldn't say dumb shit like 'That's not much.'"

"OK," Adams said. "How about, short of rape, short of penetration, it does not rise to the level of a prosecutable crime."

"Maybe it should."

"We'll leave that to the lawmakers," Adams said. "Anyway, are you saying that Boone murdered Stephenson to make this problem go away?"

"There were easier ways to deal with Stephenson, I think. But he let it go on until maybe it all threatened to blow up in his face. I'm saying it's a theory."

"That's a pretty far-fetched theory: that the commander—who could have transferred Stephenson—killed him instead. Anything else make you think he should be a suspect?"

"I've heard that Boone is a gambler, a bad one. And judging by the cash I found in Stephenson's musette bag, our dead doctor was a better gambler."

"So Boone owed Stephenson money?"

"I plan to find that out," Harkins said.

Adams sat at an empty table. "OK, try this theory on for size," he said. "Let's say Boone has been a bad commander and let Stephenson get away with stuff. Now things have reached a low point—somebody murdered one of his docs. It serves Boone's best interests and certainly the interests of the command to get this solved, right? So it could be that you and Boone are after the same thing."

"But you said he's complaining about me to the provost marshal."

"Maybe he wants an experienced investigator."

"You find one yet?" Harkins asked. That was all he wanted yesterday; now, he wasn't so sure.

"No," Adams said. "You're doing fine. You'll do fine. It's only been twenty-four hours. But I want you to keep Colonel Boone apprised of what's going on. Any big developments in the case, I want you to brief him as soon as possible. I think, and my boss thinks, that he can help. That he wants to help."

"Chain of command, all that stuff, right?"

"Right. I'll bet we can make it work for us," Adams said. He actually looked hopeful. Probably because he'd gotten more sleep than Harkins.

"OK, Captain," Harkins said. "We'll do it your way. For now."

Adams left, and Harkins walked to where Kathleen was sitting. As he squeezed onto the bench, they were joined by Alice Haus, the nurse he'd met the previous afternoon. When she sat she put her hand on Harkins' arm.

"Kathleen told me about your brother," she said. "I'm really sorry."

Harkins kept his eyes on his plate, muttered, "Thanks."

After a moment Haus said, "You kids get some rest? Ready for your day?"

"Ready for anything," Donnelly said.

"How about you, crimefighter?" Haus asked Harkins. She smiled, maybe out of sympathy for his loss, maybe because she knew what had happened in the supply tent. No secrets here.

"I'm good, thanks," Harkins said. Besides the unexpected intimacy, Harkins had gotten five hours of sleep; he felt like he'd been resurrected.

"I figured out who you look like," Harkins said to Haus. She raised an eyebrow.

"Eleanor Holm, that swimmer who won a gold medal at the '32 Olympics in Los Angeles. You know who I mean?"

Haus nodded. "Yeah? I used to swim, too."

Harkins continued. "She was on her way to the '36 games in Berlin but got yanked from the team at the last minute."

"Why?" Donnelly asked.

"Depends on whose story you believe. The head of the Olympic committee said she got drunk at a shipboard party. Holm said that the old guy made a pass at her and was pissed when she turned him down."

"Sounds like a U.S. Army field hospital," Donnelly said.

"Holm was on track to make the '40 Olympics," Harkins said. "Except that Uncle Adolf had other ideas as to what we'd be doing in 1940."

"Yeah," Haus said. "We're all a little off the course we'd planned, right?"

They were all three quiet for a moment amid the clatter of mess tins and multiple conversations. Harkins took a bite of his sandwich, used his fingers to push dripping eggs back into the bread.

"A whole generation of us not living the lives we'd planned," Donnelly said.

Harkins looked around for Colianno. Three doctors settled at a table nearby.

"I'm assisting Herr Doktor Lindner today," Haus said, nodding at the men nearby.

"Lucky you," Donnelly said. Then, to Harkins, "That guy over there. Blond hair. He's a German POW."

"The future Mr. Alice Haus," Haus said.

"He's a Kraut doctor?" Harkins asked.

"Keep your voice down. He's kind of a big deal around here."

"Why?"

"Well," Haus said, "besides the movie-star looks, he's a urologist and surgeon. An excellent surgeon."

"A urologist? Meaning what?" Harkins asked.

"You know all those movies the medics showed you in basic training?" Donnelly asked.

It took Harkins a few seconds to connect the root of the word "urology" with the frightening photos and films the Medical Department inflicted on all recruits, but when he got it, he unconsciously pressed his thighs together. Haus noticed.

"Yep, those are the ones."

"So he treats the clap?"

"He's also a surgeon," Donnelly said. "One of the best I've seen, to tell you the truth. You get shot in the dick, he's the man you want to see."

"Plus, he speaks perfect English," Haus added. "Trained in the U.S., knows about baseball, and an actual nice guy, to boot."

"And those blue eyes," Donnelly said.

"Staring at you over the top of a scrub mask," Haus said.

"So how did he wind up here?" Harkins asked.

"He volunteered to stay behind with the patients at a German field hospital when the Krauts pulled out of Palermo. That happens more than you might think. Usually captured doctors are only allowed to work on other prisoners, and they're not allowed to do surgery at all," Donnelly said.

"Then we had two GIs come in, one with blast injuries. Urotrauma. The other had been shot a couple of times, including a round that nicked the family jewels. Turns out Boone had read a couple of papers Lindner had published before the war, so Boone asked Lindner if he'd operate. Apparently, he did a great job. Saved both those guys from singing in the boys' choir."

Donnelly took her eyes off the German, looked at Harkins. "It's the wound every guy worries about, but no one talks about; plus, not too many surgeons want to spend their time sewing up penises."

"It's just not sexy," Haus said.

"Wow," Donnelly said, looking at her watch. "Not even seven and we already have a contender for worst joke of the day."

"I do what I can," Haus said.

"Boone has been pulling strings to keep him here," Donnelly said to Harkins. "We don't have a urologist on staff, and the guy became everyone's hero when he helped those two GIs."

"Why is he wearing an American uniform?" Harkins asked. "POWs, even doctors, are supposed to wear their own uniforms."

As an MP, Harkins spent a lot of time taking care of prisoners. His platoon spent three days guarding giant wire compounds near the coast where thousands of Italian prisoners awaited transport to the States. Many of them, the conscripts, had surrendered already wearing civilian clothes, carrying luggage, and calling out to the newsreel cameras, "Detroit! New York!" The latest wave of immigrants.

"Yeah, First Sergeant Drake was no fan of that either. I don't know the real reason, but it's probably easier going around in a GI uniform. He can pass for an American officer with a slight accent. Plus he's a lieutenant colonel and Boone likes him."

"He paw the nurses, too?"

"No," Donnelly said. "He comes across as a gentleman, a little strait-laced, even."

"More likely a couple of the nurses want to paw him," Haus said.

After they'd finished eating, the three doctors, Lindner among them, stood and walked past the table where Harkins sat with Donnelly and Haus. They greeted the nurses, Lindner nodding and smiling. He looked like an Aryan propaganda poster, with his blond hair and Superman chin. Harkins disliked him immediately, and it must have been obvious to Kathleen, who leaned over and whispered to him. "I like *your* blue eyes," she said.

12

3 August 1943
0615 hours

Oberstleutnant Matthias Lindner overheard the nurses use his name, was glad to see, when he stood to leave, that it was Haus and Donnelly, sitting with a lieutenant Lindner did not recognize. The women were great nurses, very competent, and he enjoyed working with them, chatting with them. Haus was an outrageous flirt, of course, but he knew it would be a terrible mistake to act on his urges or hers. Many of the Americans were suspicious of him, waiting for an excuse to complain. And First Sergeant Drake was nearly apoplectic whenever he saw Lindner in his GI uniform, so it was best not to stir up any jealousies among the American doctors who pursued Haus vigorously and fruitlessly. Lindner was not ready to get shipped out with the other prisoners, especially because of a spat over a woman. He had a job to do that went far beyond taking care of patients.

The doctors he'd been sitting with stopped outside the mess tent to talk about Stephenson's murder and their theories; Lindner withdrew with a polite comment: "Such terrible news, such an awful thing."

He picked up a discarded newspaper from a table outside the tent and tucked it under his arm, kept it there while he walked to the prisoners' compound on the edge of the hospital grounds. There were two ward tents and a kind of headquarters, which the Americans called an orderly room. Beyond that, a sleeping tent for the medical orderlies—also German POWs—who worked under his supervision, taking care of wounded prisoners. The ranking German noncom had put up a canvas wall at one end of the sleeping tent to create a small room for Lindner. It was only what he rated as a lieutenant colonel and a doctor, but it was also a kind gesture and not anything he would have demanded.

He stepped into his end of the stifling tent, sat down on his cot, then stood and paced while removing his shirt.

Stephenson's murder—he'd heard about it in between operations that morning—had jolted him, maybe even more than it had shocked the Americans. One of his colleagues suggested that Stephenson was murdered by a jilted nurse, but the rest dismissed that theory.

A surgeon named Souther even got a laugh when he asked, "How could a broad get that angry over getting her ass pinched?"

Lindner knew the story was more complicated than that. He sat on the cot and opened the newspaper, forced himself to concentrate.

It was not *Stars and Stripes,* the GI newspaper printed in theater and handed out for free; it was a two-month-old *Pittsburgh Post-Gazette,* which some soldier had gotten in the mail. Judging by its condition, it had been thumbed by scores of homesick men. Lindner scanned the front page, a mix of outdated war news—very short on details—and stories about sports, local politics, the sharp growth in steel production and the need for workers. Some factories had even put women on the shop floor. On page three he found a map showing northwestern Europe, England in the upper corner, Germany and the occupied Low Countries shaded in black. Below the map the headline read: "Allied Bombing Campaign Targets German Industry."

He didn't bother to read the short article, which, in the interests of secrecy, would reveal very little. He already knew the Allied bombers would strike his home city of Essen, part of Germany's heavily industrialized Ruhr. He wondered for the thousandth time if Liselotte had taken the children from the city—she had relatives in the country, a hundred kilometers away from the arms factories that would draw Allied bombs like flies to honey. Mail from Germany had been sporadic even before the Allied invasion of Sicily, then it had stopped abruptly. Since his capture he had sent one letter, one side of a small sheet of International Red Cross stationery. If he was lucky it would reach her in a few months, though he had long since discounted luck. He was completely cut off from his family, knew nothing of his wife or two children, whom he'd last seen in September of 1942, knew nothing of his parents and their health. Where were they? Did they have enough to eat? Were there adequate bomb shelters in the city?

Lindner folded the newspaper, put it on the floor between his feet, put his head in his hands. Sometimes, at night, he woke with a start, sure that something had happened to Liselotte, that she had screamed his name, that she was crying and huddled with the children, even that he could hear her. Sometimes he felt he might die from the uncertainty.

What he did know of strategic bombing came from a cousin, Carl, a bombardier who had flown dozens of missions over London in 1940. Carl told him that the Luftwaffe targeted docks and factories, but those were only visible when the weather was clear. On cloudy nights, or nights when they were forced off course by the RAF, they dropped their bombs over any populated area. Carl had laughed when he told Lindner that the crews called bad weather "Women and Children Nights."

Carl was listed as *fehlt* when he failed to return from a mission over Dover, England, in late 1940, though Lindner thought "missing" might be harder on the family than "lost and presumed dead."

He stood, took a warm drink from a water bottle he kept next to his cot. He closed his eyes, opened them, said aloud and in English, "I will do my duty as a doctor, and I will do everything I can for my family."

The day after the Allied invasion, Lindner had been approached by an Abwehr officer, an intelligence agent who proposed an outrageous scheme.

"You want me to do *what*?" Lindner had asked.

The Abwehr man, a Berliner named Toffen, had tried to make it sound easy, something one could do without much thought or effort.

"If high command decides to make a strategic withdrawal to the east, toward Messina or even back to the mainland, some of our most seriously wounded, those too badly injured to move, may be left behind. If you volunteer to stay with them, the Allies will put you to work as a physician. You will simply keep your eyes open. You will try to learn what you can about Allied plans for the campaign here. Or the next campaign."

"I know nothing of military operations," Lindner had protested. "I would not even know what to look for."

"You talk to people," Toffen had reassured him. "That's ninety percent of intelligence work."

"Impossible."

They'd been sitting in a café in Palermo, near the general hospital where Lindner treated patients, men with those terrible wounds. At the other tables, doctors drank liters of coffee to stay awake on their lengthening shifts.

Toffen had laughed, was still smiling when he said, "We know you studied in America. We know you speak excellent English and make friends easily."

The spymaster leaned forward. Lindner noticed that the elbows of his summer-weight suit were worn nearly through.

"We also know that no one in your family has joined the party, that your father was a critic of the government."

Lindner forced himself to sit quietly. The man sitting across from him spoke calmly, as if discussing the best ski resorts.

"Your family is in Essen, near the heavy industry centers that will be the target of Allied raids."

Lindner had nodded, afraid to speak.

"They will need special permission to move to the country," Toffen said. "I can arrange that. And you have a brother in the Luftwaffe, yes? Serving on the Italian mainland."

Lindner nodded again.

"I'm sure he'll be safe," Toffen said.

Lindner felt his hands shake, pressed them together under the table. "What if I don't find anything? What if I can't learn anything? I am not a spy, after all."

"Then someone higher up than I am will make a decision," Toffen said. "I'm sure they'll take into account that you did your best."

The very next day Toffen came for him at the hospital. Lindner had protested that wounded men were coming in and needed attention, but Toffen had dragged him off to meet a civilian, a middle-aged Italian from Rome who spoke passable German. They'd spent hours—hours in which Lindner knew young German soldiers were dying for want of a surgeon's care—explaining how he and the man would exchange signals, how the man would make funds available to him should the need arise, how they would warn each other if they thought they'd been compromised. There was an apartment, but Lindner was only to go there as a last resort, if he had an urgent message.

Lindner had been angry, incredulous that his skills were to be set aside for something like this.

Toffen finally grew exasperated. "Look, Doctor," he said. "There are people higher up who think that your loyalty is questionable. You're a little too enamored of the Americans, for instance. This is your chance to redeem yourself and do some good for your family."

That's when Lindner came to his realization. "So, I'm expendable."

"We're all expendable, Doctor," Toffen said.

When Lindner had no retort, the agent leaned back in his chair, satisfied.

"You can never write any of your instructions anywhere," Toffen said several times. "You must remember all of this. Do you understand?"

"I graduated with high honors from Leipzig," Lindner snapped, suddenly angry. "You could take every bone in the human body, pile them on a table, and I could sort and name them. Can you do that? No? I will remember your instructions."

Toffen smiled mirthlessly. "I'm sure your family will appreciate it."

Remembering the conversation now, Lindner was disgusted at how easily he'd been manipulated, how callous Toffen had been. Sometimes he hoped the agent had been killed; other times he hoped the man was still alive and would make good on his promise.

Lindner put his blouse back on and stepped outside the tent, looked over toward where the American doctors lived.

Stephenson would have a footlocker or a cabinet of some sort. Lindner wanted to see what was inside, but he could hardly do that in broad daylight. He had an entire day to worry about what the Americans might find in Stephenson's tent.

Better to focus on things he could control.

He grabbed his stethoscope and walked toward the POW ward to visit with the wounded men there.

13

3 August 1943
0620 hours

Donnelly and Harkins were finishing their breakfast when Colianno joined them, his mess kit piled with eggs, toast, and bacon.

"Where did you sleep?" Harkins asked.

"Where did *you* sleep, sir?" Colianno said.

Donnelly laughed, and Colianno smiled at her.

"I meant did you *find* a place to sleep. I'm supposed to take care of my driver, make sure you're fed and all that stuff."

"Thanks, Lieutenant. I can take care of myself pretty good."

"You know, in the German Army they'd probably shoot you for being a smart-ass."

"Yes, sir."

"And what the hell is that on your pistol belt?"

Colianno looked down, as if he needed to check. There was a standard-issue leather holster with the embossed "US," and Harkins could see the butt of a .45. But the lower part of the holster had been decorated with beads, as had the long laces meant to be tied around the wearer's thigh.

"Bought it in Palermo."

"The ridiculous holster?"

"Pistol, too," Colianno said. "I bet you could outfit a regiment just from what the locals stole and are selling."

Ronan entered the tent. Donnelly waved to her, and she joined them carrying just a cup of coffee.

"Morning," Ronan said, straddling the bench seat. "You hear about Felton? She's shipping out."

"She's already gone," Donnelly said.

"I could still use your help," Harkins said to Ronan. "I'm trying to get a read on Stephenson, so I can figure out why someone wanted him dead."

Ronan held her canteen cup in two hands, stared at the inky contents.

Harkins allowed himself a bit of hope. *She's thinking about it.*

"Let's walk over to that church," Ronan said. "See if it's empty."

The four of them stood, and Harkins said to Colianno, "Stay here." If the paratrooper was smitten, he'd be no help questioning Ronan. Besides, the nurse probably needed privacy if she was going to talk.

Donnelly, Harkins, and Ronan walked to the little chapel on the edge of the hospital compound. The churchyard wall was smashed flat in a half-dozen places, but they still went through the gate, out of respect or guilt. The sanctuary was lit by sunlight coming through the roof and the spaces where the windows had been. Fallen roof beams had crushed the pews on the right, but they found seats on the left side near the altar. They sat for a few moments, then Harkins started to speak. Donnelly silenced him with a look.

Ronan held a small cloth cap in her hands; she rotated it, tugging at the bill, turning it over. Then she drew a deep breath, squared her shoulders, and looked right at Harkins.

"Stephenson made my life a living hell from the day I arrived here. The very first conversation I had with him, we were walking into Surgery One. He stopped to let me go in first, and he put his hand on me."

Harkins raised one eyebrow slightly.

"On my rear end," she said. "And not just a pat."

When she paused, Harkins said, "OK. What else?"

"He followed me into the supply tent another time, started kissing me, putting his hands all over me, pressing up against me. Saying disgusting things about what he wanted to do to me."

Ronan looked at Donnelly, who took her friend's hand.

"I know it doesn't sound like much," Ronan said to Harkins. "But it got to the point where I was afraid to walk around the hospital compound."

Harkins felt sorry for the woman, and he knew that if one of his sisters had come home telling this story, he and his brothers would have raced each other out the door to teach the guy some manners.

But would he have killed someone?

There was either more to the story, and Ronan was not ready to tell him, or Stephenson had been killed for some other reason.

"I've heard that a number of nurses complained about Stephenson," Harkins said. "Did you tell anyone what he did?"

Ronan shook her head. "No. I knew that other women had complained, and that nothing happened, nothing changed. I thought I could just make myself keep going."

She looked up at Donnelly, and Harkins thought this would be easier on Ronan if there were such a thing as a female detective. But that seemed as likely as girl doctors.

"You know," she continued, looking at Donnelly's hand in her own. "Like we do after a rough patch of casualties. Just push all that shit down. Plus I was afraid he would hurt me if I talked; I was really afraid."

Harkins asked, "Did he ever hit you?"

"No, but he kind of let me know that he was untouchable."

"Because he was a doctor?" Harkins asked.

Hesitation. Another look at Donnelly. "I don't know. Maybe he knew something about Boone."

"Any idea what it might be?"

"Not really."

"OK," Harkins said. "Maybe it'll come to you later."

Harkins put his elbows on his knees, leaned closer. Thought about what Adams said about Boone being an ally in the investigation. Boone couldn't know that things had gotten this bad, could he?

"Moira," Harkins said. "May I call you Moira?"

She nodded. She was not crying, Harkins noticed. Tough gal. She would need all the toughness she could muster.

"I have to ask you this. Did you kill Stephenson? For what he did to you?"

"No, of course not," she said.

"If she had," Donnelly added, "she wouldn't have told you all this. Why would she make herself a suspect?"

Why, indeed? Harkins thought. There were pieces that were eluding him, angles he hadn't considered, a logical train of thought that was just beyond his reach. There had to be some way detectives juggled all these possibilities while they gathered facts, while they pulled a story from the smoky confusion.

Harkins said, "I'm sorry this happened to you, Moira. Stephenson was a genuine sonofabitch. I know what I would have done if he'd pulled that crap with one of my sisters."

She looked up at him, still hand in hand with Donnelly.

"I'm afraid I have to ask another question," Harkins said. He was thinking about legal definitions now. "Was anything Stephenson did to you . . . was anything he did criminal?"

Ronan sat up straight, angry now, her voice lower. She was trying to control herself, Harkins thought, maybe hold something back.

"He cornered me in the supply tent; I was alone. And he pulled his . . . he pulled his penis out. He had an erection. And he told me what he wanted to do to me."

Harkins shifted uncomfortably. "Did he? Do what he talked about?"

Ronan sniffled, and Harkins saw Kathleen's fingers flex, squeezing Ronan's hand. "Yeah," she said finally. "He raped me."

Later, Harkins would realize that was the point at which he should have stopped talking, but he was too focused on getting all the facts that might come out.

"Before that, did you two ever do anything sexual? Talk about doing anything?"

Donnelly stood suddenly, her eyes burning. "Come with me," she said to Harkins.

When they were outside and before she could say anything else, Harkins said, "I'm sorry. I really am. I had to ask."

"The hell you say. If Saoirse told you that story, told you some bastard whipped out his dick in front of her, then raped her, would you ask those asinine questions?"

"If Saoirse had been attacked, no one would let me be the investigator."

Donnelly crossed her arms. "Listen to yourself, Eddie. Can you forget about your precious investigation for a goddamn minute and think about the effect on her? *Jay*-sus." Then she turned and went back in the chapel.

Harkins told himself he had to ask those questions. If there were a court-martial eventually, Stephenson's behavior might come up, and Ronan—if she were called as a witness—might be exposed to worse treatment.

On the other hand, that was a lot of ifs. He shook his head, knew he was rationalizing what he'd just done.

"Lieutenant."

Harkins looked up to see Colianno coming toward him.

"Colonel Boone just sent a runner to find Lieutenant Ronan," the paratrooper said. "Wants to see her."

Harkins waited a few minutes before going back into the church. He walked up on the two women, both of whom had been crying. Donnelly had the heels of her hands pressed to her eyes.

"Moira, Colonel Boone wants to see you. He sent a runner," Harkins said.

"Why?"

"My guess is he wants to ask you about Stephenson. Maybe he heard Stephenson was bothering you. Boone is probably talking to a lot of people. If you want, I'll come with you," he said.

"So I have to tell this awful story to everybody?"

"Well, you don't have a choice; he's the commander, so you have to go, but it's up to you how much you tell him. And, who knows? Maybe talking to him can help."

"A little late for him to show interest," Donnelly said. She rubbed Ronan's upper back, just as she'd touched Harkins when he told her about Michael's death. "I'll come with you, too."

"Last night I was hoping this would all go away now that he's dead," Ronan said. "He got what he deserved."

"That may be," Harkins said. "But it's still a murder."

Ronan sat, shoulders slumped, a picture of exhaustion. Beside her, Donnelly chewed the nail on one thumb, looked at Harkins, then at her friend.

"He might be tough on you," Harkins said. "If he's really transferring nurses to make all this go away, he might lean on you. Make you want to just shut up about the whole thing."

"I don't want to tell him, you know, everything," Ronan said. "He'll just call me a liar."

"We'll play it however you want," Harkins said.

"When does he want me?"

"Now."

14

3 August 1943
0700 hours

Though it was only a short distance, Harkins had Colianno drive him and the two nurses to Boone's headquarters tent near the center of the compound. He could feel Ronan's tension, the anxiety coming off her like heat. He sat with her and Donnelly, sent Colianno ahead to see who was inside. A minute or two later, the paratrooper came jogging back to them.

"He's in there. So's First Sergeant Drake and a clerk."

Harkins had hoped to avoid Drake.

"OK," Harkins said. "Let me go in first, explain why I'm here."

Colianno helped the nurses out of the back of the jeep, squeezing Ronan's upper arm as she stepped down. Harkins turned, pushed into the tent, and found Drake sitting at a field table. The tent was about thirty feet deep and divided into a front and back room.

"What do you want?" Drake said to Harkins. "Nobody asked for you to be here."

Harkins headed for what he assumed was Boone's workspace in the back. Drake stood, tried to grab his arm as he went by, cursed when he missed.

Harkins pushed back the canvas flap and stepped through. The back wall of the tent, behind Boone's desk, was rolled up, so the space was flooded with light. Boone sat at a small field table with some papers in his hand; his admin clerk, a PFC, stood looking over his shoulder. When Boone looked up, Harkins stopped, brought his heels together, and saluted. "Lieutenant Harkins, military police."

Boone did not return the salute, but he dismissed the clerk with a wave of his hand. Harkins let his arm come back to his side.

"Colonel, I'm sure you know that I'm investigating the murder of Captain Stephenson. I've learned some things that I want to bring to your attention."

"I'm well aware of your activities, Lieutenant, as well as your lack of qualifications for the job. I've contacted the provost marshal and requested that you be relieved of your duties. Soon you'll be back doing whatever important work you were doing in support of the war effort."

So much for Adams's theory that Boone might be an ally.

"Yes, well, that may happen, sir. Until then, you're stuck with me."

Harkins turned. Ronan and Donnelly were in the front part of the tent with Drake. When Harkins motioned them into Boone's section, the first sergeant followed and stood to one side of the door.

"Why are you two here?" Boone said to Harkins and Donnelly.

"Lieutenant Ronan wants to lodge a complaint against Captain Stephenson, something you should be aware of."

"I thought we established, thanks to your keen detective work, that Captain Stephenson is deceased. Why are we bringing a complaint against him?"

"It's part of a larger pattern of behavior that involves other doctors on staff," Harkins said. "Part of my investigation."

Boone considered this for a moment, then said, "Lieutenant Donnelly, why are you here?"

"Lieutenant Ronan is in my section sir, since Nurse Felton, uh, left. I'm here to give her moral support."

Boone studied her for a moment, tapped a finger on his field desk. "You're dismissed," he said.

Donnelly, surprised but without recourse that kept her on the right side of military courtesy, turned and left.

"You, too," Boone said to Harkins.

"No, sir. This is still my investigation."

"I could have First Sergeant Drake remove you."

This wasn't how Harkins had expected things to play out, but he wasn't about to back down, either.

"He could try," Harkins said.

Boone smiled, as if he might enjoy having the big first sergeant toss Harkins.

"Lieutenant Ronan," Boone said at last. "Where are my manners? Have a seat, please."

Ronan sat in a folding chair in front of Boone's field desk. She looked like she was about to vomit. Harkins stood beside her.

"First of all, we're all terribly upset by what happened to Captain Stephenson," Boone said, his tone syrup sweet and insincere. "But I know you must be especially upset, since you and he were friends. Close friends."

Harkins was caught off guard. Did Boone really believe that?

Ronan stiffened. "We were not friends, sir. We were work colleagues."

"Oh, I'm sorry," Boone said. "I was under the impression that you and Captain Stephenson had a relationship. Were lovers, in fact."

Ronan looked like she'd been slapped. "Absolutely not."

"Hmmm," Boone said, putting a finger to his lips. Smug. "That's not what he led me to believe."

Harkins tried redirecting the conversation. "A number of the nurses told me that Stephenson forced himself on them. Tried to take advantage of them."

"That's Captain Stephenson, or, if you prefer, Doctor Stephenson," Boone corrected him. "And of course we can't hear Captain Stephenson's side, or is that unimportant to you, Lieutenant Harkins? How about you, Lieutenant Ronan?"

"No, sir," Ronan said, flustered. "I mean, yes, sir. But the doctors, some of the doctors are pigs and . . ."

She paused, and Boone asked, "And what?"

"And you let it go on. You take their side any time one of the nurses complains."

"Well, perhaps that's the way you see it. But there's more to the story, and I have a different point of view. I'm responsible for running an entire hospital, you see. If I spent my time worrying about every little lovers' spat, we'd get no work done around here."

"We weren't lovers," Ronan said, her voice cracking a bit.

"So you've said," Boone said.

"Stephenson said you'd never do anything to him," Ronan said. "Like he had something on you."

For the first time since they stepped into the tent, Boone looked surprised. Just a little, Harkins noticed, but for a moment he was off balance.

Atta-girl, Harkins thought.

"Any idea what he might have been talking about, Colonel?" Harkins asked. "Was there some arrangement between you and Stephenson?"

"Don't be ridiculous," Boone said. "How would I know what Stephenson was talking about? Or if he even said such a thing?"

Boone turned on Ronan. "What do you think will happen if you go around defaming all these people? Defaming dead men who can't defend their reputations?"

"You ordered her to come here, sir," Harkins said. "She wasn't going around bad-mouthing Stephenson. Doctor Stephenson."

"So she didn't talk to you, Lieutenant? She didn't make accusations about Stephenson? You aren't spreading rumors you've heard from other nurses?"

"I'm conducting an investigation," Harkins said. "My questions were in the normal course of things."

"Your questions have been out of line," Boone said, his voice rising. "I think you're an irresponsible gossip and part of the problem."

Boone stood suddenly and walked around to the front of the field table. Ronan flinched, had to bend her neck backwards to look him in the eye.

"I'll tell you what will happen if you keep spreading these stories, Lieutenant Ronan. You'll be dragged in front of an investigating board. All men, maybe one token nurse. And they'll start firing questions at you."

Boone waited a beat before asking, "Did you ever flirt with Captain Stephenson?"

"No," Ronan said, wilting a little more. "I try to be friendly with everyone, get along."

"Did you ever have a drink with him?"

"Some of the nurses did when he offered. Nurse Whitman."

Harkins thought he saw Boone's right eyelid twitch, barely a tell.

"Let's keep poor Nurse Whitman out of this, all right? I asked if you drank with Doctor Stephenson. Did you ever go to him for help or advice?"

"Just to talk about medical procedures."

"Colonel," Harkins said, trying to intervene, "the nurses' complaints will all be part of my report to the provost."

"The allegations, you mean," Boone said. He turned back to Ronan. "How many sexual partners have you had in your life, Lieutenant?"

Ronan flinched, like Boone had taken a swing at her.

"How many sexual partners have you had since joining the army? How many encounters with each man? Feel free to approximate if you've lost track."

"Let's go, Moira," Harkins said.

When she began to stand, Boone snapped, "Sit down, Lieutenant."

Ronan sat.

"You know it's against regulations for you to have sexual relations with a superior officer, don't you?"

"I didn't have *relations*—"

Boone cut her off. "I asked if you were aware of the regulations, Lieutenant."

Ronan squeezed her fists, looked down into her lap. Harkins thought he saw a tear spot her trousers.

"Let's see, what else will a board of officers, a board of male officers, likely ask you? How about, 'What did you expect would happen, working side by side with men in the prime of life, in a war zone, under tremendous pressure? Didn't you think they would want to have sex with you?'"

"That's enough, Colonel!" Harkins said. It came out sounding like an order, but one that Boone was not obliged to obey.

"How about, 'Do you wear the government-issued underwear, or do you wear personal items you brought from home?'"

Boone went on. "Did you tell him to stop? Did you fight him? Scream?"

Harkins stepped around Boone and took Ronan's arm, helping her to her feet. She wobbled a bit as he walked her to the door of the small office section.

"Were you a virgin when you joined the army?" Boone said to her back.

Drake stood by the door, looking embarrassed. The first sergeant held the flap open for them as Harkins helped Ronan through. Drake followed them. When they were outside, Harkins turned on the first sergeant.

"You tell that cocksucker that I am not fucking going away. I may be a traffic cop, but I will burn this fucking place down, and him with it."

Harkins turned away and so did not hear Drake say, "Yes, sir."

15

3 August 1943
0730 hours

Colianno and Donnelly were outside, waiting in the jeep. Harkins helped Ronan into the back and the four rode in tense silence back to the nurses' tent. Harkins got out when the women did.

"You did a good job back there," Harkins said to Ronan. "I know that was tough."

Ronan brought her right fist up in a roundhouse punch that caught Harkins just above the left eye. He was so surprised that he didn't even turn his head.

"You don't know *shit* about what I went through back there, or what I went through with that bastard Stephenson!" She strained, red-faced, spittle flying from her mouth. "He pushed my face into the dirt! Nearly broke my arm pulling it backwards! Kicked me from behind to get my legs apart! And after . . . after he asked me if I fucking *liked* it!

"You walked me right into that ambush back there. 'Maybe it will help,' you said. As if he would fucking help. He hasn't done a single thing, hasn't lifted a finger to help one nurse. What the hell was I thinking?"

She threw another punch, a weak jab. Harkins leaned back so that she barely connected. When Ronan turned away, Colianno got out of the jeep to walk her to her tent, but she waved him off and hurried away, head down.

Donnelly approached Harkins and looked at the cut above his eye. He dabbed at it with his fingers, which came away bloody.

"I ought to punch you in the other eye," she said. "Why did you let Boone get away with that? I told you to be careful."

"You heard all that?"

"You're goddamned right I did. I listened from the other side of that door." Donnelly studied him, eyes narrowed. "You knew that was going to happen. You had to, since you asked essentially the same stupid questions."

"No," Harkins said. "I tried to warn her."

He wanted to mention Adams, the instructions from the provost to seek Boone's cooperation, but he knew it would sound like an excuse.

"But I have seen defense attorneys, even detectives, ask those questions of rape victims. She has to be ready for that, and worse."

"But now you know what your questions sounded like to her," Donnelly said. "You and Boone were reading from the same hymnal, it's just that he was more outrageous."

"Boone had to be told to his face if anything is going to change around here."

"You got more than that," Donnelly said. "Maybe you wanted to poke the bear. Maybe you wanted to see what Boone would do when confronted, what you were up against. Maybe see if Boone should be on your list of suspects."

Harkins looked at her, and for a moment, in spite of the surroundings and her uniform and her knife-cut hair, he saw a seventeen-year-old girl in a pleated skirt who'd stood up to a bully, a priest who wanted to use a switch on her little brother's backside.

"You used her to bait him, Eddie."

"Jesus, Kathleen. I didn't use her as bait. Somebody had to speak up. It can't just be a bunch of nurses sitting around and bitching into their coffee cups. I had to ask the questions I did."

"You keep telling yourself that."

"I just wasn't ready for Boone to go on the offensive."

"Well, you better be ready from now on, pal," Donnelly said. She poked him in the chest with each word of her next sentence. "I don't want her exposed to any more of his shit."

"OK, I'm sorry," Harkins said. "I really am. He caught me off guard."

"I will beat your ass, Eddie Harkins; don't think I won't."

Donnelly stepped back, drew a long breath, let it out. "You got my Irish up, boy-o."

"I see that. What about your friend?" he asked, touching his eyebrow again. "She's got a temper. Is she capable of violence?"

"You mean did she shoot Stephenson?"

Harkins stayed quiet.

"If she did, it's only what he deserved."

"Maybe," Harkins said.

"Did you deliberately provoke her?" Donnelly asked. "With that stupid comment about you knowing how hard that interview was? Were you trying to see if she'd lose it?"

"No," Harkins said.

Donnelly didn't respond to that.

"She said that Stephenson maybe had something on Boone," Harkins said. "And that's why Boone let him get away with so much bullshit. Any idea what she was talking about? What Stephenson had on Boone?"

"None," Donnelly said.

"Ask her, would you?"

"OK, but give her a little time," Donnelly said.

"She going to be all right?"

Donnelly gave out a sad little laugh, looked around at the rows of tents, with their bandaged and drugged residents visible through the open side walls, the broken bones and gunshot faces and missing limbs. "Any of us going to be all right after all this?"

She turned and walked toward the nurses' tent. Colianno, who'd been standing nearby, listening, came up beside Harkins.

"Slugging you isn't the same thing as shooting someone at close range," the paratrooper said. "Believe me, I know. Anyway, I don't think Lieutenant Ronan could do that."

"You're probably right," Harkins said.

"You need to get that cut checked, Lieutenant."

When Harkins didn't respond, the paratrooper pointed over his shoulder with his thumb. "OK if I go grab my gear? I'd like to keep it with me in the jeep."

Harkins nodded, glad to be left alone for a moment.

It had been a classic screwup. The questions he thought were reasonable were not; it's just that he'd heard them so many times before that they seemed normal. It was only when Boone turned the same questions into an assault that he saw what he had done to Ronan. What he would never do again, he promised himself, if he lived long enough to become a detective.

He put his hand to his eyebrow; it was still bleeding.

"Well, guess I deserved that."

He wondered if this made any sense at all. He was trying to pin a rape on a dead guy. Would bringing all that out in the open help Ronan?

Would it make things better for the other nurses if Boone's terrible leadership were exposed? It sure looked like Stephenson had already been dealt rough justice.

"Justice," an old cop had told him when he was an unspoiled new hire at the Philadelphia PD, "don't always look like what you expect."

He stepped into a slice of shade beside one of the tents, took a pull of warm water from his canteen, remembered when he figured out what the old guy meant.

On foot patrol, a summer night, using his shoulder to bust open a locked door, crashing into the vestibule of an apartment building. A man, middle-aged, skinny, sweating through a stained undershirt, pants around his ankles, turning toward Harkins and away from a girl on the floor, who immediately pulled herself into a tight ball.

She was fourteen, they learned later, at the hospital. Had wandered into the wrong building looking for a friend's apartment. The cops—Harkins, another patrolman, and a sergeant named Healy—told the girl's father that the suspect had fled up the stairs, that he'd fallen from the roof while trying to escape. Six stories. Hit the concrete like a ripe pumpkin.

But the man had not run. He was drunk, for one thing. When the cops busted in, he tried to get away, stumbling up the stairs and holding his pants as he climbed.

Sergeant Healy had watched him from the first floor, one hand on his pistol, the other on the bannister, before turning to Harkins and the other patrolman, both of them rookies.

"Which one of you has a sister?" the sergeant asked.

"I do," Harkins said.

"Find something to cover her up," Healy told the other cop, then motioned Harkins to follow.

They caught up with him easily on the second floor, still fumbling with his pants. Harkins yanked up the man's trousers, held them as the two cops, one on each arm, kept climbing, the man dragging his feet, not realizing what was happening until the fourth or fifth floor, even then too drunk to resist.

Harkins figured they were going to beat him, maybe with their fists, maybe with the nightsticks they were carrying.

When they reached the roof and Healy kept going toward the edge, Harkins finally asked, "What are we going to do, Sarge?"

"Shut up, kid," Healy said.

And Harkins kept walking, matching Healy stride for stride, unable to stop himself, the drunk in between them, blubbering some apology.

At the edge of the roof, Harkins simply let go of the man's arm as Healy pulled him free and shoved him over the edge. Then they turned back to the stairwell, and Harkins saw a woman watching them from an apartment window in a taller building next door. She nodded at him, retreated back into the gloom. After his shift, Harkins, his shoulder a knot of pain, went to his parents' house and hugged his sisters, wordless.

16

3 August 1943
1030 hours

"You've got some other scars here," the doctor said, pointing with his forceps and curved needle to the three other places on Harkins' forehead where he'd been stitched in the past.

"Golden Gloves boxing. Took me a while to learn to block with my arms and hands, not my face."

"So you unlearned that lesson today?"

"Something like that," Harkins said.

"I hear you knew Nurse Donnelly before the war."

"Yeah, we're from the same neighborhood, same schools."

"I have two medical school classmates here on Sicily. I ran into one of them before we left North Africa. And I have a brother in the Pacific."

Harkins studied the doctor. Was it possible he'd heard about Michael, was trying to strike up a conversation?

"He a doctor, too?"

"No. He's a lieutenant in the marines. Wounded on Guadalcanal last fall. Spent two months in navy hospitals in Hawaii. Then they sent him back to the front. Some other island no one has ever heard of before."

Harkins paused. Everyone was worried about someone. "Tell me, Doc, were you friends with Captain Stephenson, the guy who was murdered yesterday morning?"

"Well, I knew him, of course. There are only eighteen doctors here at the hospital when we're fully staffed."

"What did you think of him?"

The doctor studied Harkins a moment. He was a bit older than the other surgeons, though he only wore captain's bars. Hair long gone, same exhausted look as everyone else on staff, he'd introduced himself as Doctor Trennely. The nurses called him "Good Guy" Trennely. Harkins figured he kept his hands to himself.

"Let's say I did not have a high opinion of him, as a person. As a knife, he was great, the times I worked with him."

"Can you elaborate?"

"Well, if you're any kind of investigator, and I'm going to assume you are, you'll already have found out that Stephenson was always on the prowl, always looking to shack up with some nurse. I mean, some of them are flirts; I guess they like the give and take. I don't know. But he wasn't kind to the women, as far as I could see.

"I also heard that he tried scrubbing in once when he was drunk," Trennely said. "As you can imagine, we're very touchy about our professional standards as doctors, as surgeons. I didn't see this, mind you, I heard about it later. But that would have been a *serious* infraction."

"Grab-ass was acceptable, though? Professionally, I mean."

Trennely paused, made eye contact, didn't say anything.

"He ever lose a patient, maybe made a mistake, and someone wanted revenge?" Harkins asked.

"No. I don't know. I mean, I wouldn't have any way of knowing that."

"He cheat at cards?"

Trennely looked surprised at the question. "What?"

"Forgive me, Doc, but the guy was a major-league horse's ass. Guys like that tend to have other problems, too."

"I don't play cards with the other surgeons."

"Why not?"

Trennely looked at him and smiled. "I just never learned. Always a bit embarrassed about it, to tell you the truth."

"Was Stephenson the only doc bothering the nurses?"

"I think it's safe to say he was the worst offender."

"But there were others."

Trennely hesitated, weighing whether he was being a gossip or a helpful witness. "Wilkins."

Harkins wrote the name in his book. "What about Lieutenant Felton? He ever bother her?"

Trennely laughed, yanked hard on the suture. Harkins flinched, figured the doc mostly worked on people who were under anesthesia.

"She didn't take any guff from Stephenson, Boone, or anybody else."

"That why she got transferred?"

"No doubt."

He finished his work, tied off the suture with a couple of quick twists of his fingers and hands, and told Harkins, "Keep that as clean as possible, which I know is kind of a joke out here. If it gets painful, tender, that might mean infection, so make sure you come back."

"Thanks, Doc."

Trennely rolled his instruments into a soiled cloth. "You close to catching the guy who did this? Who shot him?"

"Was it you?"

Trennely looked panicked for a moment. "No, absolutely not!"

"Well then, I'll cross you off the list, and I guess that makes me closer."

Harkins walked outside, saw a jeep parked next to his own, Colianno talking to someone. As he approached, he saw that it was Captain Adams, the contract lawyer turned deputy provost. Harkins saluted.

"Lieutenant Harkins," Adams said. "Based on what Private Colianno has told me, it sounds like you're making some progress. I'm glad to hear that, and your replacement will be, too."

"My replacement?"

"Investigator. I found a guy in the Seventh Army Headquarters who was with the Georgia Bureau of Investigation. I got his boss to assign him to the provost marshal. You'll be going back to your unit."

"No, sir. Tell him thanks, but no thanks. I want to see this through."

Adams looked surprised. "You were dead set against being the lead in this. You even made a big deal, said you weren't qualified."

"I was exhausted, talking crazy. I'm on it now, and I don't want to let up. I can get this done quickly, before your Georgia boy can get his gear packed to get over here."

Adams looked perplexed. "I don't understand."

"Look, Captain. I appreciate your trying to help me. But this place is a mess, and I've started to make progress. Got some momentum."

"On the murder?"

Being a team player had already burned Harkins once today. Should he trust Adams? The guy was being straight with him, but he was as inexperienced as Harkins when it came to investigations.

"On the murder and some other things."

Adams took off his helmet and glasses, wiped his balding head with a kerchief. Harkins looked into the back of the jeep, where Colianno had stashed an M1 Garand next to the carbine he'd already come up with. The paratrooper was hoarding weapons.

"It might not be that easy. Colonel Boone called the provost again this morning to complain about you. Says that you're asking all sorts of inappropriate questions of the nurses, stirring up trouble that has nothing to do with the murder. He says you're clearly unqualified."

"That's because I rattled his cage."

"Meaning what?"

Harkins looked at Colianno, who sat in the jeep, one hand resting on the steering wheel, listening.

"Take a walk, Colianno," he said.

When Colianno was out of earshot, Harkins faced Adams. "Look, Stephenson raped one of the nurses. He told her, or at least implied, that Boone would never do anything about it because he, Stephenson, had something on Boone."

"Jesus. What did Stephenson have on him?"

"I don't know, but I intend to find out. The way the doctors chase the nurses, this hospital has been a nightmare place for these women to work. Before my little run-in with the colonel this morning, I thought maybe Boone didn't know how bad things were."

"And now?"

"Whether he knew or not, I don't think he's at all interested in changing the way things are."

Adams chewed the inside of his cheek. "What does that have to do with your actual job of finding the murderer?"

"I think it's all tied together. If Stephenson really did have something on Boone, and then Stephenson started attacking these women because he thought he had free rein, then maybe Boone decided to get rid of the problem."

"So Boone is a suspect?"

"One of them. Stephenson pissed off a lot of people."

Adams put his glasses back on slowly. "You think other women were attacked?"

"Yes, sir. Maybe not raped, but threatened; they sure didn't feel safe."

"I already told the provost I was replacing you." Adams drummed his fingers on the hood of the jeep. "But."

Harkins waited, then said, "But?"

"But he left for a big planning meeting in North Africa a couple of hours ago. Big brass talking with the Brits about the next campaign; mainland Italy, I guess. He'll be gone a day or two. I might be able to stall him, put my Georgia boy on ice for a bit, but you're going to have to wrap this up fast."

"Thanks, Captain."

"You won't be thanking me if we both wind up in hot water."

"I'll get my notes written up and make sure you get a copy," Harkins said. "But I'm not going to keep Boone briefed."

Adams retrieved his canvas briefcase from the front seat of Harkins' jeep. "You know, I once left a job because my boss patted my wife on the ass as we were walking out the door of a company party. The next day I went into his office and told him that made her uncomfortable and that I wasn't happy about it either."

Harkins tried to picture Adams confronting a boss. Confronting anyone. "What happened?"

"He told me that women like that kind of attention, that she only complained to me because she didn't want me to think she was flirting. I told him to go fuck himself. Took me three months to find another job, and I took a pay cut." Adams looked at Harkins and smiled. "But, *damn*, that felt good."

Harkins smiled. Adams wasn't so bad.

"You know," the lawyer said, "you must be doing a pretty good job."

"Why's that?"

"'Cause if you were a real screwup, and if Boone didn't want things to come to light, he'd be fighting to have you stay on the case."

17

3 August 1943
1330 hours

After Adams left, Harkins spent an hour typing up his notes in the nurses' admin tent. The need to concentrate calmed him a little bit.

"You type really fast," Colianno said as he came in. He dropped an envelope on the table. Crime scene photos.

"Took typing in high school."

"'Cause you knew it would be useful doing police reports?"

"No, because the class was full of girls. Learning to type was icing on the cake."

"Was Lieutenant Donnelly in your class?"

Harkins pulled the sheet and carbon copies from the roller, tapped the edges on the table. "You're really taking to this detective stuff, aren't you?" he said. "How about you just get the jeep, and we'll go find these other doctors."

When Colianno didn't move, Harkins looked at him, waiting.

"Lieutenant Donnelly told me about your brother. I'm real sorry."

"Thanks."

"Last night, after that Kraut plane almost gave you a haircut, you were smiling; a little later, I mean."

Harkins leaned back in the folding chair. "Yeah, I don't know what that was about, to tell you the truth."

"Couple of the guys talked about that feeling," Colianno said. "After a fight, or a close call. They felt like laughing, or they did laugh, just cracked up. One of our sergeants said it's because you're just glad to be alive. That you shouldn't feel bad about it."

"Thanks, Colianno," Harkins said.

When the paratrooper left, Harkins looked down at his hands. He would never forget the image of that burning aircraft headed straight for him, and he wondered if Michael had seen the torpedoes coming at his ship.

"Shit."

He pulled out the crime scene photos. They were grim, as he expected. Harkins had seen these kinds of photos used in court, and he knew that investigators sometimes put them on bulletin boards in their squad area, but he wasn't sure what he could glean from them.

"Still not a detective," he told himself.

Harkins put one copy of the report in an envelope, wrote "Captain Theodore Adams, Deputy Provost" on it. He put the other two copies in a folder on the field table, then used a brick to weigh it down in case the wind picked up. He grabbed his gear and headed out the door, then looked back to where the reports lay.

In a precinct house, a detective would keep this kind of stuff locked up in a cabinet, but there was no such place here. He grabbed the file folder and was about to stuff it in his musette bag when he saw a crate labeled "Records," with patient folders in Kathleen's handwriting. He wrote a note asking her to hang on to the file, then hid the paperwork in her collection of similar folders.

When Harkins stepped outside, Colianno started the jeep and put it into gear. Before they rolled, he looked up and said, "Uh-oh."

Harkins looked up and saw First Sergeant Drake approaching. The big man waved when he saw Harkins.

"You want me to drive away?"

"Nah. Let's see what he wants."

"Some stuff going on you should know about, Lieutenant," Drake said.

Harkins and Colianno looked at each other. *Lieutenant.*

"OK, First Sergeant."

"OK if your troublemaker hears this?" Drake asked, pointing a thumb at Colianno.

Harkins nodded. "He's been quite helpful, actually."

"Colonel Boone is pushing to get rid of more of the nurses. He told the clerk to start typing up the paperwork. Ronan, Donnelly, Melbourne. Couple of others."

"All the ones who have something to say about Stephenson."

"All the ones you need to keep around, I figured."

"Can you stop him?"

"I can delay. Send the clerk away for half a day, have him do a bad draft, that kind of thing. But no, I can't actually stop him, and you can't, either. He'll say this is for the good of the hospital and the patients. He'll put in a request for replacements, trading nurses with other teams, and he'll probably get his way. He's still the boss."

"For now," Harkins said.

"You got a plan?"

"I have to talk to some of the other docs," Harkins said. "You ever see any stuff around here looks like it was taken from a church?"

"Sure," Drake said. "Doors and benches, stuff like that."

"Nothing gold?" Harkins said. "Nothing that looked like it could be sold?"

"No."

"Do you know what Stephenson might have been talking about when he told Ronan that Boone would never stop him? Did Stephenson have something on Boone?"

"I don't know," Drake said. "You planning on talking to Lindner?"

"The Kraut doctor?"

"Yeah. He and Colonel Boone and Captain Stephenson talked a lot, met a few times. And today Boone and Lindner went for a ride."

"Where?"

"Nowhere, probably. Riding in a noisy jeep someplace out of the compound is about the only place you can talk without ten people overhearing you. But Boone was pissed off when he got back, and Lindner didn't look too happy, either."

"What's your take on Lindner?"

"Excellent surgeon. Saved a couple of guys with scary wounds. Drives me crazy that he wears a GI uniform—he put a little *P* above the pocket, for prisoner. And I don't like that he comes and goes just like our doctors. But Colonel Boone likes him. In fact, Colonel Boone has called in a few markers to keep Lindner here."

"Because he's a good surgeon?"

"That's the story," Drake said.

Harkins' circle of people connected to Stephenson was growing. He wanted to eliminate at least a few names.

"OK, thanks, First Sergeant. Thanks for the information. Glad you're on our side in this."

Drake looked surprised. "Your *side*? What is this, high school? I ain't on your fucking *side,* Lieutenant. That dead doctor probably got what he deserved, you ask my opinion. This is about Colonel Boone. What he's doing to the nurses is wrong. We're down almost a third of what we need to do all the surgeries these wounded kids need. And in case you ain't noticed, the war hasn't slowed down any. Jesus H. Christ."

Drake turned and walked away, muttering something about amateurs.

When Harkins looked at Colianno, the paratrooper said, "So, is he still on your shit list?"

18

3 August 1943
1400 hours

"Let's go talk to these other docs," Harkins said when he climbed back into the jeep. He took off his helmet and rubbed his eyes. He was operating on four or five hours of sleep in the last forty-eight. He poured water from his canteen into a kerchief and used it to wipe his eyes, the back of his head.

He turned in his seat to check out Colianno's growing arsenal. He'd added a trench knife, the handle made out of studded brass knuckles. There was a small wooden ammo crate with three hand grenades rolling around inside.

"You got a thing for firearms, don't you?"

Colianno looked at him, then turned back to the road. "I lost my weapon in the jump," he said. "Plane was going too fast and when I went out the door the prop blast tore everything off of me. Weapons carrier, musette bag, bayonet. I was on the ground, by myself, and in the dark without a weapon. Makes an impression on you. Next time we jump, I plan to have a few extras."

"Where will next time be?"

"Seems pretty obvious we gotta go to the mainland from here. Of course, the Krauts don't know where we'll land. Long as we keep that a secret, we got a chance."

"Better you than me," Harkins said, looking up. "Turn here. Let's go back to where they found the body."

There were slit-trench air-raid shelters scattered around the compound, with a cluster near the nurses' tent and another by the enlisted men's tents. Colianno parked the jeep next to the trench nearest where Stephenson was shot. It was thirty feet long by two and a half feet wide, with sandbagged walls on one side and a rim of sandbags, piled four high, all around the upper edge.

Harkins got out of the jeep and walked to the spot where Stephenson's body had been sprawled, carrying the envelope of crime scene photos. Pulled out two shots of the corpse, laid them on the ground, oriented as the body had been.

"He was running in this direction, right? Toward that shelter right there."

"Looks like it, I guess," Colianno said.

Harkins turned. "So where was he coming from?"

Together they retraced what Harkins thought might have been Stephenson's last steps, back to a T-shaped intersection of two narrow passageways. Directly in front of them was a medium tent with its sidewalls staked down to keep the dust to a minimum. They looked inside, saw clean linens wrapped in heavy brown paper, piled on wooden duckboards.

Harkins turned right. In that direction were two more supply tents, sides staked to the ground, then a large sleeping tent for the hospital's NCOs.

Harkins led them back to the T intersection, figuring that Stephenson had to have come from one of the arms of this T. They walked about fifteen yards, canvas walls on either side of them formed by the sides of surgery tents 1 and 2, which were always closed against the dust and flies.

"He could have come out of one of these," Colianno said of the surgery tents.

"He would have to crawl underneath," Harkins said. "Why do that when he could use the front entrance? They're both staked down, too."

Harkins studied the bottom of the tent to see if there were any obvious gaps. When he looked up, he saw Alice Haus come out of the next tent.

"Hey," he said. "Alice."

She stopped. "Lose something?"

"What's that tent you just came out of?"

"It's the back side of the nurses' tent. Somebody cut a giant slit back here on one of those hot nights, and now we use it as a door. We pull it shut, because if First Sergeant Drake sees it he'll have a heart attack and will make us buy Uncle Sam a new tent."

Harkins walked to where she was standing. The makeshift door was hidden; someone had figured out how to make it stay shut with a quick pull by looping a tie-down cord over one of the tent stakes.

"All the nurses live here?"

"About half, I'd say."

"Kathleen?"

"No."

"Moira Ronan?"

"Yeah, this is her tent. Why do you ask?"

"Any doctors' tents around here?"

"No, they're on the other side of the compound," she said, pointing north. "I gotta run, OK?"

"Sure, thanks."

When Haus was gone, Colianno asked, "You think he was coming from the nurses' tent?"

"Don't know. If he was in there, maybe someone saw him."

"But he could have been coming from anywhere. You can get to this spot from anywhere in the compound."

"You're right. But he sure had a thing for nurses, so this just looks fishy to me."

Harkins looked at one of the photos in his hand, a close-up of the exit wound, Stephenson's exploded head. He wondered how Stephenson became the kind of man someone wanted to murder. Did that kind of thing happen in stages? Small steps? Did he know what he had become? Was there a split second when he felt the muzzle of the pistol at his head and realized his sins had caught up with him?

Harkins put the photo back in the envelope, looked around once more. "Let's go see if we can find Doctor Wilkins."

The doctors lived three men to a pyramidal tent, which gave them each about twice the space that the nurses had in their one giant tent filled with cots, and three times as much as the enlisted men.

"Rank hath its privileges," Colianno said as they rolled up. They could see inside three of the tents in a row of five. Apparently the doctors' tents were not subject to inspection, as the nurses' tents were, since there was laundry hanging from every guy wire and post within sight. Inside, books, magazines, and letters were scattered about, along with uniform items and the occasional piece of furniture liberated from an Italian home.

Harkins and Colianno walked down the row, reading hand-lettered signs the docs had used to name their castles. Shangri-La, Hoochy-Cootchy Hut, The Nite Club.

"Those are some stupid friggin' names," Colianno said.

A mail orderly came out of one of the tents.

"Where's Captain Wilkins?" Harkins asked.

"With a couple of the other docs, playing cards down there." He pointed to a tent fly that had been erected above a small fountain. As Harkins and Colianno approached, they saw that four men were playing cards on a piece of wooden packing crate propped over the center of the circular base. All four had their shoes off, their feet in the bubbling water.

"Gentlemen," Harkins said as he approached. Two of the men looked up.

"I'm Lieutenant Harkins, military police. I'd like to ask you a few questions about Captain Stephenson."

"I'm out," one man said to his partners, folding his hand.

Another doc, this one with an almost comically large mustache, a caricature of Pancho Villa, said, "Coward! You're going to have to stay in at least one hand so I can take the rest of your money."

They'd been drinking, that much was clear. *Maybe they don't go on duty until this evening,* Harkins thought. Then, *But what if casualties start coming in quickly?*

One way for Harkins to gauge his own degree of exhaustion was to see how quickly he got pissed off at some asshole. He already hated these guys.

Harkins nodded at Colianno, who retrieved Stephenson's musette bag from the jeep. When Harkins had it in hand, he called the poker players again.

"Gentlemen, I said I'd like to have your attention for a few moments."

"He's not doing anything," Mustache said, pointing at the man who'd folded. "He can talk to you."

Harkins walked up to the card game and swung the canvas bag, clearing the table of cards and chips, which scattered to the ground and into the fountain.

"What the hell?"

"Who the fuck do you think you are?"

"I told you who I am and what I'm doing here. Now I'd like a little goddamn cooperation, if you don't mind. I'm tired and hot and, in case you haven't noticed, I'm the only one here wearing a pistol. I haven't shot anyone in days, but that could change."

"All right, tough guy," Mustache said. "What do you want to know?"

"Are you Wilkins?"

"No, that's me. And it's *Captain* Wilkins to you."

Wilkins had been sitting with his back toward Harkins. Another big man, like Stephenson. Hairline creeping down toward thick eyebrows, a dark beard that gave him a menacing look. He wore a sleeveless olive drab T-shirt, and Harkins could see a Saint Christopher's medal nested in a mat of dark hair on his chest.

"All I've been hearing about Captain Stephenson is that people didn't like him," Harkins said, pulling out his notebook.

"That's because he drank too much and thought with his dick," Mustache said. "And that's Souther, S-O-U-T-H-E-R."

"Sounds like you're spending all your time talking to the nurses," Wilkins said.

The other men laughed, and Souther said, "Yeah, *talking*."

"You got another story?" Harkins asked. "That's what I'm here for."

"Look," Wilkins said, "Stephenson was a pain in the ass. But a lot of that stuff, the nurses bring that on themselves."

"How's that?"

"By saying no all the time," Souther said. Another round of laughs.

Harkins' patience was gone. He would have to separate these men to get anything useful out of them. Get them when they were sober.

"Any of you seen this before?" Harkins asked, pulling the gold paten from the musette bag.

"Yeah, Stephenson tried to use it to settle a debt the other night." This from one of the men who had not spoken yet.

"Tried?"

The speaker, narrow shouldered and sweating even more than the others, said, "I recognized it. He got that from a church somewhere, so I said he couldn't use it."

"One thing to steal wine," Souther said. "Or furniture. But you can't show up here with stuff you stole from a church, bombed out or not."

"Any of you ever see anything else he had, or anyone had, like this? Gold? From a church?" Harkins asked.

No response. So Harkins continued, "Does Colonel Boone gamble?"

"Some," Souther said. "Not much good at it."

"He owe anyone here money? Colonel Boone, that is."

Two of the men looked down at the table. After a pause, Souther said, "Nah, we're all pretty even up these days."

"OK, so we're all friends here," Harkins said. "Let's go back to the nurses. Captain Wilkins? You play grab-ass with the nurses, too?"

Wilkins looked at him, trying to give Harkins the cold stare. Another big man used to intimidating people without even trying.

"I get paid to stitch wounded boys back together," Wilkins said. "Not to be a choir boy."

"Look," Souther said. "Some of these nurses get around, like—what was her name?"

"Whitman," one of the men said.

"Yeah," Souther continued. "Whitman got around, and a couple of other nurses have had happy relations with some of the docs. And it's not just the docs getting action, is what I hear."

More drunken giggles.

"So it goes on, you know. It's up to us to figure out which ones are game and which ones aren't."

"So how do you figure it out? Grab 'em first and see if they complain?"

"Jesus H. Christ," Souther said. "Who are you, the goddamn pope? We're out here working our asses off, we deserve a little break now and then."

Wilkins was still giving him the hard-guy stare, something he'd cribbed from an Edward G. Robinson movie.

"I'll come back around when you guys aren't in your cups," Harkins said, turning to the jeep.

"Speaking of a little break," Wilkins said to his back, "that Kathleen Donnelly is a nice piece of ass, if you like them skinny Irish wenches."

Harkins spun around and took two fast steps toward Wilkins, who tried—too late—to get out of his chair. Harkins hit him with a right-left-right combination, not holding back, but launching his full body weight onto the bigger man. Then he grabbed Wilkins's windpipe with his left hand, pressing his thumb against the man's Adam's apple, smashing the doctor's face with his right fist.

Colianno pulled him off after a few seconds. Wilkins did not get up, but Souther bent over him, then looked at Harkins and said, "I'll get the military police after you, you sonofabitch!"

Harkins yanked his pistol from its holster, pointed it at Souther, then at the prone Wilkins, back at Souther until the doc put his hands up.

"*I'm* the fucking military police!"

The docs didn't move for the few seconds it took Harkins to get control of his breathing. Colianno stood beside him, waiting.

"Let's go," Harkins said. He turned his back to the doctors, but he did not holster his weapon, just walked away holding it beside his leg.

"Pretty smooth back there, Lieutenant," Colianno said. He did not look at Harkins, but kept his eyes straight ahead as the two men walked away side by side.

Harkins thought Colianno might have been smiling when he said, "Learn that in MP school, did you?"

19

3 August 1943
1600 hours

Harkins and Colianno were waiting when Ronan came out of the surgical tent. The lower parts of her trousers, the part not covered by a surgical gown, were blood-spattered. Red creases marked the sides of her face where the strings of the surgical mask had been tied. She rolled her shoulders, trying to work out the knots from a few hours of standing with her arms held above a patient on the operating table. She walked beside another nurse and, as far as Harkins could tell, they talked about putting some guy's jaw back together. When she saw Harkins, she stopped.

"What the hell do you want?" she said.

"I wonder if I could have your help for a few minutes," Harkins said.

Ronan looked at Harkins, then at Colianno, then back. "I just got finished assisting in a five-hour surgery," she said. "I'm not up for any more of your bullshit."

"Look," Harkins said. "I'm sorry about what happened earlier. I didn't know Boone was going to do that. This will only take a few minutes, and we'll take you back to your tent."

Ronan sighed, said good-bye to the other nurse, then climbed into the jeep. They drove the short distance to the murder scene. When Colianno parked, the three of them got out and Harkins walked to the spot where the body had been found. Harkins thought Colianno whispered something to Ronan, but he couldn't be sure. The nurse looked tense; Harkins wondered if she'd take another swing at him.

"So where were you when the air raid started?"

Ronan looked around, back toward the T intersection of dirt paths that led, Harkins had found this morning, to the nurses' tent.

"Coming back from the latrine."

"Heading from the latrine to where?"

"To my tent. I'd just gotten off a night shift and wanted to get some sleep."

"So you hadn't reached your tent yet and, what? Was there an air-raid siren, or did you hear the *ack-ack* first?"

"I don't remember," she said. "Is that important?"

"I don't think there was a siren, Lieutenant," Colianno offered. He stepped closer to Ronan, so the two of them were side by side, facing Harkins. "Those quad fifties opened up, one of them, at least. Then the others joined in."

"I'd like to hear what Lieutenant Ronan remembers," Harkins said.

"I don't," Ronan said, exasperated. "Remember, that is. Not the exact sequence, anyway."

"OK," Harkins said. "Let's assume it was the *ack-ack*. That was certainly loud enough for everyone to hear, right? Private Colianno says he didn't go to any shelter because he figured it would turn out to be a false alarm. Is that what you thought, or did you take it seriously?"

"No, I took it seriously. We were bombed when we were on the beach, D plus two or three. Scared me plenty."

"Yeah, I'm with you," Harkins said, trying a smile. "Private Colianno thinks the Luftwaffe is finished, at least in this campaign, but hell, I wouldn't want to get killed by the last Kraut pilot to make it into the air."

Ronan stared back at him, expressionless.

"So you started running right away?" Harkins asked.

"I guess so, yeah."

"Toward the shelter?"

One corner of Ronan's mouth twitched. She looked like she wanted to slug him again. Beside her, Colianno shifted his weight from one foot to the other, back again.

"I ran toward my tent first."

"Why?"

"I didn't have my helmet with me," Ronan said. "We're not supposed to be out without them, but I didn't bring mine to surgery that morning. And the shelter doesn't have overhead cover, so we need them."

"I see."

"I ran into the tent and back out again, quick as that."

"And did you run for this shelter?" Harkins said, pointing with his thumb to the air-raid shelter Stephenson never reached.

"Yes."

"Anyone else running with you? Alongside you? Behind you?"

"Of course," she said. What little patience she'd had was exhausted. "There were all kinds of people running every which way. A bunch of them headed for the same shelter as me."

"So you didn't see Stephenson?"

"No." Then, "Well, later, after the 'all clear' had been given."

She pointed at the spot beneath Harkins' feet. "He was right there. Just like you found him."

Harkins said nothing for a long moment, just looked at her with the hint of a smile. Then, "OK," he said. "Thanks. I appreciate your help."

"I'll bet," Ronan said. She looked at Colianno, then turned and headed down the alley between tents, heels scuffing little clouds of dust. When she was gone, Colianno turned to Harkins.

"Were you trying to get her to punch you again? See if you could egg her on?"

Harkins turned and walked to the jeep. "Can't deny she's got a temper."

"Everyone has a temper if they're pushed far enough. You, for instance. You went crazy on that doctor. I hadn't pulled you off, you might've killed him."

"You may be right," Harkins said, embarrassed that Colianno had seen that. Not that Wilkins didn't deserve what he got.

When he reached the jeep, Harkins leaned over, hands on the vehicle's sun-beat hood, stretching his back.

He doubted that his uncle Jimmy, the brawler, entertained any second thoughts about his behavior, unless it was to figure out how he could hand out a more effective beating. Jimmy had created his own black-and-white world, and he liked it there. You had your family and friends, and to hell with everybody else. When his blood was up, Harkins' uncle was unburdened by reason, uncaring of consequences.

And for a moment back there by the doctors' tents, that had been Eddie Harkins, waving his goddamn pistol like a gangster.

"So?" Colianno stood beside him, clearly wanting Harkins to see that Ronan was not that crazy.

"If I can't keep my head when Wilkins makes a smartass remark about Kathleen," Harkins said, "a completely predictable remark for an asshole like him—how much harder might it be for her to keep her cool?

She was the victim of a terrible crime. If that doesn't make you lose your head, what will?"

Colianno and Harkins grabbed some chow in the mess tent, then Colianno disappeared with the jeep while Harkins typed his notes. When the driver came back, he had a tommy gun slung over his shoulder. Harkins looked, didn't ask about it.

"I found the other driver who took Stephenson to Palermo," Colianno said. "Get this, Stephenson went to that whorehouse with that Kraut doctor, the POW."

Harkins looked up from his notes. "You sure?"

"Hard to get that one wrong, him being the only Kraut doctor here. The driver said they went together, described the same place. Stephenson got piss-drunk, the Kraut stayed sober. But he did go inside."

"That's strange," Harkins said. "The nurses describe Lindner as a gentleman. Kind of straitlaced. What's he doing hanging out with a piece of shit like Stephenson? The driver say what the two docs talked about during the ride?"

"Guy said they talked German; can you believe that?" Colianno said.

The driver stepped into the tent, pulled up a wooden crate stenciled 11TH FH.

"OK if I sit down, Lieutenant?"

Harkins nodded and Colianno sat, held the tommy gun between his knees and pointed safely upward. Harkins noticed there was no magazine in the weapon.

"What kind of place is this, where this POW runs around like some fancy-ass American colonel?" Colianno asked. "Everybody talking fucking German. You ask me, this is where you should be looking. Lindner and Stephenson."

"And not at Lieutenant Ronan?"

Colianno didn't take the bait. Probably figured his feelings for Ronan were already pretty clear.

"Maybe Lindner's a fairy. Maybe he made a pass at Stephenson and, when he got turned down, killed him to keep it from coming out."

"That's quite a theory," Harkins said. He couldn't suppress a smile. "Anything to make you think that? Lindner flirting with any of the enlisted men?"

"No, but he's really neat, you know. How he dresses, I mean. Plus, he's a dick doctor, right?"

Harkins chuckled, went back to typing.

Colianno put the tommy gun across his lap and used a rag to wipe some dust off the slide.

"You know what I can't figure out?" Colianno said. "Guy like Stephenson, obviously a grade A asshole, and the most people want to say about him is that he got fresh with the nurses. Those other docs this morning, the only complaint they had was that he tried to use a stolen paten instead of cash in a card game."

"So?"

"There had to be other stuff, don't you think? Like, I don't know, he treated the orderlies like shit, or stole stuff?"

Harkins stopped typing.

"Yeah, I've thought about that," Harkins said. "Though the only thing we've found—besides the paten—is that no one wanted to share a tent with him."

"Just seems strange, is all I'm saying."

"There was this trial in Philly three, four years ago," Harkins said. "Guy was a principal of a school, a deacon in his church, president of his local American Legion. Married, two or three kids."

Colianno was still absentmindedly wiping down the weapon, but his eyes were on Harkins.

"Turns out he was a killer. Picked up working girls, murdered them, buried them over in Jersey, the Pine Barrens."

"So, you think Stephenson might have been doing other stuff, stuff he hid?"

"Maybe," Harkins said. "Could be that the other docs didn't see, or didn't want to see, the worst that Stephenson was capable of. Could be that they saw it and just didn't think it was all that bad."

Harkins looked back down at his notes, pencil scribbles on sweat-stained paper. "One thing's for sure," he said. "Something he did pissed somebody off."

20

3 August 1943
2100 hours

It was full dark when Harkins went looking for Donnelly in the nurses' sleeping tent. He knocked on the pole by the door and waited like a suitor until a nurse came out and told him Kathleen wasn't there. He returned to admin, by the church wall, asked Colianno to wait, and walked the last few yards from the compound's main street. When he passed the tent where he and Donnelly had spent the previous night, he noticed that all the tent's flaps were down again, and there was a dim glow from a kerosene lamp visible at the doorway seam. He wasn't proud of the impulse, but he wanted to call her name at the doorway, see if she was in there. He even stopped for a moment. Then he walked to the admin tent, where Donnelly and a clerk were transferring information from casualty tags to larger forms.

"Take a smoke break, Dale," Donnelly said to the clerk.

The soldier left the tent, and Harkins checked to make sure he wasn't close by and eavesdropping. When he turned back to Donnelly, she was massaging her neck muscles. There were four piles of the large tags on the table. Medics at the forward aid stations tied them to wounded GIs; there were notes about the treatment and drugs the wounded men had received. A number of the tags had blood on them.

"How long you been doing that?"

"Since 1935, feels like."

"You going to finish soon?"

Donnelly smiled. "Sorry, the supply tent is in use. Besides, you're still in the doghouse."

"I meant so you could get some rest."

"Sure you did." She stood, stretched, leaning backward, then sat down again and put her feet on the clerk's chair. She was wearing men's shoes.

"Nice," Harkins said.

"Yeah, aren't they? The quartermaster doesn't stock women's shoes or even shoe sizes. These are the smallest men's shoes, and I have to stuff the toes with cotton bandages."

She pressed her feet together, side by side, moved them back and forth like windshield wipers.

"I can't believe how much time I used to spend thinking about clothes, buying clothes, ironing clothes, washing my hair, putting on makeup, fussing with my hair. Now a sponge bath out of a helmet is a luxury."

"Certainly is," Harkins agreed.

"Enough. Have a seat," she said, indicating a crate marked with a caduceus and a large US.

"I hear you got in a tussle with a doc named Wilkins," she said. "That right?"

"He had it coming."

"Uh-huh."

Harkins was silent. Donnelly sat with her arms folded, obviously waiting for him to go on.

"What?" he said.

"Want to tell me what it was about?"

"A couple of them were bad-mouthing the nurses."

"Any nurse in particular?"

"Whitman."

"Don't be coy, Eddie. There are no secrets around here. I knew when we shacked up that word would get around."

"And that doesn't bother you?"

"Apparently not as much as it bothers you."

Harkins wiped his forehead with his sleeve.

"Eddie, it's sweet that you care. Really. But this isn't high school, and it certainly isn't the neighborhood. You and I aren't going to see each other in church. My dad and brothers aren't going to come looking for you."

She leaned forward, touched his knee, smiling the way you might smile at a kid brother who hadn't yet made sense of the world.

"Is that what we did?" he said. "Shacked up?"

"Well, we're not engaged. If we were going to be located close to each other, if we could see each other—which I would enjoy—it would be different," she said. "Of course, I'd have gone about it in a completely different way. I wouldn't have hopped into the sack with you a few hours after seeing you for the first time in years."

"I just don't want to be responsible for you getting a bad reputation," Harkins said.

Donnelly laughed. "All the shit that's going on here and you're worried some asshat doctor thinks I'm a floozy?"

"So I shouldn't worry about it?"

"You're a great guy, Eddie, always have been. But I don't need a boyfriend right now. I had two patients die on me today, right on the operating table. I got bigger fish to fry."

"What did you want, then?" Harkins asked.

"I just wanted to be held for an hour or two. Like you."

For many people, the war had broken strictures that had been in place for a long time. Single women like his sisters were working in factories, driving trucks, living on their own. Probably half the guys in uniform had told some woman a version of "I'm shipping out and want something to remember you by."

"Look, even if I didn't do what I wanted," Donnelly said, "even if the nurses didn't fool around, the same docs would just make stuff up anyway. At least I got to have fun. OK?"

"OK," Harkins said again, though he wasn't sure he was OK with it at all.

"So what have you done today to win the war?"

Harkins leaned back, stretched his tired legs in front of him. "Colianno found out that your Kraut doctor friend went to the bordello with Stephenson."

"That's an odd pair."

"That's what I thought. Is Lindner friends with any of the other docs?"

"I don't really know. I know he talks to absolutely everyone. He's always in there chatting with the GIs who come in. Says he wants to practice his English, plus he's just friendly."

"Mind keeping an eye on him for me?"

Donnelly smiled. "Sure. I bet we could get Alice to move into his tent."

"I'll bet we could."

Harkins paused, then said, "You know, I was kind of surprised to hear you guys talk about him like you do. Like he's a friend."

"I knew you found that strange, the way you reacted when you saw him in the mess tent," Donnelly said. "I guess we just think of him as a surgeon first. He's kind of powerless since he's a POW. Maybe he figures if he gets shipped back to the States he won't get to do surgery, so he's careful not to attract too much attention."

"You know anything about him, other than the professional stuff?" Harkins asked.

"You mean like family? Not really. Although . . ."

"Although?"

"Now that you mention it," Donnelly said, "besides you, he's the only other person I've told about wanting to go to medical school. Maybe a nurse or two, but Lindner and you are the only men."

"What did he say?"

"Well, if he thought it far-fetched he didn't say anything to me. But now that I think about it, it's strange that I feel more comfortable telling a so-called enemy than telling my own male colleagues."

"Doesn't say much for your colleagues, I guess," Harkins said.

"I can't figure out why he'd go anywhere with Stephenson, especially to a bordello."

"Colianno thinks the Kraut is a fairy, and that he killed Stephenson when Stephenson turned down his advances."

"Well, I don't know about him being a fairy, but if he isn't, he certainly doesn't need to go to a bordello. Half the nurses here would sleep with him if he asked."

"Has he? Asked, I mean."

"If he has, the nurses aren't talking about it. But it's pretty hard to keep secrets around here."

"So I've noticed," Harkins said. "Anyway, I'd just like to know what he's up to, what connections, if any, he's made. He seems to have a lot of freedom."

"Yeah, he does come and go as he pleases," Donnelly said. "Even I think that's a bit odd. Maybe he gets special privileges because of what he can do in surgery. He's a whiz on the whizzer."

"You definitely need some sleep."

"There's something else you should know about all the shit that's been going on here," Donnelly said. "Though I'm not sure you can do anything with it, and you have to promise me you'll keep it to yourself unless we agree otherwise, OK?"

"OK."

"Whitman didn't choke to death, like everybody thinks. I'm not sure exactly what killed her, or who killed her, but I think Boone was somehow involved."

"Go on," Harkins said.

Donnelly took a deep breath. "I did an autopsy on her before they took her to the cemetery."

Donnelly said it like it was a momentous announcement.

"Isn't that routine in something like this?"

"A healthy young woman dies back in Philly? Yeah, maybe they do an autopsy," Donnelly said. "Not here. We're not really equipped for forensic pathology. Most of our deaths, it's pretty obvious what killed them."

"OK, so you did an autopsy."

"I did a half-assed autopsy, a field-expedient autopsy."

"OK."

"Eddie, I'm not authorized to do anything like that. I'm not a doctor, and someone in authority would have to order an autopsy."

"All right, I see. So you could get in trouble."

"Exactly. Which is why you have to keep this to yourself."

"What did you find?"

"No vomitus in her trachea."

"What does that mean?"

"It means she didn't choke on her own vomit. But that's what Boone wrote on her chart, which is the closest thing we have to a death certificate."

"Is it possible that the first people to find her jumped to that conclusion, and then it caught on?"

"Yes, of course that's possible. But Boone is supposed to know better. He's not supposed to just go by what a bunch of medical orderlies tell him, or even what some nurses tell him."

"If Boone knew that she didn't choke but that's what he put on the chart, what? You think he's trying to hide what really happened?" Harkins asked. "She was drinking with Stephenson that night. Maybe Boone was trying to cover something Stephenson did."

"Maybe. Or maybe Boone was the father of her baby, and for some reason he didn't want that coming out. He's married, I think."

"Whitman threaten to expose him? Everything I heard about her, she was too nice for that kind of game."

"Look," Donnelly said. "I'm sorry this leaves us with more unanswered questions, but I wanted you to know. I wanted someone besides me to know."

Harkins reached across and squeezed her knee. He knew what it was like to carry secrets.

"OK," he said, standing. "Colianno and I are headed back into the city. Talk to the madam again. So, you'll ask around about Lindner?"

"OK, chief, I'm on the case," Donnelly said, bringing her fingers to her eyebrow for a mock salute. "Tell me, Lieutenant Harkins, is there a reward involved?"

Harkins was operating on about eight hours of sleep in the last seventy-two. It was, he thought, a testimony to the glories of nature that he still felt a stirring at Donnelly's teasing.

"I guess we'll have to see how you perform. I'll stop back later if you think you'll be awake."

"Yes, unfortunately." She patted the pile of casualty tags.

"Don't you have clerks to help with that?"

"Yeah, but a nurse has to check, make sure the information is transferred to the patient chart correctly. I sent the last clerk away after he'd been at it for seventeen hours and was drooling on the pages. The guy outside on a smoke break has been at it for ten hours."

She lifted a pile of tags, straightened the strings on the ends.

"And there are always more coming in."

21

3 August 1943
2200 hours

Harkins and Colianno went into the bordello behind three noncoms wearing the shoulder patch of the Forty-Fifth Division. The madam gave the three a coy smile—hustling men was her business—but when she saw Colianno she beamed. She ignored Harkins completely.

After a few minutes of rapid-fire conversation, Colianno kissed her hand and gave her a musette bag. When the two GIs walked outside, Harkins asked, "What was in the bag?"

"Cigarettes, chocolate, that kind of stuff."

"Ready for anything, aren't you?"

Colianno shrugged. "You don't have to be a genius to figure out that these people are glad to have a few luxuries. I could probably conquer the island with a couple dozen pairs of silk stockings."

"So what did you find out?"

"Lindner was here. Came with Stephenson two nights before he was killed. Stephenson was drinking, was drunk when he arrived, and he went upstairs with two girls. Lindner didn't go up."

"Is that why you think he's a fairy?"

"I asked Senora Pescetelli, 'cause she provides, you know, that service, too. Guys who like guys. She doesn't think so. Maybe he was afraid of getting the clap. Anyway, Lindner had a medical bag and he treated some of the women for some minor stuff. The senora was very grateful. I asked if she knew he was a Kraut, and she said it didn't matter to her. He and Stephenson left within an hour."

Harkins walked outside, Colianno following. They paused on the narrow step at the front door.

"I still can't figure out why a proper German doctor is hanging around with an ass like Stephenson."

"Maybe he caught a ride here to treat the girls," Colianno said.

"Maybe," Harkins said. "You know, I wasn't expecting a connection between Lindner and Stephenson. But now that we've found one, I wonder who else Stephenson was connected to. Boone has been pulling strings to keep Lindner at the hospital, instead of letting him get shipped out with the other POWs. I wonder if the three of them are connected."

"Well, Colonel Boone sure ain't going to answer any questions for you, but the Kraut will. I mean, he has to, right?"

"Yeah," Harkins said. "He doesn't have much choice, although he could lie about his connection to Stephenson."

On the street beside the brothel, the same two boys Colianno had hired to guard the jeep the day before sat in it. Three GIs stood close by, identifiable in the weak moonlight by the silhouettes of their helmets.

The boys started talking to Colianno immediately, sounding nervous. Colianno calmed them, handed over a GI sock filled with C-ration cans. The boys scattered into the darkness.

"Help you find something?" Harkins asked the figure standing closest. He was shorter than the other two, and even in the dark he looked like the leader.

"Who're you?" the man asked.

"Lieutenant Harkins, military police. Who are you?"

The street was empty, the shops closed up for the night, no one visible in the second- and third-story windows. Harkins and Colianno were alone with three shadows.

"We're looking for a paratrooper by the name of Colianno, talks dago real good," the leader said. "Sounds like we found him."

Harkins felt Colianno stiffen beside him, as if ready to run. Or fight.

The man clicked on a flashlight with a red filter, pointed it first at Harkins and then at Colianno. Harkins could see, in the reflected light, that the man had a shotgun in his hand; not an army-issue weapon, but something sawed off.

"Turn that light off," Harkins said.

The GI waited an insubordinate few seconds before clicking off the flashlight.

"What's with the shotgun?" Harkins asked.

"Oh, this here is what the dagos all use to kill one another. It's called a, uh, what's it called, Sammy?"

One of the other men said, "A *lupara*."

Harkins put his hand on his pistol, unbuttoned the leather flap covering it. Colianno was wearing his pistol, but did not reach for it.

"What do you want?" Harkins asked. Colianno still had not spoken.

One of the other men said, "Not here. This guy's a friggin' MP."

Harkins asked again. "I said, what do you want?"

"I got no beef with you, Lieutenant."

The man half turned. "You're Colianno, right?" He held the shotgun in his right hand, by the balance point. Colianno did not answer.

Harkins eased his pistol from its holster, not trying to hide the motion, but not moving too quickly, either.

"I know what you did," the speaker said to Colianno. After a few seconds he stepped back into the shadows, and Harkins could just make out another jeep, a few yards away, a fourth figure in the driver's seat. The man who'd been doing all the talking got in the front passenger side, the others in the back.

"We'll be seeing each other again," he said before tapping the driver on the arm. The jeep backed, did a quick K-turn, and drove away.

Harkins let out a breath. Colianno still had not moved.

"You OK?" Harkins asked.

"Yeah."

"Want to tell me what that was about?" He pushed his pistol back into its holster, buttoned the leather flap.

"Not really," Colianno said. "It's my problem, Lieutenant."

"The guy had a shotgun, Colianno. Maybe came out here to shoot you, for Christ's sake. Make it look like some local did it."

Harkins heard his pulse in his ears as the adrenaline coursed through his limbs, felt his face flush. He had a sudden mental image of Michael, wondered if his little brother had been alone when he realized the end was coming.

"I'd like to know what the hell we're dealing with."

After a quiet moment, Colianno said, "You want, you can send me back to my unit."

"They don't want you. I'm stuck with you, thanks to my do-gooder brother."

Colianno stood in the dark, infuriatingly silent.

"Shit, let's go," Harkins said, climbing into his own jeep. "I'd probably wind up with a replacement that was even more of a pain in the ass. But you're going to have to deal with those guys sooner or later."

22

3 August 1943
2345 hours

It was nearly midnight when Colianno dropped Harkins off at the admin tent, where he'd left Donnelly working on the casualty tags.

"Where are you going to be?" Harkins asked his driver.

"There's a spare cot over in the enlisted tent, where the orderlies stay. I'll be over there."

There was a quarter moon, but Harkins could not see Colianno's face in the shadow cast by his helmet. He suspected the paratrooper was going to look for Ronan.

"Be back here before first light," Harkins said. He pulled his musette bag from the backseat and walked into the admin tent. Donnelly was there, seated at the same table, an even bigger stack of bloody casualty tags in front of her. Patrick Harkins sat on the crate beside her, reading from the cards as she transcribed names. They both looked up when Harkins came in.

"Pat," Harkins said.

The priest stood, pulled his brother into an embrace. Harkins felt a sudden catch in his throat. He started to speak but choked on the words.

"Kathleen told me you got a letter from Da at yesterday's mail call," Patrick said. "So did I."

Patrick held his brother at arm's length, looked into his eyes, his big hands squeezing Harkins' shoulders.

"I'm so sorry, Pat," Harkins managed.

Kathleen slipped past them, out of the tent, left them alone.

"You know he would have joined up anyway," Patrick said. "He'd have found a way."

"But I made it so much easier," Harkins said. He'd found his voice but his eyes were swimming, his nose running. He swiped at his face with a sleeve. "Maybe if he'd waited a year like we asked he wouldn't have been on that ship."

"He'd have been on some other ship, though," Patrick said.

Harkins sat down heavily on a wooden crate and put his head in his hands. Patrick pulled up a folding chair and sat in front of him, their knees almost touching. After a minute or two, Harkins looked up and said, "How are you doing?"

"I'm kind of in shock, you know. I hadn't seen Michael in eight, nine months. Then this letter comes, but it doesn't feel real yet."

"Were you worried about him?" Harkins asked. "He was just a kid."

"Sure. Worried about him, worried about you, worried about the old folks. Difference between you and me is that when I worry, I pray a lot."

"Helps?" Harkins asked.

"I think so."

Harkins wiped his face on his other sleeve, which was just as filthy. He hadn't changed his clothes in three weeks.

"Mom will never forgive me," he said.

"She will," Patrick said. "She believes in redemption."

"Wish I did."

They sat like that for a few more minutes. When Harkins looked up he was struck with a sudden realization. Patrick and Michael looked so much alike that, as long as his paratrooper brother survived the war, he'd always know what Michael would have looked like had he aged, too.

Kathleen knocked on the tent pole by the door. "OK to come in?" she asked.

Harkins mopped his face again. "Yeah, sure. Come on."

"You guys OK?" she asked when they were all crammed inside.

"Just peachy," Harkins said, looking up and trying a smile.

Patrick stood and picked a musette bag off the floor. HARKINS was stenciled on the side, along with a hand-drawn cross.

"That your salvation kit?" Harkins asked.

"Might save your sanity, if not your soul," Patrick said as he reached inside and pulled out two of the paperback books. "Saw these in a pile of gear the guys were getting rid of and grabbed them for you."

Harkins took the books: Mark Twain's *Huckleberry Finn* and Jack London's *White Fang.* The back half of *Huck Finn* was swollen where someone had dropped it in a puddle or got caught in the rain. Harkins had read both books before—*Huck Finn* several times—but was glad for the gift.

"No catechism available, huh?" Harkins said. He wanted to talk about anything but Michael and how he helped send his younger brother to sea.

"If I thought you'd read it I'd scare one up," Patrick said.

Harkins looked at Donnelly. "My brother worries about my immortal soul," he said.

"Speaking of your immortal soul," Donnelly said, "Patrick, ask him where he's been."

Patrick looked at Donnelly, then his brother.

"A whorehouse," Harkins said. "My second visit today, in fact."

"I'll just assume this has to do with the investigation," Patrick said. "Kathleen has filled me in on what's been happening."

"I found out something interesting about Herr Doktor Lindner, too," Kathleen said.

"You've been busy," Harkins said. "You managed that without leaving this tent?"

"I'm just that good. And two other nurses visited me right after you left."

Harkins dragged another crate from the shadows and sat down beside Patrick. He looked at his brother, then at Kathleen. Would he have told her about Harkins' role in getting Michael the forged birth certificate, getting Michael killed?

He wondered if someone could die from shame.

Harkins put his hands to his face.

"You OK?" Kathleen asked.

"Sure, sure."

"Turns out Lindner is treating a pretty senior American officer for the clap," she said. "A general. Very hush-hush."

"I imagine that would be," Harkins said. "Why would the general use a prisoner?"

"Lindner is an accomplished urologist, for one thing. The other reason might be that the guy can get rid of Lindner at any time. Just ship him back to the States with the next batch of POWs."

"So who's the general?" Harkins asked.

Donnelly looked at Patrick, then back at Harkins. "You know I can get into a lot of trouble like this, gossiping about patients? Is this really part of the investigation?"

"Kathleen, I had a couple of hours' sleep in the last three days. The last thing I want to do right now is chat about something that isn't going to help me. So, yes, this is part of the case."

"What about you, Patrick?" she asked.

"I can go outside."

"No, stay," Harkins said.

"Then we'll call it secrets of the confessional. You have anything you need absolution for, Kathleen?"

Patrick smiled, and Harkins thought, *There's no way she told him about that.*

"Pure as the driven snow, Father."

"Can we get back on track here?" Harkins said.

"OK, OK," Kathleen said, holding up a hand. "The general is named Glass. He's a supply guy."

"I know that name. He's in charge of logistics for the next big operation," Patrick said. "Which I assume is the invasion of the mainland."

"How do you know that?" Harkins asked his brother.

"Because in airborne operations, we spend all our time talking about how many airplanes are available, 'cause that determines how many guys we can put on an objective, on an operation."

"The chaplains talk about that?"

"Not so much, but we bunk with the other captains, and they obsess about it."

Harkins chewed the inside of his lip to keep himself awake.

"Treating someone for the clap require multiple visits?" he asked.

"In most cases, yes," Kathleen said. "Why do you ask?"

"I want to know if Lindner will be going back to see General Glass, or if he's finished."

"I don't think the course of treatment is finished, no."

"How do you know?"

"The pharmacist. He and Lindner had some conversations about treatment."

"OK, let me think about it."

"So," Patrick said. "Kathleen tells me it's all over the hospital that you punched a doc named Wilkins, maybe wanted to shoot him."

"No maybe about it; I did want to shoot him," Harkins said. "The important thing is that I didn't."

Patrick shook his head. The big priest, who was a bruising boxer, a nearly unstoppable force, had rarely been in a fight outside of the ring, and could not understand why trouble followed his younger brother.

"What was that about?" Patrick asked.

Harkins shrugged. "He asked for it."

Patrick was silent, probably disappointed in his brother, but cutting him some slack. They'd both gotten terrible news.

"Yeah, yeah, I know," Harkins said. "That's Uncle Jimmy's line."

He stood, pushed back the crate he'd been sitting on. There was a bundle of GI blankets on a shelf. He pulled one out and spread it on the ground.

"You going to sleep right there?" Donnelly asked.

"Is that OK? 'Cause if it isn't, you'd better tell me in the next ten seconds, because I'm going to be out like a dead man."

"There is one other thing," Patrick said.

Harkins sat down on the blanket, pulled off his boots and socks. "Is it going to require me standing up?"

"It's about Colianno," Patrick said.

"Yeah, I wanted to thank you again for sticking me with your save-a-private, save-the-world idea. It's bad enough he's always ready to get into a fight. Now we have guys coming out looking for him."

Harkins told Patrick and Kathleen about the GIs who'd shown up outside the bordello, looking for Colianno.

"There's a rumor going around the regiment," Patrick said. "You know those groups of paratroopers I told you were wandering around lost on D-Day?"

"'Cause the jump was scattered," Harkins said.

"Yeah. Well, there's a story that, in one of those groups, one paratrooper killed another."

"Jesus," Donnelly said.

"And it was the group Colianno was in?" Harkins asked.

"I think so."

"But it's a rumor, and you don't know how Colianno is involved. Got anything more concrete than that? Because that's pretty weak."

Harkins was a bit surprised to hear himself defending Colianno, or at least looking out for him.

"No. I've identified two guys who were on that patrol, but neither one of them is talking about it. To me, anyway. I'm still trying to figure out who else might know something."

"Isn't this something you should turn over to the commander? No offense, but you're the chaplain."

Patrick shrugged. "You could say chaplains have a broad mandate. I can pretty much go where I want if I can call it 'taking care of the troops.' That's why I'm always riding around visiting our guys in the hospital."

"I could use your help as a detective," Harkins said. "You can go around talking to people for me. They'd probably trust a priest more, anyway."

"Anyway, I'm going to talk to the CO in the morning. I wanted to give you a heads-up. Something else, too."

"Great. Can't wait to hear what tops the fact that I might be riding around with a homicidal maniac."

"Our regimental commander, Colonel Gavin, is putting Colianno in for a Silver Star for his action at a place called Biazza Ridge."

"That's a big deal, right?" Donnelly said.

"It means he did something pretty remarkable during a fight," Patrick said.

"Besides the possible fratricide, you mean?" Harkins said.

Patrick reached into his musette bag again, pulled out a small silver flask. Harkins recognized it: their father had given one to each of his two oldest sons, engraved with their initials, when they completed basic training. Eddie Harkins' flask had been stolen on board the troop ship en route from the States to North Africa.

"Kathleen?" Patrick asked, offering it to the nurse.

"Don't mind if I do, thanks." She raised the flask in a toasting gesture but seemed hesitant to say anything.

"To Michael," Patrick said.

"To Michael," she said. She put the flask to her lips and took a dainty pull. "Where do you get whiskey out here?"

"We paratroopers are resourceful," Patrick said. He offered a drink to his brother.

"Michael," Harkins said before he drew a long sip. Then he turned the flask to see where it had been engraved. On the side opposite the "PH" someone had scratched paratrooper wings, the kind Patrick wore on his uniform blouse. The work was primitive, like a jailhouse tattoo.

Harkins wondered if Michael had eventually gotten the same gift from their father. Wondered if it was on the bottom of the Pacific.

After Patrick made his toast he asked, "So how's the investigation going? I mean, in general."

"Sometimes I feel like I'm making progress, but then I learn something that has me going in another direction, and I just wind up being more confused. Chasing my tail. One thing for sure, now I know why it takes so long to become a detective, I mean a real detective, back home."

"You feel like you're in over your head?" Patrick asked.

"All the time. I'm just stumbling around, asking dumb questions."

"Why are they dumb questions?" Kathleen asked.

"Well, they may or may not be dumb, but anybody I talk to has only one perspective. It's like, if two people see the same thing, you're going to get two completely different stories from them," he said. "And then, of course, some people are just going to lie."

"So what does a detective do?" Patrick asked.

Harkins, who could feel sleep coming over him like a heavy blanket, was not sure he heard the question.

"What is the nature of a detective?" Patrick said.

"This sounds like something from one of those philosophy classes you had to take," Harkins said. He teased his brother, but was jealous of Patrick's education. "Some pope write this?"

"A Roman emperor, actually," Patrick said. "So, what does a detective do?"

"Asks questions," Kathleen said.

"That's a technique," Patrick said.

"A detective tries to find out what happened," Harkins said. "And if there has been a crime, who is responsible."

"A detective compares stories, right?" Kathleen asked. "To see if one contradicts another."

"Yes," Patrick said. "He might try to trip people up by pointing out inconsistencies in a story."

"Sometimes detectives lie to people they're questioning," Harkins said. "I've seen that myself. They pretend to have information they really don't have. Once I saw a detective tell a suspect, 'We don't need your statement. Your partner already told us what happened, and he fingered you.'"

"Isn't that the plot of every gangster movie?" Kathleen said.

"It works, though," Harkins said. "Sometimes you ask them the same question, to see if they contradict themselves, because it's hard to keep track of the lies. Sometimes you hit them with an unexpected question."

"What's your favorite Shakespeare play, Kathleen?" Patrick asked.

"Well, that was an unexpected question. I've got to go with *Henry the Fifth*."

"Not *Romeo and Juliet*?" Patrick teased.

"Teenage lovers who kill themselves? No, thanks," she said. "Give me a good battle speech any day."

"Eddie?"

Harkins' favorite play was *Hamlet,* and Patrick knew it.

"The play within the play," Harkins said. "Hamlet makes the king and queen—who were they? Gertrude and . . ."

"Claudius," Patrick said.

"Hamlet puts on a play at court that shows how his father was murdered, and his mother and her new husband, who murdered the old king, go a little crazy," Harkins said. "Plus there's a lot of talk of ghosts, which I like."

"So you're going to, what? Put on a play?" Kathleen asked.

"Nah. Hamlet had a theory, which I don't have yet," Harkins said. "The important thing was he kept after his suspects, challenging their stories and their memories, until the façade started to crack."

"I doubt if every detective knows exactly what he's doing all the time," Patrick said. "If the case is complicated, and it seems like this one is, I'll bet they just keep stirring things up until something gives."

Harkins thought about a detective he knew named Kilgore, a squad room philosopher. Kilgore said a detective has to keep moving "like a shark."

"Why like a shark?" Patrolman Harkins had asked.

"Shark stops moving, it can't breathe. A detective stops moving, the investigation dies."

At the time, Harkins didn't know enough to ask a follow-up question, like "What if you don't know what direction you should move?"

"Guess I'll keep stirring things up, then," Harkins said, falling back. "Besides, I'm too bullheaded to give up."

He'd forgotten to remove his pistol belt, so his canteen jabbed him in the ribs, but he could not muster the effort to sit up again.

"First, sleep."

23

4 August 1943
0010 hours

True to his word, Harkins was asleep a few seconds after lying back on the blanket. Kathleen walked outside with Patrick.

"I worry about my brother."

"Yeah, he worries about you, too," she said. "Maybe he'll get this investigation wrapped up soon and he can go back to some other duties."

"You mean what he called 'unfucking fucking traffic jams'?"

Tired as she was, Kathleen had to laugh. "Father, you shock me."

"Yeah, I shock myself sometimes."

Kathleen, who could no longer see his face in the darkness, heard a bit of sadness.

"Michael's death is eating him up, for sure," Patrick said.

"You, too?"

"Yeah, but Eddie's got a bigger burden."

"How's that?"

Patrick looked at her for a moment, then shrugged his big shoulders. "I should probably shut up," he said. Then, "You know, after this war is over I might not be suited for going back to some sleepy little parish."

She stepped close, put her hand on his arm, and stood on her tiptoes to kiss Patrick on the cheek. "That'll be a good problem to have," she said. "Worrying about what to do after the war."

"See you, Kathleen."

"See you, Patrick."

The priest walked away, headed back to the unpaved main street where he'd left his jeep.

Kathleen turned to go back to her stack of casualty tags, then decided to use the latrine. Too much coffee.

She skirted the edge of the compound—the women's latrine was on the far northeast corner. She looked at her watch, but it was too dark to see the face. The guys were issued watches with luminous dials, numbers that glowed faintly; nurses had to supply their own watches. Brenda Felton had taken at least two government-issue watches from dead soldiers, handing them out to nurses, saying those boys didn't need them anymore, while the nurses did.

She was thinking about one of the men who had died that day on her table. His torso was nearly shredded but his face had been untouched and showed no sign of the terrible pain that had been visited on him. His dog tags had been torn off; unless one of his buddies was also in the hospital and could identify the body, he'd probably end up buried as an unknown. Whenever she heard that term she thought of the family, left ignorant of what had happened to the son, father, brother who had walked out the door one day and would never return.

Kathleen felt rather than heard a footfall behind her. Before she could turn, she was shoved forward, her foot caught from behind. She didn't even have a split second to throw her hands in front of her and so hit the ground stretched out, her face in the gravel, all breath punched from her chest. Then there was a weight on top of her, a big hand on the back of her head, then something cold and hard, and she knew it was the muzzle of a pistol pressed to the base of her skull. Everything was darkness; there was no sound except her lungs trying to find air, no conscious thought until there came unbidden a complete sentence: *This is how I die.*

Her attacker pulled the pistol's hammer back, the click distinct as a thunderclap. She tried to buck the man off, tried twisting to see his face, but he pressed her skull as if trying to crush it with one hand.

She kicked her feet to the side, trying for some leverage, and the man let out a snort that might have been a laugh at her efforts.

Then he pulled the trigger.

When she felt the urine hot in her pants she realized the pistol's chamber had been empty, and by the time she formed that thought, he was gone.

24

4 August 1943
0030 hours

As soon as Kathleen Donnelly limped back into the admin tent and woke Eddie Harkins, she knew she'd made a mistake.

"What the hell happened to you?" he said, instantly awake and on his feet. He helped her into the only chair and turned up the kerosene lamp, which she'd left lit. He leaned in, examined her bloody nose and already swelling lip.

"Jesus Christ, Kathleen! Who did this?"

"I don't know," she said, looking at her hands, her left palm a bloody scrape. Mentally, she was already past flipping through suspects and on to the danger other nurses might be in.

"Was it one guy?" Harkins was furious, eyes wide, breath shallow. His pulse was probably through the roof. "I'll bet it was that shit Wilkins. I'll kill him."

"Stop," Donnelly said. She had to buy some time, figure out a sensible approach that didn't start with a shootout. "Fill that basin with water and bring me that packet of towels," she said. Harkins buckled on his pistol but did as instructed.

She tasted salt, put her hands to her mouth, felt the wetness below her bottom lip, where she may have bitten herself. She probed the sides of her nose with shaky fingers. It was swelling, but did not seem to be broken.

"Did you see anything?" he asked. "Did he say anything?"

"Where's Colianno?"

"He asked where Colianno is?"

"No. *I* want to know where Colianno is. I want him to find Ronan for me. She might be in danger, too, so I've got to get her out of here."

"Both of you have to go someplace safe."

"I'm not going anywhere," Donnelly said.

"Jesus, Kathleen. We're not playing games here. I'm going to get you out of here, and I'm not taking no for an answer."

"Nobody asked your fucking opinion, Eddie," she shot back, the adrenaline boiling up in her, coming out aimed at him. "We're down three nurses, and we'll be down a few more if Boone gets rid of Savio and Melbourne. We can't be any more shorthanded around here without putting the patients at even more risk."

"And you're not at risk?" Harkins demanded.

"We're all at risk," she said. "I'm a soldier too, you know."

The sentiment surprised her, because that's not how she thought of herself. She was quite sure she'd never referred to herself as a soldier, and it sounded contrived, a little corny. But it was also true that her duties went far beyond nursing.

"I'm responsible for Ronan since Felton left, and I'm not going to have her walking around here with some maniac on the loose. She's the bigger threat to Boone, or Wilkins, or whoever is behind all this shit."

"She won't be at risk after I shoot those two bastards."

"And what if it's not either one of them? What if it's someone you don't even suspect yet? Then what? You feel better but this place is still screwed up?"

"I'm going to yank them out of bed, see if they have alibis."

"No, first things first. Find Colianno, find Ronan. Neither Wilkins or Boone is going to talk to you. They'll just deny everything anyway."

"Do you think it was one of them?"

"Well, they're both pissed off at you, that's for sure, and this might be about getting you to back off. I mean, if it were about me, he would have done something more."

"Did he try to, you know . . ."

"Rape me? No. And he obviously didn't want to kill me, because he could have."

She decided in that instant that she wouldn't tell Harkins about the pistol, the empty chamber, the certainty she was about to die.

"Eddie, you've got to promise me you'll give yourself time to think first, time to cool down before you go rattling Wilkins or Boone. That might be exactly what he wants."

"Who?"

"Whoever did this to me probably knew about you and Wilkins, and certainly knows about the investigation. Hell, I'm not a problem for Boone, so the only good reason to attack me is to distract you, maybe goad you into flying off the handle. Maybe Wilkins is waiting for you somewhere, plans on shooting you when you attack him."

Harkins was quiet for a moment, and she hoped that meant he was thinking about slowing down.

"We've got to take a longer view," Donnelly said. "Not react in the moment."

"Lindner," Harkins said.

"What about him?"

"Lindner was connected to Stephenson, went to the bordello with him. I'm going to pull Lindner's chain a bit, see where that gets us."

Harkins stepped close to her, dipped a towel in the basin he had filled, used a corner to wipe grit from her cheekbones. "Anything broken?"

"I don't think so," she said. "Mostly I was just scared. Angry, too."

"You fought?" Harkins asked.

"You're goddamn right I fought. And I'm not done, either. But we've got to be smart about this, Eddie."

"OK," he said.

"Let's go find Ronan."

Donnelly stood, brushed off the front of her uniform. Her trousers were stained in the front; if Harkins noticed, he didn't say anything. He pulled his pistol from its holster, yanked the slide back and checked the chamber, where a .45 round gleamed dully.

"All right," he said over his shoulder as he pushed aside the tent flap. "We'll do this your way for now."

Donnelly found Ronan asleep in the nurses' tent, along with six other women snoring and stretched across their cots, no air stirring in the August night. Ronan slept facedown, one arm above her head, the other hanging off the side of the cot. Donnelly touched her shoulder, which was slick with perspiration.

"Moira, wake up."

Ronan opened an eye, rolled onto her side and then immediately into a sitting position, ready for an emergency, though not the one Donnelly brought.

"Get your stuff," Donnelly said. "I want you to come with me."

Ronan lifted her shoes, shook them to make sure she didn't put her foot on top of one of the spiders that liked to climb inside, then jammed a foot into each. She'd been using her blouse as a pillow; she shook it out and put her arms in, began buttoning it.

"We have mass caz?" she asked Donnelly.

A "mass caz" meant mass casualties, a wave of patients and all hands turn to.

Two other nurses watched them now, so Donnelly lowered her voice. "Grab your duffle and the rest of your gear."

Ronan knew now that she wasn't going to lend a hand in surgery; she was moving. She was suddenly wide awake, and it took her less than a minute to stuff all her belongings into the duffle bag, which was less than half full when she finished.

There was a small light hanging from a central tent pole. When Donnelly walked past, Ronan said, "What the hell happened to your face?"

Donnelly didn't answer, just led Ronan out of the tent. Outside, Harkins had already found Colianno, and the four of them climbed into Harkins' jeep, the nurses crammed in the narrow backseat.

"We can't go to the admin tent," Donnelly said to Harkins.

"Where to, then?"

"Let's go to the ward tents. Good Guy is on duty, and there'll be a couple of nurses and some orderlies, too. A crowd. I think that's what I need right now."

Ronan did not ask any more questions as they drove, and she followed Donnelly quietly into one of the two big ward tents. There was very little going on, a couple of nurses moving about, checking on patients. Most of the men appeared to be sleeping.

"Doc Trennely here?" Donnelly asked one of the women.

"He's asleep in the corner," the nurse said. She took Donnelly's chin between her thumb and forefinger, examined the scrapes and bruises. "Want me to clean that up for you?"

"No, thanks," Donnelly said.

"Doc Trennely told us to wake him right away if anything changes with one of the patients," the woman said. She checked out Harkins and Colianno, then Ronan with her duffle bag. "Shall I wake him?"

"No, that's OK," Donnelly said. She wanted as little attention as possible, and the ward in the middle of the night was about as quiet a place as you could get and still be around enough people that you weren't going to be attacked again.

"You're going to wait here for me, right?" Harkins asked Donnelly.

"Yes." She looked at her watch; it was nearly 0230. "I'm going to want her out of here before dawn," she said, tilting her head toward Ronan, who stood whispering to Colianno.

"You have someplace in mind?" Harkins asked.

"Not yet. We've got two hours to come up with a plan to get her someplace safe."

"OK."

"Where are you going right now?"

"Talk to First Sergeant Drake," Harkins said. "He's going to want to know about this assault, and he'll know where Boone is now and maybe where he was a few hours ago."

When she looked around, Donnelly saw Colianno put his arm on Ronan's shoulder. It was no secret the paratrooper was sweet on her. The gesture looked comforting, and she thought about what she'd told Harkins about why she'd slept with him. She'd wanted to be held. She wanted it still.

Harkins pulled a pistol from the back waistband of his pants, a revolver, like a policeman might carry. "You know how to use this?"

"Point and shoot?"

Harkins showed her the thumb safety, showed her how to pull the hammer back. The noise made her think of her attacker, who had wanted to terrify her.

"Click, point, shoot," he said.

25

4 August 1943
0300 hours

Harkins took Colianno with him to find First Sergeant Drake, though the paratrooper clearly wanted to stay behind with Ronan and Donnelly.

"They'll be fine in the ward tent," Harkins said. "There's got to be a dozen people in there, not even counting the patients."

Colianno hit the jeep's starter and pushed it into gear.

"You *think* they're going to be OK," Colianno said, "but since we don't know who jumped Lieutenant Donnelly, we don't know for sure. Could have been one of the docs on duty, or one of the orderlies in the tent right now with them. You should have left me with them, Lieutenant."

Harkins got into the passenger side of the jeep. "I need you with me to make sure I don't shoot Wilkins and Boone on sight."

"Is that supposed to be a joke?"

"We'll come back as soon as we can. Before dawn, for sure."

"OK," Colianno said. "Where we going?"

"Let's go wake up First Sergeant Drake."

Drake's sleeping tent was near the middle of the hospital compound, in line with the tent that held both the orderly room and Boone's office, a supply tent for nonmedical supplies, and, just a few dozen yards way, Boone's sleeping tent. Harkins wanted to approach on foot, so he had Colianno park the jeep on the hospital's main street.

"First Sergeant?" Harkins said as he knocked on the post beside the door flap. "It's Lieutenant Harkins."

Drake reached the door so quickly Harkins wondered if he'd been waiting for visitors. The big man appeared in a T-shirt, boxer shorts, and his GI shoes, no socks.

"What's the matter?" he asked Harkins.

"There's been an assault. Can I come in?"

"Shit," Drake said. He turned away from the door and Harkins followed him inside, motioning for Colianno to wait.

Drake used a match to light a kerosene lamp, then adjusted the wick until there was enough light for Harkins to see. There was a cot with a single sheet, a lumpy pack of some sort that Drake might have been using as a pillow, a field desk piled with papers held down by rocks functioning as paperweights.

"Who got attacked?" Drake asked.

"Nurse Donnelly."

Drake sucked his teeth. Harkins could see that it irked him—was a blot on his professionalism—that the hospital seemed to be spinning out of control.

"How is she doing? She hurt?"

"Shaken up, I guess. No major damage that she'd admit to."

"She's a tough one, Donnelly is," Drake said. He found his pants in a tangle on the floor, shook them out, pulled them on one leg, then the other, stepping back into his shoes. "Surprised you came to me first," he said.

Harkins knew what the first sergeant meant. "Yeah, she made me promise not to just start shooting people."

"I heard all about you and Captain Wilkins. You think it was him? Maybe he was pissed because you beat his ass today?"

"I don't know, but sure as hell he isn't going to talk to me. Neither will Boone."

"Colonel Boone?"

Harkins thought about how embarrassed Drake had been listening to Boone's verbal assault on Ronan. "You saw how agitated he was when Ronan talked about Stephenson. You saw what he did to her."

"Still," Drake said, sounding less and less sure. "That's a long way from attacking a nurse. Besides, Colonel Boone was gone for part of the night," Drake pointed out. "What time was this attack?"

"About twelve thirty or so."

Drake looked at his hands. His life would be easier if Boone had an alibi. "He might have been back by then."

"Where did he go? Off-compound?"

"He took that Kraut doctor, Lindner, with him about twenty-one hundred, twenty-one thirty or so. They drove out through the front gate."

"Any idea where they went?"

"No, but it isn't the first time. I already told you that Colonel Boone has pulled some strings to keep Lindner from getting shipped back to the States, like every other POW we've had come through here."

Harkins studied the big man. Drake clearly did not like him, but, as Felton said, he was completely predictable when it came to protecting the work done at the hospital. Drake knew what his most important mission was, and it was not shielding doctors from the law.

"What do you know about Stephenson and Lindner?" Harkins asked. "Did you know they went to a bordello together?"

"Yeah, I heard that, but I don't know what to make of it. Stephenson was out of control in so many ways."

"I need your help, First Sergeant."

Drake looked at Harkins without changing his expression.

A long ten seconds went by before he said, "What?"

"Remember when Ronan said Stephenson was untouchable because he had something on Boone? Can you help me find out what that was?"

Drake didn't answer, and in the silence after Harkins' question, the two men heard someone outside. Drake held his finger to his lips, then walked to a back flap of the tent. Opening it, he stepped outside and closed the flap behind him, so that he'd be clear of the light. Harkins did the same thing at the front of the tent, but saw nothing. When he came back inside, Drake was already sitting on his cot again.

"See anything?" Harkins asked.

"Not even sure I heard anything, to tell you the truth. Getting paranoid, I guess."

"Where do you think Lindner goes when he leaves here?"

"I know he's treating some colonel or general," Drake said. "And given his specialty, I'd say the brass has the clap."

This confirmed what Donnelly had told Harkins.

"Is that all he does? Goes there and comes back in?"

"I don't know. He gets picked up in a staff car and taken into the city. What he does beside that is anybody's guess. Colonel Boone has given him all kinds of privileges that the Kraut shouldn't have."

"He ever go into the city any other way? Take a jeep and driver, maybe?"

"He did with Stephenson, but not by himself, as far as I know. But it's possible he caught a ride with an ambulance or one of our trucks. The drivers all like him."

"They don't care he's a Kraut?"

"Not since he saved that guy's dick, the one who came in here all shot up. He's a regular hero."

It was the same story Donnelly had told him. "So I hear," Harkins said.

Drake rubbed his face with meaty hands. "You know, I used to think I had a handle on what happened here. I used to think it was the enlisted men who would give me trouble." Drake looked at Harkins again. "I'll help you to the extent I can. I can't drop everything and start working for you. And I won't be disloyal to the colonel, won't work against him unless I think he's got something other than the best interests of the command in mind, the best interests of the patients."

"I understand," Harkins said. "Thanks."

Harkins turned to go. Drake called him back.

"Lieutenant," he said. "I just need all this stuff to go away. I need to get a full complement of docs and nurses so we can concentrate on what Uncle Sam is actually paying us to do, you know?"

"I do, First Sergeant."

"And if that means we have to get rid of a few bad apples, well, let's make it as quick as possible, OK?"

When Harkins and Colianno made it back to the ward tent, they found Donnelly and Ronan awake and working, changing bandages on a kid with what looked like a half mile of white gauze wrapped around his chest.

"We weren't about to go to sleep," Donnelly said when Harkins gave her a quizzical look. The four of them stepped outside.

"I could sleep for a year," Harkins said, running his hands across his face. He'd have to shave today, and he wanted badly to brush his teeth, which felt like they were wearing little fur coats.

"What's Boone's next move?" Harkins asked. He stood, paced in front of the two nurses and his driver. "He's getting rid of nurses; he got rid of Felton, and I think you're next, Moira. Stephenson's gone. Who else has been either close to Boone or causing him trouble?"

"The Nazi," Colianno said.

"Lindner?" Donnelly asked.

"Sure," Harkins said. "Drake confirmed that Boone was pulling strings to keep the Kraut doctor here. Then there's this whole Stephenson and Lindner at the bordello thing."

Harkins caught a whiff of coffee brewing down at the mess tent. He lifted his face after the scent.

"OK, now what?" Donnelly asked.

"Last night Boone and Lindner left the compound, and Drake told me sometimes Lindner leaves on his own. I want to find out where he goes."

"He has that patient I told you about," Donnelly said.

"The clap case, yeah, but maybe there's something more."

He turned to Colianno. "You have relatives in Palermo?"

"Cousins by the dozens," Colianno said.

"Can we get some to help us?"

"Sure."

"And you trust them?"

"With my life."

"And they speak English?"

"Not a word."

"OK," Harkins said. "We can still work with that. I want them to follow Lindner when he goes to see his patient. See if he goes anywhere else."

"Do we know when he's going? To this patient, I mean," Colianno said.

"In the morning," Donnelly said. "He asked one of the American docs to cover his ward, the POW ward, in the morning, from seven to noon."

"OK," Harkins said to Colianno. "You've got to find out where this general is, get your cousins in place there by seven."

"You have someplace Moira can go for a while?" Donnelly asked Colianno. "Away from the hospital?"

"You want to help her go AWOL?" Harkins asked. This wasn't part of the plan taking shape in his mind, but he appreciated the simplicity of it. If Ronan disappeared into the city, using Colianno's contacts, they would not have to worry about her being attacked or transferred; it would buy them a little time. Of course, she could also be court-martialed for going AWOL.

Colianno looked at Harkins, who shrugged and said, "Honestly, I don't have a better idea right now. Moira, what do you think?"

"How long would I have to stay away?"

"Until I get some answers about who attacked Kathleen, and what Boone's next move might be."

"So you don't know how long," Ronan said. "What about the shortage of nurses?"

"We'll have to make do for a while," Donnelly said.

Around them, the compound was beginning to stir with the early-morning rituals.

"It'll be light soon," Harkins said. "Let's get you out of here. We can always bring you back."

Ronan looked around. It was almost light enough to recognize people at a distance, and to Harkins it looked like that helped her decide.

"OK," Ronan said.

Harkins wanted to move fast now. "You got someplace in mind she can stay?" he asked the driver.

"Yeah."

"OK, take her there first, before you go looking for your cousins. I'd like to have you and them positioned as soon as possible, start following Lindner when he leaves this patient," Harkins said. "I'm going to ask him about Stephenson and Boone and what all the hush-hush is about. Maybe he'll give me something; maybe the attention will shake him up, cause him to do something."

When he said it out loud, Harkins thought it sounded like a long shot. He wondered if the detectives he knew back in Philadelphia also had these little crises of confidence.

"Anybody has a better idea, now's the time to say so."

They were all silent for a moment. A few feet away, a wounded soldier moaned in some nightmare, then woke with a start, sitting straight up, face contorted in fear, hands in front of him as if to ward off a blow.

"No! Don't!" he shouted.

The soldier looked around, saw where he was, then lay back down. When it was quiet again, Donnelly turned to Harkins. "I want to go with Moira," she said. "Not that I don't trust you, Colianno, but I want to make sure she's OK. Then I have to get back here for surgery."

"I'd rather you stayed here in the compound," Harkins said.

Kathleen put her hand on his arm. "I know you would, Eddie. Moira is my responsibility now."

Harkins knew he wasn't going to win this argument. "OK, OK. But we'll lose a lot of time if Colianno has to drive two of you into the city, then drive you back, Kathleen, before he looks for his cousins. Can we get you another driver? Is there someone you trust?"

"Yeah," Donnelly said. "One of the medical orderlies owes me a favor and he can sign out a jeep."

"All right," Harkins said. "We all know what we're doing, right?"

Donnelly snorted. "Well," she said, "we all know what we're doing *next*, but that's about as far as I'd go."

26

4 August 1943
0400 hours

Eddie Harkins hurried to where the doctors' tents were lined up, looking over his shoulder at the eastern sky, which was bloodred with the dawn.

"Red sky at night, sailor's delight," he said to himself. "Red sky at morning, Captain Wilkins take warning."

He expected to find some people stirring—there were doctors on duty twenty-four hours—but he didn't run into anyone. He checked inside the first two tents, shining a red-filtered flashlight on the men stretched out on their cots. In the second tent, one of the docs appeared to be awake and masturbating. When Harkins hit him with the light he turned toward the tent wall, but didn't say anything and didn't stop.

Kathleen wanted him to think clearly, not give in to anger. What he thought was this: Wilkins was never going to admit anything to Harkins. And if he wasn't going to get anything useful from Wilkins, he wanted to at least give the doctor something to consider, maybe give him pause the next time he was tempted to play tough guy. A clear, straightforward message that would come in handy.

Wilkins was alone in the third tent, on his back, mouth open, arms folded across his chest, one leg dangling toward the floor. In three quick steps Harkins was inside, pistol drawn. He put one hand on Wilkins' mouth and thrust the gun muzzle deep into the soft flesh beneath the doctor's chin.

Wilkins woke, eyes suddenly wide, the irises framed in a white ring. He reached for Harkins' arms, then settled back once it registered that the MP held him at gunpoint.

"Somebody jumped Kathleen Donnelly this morning, shithead," Harkins said.

He leaned closer, bent over Wilkins and the cot. He could smell the man's breath, could see fear.

"I don't care about the why, but I will find out the who," Harkins said. "Then it's going to be a party."

Harkins backed out of the tent, put his weapon in its holster, and turned toward the POW encampment.

The prisoners lived in their own section of the hospital compound, with a military policeman manning a flimsy gate that couldn't stop a determined toddler. Behind the MP, a few strands of barbed wire were nailed to some shaky fenceposts. It was pretty clear no one expected the prisoners to try to escape. The only ones healthy enough to run were the medical people—and according to Kathleen they were, to a man, dedicated to their patients, who were fellow prisoners. Once a POW got well enough that he might think about walking to Palermo, he got shipped out for the States.

"Morning, Lieutenant," the MP said when Harkins drew close. He saluted, and Harkins returned the courtesy.

"I'm here to find the Kraut doctor, the colonel."

"The dick doctor," the MP said, smiling. "Guy knows a lot about baseball. You know, for a Kraut." He was tall, with a strong Boston accent. Harkins couldn't see him well in the dawn light, but he knew the kid was smiling. Easy duty here.

"The very one. You know if he was out of the compound last night?"

"I just came on at zero-three, sir. Nobody in or out while I've been here."

"OK, so where do I find Colonel Lindner?"

"You gotta go to their orderly room, Lieutenant," the soldier said, pointing over his shoulder at a small walled tent. Harkins could see a kerosene lamp lit and perched on a field table. "We're not supposed to let people go walking around through their compound."

"Oh, is that right?"

"I'm not here to keep them in, Lieutenant. I'm here to keep GIs out."

"Somebody afraid we'll disturb their beauty sleep? The Kraut POWs get to make their own rules now?"

The MP shifted his weight from one foot to the other. "Not quite."

"Well?" Harkins asked.

"Some drunk GI went into one of the compounds down near Gela. Shot three unarmed POWs before they could take his pistol away. Killed them. Said he was pissed that they were going to the States and he had to stay in goddamn Sicily."

"Damn," Harkins said, looking back over the MP's shoulder. "OK, then. Is someone on duty there?"

"Just head over there, Lieutenant. Someone will come along shortly."

Harkins went to the orderly room tent and waited outside. Within a couple of minutes a German noncommissioned officer approached, slapped his heels together, and said, in clear but heavily accented English, "Can I help you, sir?"

The man's tunic had been torn and repaired and appeared to be spotted with dried blood. But all the buttons were fastened and his face was clean and shaved.

"Lieutenant Colonel Lindner," Harkins said. "Show me his tent."

"Yes, sir," the noncom said. "He is not there, sir."

Harkins cocked his head. Was Lindner already out of the gate? Did he even come back after his ride with Boone?

"Where is he?"

"Morning rounds, sir. Please come with me."

Harkins followed the German to the ward that held the POWs recovering from surgery or illness. Lindner, followed by an orderly, was moving from patient to patient, looking at paperwork on a clipboard he carried. Lindner spoke to the soldiers who were awake. When he came to a patient whose head was wrapped, his eyes completely covered in bandages, Lindner sat on the edge of the cot and put his hand on the man's chest as he spoke.

Harkins, who had envisioned himself dragging the colonel out of bed, decided he could wait.

Finally, Lindner noticed him standing by the entry. The doctor finished with a patient, then gave some instructions and his clipboard to the orderly.

"You are here to see me, Lieutenant?" Lindner said as he approached. He looked serious, maybe a bit anxious.

"Do you know who I am, Doctor?"

"You're investigating the death, the murder, of Captain Stephenson, correct?"

"Yes," Harkins said. "Let's step outside, shall we?"

The two men walked along a narrow footpath between the ward tent and what looked like a sleeping tent for the orderlies. Harkins could hear morning chatter inside—in German, of course.

"You left the compound with Colonel Boone last night," Harkins said. It wasn't a question.

"Yes. Colonel Boone asked me to accompany him to Palermo. The American medical service is taking over the municipal hospital, the one I ran before the invasion, and he wanted to get my input on a few things."

"So you just went to the hospital and came back?"

"Yes."

"What time was that?"

"We left around twenty-one thirty, maybe a little before, and were back shortly after midnight."

"Colonel Boone go anywhere else? Maybe after he dropped you off?"

"I wouldn't know, Lieutenant. He certainly does not share his plans with me."

"You've become pretty friendly with Colonel Boone. He gives you all kinds of privileges that most prisoners don't get. The American uniform, the freedom to leave the compound."

"Colonel Boone has indeed been very kind to me, and I know that this is against the wishes of First Sergeant Drake. Colonel Boone was familiar with some of my published work—from before the war—and I was able to be of some assistance on some particularly challenging surgical cases."

The two men reached the end of the short walk, where there was a sign in German. In smaller letters, like a subtitle, was stenciled LATRINE. They turned and headed back, simply pacing now. The older man spoke proper schoolhouse English. Harkins found himself matching the doctor's speech patterns, which annoyed the cop a little. The Germans were all so formal, so by the book. It made Harkins want to cuss and slouch and dress like an unsoldierly slob.

"Yeah, I understand you had quite the reputation as a surgeon, and that your work here has been very good as well," Harkins said. "Captain Stephenson had quite a reputation, too. Though not a good one."

Lindner looked at Harkins, perhaps anticipating the next question.

"And yet you and Stephenson made at least one trip together into Palermo, to a bordello." Harkins took off his helmet, held it in the crook of his arm as he wiped his forehead with the other sleeve.

"Captain Stephenson told me some of the women had urinary tract infections, and he wanted to know if I could help them."

"But he was there as a client," Harkins said. "You don't strike me as a man who visits brothels."

Lindner stopped walking, kept his hands behind his back as he turned slightly to face Harkins. "Loyt-nant," he said, using the German pronunciation before correcting himself. "Excuse me. Lieutenant."

"Yes, Herr Doktor?"

"Colonel Boone and I are not friends, as you suggest. We are something closer to colleagues. Peers, when it comes to medical questions, I suppose, and he has treated me with respect. But I am still a prisoner of war, and subject to his decisions as the local commander. I have remained here at the hospital because I am useful. I have no doubt that I will be shipped out with the other prisoners when this hospital moves forward, if not before."

"And Stephenson?" Harkins asked. "Was he a friend?"

"I doubt if Captain Stephenson had any real friends," Lindner said. Harkins thought about the dead man's tent, where he bunked alone.

"I am sorry, I know it is not polite to speak of the ill and dead."

"It's not polite to speak ill *of* the dead," Harkins corrected him. "But let's not worry about Stephenson's delicate feelings. What did you think of him?"

Lindner looked to his right. A few feet away, a POW left the sleeping tent, wearing a T-shirt, a towel draped over his arm like a waiter in a fancy restaurant.

"I thought he was deeply insecure. Manipulative. Selfish. Not above using people to satisfy his own base needs."

"He was a fucking pig," Harkins said.

Lindner studied Harkins for a moment. Harkins doubted the good doctor ever used the word "fuck."

"You a Nazi, Doctor?"

Finally, Lindner seemed caught off guard. "What?" came out "Vat?" He blinked a few times, used both hands to pull on his lab coat.

"Are you a member of the National Socialist Party? Is that required of someone of your rank? Your stature?"

Lindner regained his composure. "I am not a Nazi. As I'm sure you can imagine, there will be very few Germans you encounter, especially

German prisoners, who would admit such a thing if it were true, so I would not be surprised if you don't believe me."

"You're right, I'm sure," Harkins said.

"I have other patients to see, Lieutenant, so if that is all."

"Oh, Doctor, we're finished when I say we're finished. You're still a prisoner, remember?"

Lindner tilted his head agreeably, put his hands behind his back again. "As you wish," he said.

"Why did you stay behind when the rest of your people pulled out?"

"There were hundreds of wounded who were too badly injured to move. I volunteered, as did a number of the orderlies you see working here. We knew the Allies would take care of our wounded and that we would be able to help with that care."

"But if you're such a big-shot surgeon, why would they leave you behind? Why not some wet-behind-the-ears doc just out of medical training?"

"Wet ears?" Lindner said, the *W* sliding toward a *V* sound. Harkins was starting to think the slip-ups were a tell.

"Wet behind the ears. It means someone new to a field, inexperienced."

"I see. Strange expression."

"Well?"

Lindner looked into Harkins' eyes. "I have no idea," Lindner said. "Maybe it was important that it be a volunteer. Maybe the younger doctors were afraid."

Harkins had already decided not to ask Lindner if he was treating a senior American officer. If Colianno was able to deliver, there'd be a tail on Lindner this morning, and he didn't want the German to be suspicious.

"Was Stephenson blackmailing Colonel Boone?"

"I don't understand."

"Stephenson was getting away with a lot of shit. Boone should have stopped him, maybe even court-martialed him. But Boone didn't. He let Stephenson go on. I'm wondering if Stephenson knew something about Boone that Boone had to keep quiet."

"I wouldn't know anything about that," Lindner said, "anything" coming out a little like "any-sing." The doctor's perfect English slipped when he was under pressure. Or lying.

Harkins smiled at Lindner, but said nothing more.

"May I go to my patients now?"

"Sure, sure," Harkins said. Friendly now. "I appreciate your time this morning."

Lindner brought his heels together. Prisoners didn't rate salutes from Americans, so Lindner nodded and turned to go.

"Oh, one more thing, Doc," Harkins said. Lindner faced him again. "Who do you think killed Stephenson? And why?"

"I do not know, Lieutenant," the doctor said, smiling, his accent perfect again. "But I am sure you won't rest until you find out."

Lindner turned back to the ward tent, the tails of his lab coat trailing behind.

"You're goddamn right about that," Harkins said under his breath.

27

4 August 1943
0700 hours

Colonel Walter Boone's morning had started out well enough. He and Lindner had put in an appearance at the municipal hospital in Palermo, made sure plenty of people saw them there together. Then the two men rehearsed the story Lindner was to tell when that beat cop, Harkins, started asking questions. Lindner had repeated the alibi back flawlessly—he was a smart guy—and Boone felt a little less vulnerable. His orderly brought him the news about Donnelly being assaulted, and it was just a few minutes later he heard the scuttlebutt about Harkins showing up at Wilkins' tent, making some sort of threat.

Perfect.

Harkins obviously figured Wilkins had assaulted Donnelly. The two men had had words that previous day, and Harkins, applying the kind of bovine, simplistic thinking that Boone thought drove most police officers, had naturally assumed that Wilkins had lashed out. Apparently, the cop thought everyone lived by the same gutter-justice code, the tit-for-tat exchange of threats and violence. The more attention Harkins paid to Wilkins, the better for Boone.

But the colonel still had something eating at him like an ulcer: Ronan's comment that Stephenson felt safe doing whatever he wanted because he had something on Boone.

Was the little tart clever enough to make that up? Was she bluffing?

He stood in the door of his sleeping tent, absentmindedly buttoning his shirt and staring out across the compound.

What was the name of that philosopher? The "somebody's razor" guy.

Two soldiers walked by. "Morning, sir."

Boone nodded at them, turned back into his tent.

The simplest explanation is the most likely, or something like that.

He drew a deep breath, his heart suddenly fluttering, as if he'd had too much caffeine.

I have to assume Ronan knows something. All the nurses talk to one another. What else do they have to do except gossip?

There was a knock on the post by the door flap. "Colonel Boone?"

He turned to see Captain Palmer, the head nurse, standing with her fatigue cap in her hand, worrying the brim. She reminded him of a little bird; she never stopped her nervous movement, the fidgeting.

"Yes?"

"We have a situation with Nurse Ronan."

"What the hell does that mean?"

"She seems to be missing. AWOL, I mean."

"What? What are you talking about?"

Boone had never heard of a lieutenant going AWOL, much less a nurse, an American woman who was now, possibly, somewhere in a foreign city.

"Are you goddamn sure?"

"The other nurses said she packed her gear about oh three hundred this morning; all her uniforms, bedding, everything. Her cot is empty. Told a couple of people that she'd be gone for a few days, but they shouldn't worry about her."

"Was anyone with her?"

"I'm not sure, Colonel."

Maybe the assault on Donnelly had scared her. Whatever the hell was going on, Boone figured that Harkins was involved, and that mouthy paratrooper he'd picked up as a driver. They were all lining up against him now. Donnelly too.

"Where the hell could she have gone?"

"I don't know, sir. But First Sergeant Drake is going to look for her."

Drake.

The first sergeant had dragged his feet getting the transfer paperwork ready, Boone now saw. Drake, usually a model of efficiency, had given him some bullshit story about the clerk having to retype the orders.

Harkins had gotten to him, too.

"Where is Drake now?"

"Headed to the motor pool, I believe," Palmer said.

"Where's Donnelly?"

"Nurse Donnelly is scrubbing in for surgery this morning."

"Did you ask her where Ronan is?"

"Yes, sir. She said she doesn't know."

I'll bet, Boone thought.

He looked at Palmer, who was still twirling her fatigue cap, folding the edges, pulling them open. She had never connected with her nurses; none of them seemed to like her. She stayed clear of the hard, dirty work the nurses did on the ward, changing bandages or helping wounded men move position so they didn't get bedsores.

"Who's on the ward right now?"

"Doctor Trennely was on last night," Palmer said.

"Tell him he has to stay on duty. Tell him I've been called away."

"Sir, we haven't received any new nurses. We're terribly shorthanded. Are we expecting any more to come in? Replacements?"

It was her whining that pushed him over the edge.

"Do I look like the fucking personnel desk to you? Nurse staffing is your responsibility. If you're shorthanded, you might have to do some actual goddamn nurse's work for a change. I suggest you scrub in, Captain."

Palmer looked like she was about to cry, which made Boone's blood boil.

"Jesus!" he said. "Get out of my sight before you start blubbering."

Boone went back into his sleeping quarters, opened his footlocker, and found his pistol, wrapped in an oily T-shirt. He jammed a magazine into place and pulled back the slide, chambering a round. He slid the weapon into its holster, then buckled the belt around his waist. It was unusual for a doctor to wear a sidearm, but once he was outside the gate no one would think anything of it.

With his helmet tucked under his arm he hurried to the motor pool, where he grabbed a corporal. The man wore mechanic's overalls and a grease-stained fatigue cap.

"Was First Sergeant Drake just here?" Boone asked. The corporal looked a bit startled, and Boone figured it was because the colonel never visited the motor pool, even though it was part of his command. Drake had asked him to at least put in an appearance from time to time, had stressed that the drivers and mechanics wanted to see he cared about them.

"I'm a surgeon," Boone had told him. "Not an oil monkey."

Drake never asked again.

"What did he say?" Boone asked the corporal.

"He wanted to know if one of our guys drove some nurses into the city this morning."

"Smart man," Boone said to himself. Unlike Harkins, who had his own jeep and driver, the nurses had to rely on motor pool vehicles and drivers to get anywhere. "And did they?"

"Yes, sir. One of our guys took Nurse Donnelly into the city. They were both back within an hour, hour and a half."

"Where is this man? I want to talk to him."

"Well, that'll be a bit of a problem, Colonel, you see—"

"Don't give me that shit, Corporal," Boone said. Two soldiers who'd been heading toward them stopped and headed in the opposite direction.

"No, sir. I mean, yes, sir. It's just that the first sergeant took that same driver—his name's Gallegos—he had that same driver take him back into Palermo. He wanted to see where Nurse Donnelly had gone."

Boone smiled. "How long ago did they leave?"

"Couple of minutes, sir. You could probably catch up if you need to."

Just then another jeep pulled up, the driver apparently wanting to talk to the corporal. The driver saluted Boone.

"Out of the jeep," Boone said.

"Sir?" the man said.

Boone turned to the corporal. "I'm taking this jeep."

"You heard the colonel," the corporal said to the startled driver. "Unass that jeep."

The GI scrambled out, and Boone swung into the driver's seat and, without another word, took off in the direction of Palermo, a rooster tail of dust behind him.

28

4 August 1943
0900 hours

The army staff car was not subtle. A big Dodge painted olive drab, white stars stenciled on the doors, nearly twice as long as a jeep. When it stopped outside the gate, the driver jumped out and used a rag to wipe some of the road dust from the windshield. The rest of the car looked like a powdered confection.

Oberstleutnant Matthias Lindner waited, as instructed, in the registration tent near the entrance to the hospital compound. When he saw the general's aide exit the front passenger door, he walked outside.

"Colonel," the aide said. Courteous, not friendly.

"Lieutenant," Lindner responded. The aide opened the rear door and Lindner climbed in. It had to be over one hundred degrees in the car, but rolling down the windows on these dirt roads was an invitation to be suffocated by the dust. Instead, Lindner thought of a cool place and pressed a handkerchief to his nose.

"Lot of traffic this morning," the aide said. "It's going to take us a little longer to get there."

The aide's name was Cohen, a pleasant young man from Boston. A Jew. Lindner wondered if his patient had chosen a Jew to fetch him just to get under his skin. Lindner actually didn't mind. Cohen was well-read, spoke passable German—better than the gutter German Stephenson had been so proud of—and had studied philosophy at Columbia before the war.

Lindner had never gone in for the Jew-baiting that swept the Third Reich in the years before this war. His father said that the National Socialists were using the Jews as scapegoats, as the "Other," in order to give ignorant Germans something to focus on while Hitler consolidated power.

"Classic demagoguery," his father had said. "And the sausage eaters don't even know they're being sucked in." "Sausage eater" being the elder Herr Lindner's catchall name for mindless followers, whatever their social status.

Lindner had gone along with the times, of course, laughing at the coarse jokes, applauding lazily when some party hack talked to the staff about cleansing the hospital of dirty Jewish doctors. He had looked the other way as colleagues were tossed out of their positions, had held his tongue, had offered no one a hand. He'd needed his job, of course. Had a family to support. Sometimes, though, when he woke in the middle of the night, a sour taste of shame rose up in his throat.

"Doctor."

Cohen had turned around in the front seat, was facing Lindner, who had been daydreaming.

"Yes?"

"Do you live with the other POWs, or with the American doctors? At the hospital, I mean."

Lindner looked out the window, which was nearly opaque with dust. "With the prisoners."

Cohen and the driver exchanged looks, and Lindner was surprised to realize that Cohen did not like him. He worked hard, especially with the Americans, to be friendly.

The driver, whose name Lindner did not know and did not care to learn, spoke. "They're going to stick you on one of those troopships, Doc. Ship you back to the States. I hear they got German POWs doing all kinds of work, building army bases and such. Draining swamps. Sweat your balls off in Texas or Louisiana or some other hellhole. Should be lots of sick Krauts for you to take care of."

The man clearly found the picture amusing. Lindner did not respond.

"That's if your ship don't get sunk by one of your own U-boats." The driver laughed, slapped the steering wheel with a meaty hand. "Wouldn't that beat all? Come all this way and get done in by your own side."

"That's enough," Cohen said to the driver.

They dropped down to the coast road, the Via Messina Marine, which the Americans had marked with wooden signs saying OCEAN DRIVE. They turned left, away from the waterfront, into the heart of the old city. The American brass, like the Germans before them, always took the best properties for their headquarters.

To the right of the car, the Chiesa Santa Maria Maddalena, ancient, thick walled. On the left rose the grand Palazzo dei Normanni, begun in the ninth century and named for the Norman nobles who battled the Saracens for control of the island. Palermo had been a city and a trading port for over a thousand years: the Phoenicians, the Carthaginians, the Greeks, the Romans, the Arabs, then the northern Europeans. Each civilization had left traces in the place names and architecture, and then had passed to ash and dust.

Twenty-five hundred kilometers to the north, Hitler had promised his people a Thousand-Year Reich. Lindner doubted it would last another five.

He shifted from the right to the left side of the car to look out the other window, to see what this city might tell him about thousand-year empires.

So much beauty here, Lindner thought. And on his visits to the city, Stephenson had wanted only wine and women.

South of the palace and bordering the Parco d'Orléans, there was a three-story office building that had been taken over by the Americans. Inside, Lindner's patient waited.

Cohen got out when the car pulled to the curb, and opened Lindner's door. The aide wore a pistol, as he always did, and Lindner wondered if Cohen would shoot him if necessary. Probably. Maybe even happily.

"You know the way, Doctor," Cohen said. "We'll be here when you're finished."

Lindner walked into the cool lobby, with its giant marble tiles and iron-railing staircase. On the second floor he walked past an office marked G4 and entered the door to an adjacent, private office. Brigadier General Truman Glass was huddled over a map, standing amid piles and rolls of papers and maps. He was surrounded, in fact, by a sea of planning documents. Lindner stood quietly until Glass acknowledged him.

"Herr Doktor Lindner," Glass said. He walked to the door that led to an adjacent room, which Lindner knew contained a half-dozen desks and twice that number of scribbling clerks and junior officers. Glass locked the door.

"I don't mind telling you that I'll be glad when our little meetings are over," Glass said.

Lindner smiled, set his medical bag on the table, walked to a sink in the corner, and washed his hands. By the time he turned around, Glass had removed his pants, was standing in only his boxer shorts. The general was a big man, with a bald head and exceptionally hairy chest, back, and arms. He'd once told Lindner that he could have gone to medical school, but decided on business instead. Wanted to make "a whole shitload of money," an American expression Lindner had never heard before. When the war came along, Glass volunteered his service and expertise in logistics.

"You know what the GIs call this?"

Lindner was confused. "This?"

"This routine. Having a doctor or medic check your pecker. They call it a short-arm inspection. Ha ha ha!"

Lindner wasn't sure what that meant, then figured out that the penis was the "short arm." He still did not find it funny.

Lindner went to a closet and dragged out a red case marked VENEREAL PROPHYLACTIC UNIT, MEDICAL DEPARTMENT, UNITED STATES ARMY.

Glass, one of the senior American supply officers on Sicily, kept for himself a kit designed to treat scores of men. Lindner wondered if any GIs were going without.

He pulled out a white basin, two small towels, and a bar of soap, and handed them to Glass. There was a large pitcher of water on the floor, which the doctor used to half fill the basin. "Wash first," he said.

Glass soaped his penis, his pubic hair, his lower abdomen.

Lindner put on the rubber gloves, got out the syringe and jar of ointment. He filled the syringe, then set it aside. "OK then," he said. "Let me take a look."

Glass still had some yellow discharge from the end of his penis. Lindner handed Glass a small gauze. "Wipe. Gently."

"It's sore. Hurts like hell when I piss," Glass said. He grabbed himself with one hand, leaned forward to see over the bulge of his stomach. "But some days are better than others. Doesn't hurt as much. Means I'm getting better, right?"

"Yes, sir, I suppose."

Lindner had heard that the Allies had a new drug that fought infection, penicillin, but it was still hard to come by. He wasn't sure he'd use it on Glass anyway, since he wanted to treat the general over a number of visits.

Glass was careless in leaving papers lying about.

Lindner took the general's penis in his gloved hand, inserted the syringe into his urethra and pushed the plunger. Glass' knees buckled, but he was too proud to cringe.

"Holy fucking Christ!" he said, his teeth clamped shut so they wouldn't hear him in the next office.

Lindner handed him a clean gauze. "Hold this on the tip. Blot, but don't wipe."

While Glass was focused on his penis, Lindner looked up. There was a rollaway blackboard against one wall, with columns of numbers marked with designations starting at D – 20 on one side to D + 20 on the other. The horizontal rows were marked with Roman numerals, which is how the Americans categorized classes of supply.

"Are you using the condoms I gave you, General?" Lindner asked. It turned out that Glass, like Stephenson, had an appetite for prostitutes. No doubt he'd caught his disease that way; Lindner was concerned he was spreading it to other unfortunate women.

"I hate those fucking things," Glass said. "They ruin every good sensation."

"And so it burns when you urinate. How is that sensation?"

"I'm going to start hiring virgins," Glass said. "So I can't get anything."

Lindner looked up at his patient, the man's eyes like dark marbles beneath a single thick brow that stretched from one side of his face to the other. Could the American be so naïve as to think that the women offered as virgins really were virginal?

"Or maybe I'll just get a Frenchie," Glass said.

The GIs Lindner treated were all obsessed with what they called "Frenchies," being pleasured orally. In his time studying in Boston, he'd been surprised to learn that the act was considered so exotic that the Americans gave it what they thought of as the ultimate libertine designation, ascribing it, as they did all things sexually exotic, to the French.

Lindner's father, also a surgeon, had never understood the son's selection of urology as a specialty. Some of his medical school classmates had ridiculed him, and he knew the Americans regularly referred to him as the "dick doctor." But the fact was that he could help men who had suffered life-altering wounds. Of course, there were the patients he could not help, for whom no minor skin graft would replace what they'd lost. They committed suicide in staggering numbers.

"Stop daydreaming," Glass said. "You can fucking do that when I'm not standing here with my dick in my hand."

Glass held out the gauze, soiled with his discharge, to Lindner. The doctor, still sitting and, unfortunately, at eye level with Glass' diseased member, knew there was a trash can right behind the general. This was part of Glass' way of showing who was boss, even though he was the patient. Lindner held out his gloved hand and took the gauze, then dropped it in the rubbish.

"How many more visits?"

"Three or four, I think, depending on how you progress."

"I'm going to be a little harder to reach next month. The war goes on, you know."

Lindner said nothing, hoped his expression did not betray that this is what he was interested in, was the reason he was willing to endure Glass' pettiness.

"Did your hospital lose a lot of supplies to theft?" Glass asked. He often posed questions about the German services of supply, bragged about everything the Allies had at their disposal, as if he had created it all himself.

"Yes, General. The Sicilians were mostly interested in gasoline, it seemed. The garrison commander here in Palermo made an example of one young man who was caught stealing food from an officers' mess."

Glass was intrigued now, as Lindner expected. "What did they do?"

"Shot him on the street in front of the palace. They displayed his body with a sign around the neck. 'Thief' in German and Italian."

Lindner had concocted the story because it confirmed Glass' opinion of the Germans: that they were both ruthless and admirably direct.

"Hah," Glass said. "We should do that. We're hemorrhaging supplies on this goddamn island. Stuff gets stolen from right under our goddamn noses. You can buy it back on the street from those black market fuckers."

Lindner emptied the basin in the sink, spilling some on the floor. He felt a queasy excitement. He was about to push Glass as far as he ever had, perhaps coming close to asking one question too many.

"It was worse in Naples," Lindner said. "Those people stole everything. Our police units rounded up thieves by the dozens."

"Shoot them, too?"

"I don't know," Lindner said. "I think they put them in prison. Probably still there."

"I'll deal with that when I get there," Glass said.

Lindner waited, but Glass said nothing else. Lindner could see that the general's attention was being drawn back to the papers on his desk. Soon he would dismiss the doctor. Lindner needed more time.

"Can I put my pants on now?"

"Not quite, General," Lindner said. He looked inside his medical bag, spotted a small glass jar. "I need a urine sample."

He was improvising now, sloppily. The conversation with Harkins had thrown him. Of course the urine sample should have been taken before the medicine went in, but maybe Glass wouldn't notice. The general looked at him for a moment—Lindner had never asked for a sample before—but finally he took the bottle and retreated to a water closet in the corner of the room.

Lindner stood and walked to the general's desk, where Glass had left papers and maps and notebooks scattered about. He was queasy with fear as he reached out and turned over a thick stack of papers bound with a metal clip.

The title read *Fuel Handling to D+10*.

"Goddamn it to hell!"

Lindner dropped the papers, expecting to see Glass storming from the closet, but the general was only complaining about the pain of urination.

"Sonofa*bitch*!"

Lindner reached over the desk with two hands, picked up another stack of unruly papers to see a map buried beneath. A quick glance to the corner told him Glass was not finished yet.

He was looking at Sicily, the island marked with red and blue phase lines that marched from Palermo toward Messina, nearest the boot of the mainland. A date scrawled in the corner told him the map was already four days old. Lindner reached to see what was below it when a drop of sweat rolled down his nose and splattered on Sicily. He tried blotting the moisture, but his fingers were damp, too. Lindner quickly brushed his sleeve across his face.

"Lindner! You Kraut bastard!"

Lindner looked up. Glass was still behind the thin door.

"How much do you need in this goddamn jar?"

"Up to the line, General."

Lindner peeled back the map of Sicily. Below it was a nearly transparent overlay, a smaller scale map rendered in pencil, with no names or cities, no named rivers or roads. It was a sketch of military symbols to be placed over a map, like tracing paper. Without the map below it, Lindner wasn't sure what he was looking at.

"Lindner!" Glass screamed. "Goddamn. You can make do with less than that, right? I'm not quite up to the line. I just took a piss right before you showed up."

Lindner did not want to release the general just yet.

He turned his head, looked at the map overlay from a different angle. Suddenly the shape made sense. A bay of some sort, with a jagged beak of land on the north end jutting into the sea; a long, nearly straight stretch of coast, divided into segments by hashed lines. An invasion beach and its sectors for side-by-side assault units. A curly line running from the mountains—a river? But where was it? Had he even seen it before? The overlay was not marked with a name, but merely with a number. *Copy 12 of 50.* It was like trying to identify a person you'd seen once or twice in your lifetime from a line drawing of a silhouette.

"Lindner, you Nazi sonofabitch! Are you out there?"

"I can make do, General."

"Thank God almighty. I feel like I'm pissing fire ants."

Lindner moved the papers back in place. There was the damp spot where his sweat had dripped on the map. Glass still had not come out from the water closet.

Then Lindner knew.

The Gulf of Salerno. South of Naples, where Glass promised he'd deal with thieves and black marketers.

The Allies were going to invade the mainland at Salerno.

Of course! It made sense. The Germans and those Italians who had not surrendered were escaping Sicily across the narrow Strait of Messina, right onto the toe of the Italian boot. It would not make sense for the Allies to plunge across at such an obvious place. They would try to deceive the Germans as to where the inevitable assault would be. Salerno, some four or five hundred kilometers north along the coast, would be a surprise, and it would save the Allies from having to fight their way up the entire length of mainland Italy.

Just as Lindner was admiring the simplicity of the plan, Glass banged open the thin water closet door with his shoulder, head down, pulling up his undershorts. Lindner took a quick step away from the desk and nearly bumped into Cohen, the aide, who had appeared behind him.

"Can I help you with anything, Doctor?"

Lindner's breath left him. How long had Cohen been there?

"No," he managed. "No, thank you."

Lindner turned back to Glass. "Will you be around for another week, General?" he asked.

Cohen stepped around to the desk, straightened the papers there as he studied Lindner.

Glass, his eyes marked with pain, looked hard at the two men. "Why?"

"I can set up the last two treatments for you, hand it off to an American doctor if you prefer. But you don't want to stop now. You'll want to finish."

"I don't trust the American doctors to keep their goddamned yaps shut," Glass said. "Whereas if you talk, I'll slap you into the hold of one of those POW ships. You'll wind up in East Jesus, Idaho, or some goddamn place. Besides, we don't have time for that. I need to be finished by September first, because I don't want to go through this horseshit again, that's for sure."

When Glass mentioned the date, Cohen looked from his boss to Lindner, as if trying to see if the date had registered with the German.

"I'll bet if you put a German general through this bullshit," Glass said, handing the jar of urine to Lindner, "he'd have you shot for making him piss lightning into a bottle."

"Quite possibly," Lindner said. His hands shook; he gripped the bottle to steady them.

"What's up?" Glass asked Cohen.

"Looks like the locals stole a couple of tons of canned food from the depot just above Gela," Cohen said to Glass, handing over a typed sheet.

"Bastards!" Glass said. He took the report from Cohen. "Doctor Lindner here tells me the Germans used to shoot thieves. What do you think about that, Lieutenant?"

Cohen didn't answer right away. He studied Lindner, who packed his instruments, then looked down at his boss's desk just a few feet away. He walked over, lifted the report on fuel handling, glanced at the map of Sicily. When he got to the overlay, he yanked it out and rolled it up, turning his back toward Lindner so the German could not see the sheet.

"I don't know that we want to be in the business of shooting thieves, General," Cohen said. "Spies, though. It might be useful to shoot a couple of spies."

29

4 August 1943
1000 hours

Boone caught up with Drake's jeep on the road to Palermo when the first sergeant got stuck behind a convoy of trucks. He kept Drake in sight—without getting too close—and followed him into a dense grid of streets a few blocks west of the waterfront and just south of a patch of green marked with an ancient sign that said VILLA TRABIA.

Boone watched from an intersection three blocks away while Drake's jeep pulled onto a sidewalk. The first sergeant's driver pointed to a building Boone could not see, then Drake got out of the vehicle and, looking at his watch, gave the driver some orders, probably telling him when to come back.

There was no military traffic in this neighborhood, so Boone was wary of getting too close. He watched Drake through binoculars he'd found in the jeep, and when Drake's driver pulled away, Boone got out and followed the first sergeant on foot. There was some shade on one side of the street, but otherwise the heat bounced off the stone buildings and ricocheted around the tightly packed space. There was no breeze from the sea, no greenery along the avenue, no one moving outdoors except for Americans; there was just stone and dog shit and the occasional sound of someone speaking inside one of the oven-hot apartments.

With Drake out of sight, Boone hurried along so as not to lose him, and was soon drenched in sweat, his shirtfront dark. He turned a corner into a residential area and saw Drake step into the street to get a look at the second story of a building. The first sergeant did not see him. Drake entered a courtyard. Boone, after waiting a few seconds, followed.

On a gatepost were a few brass frames for hand-lettered signs showing the names of the residents. The third one Boone inspected said COLIANNO.

"Well, that was helpful."

Drake was out of sight behind some shrubs in the center of the courtyard. The apartments were arranged around a square, forty or fifty feet to a side, with doors leading directly onto the courtyard from the first-floor flats, and a balcony that led to the second-floor rooms. Boone climbed a staircase to his left, being careful to stay in the shadows. As he'd hoped, he was able to look down on Drake, across the courtyard and standing in front of one of the ground-floor apartments.

Drake knocked on a door, and Boone heard what sounded like a question in Italian. Almost a minute went by before the door opened, revealing a tiny old woman in a shapeless housedress. The woman looked Drake up and down, then scanned the courtyard before closing the door again, leaving Drake standing there with his helmet under his arm.

Then Boone heard a woman's voice with an American accent say, "Dominic?" When the door opened again, Second Lieutenant Moira Ronan, absent without leave in a combat zone and in danger of being declared a deserter, stepped into view.

"Oh, shit," she said.

"I'm glad to see you're safe," Drake said. "I was worried."

Boone was surprised at how clearly the conversation carried to the second-floor gallery.

"I don't want to go back there, First Sergeant," Ronan said. She wore a GI undershirt and her uniform trousers and shoes. She crossed her arms tightly, which made her look anything but defiant.

"Look, I'm sorry about what happened with Colonel Boone," he said. "All those questions, I mean. That was a terrible thing to do."

Ronan lifted her chin, wiped a drop of sweat off with the back of her hand. It was desert hot in the courtyard. The old woman stepped out of the apartment and past Ronan, shuffling out of the courtyard to the street.

"I didn't want to get shipped off to North Africa. He blames me, blames the other nurses."

You're goddamn right, Boone thought.

She was quiet for a moment. Then, "All that shit he let happen."

Drake stood quietly. A cat came out from the open door and rubbed against his leg.

"What did Stephenson have on Boone that kept Boone quiet?" Drake asked.

Boone held his breath. Then the door behind him opened and a woman coming out of the apartment yelped, surprised to see an American soldier crouching beside her door. She ducked back inside, slamming the door behind her.

Boone looked over the edge of the balcony; Ronan and Drake were gone, the door to the apartment shut.

"Shit," Boone said, going down the stairs two at a time. He glanced out through the gate to see if they'd left the courtyard, but the street was empty.

He was frantic now. If Drake hadn't colluded with Ronan and the others, he was about to start. They were ganging up on him. He had not come this far and worked this hard to be destroyed by gossiping nurses.

Boone pounded on the door.

"Who's there?" Drake asked.

It was a ridiculous question, and Boone laughed. "Colonel Boone. Open the door, First Sergeant."

There was shuffling inside, talking, Drake giving instructions to the woman, no doubt.

"I said open the goddamned door, First Sergeant!"

Drake waited another moment, then slid back the iron bar on the door.

"Where is she?" Boone said as he barged in, nearly hitting Drake with the door.

"She's not here," Drake said.

Boone stomped around the front room, then pushed through the curtain that separated it from the only other room in the back. There was a window, big enough for Ronan to climb through. Boone pushed the shutter open, but the back alley was already empty. When he turned, he caught a glimpse of himself in a mirror. He looked like a patient he'd seen recently, a GI who'd taken a handful of the army's stay-awake pills: eyes wild, face flushed.

"But she was here, wasn't she? Whose place is this? Who brought her here?"

"I guess it was Colianno, that paratrooper who drives the MP lieutenant around."

"So she's fucking a private now?" Boone said. "And that little tramp has the nerve to smear my command?" Boone was beyond angry. He felt like his heart was about to jump from his chest. His hands shook; he saw spittle flying from his lips.

"Why did you come here, Colonel?" Drake asked. He was looking at Boone's pistol.

"We have to stop her," Boone said, as if it were obvious.

"I came to find her and bring her back. Then you obviously followed me. Why did you think you needed to come out here?"

"Look, Drake, you and I both know that Stephenson wasn't the only asshole doing what he was doing. If Ronan takes this complaint—and that's all it is, an allegation—if she takes this to the corps level or even up to the Seventh Army surgeon, we're all fucked."

"I'm not."

"You think your hands are clean here? There isn't anything that goes on in that hospital that you don't know about. You knew that Ronan was shacking up with that wop paratrooper. I'm not the only one who can be accused of not taking appropriate action."

"You're the commander," Drake said.

There was a sound in the next room, maybe the cat Boone had seen. Startled, he pulled his pistol.

Later, Boone would tell himself that it wasn't until that moment that he realized why he'd come, why he wore a sidearm.

"Where is she?" he shouted. "Where the fuck is she?"

Drake's voice was surprisingly calm when he asked, "Did you kill Stephenson, Colonel?"

Boone stopped his rant and looked at Drake closely. When he pointed the pistol, Drake lunged, grabbing for the barrel. Boone heard the report, felt the slide jump back and forward again under Drake's hand as they struggled.

Then Drake bent forward, air rushing out of him as he fell heavily, his knees hitting the floor like pile drivers.

Boone stepped back. He could see Drake's eyes move. Looking for the pistol? Looking for help? He was still alive, his eyes tracking Boone's shoes as the colonel stepped over him and out the door.

30

4 August 1943
1030 hours

Lieutenant Cohen walked Lindner back to the street and the waiting staff car. There was a woman selling flowers from a pushcart, and some Sicilian men clearing rubble with shovels and wheelbarrows. Other men stood or sat in the shade, and Lindner wondered if they were hoping to be hired by the Americans.

Dozens of soldiers hurried into and out of the headquarters building. Lindner doubted anyone noticed the small *P* above the breast pocket of his American uniform. Of course, he wore no insignia of rank or unit patch, either, but the average GI paid little attention to wearing the uniform correctly. They were always adjusting things, adding and subtracting pieces to suit their work and comfort. They hardly looked like soldiers.

And yet they're winning the war, Lindner thought.

"I'm not going back to the hospital with you," Cohen said. "Sergeant Cordell here will drive you."

Lindner looked at the driver, who stood on the opposite side of the big car, smoking a cigarette. When Cohen called him, he flicked the butt away and stood at what probably passed for the position of attention in the American army.

"Got that, Sergeant?" Cohen asked the driver.

"No problem, Lieutenant. I'll take care of him."

Lindner reached for the door handle, but Cohen leaned in front of him. "Let me get that for you," he said.

Before he opened the door, Cohen, whose face was just inches from Lindner's, looked the doctor in the eye for a long few seconds. "You know, Doctor, it's not like we need a reason to put you on one of those

POW ships," Cohen said. "You've been useful up to this point, but that could all change."

"Of course, Lieutenant," Lindner said.

Cohen yanked the door open and Lindner climbed into the hot car. The lieutenant, standing curbside, was still studying him when the driver put the car in gear and pulled away.

Lindner felt as if he'd been holding his breath since Cohen came up behind him at Glass' desk. He wanted Cohen to find some American doctor to treat Glass. He wanted to go back to the ward and lose himself in work. He would even prefer, he admitted, one of the POW ships headed for America. But none of those things were in the cards. He finally had a piece of useful information, or so he thought, and he had to pass it along if it was going to do any good for him, for his family back in Essen, for his brother in Italy.

He felt sick to his stomach, but it was possible, at least, that the terrible burden of waiting might, at last, be over. First, he had to gather his courage.

"Sergeant, I wonder if we might make a small detour," Lindner said.

"I don't know if that's a good idea, Colonel," the driver said.

"It's Sergeant Cordell, correct?"

"Yes."

"Well, you see, I was stationed here in Palermo for many weeks before the invasion. Time enough to develop relationships with some of the locals. One in particular."

Cordell looked at him in the rearview mirror, and Lindner could see the man was smiling. "Hot damn, Doc!" he said, slapping the steering wheel again. "You got a little piece of dago tail stashed somewheres? You want to pay her a visit?"

Lindner swallowed. He wasn't sure which was more distasteful: lying to this man or allowing the American to think he was no better than any rutting twenty-year-old. No better than the late Captain Meyers Stephenson.

"There is a woman, yes. And I would like to visit, if you could see fit to drive me a bit out of the way and perhaps wait for me. Just a short time."

"I know what you mean about short time, Doc. I mean, I'll bet it's a medical fact that a guy with blue balls can only last a minute or so next time he's with a woman. Am I right? Right?"

Lindner wasn't sure what the driver was talking about, since the point of the conversation seemed to turn on the meaning of the term "blue balls," but Cordell wanted to be right.

"I believe you are correct," Lindner said.

"Say, is your friend a working girl?"

"Sorry?"

"I'm just wondering if there was another woman around who might make this worth *my* time and trouble," Cordell said. "I'm taking a risk here. Lieutenant Cohen is pretty straitlaced, doesn't even drink, if you can believe that. Anyways, I could get in trouble. So I was thinking that maybe there was a little something in it for me."

The driver was asking if Lindner's imaginary friend was a prostitute. He wanted to know if other women were available.

"I'm sorry," Lindner said.

"Oh, well. I reckon it don't hurt to ask," Cordell said.

Lindner had Cordell drop him alongside the steep rock topped by the Castello Utveggio, a palace that had been turned into a hotel and, before the invasion, was a billet for German officers. He looked up at the crenelated tower and wondered if the Americans had moved in, wondered if they also co-opted the best properties.

Lindner walked south along the waterfront by the Grand Hotel Villa Igiea, where he had enjoyed a few meals during his time in Palermo, before the Allies came. He turned back to admire the view of its stone tower and, below it, the recently tidied outdoor restaurant. There were a few civilians and a handful of Americans; officers, he judged. About twenty yards back along the sidewalk, a young man in a rakish hat looked directly at him, then turned in to the garden and headed down the steps toward the waterfront.

Lindner moved along the seawall, turned west into a side street just past the hotel proper. Just ahead of him was a block of four apartments in a sand-colored building. Lindner turned back at the corner, looking for the man in the hat, the one he'd seen at the garden, but there was no sign of him. He ducked into the shadow of a doorway, waited nearly a minute, then stepped back out into the street. His imagination was getting the better of him, but he wasn't imagining its effect: His pulse hammered away as if he'd just run a mile.

Lindner walked toward the apartment block. The entrance was in the center on the ground floor and led to a tiny, pleasant courtyard with four lemon trees. He had no idea if his contact would be there, did not even know if the man lived there or just visited, but he'd been told to come when he had an urgent message. And Doctor Lindner had an important message.

He believed the war was already lost, that the Nazis had destroyed Germany for the second time in a century not half over. He believed the moral answer would be to help the Allies advance to a quick victory, save the Fatherland from a prolonged struggle that would leave it in ruins, its cities bombed, its people homeless and hungry.

But Lindner also believed that the Abwehr and the Gestapo would kill his younger brother, would deny his family the permits necessary to travel to the countryside if he failed to produce any intelligence at all.

But what if the Germans adjusted their defense of the mainland based on his report? Would they move the Luftwaffe antiaircraft units into the very zone that was to be attacked? What if his report put his brother into even more danger? What if he got Albrecht killed?

Lindner reached the entryway to the apartment block just as the young man he'd seen earlier came around the corner in front of him. The civilian had circled the building and removed the hat, but the hatband had pressed a red line into his forehead. Terrified, Lindner turned immediately and walked away as quickly as he could without running.

31

4 August 1943
1100 hours

Harkins spent the morning tying up a loose end, corroborating Colianno's story about where he was the morning of the murder. The two soldiers he'd claimed had been with him that morning—men who'd also ignored the air-raid warning—had both returned to their units. Marshall, a First Infantry Division artillery soldier, was back in the fight, his unit on the move behind the Allied advance. It would take days to track him down.

Harkins sent a message to Patrick to find the other soldier, a paratrooper from Colianno's own regiment. In a conversation with the chaplain, Private Eugene Harris confirmed that he, Colianno, and the artilleryman, Marshall, had ignored the air-raid warning and had spent the time packing their gear for discharge.

Harkins found Gallo, the doctor he'd seen the morning of the murder, the man who said that Stephenson had been right behind him, running for the same shelter. It was another dead end, and it reminded Harkins why so-called eyewitnesses often turn out to be unreliable. Gallo couldn't tell Harkins how far back Stephenson had been, did not hear what, if anything, Stephenson had been saying, couldn't even say for sure if Stephenson had been headed for the same shelter trench.

By the time Colianno came to pick him up, Harkins felt he'd wasted the better part of a day with nothing to show for it.

"Learn anything new so far?" Colianno asked when Harkins climbed into the jeep.

"Not a goddamn thing. You?"

"We'll know soon enough."

Colianno dropped Harkins off on the waterfront at a sidewalk café owned by a cousin, told him to wait while he retrieved the other cousins, the men he'd sent after Lindner. Harkins thought he'd be conspicuous, an American officer sitting around sipping coffee in the afternoon, but it turned out that there were plenty of GIs killing time in Palermo. He wondered about his own platoon—he'd been temporarily assigned to the provost marshal's office, thanks to Captain Adams' paper shuffling—and was surprised to find he missed them.

He'd finished half of a tart lemonade when Colianno pulled up.

"How'd it go?" Harkins asked before the four men had dismounted. He had a couple of theories about what was happening at the hospital, and he wanted to drop the ones that did not look promising. Having Lindner followed had seemed like a stretch, a little desperate.

"Not good," Colianno said. "The Nazi doc saw them following. Saw Enzo."

At the mention of his name, the youngest cousin dropped his head. *"M'â scusari."*

"They followed him to an apartment building, and it looked like he was going inside. Maybe there's something going on in there."

"How big an apartment building?" Harkins asked.

Colianno posed the question, got an answer. "Four."

Harkins looked at the cousins. The oldest, Colianno had told him, was twenty-three, the youngest and brightest only sixteen. Same age Michael had been when Harkins helped him lie his way into the navy.

"OK," Harkins said. "I have an idea, but maybe they leave Enzo home this time."

"He's real sorry," Colianno said.

"I'm sure he is. I'm more worried about the fact that he's been made. Lindner has seen him, knows that Enzo was following him."

Colianno spoke to Enzo, put a hand on the young man's shoulder. Enzo protested, but eventually nodded his head in agreement.

"What's the plan, boss?" Colianno asked Harkins.

"Think they can find out who lives in those four apartments?"

"Then maybe we can link someone back to Lindner?"

"Something like that," Harkins said. "I want to know what our German friend is up to."

While Colianno was explaining what he wanted his cousins to do, an army ambulance stopped along the waterfront and Kathleen Donnelly got out. She told the driver to wait for her on a side street, then walked toward Harkins.

"This where the brain trust is meeting?" she asked.

She had changed into a clean uniform—no bloodstains—and had her hair wrapped against the dust in an olive drab scarf that had once been an arm sling.

Harkins stood, checked the impulse to kiss her, and instead pulled up a chair for her. "How'd you find us?"

"Dominic pointed out this place when we came out here with Ronan. Said his cousin owns it."

"So now you're taking in the sights?" Harkins asked.

"No. I came out to tell you that it looks like Boone is no longer enamored of Herr Doktor Lindner."

"What do you mean?"

"First Sergeant Drake's clerk came to the admin area, looking for Drake, who has been gone all day. Very unusual. Anyway, the clerk said that Boone told Lindner to ship out with the next batch of prisoners."

"Did they get another dick doctor?" Colianno asked.

"No. We're down two docs and three nurses, by my count. And we're getting ready to jump."

"What's that?"

"We got a warning order to be ready to jump forward, relocate the entire hospital somewhere closer to the front; shorten the ambulance ride for the patients who need care right away. We try to stay no more than twenty-five miles or so back from the fighting."

"So you just pick up the whole hospital?" Harkins asked. There had to be tons of tents and equipment, not to mention two hundred–plus patients, some of whom were in bad shape and probably could not be moved.

"We have three platoons, and we usually move one at a time. Leapfrogging. We support the First Division and their attached units, but I guess somebody else is covering while we move the whole hospital. "It *is* a giant goat rope. All those vehicles getting loaded up. Everything has to be labeled correctly and put in the right trucks. We have to discharge or move our patients. We have to send people forward to scout another location, and when we get there we have to set up right away and be ready to receive patients. We're actually pretty good at it, compared to other hospital units, but it's still FUBAR."

"And when does this happen?"

"We've been given a warning order. Could be anytime in the next twelve hours, or we could sit around here for another week. It'll be a lot harder if Drake isn't back by the time we start. He's the ringmaster of this operation."

"Is there any way Boone is behind this move?" Harkins asked.

"What do you mean?"

"Well, it's just that he's been trying to make it as hard as possible for me to talk to nurses and doctors. I'm wondering if collapsing the whole hospital into a circus train is part of that."

"Nah," Kathleen said. "The rumor mill says that the Brits are stalled over on the east coast of the island, and that Georgie Patton is pushing everybody hard so that he can beat them to Messina."

Messina, the island's third-largest city, sat at the apex of a triangle pointed at the toe of the Italian boot and was the main objective of Montgomery's British forces. The Americans were supposed to guard Monty's left as he pushed the Germans and Italians back. But George S. Patton, commander of the newly minted Seventh Army, wanted to be no man's second. He was racing to outstrip the British advance, driving his American units along the rugged northern coast and fighting through successive German defensive lines. The hospitals were full of wounded men who'd made down payments on the stateside headlines Patton envisioned for himself as he beat the British.

"Anyway, moving is just part of what we do, you know, depending on how the fighting is going," Donnelly said. "But I see your point about all the confusion, the nurses being shipped out and such, everything making it harder for you, too."

Harkins looked out at the water, where U.S. and Royal Navy ships lay at anchor while smaller craft dodged back and forth to the port. The Germans had blown up most of the port infrastructure to make things as difficult as possible for the Allies. Still, tons of materiel made it to shore every hour, everything from flashlight batteries and cotton swabs to locomotives and rail cars. Harkins had heard that as much as twenty-five percent of it disappeared into the black market, stolen by Sicilians, who were, in some cases, helped by GIs.

"Can you stay and have something to eat with us?" Harkins asked Donnelly.

She stood up, waved at the ambulance driver who was parked waiting for her. "No, thanks. I've got to make sure all the admin stuff and patient records get packed up. And I'm backup surgical nurse tonight, too."

"You know," Harkins said, "before I came to the hospital I would have guessed that you guys have it pretty easy. Tents with cots. A mess tent and cooks. But you must be exhausted all the time."

The ambulance pulled up next to the café. Donnelly opened the door and stood on the running board, in her men's shoes and outsized trousers, with road dust in her hair and in the tiny wrinkles beside her eyes. She looked ten years older than her age, but Harkins saw something else, too. She was fully engaged, completely alive, thoroughly dedicated to her patients.

"You know what we say in the U.S. Army Nurse Corps, right?"

"What's that?"

"I'll sleep when I'm dead."

32

4 August 1943
1230 hours

There was nothing on the menu board at the café, and the owner told Colianno there was a shortage of everything. Trade with the eastern end of the island was impossible because of the battle lines, and the roadways on the Allied, or western end, were clogged with military traffic. The American navy kept most fishermen bottled up in Porto Palermo, and two hundred thousand GIs—all sick of army food—ate anything they could buy, steal, or otherwise get their hands on.

Colianno haggled with the café owner and finally came to a compromise.

"He's charging us four times as much as he usually does."

"Maybe it's a tax for invading his country," Harkins said. "What'd we get?"

"Polpo bollito. Probably fresh out of the sea this morning, or so he says."

Harkins looked out at the harbor, large sections of which were streaked with the silver and blue of fuel oil leaked from sunken ships.

"Hope it doesn't come with any of that shit that's spread all over the water."

The café owner brought out a ceramic pitcher of wine and two mismatched glasses. Colianno poured them each a few fingers.

"My brother told me that your regimental commander put you in for a Silver Star. Something about you pulling a wounded guy out of a foxhole while a tank was trying to run over him."

Colianno did not respond, but called to the owner, who appeared with a pitcher of water.

"Is that what happened?"

The paratrooper sipped his wine, took a big swallow of water. "The tank was trying to run over a bunch of us. Did run over a few foxholes. The guys who'd dug deep enough were OK."

Harkins figured that meant that some had not dug deep enough.

"And the guy you pulled back?"

"Name's Quint. He took a bunch of shrapnel in his back, legs, and ass from mortar rounds the Krauts were dropping on us. He couldn't get out of the hole," Colianno said. "The tank was headed for him—I'm pretty sure the Kraut driver spotted Quint's foxhole and mine, which was right next to his. Anyway, the tank stopped to shoot at something behind us, so I jumped up, ran over there, and yanked him out by his feet. Pulled him back about thirty yards. Must have hurt, because he screamed the whole time. I guess I kind of dragged him on his face. It'd be an improvement."

"He make it?"

"Last I heard, yeah. He was complaining about eating dirt while I was pulling him. Ungrateful shit."

Harkins laughed, thinking Colianno meant it as a joke, but the private was not smiling. "He's your buddy, though, right?"

"Fuck, no. I hated that bastard. He and I tussled all the time in North Africa. He was always bellyaching about something. Easily the biggest eight ball in our squad."

"But you risked your life to save him."

Colianno looked at Harkins as if the lieutenant had missed something obvious. "So?"

"So doesn't that strike you as—I don't know—strange? Surprising? Unexpected?"

"No."

Harkins waited.

"Look, Lieutenant. I don't know what it's like in the MPs, but in an infantry squad, you have to depend on the guy next to you, and he's gotta know he can depend on you." Colianno shrugged, as if the thought were just occurring to him. "I'd take a bullet before I'd let one of my guys down. Even a bastard like Quint."

The food arrived, modest portions of something white and boiled. Harkins looked at his plate and thought about what Colianno had said. The response—*I'd take a bullet*—sounded like something Hollywood would come up with. But Colianno had actually been shot at, had risked taking a real, not a movie, bullet.

"What is this?" Harkins asked.

Colianno stuffed a forkful into his mouth, breathed around it because it was hot, said something that sounded like *ball piss.*

"What?"

Colianno swallowed and said, "Boiled octopus. And if you're going to be a pantywaist and not eat yours, I will." Colianno shoved another, smaller bite into his face. "You Irish don't know a thing about what good food is," he said.

"You know," Harkins said, "a Silver Star might get you home faster when this is all over. I hear they're going to award points for campaigns, decorations, wounds; and guys with the most points will go home first."

"Bad luck to talk about that kind of stuff. You stop paying attention to what's going on in front of you, you're liable to get killed."

Harkins poked at the octopus with his fork. "I got an uncle," he said. "Actually my ma's uncle, who was in the Great War. Only reason we knew he had any medals was because us kids used to go through his old duffle bag when he slept on our couch."

"He lived with you?"

"In between jobs or girlfriends," Harkins said. "My ma told me that when he came home from the war he just sat on his mother's back stoop every day, all day, drinking coffee and smoking cigarettes. For eight months. Anyway, when I joined up I went to see him. He's in pretty bad shape now, but I thought he could give me some pointers about the army, you know? About the war."

"So what did he say?"

"Said it was all bullshit, all of it. Said those guys you hear down at the American Legion talking about the war weren't anywhere near the real thing."

"That part sounds about right," Colianno said. "I can already see that with guys in my unit. The guys doing the most talking are the most full of shit."

"I asked my uncle about combat. He said, 'I went where I was told to go, I did what I was told to do, and I was scared shitless all the time.'"

Colianno laughed and said, "Your uncle's a friggin' genius."

Harkins was about to agree, when they were interrupted by a small boy who ran up to their table. He panted a few sentences to Colianno, who asked two questions.

"Let's go," Colianno said, standing and pushing the table away. "There's been a shooting at my aunt's place."

The military police had the street blocked by the time Colianno and Harkins pulled up. Their vehicle wasn't yet stopped when Colianno jumped out and ran to a ground-floor door, where an MP sergeant stood. Harkins followed and could see inside, where a body too big to be Ronan lay covered with some sort of cloth.

Colianno asked the sergeant, "Any others?"

"Ain't one enough?" the sergeant said.

Harkins took Colianno by the elbow, pulled him out of earshot of the MP.

"OK, so that's not Ronan," Harkins said. Colianno looked like he might throw up.

"Let's figure out how we want to play this. We don't want to lead the MPs to Ronan, right?"

"I showed her a second house, another place to hide if somebody found out about this one. She's supposed to go there if things go south."

Harkins, impressed, said, "Good. That's great. So if she's not around here somewhere, we'll go look for her there. If she is here, let me do the talking and I'll see if I can't bullshit our way out of this situation. What I don't want is for us to be ordered to sit around waiting to be questioned. Let's play ignorant."

"That shouldn't be hard," Colianno said. "Let's make it quick, OK?"

Harkins reached into the pocket on the back of his seat and fished out his MP brassard, the armband that identified him as a military police officer.

There were four MPs in the courtyard. A tall PFC had one of the English-Italian phrasebooks issued to the invasion force and was trying to question an old woman in the entryway of an apartment. She could not have been five feet tall, and when she spoke, Harkins noticed that she had only a few teeth clinging to her gums, lonely sentinels manning an abandoned outpost.

Colianno saw this little farce, walked up and offered to translate.

Harkins approached the unhappy-looking sergeant in the doorway. He did not recognize any of the men, who were from another military police unit.

"I'm Lieutenant Harkins."

The sergeant saluted, stepped out of the doorway. Behind him, Harkins saw a body covered in what he now saw was a tablecloth, GI shoes sticking out from below. Blood had soaked a large circle in the center of the cloth, had leaked out onto the floor in a small, dark river.

"I'm Sergeant Sutherland, and I'm glad you showed up, Lieutenant. We got flagged down while on patrol, and I'm not really sure what to do here."

"Lot of that going around," Harkins said. "Unfortunately, I'm not here to take over the investigation. You should send for the provost, if you haven't already."

Harkins stepped through the door, and Sutherland stepped back to make room for him to pass. The body lay in the middle of a small front room; a tiny table and chair had been knocked over, perhaps in a struggle. The rest of the apartment appeared to run straight back, shotgun style.

"No sign of anyone else?"

"No other bodies; other than that I haven't had a chance to look around much."

Closer to the body now, Harkins saw that the dead man had to be over six feet tall.

"Shit," he said. Then, to Sutherland, who was, however reluctantly, in charge of the crime scene, "Mind if I have a look?"

The sergeant shook his head, and Harkins squatted beside the corpse, pulled the tablecloth back from First Sergeant Drake's face.

"You know who that is?" Sutherland asked.

"First Sergeant Irwin Drake, Eleventh Field Hospital, just up the hill south of the city."

Harkins looked at Sutherland, who stood with his thumbs tucked into his pistol belt, looking worried and clueless.

Probably what I looked like standing over Stephenson.

"You'll want to write this down, Sergeant."

The noncom pulled out a pencil and pocket notebook. Harkins was repeating the information when Colianno walked in. The paratrooper looked at the body, then at Harkins, made a *come outside* gesture with his head.

When the two men were out of earshot of Sutherland, Colianno said, "It was another GI. The old woman across the courtyard told me she heard someone pounding on my aunt's door. Tall, skinny guy in an American uniform. He went in, there was some loud talk in English, then a gunshot, and the tall guy ran out."

"Did you share all this with the MPs?"

"Not yet. I told them that she heard a gunshot and saw a man running. I left out the fact that he was a GI, left out the description. Thought I'd see what you wanted to do first."

"Did the neighbor see what happened to Ronan and your aunt?"

"No. I figure they must be at the other safe house."

"We'll check there, then head back to the hospital to see where Boone is," Harkins said.

"You think it was Boone?"

"Tall, skinny American," Harkins said. "Maybe Drake came looking for Moira, and Boone followed him."

"How did Drake find this place?"

The two men looked around, and Harkins spotted the jeep at a nearby intersection, the driver looking dejected as he spoke to an MP. He pointed. "Drake used the same driver Kathleen used, I'll bet."

"Goddamn it," Colianno said.

"Still doesn't explain why Boone would shoot Drake, if that's what happened."

"He's on a goddamned Bonnie and Clyde shooting spree, you ask me," Colianno said. "At least Stephenson got what he deserved."

"Drake didn't," Harkins said. "Didn't deserve this."

The second safe house belonged to another of Colianno's family members, a cousin named Giovanna. On the short ride over, the paratrooper explained that Giovanna's husband had been drafted into the Italian Army and had died of dysentery in North Africa in 1941.

Colianno parked the jeep on the sidewalk next to an old woman who was sitting on a low stool, selling fruit from a basket at her feet. Colianno killed the engine and greeted her, but the woman yelled something unfriendly back. She kept up an angry patter as the Americans walked away.

"She upset you almost ran over her toes?" Harkins asked. When Colianno didn't answer, Harkins asked, "What'd she say? *Infamia?* What's that?"

Colianno stopped, looked back at the old woman, then at Harkins. "It means something bad somebody does. There's a word in English. Infamy, like FDR used in his speech."

"'Cause you parked on the sidewalk?"

"No, Lieutenant. It's because I'm Italian—I have a Palermo accent, like my parents. But I'm here as an invader."

The woman, seeing that they'd stopped, struggled to her feet, still complaining. Harkins watched her.

"What's she saying now?"

"She asked if I killed any Palermo boys."

Colianno turned and trotted ahead, leaving Harkins thinking about the position the paratrooper was in, here in his parents' country.

Jesus, Harkins thought.

Harkins followed his driver into a courtyard, where Colianno was already knocking on a door. Ronan answered, threw herself into Colianno's arms, and sobbed into his neck for nearly a minute.

I guess the charade is over, Harkins thought as he stood by awkwardly.

When Ronan pulled herself away, she looked at Harkins and said, "Sorry." He wasn't sure if she was apologizing for the tears; for the fact that she was AWOL; or for her relationship with Colianno, a private.

They walked inside and Harkins said, "First Sergeant Drake is dead."

"Jesus," Ronan said. She sank into a kitchen chair, put her head in her hands.

"Do you know who shot him?"

"Had to be Boone. He came to the door while I was talking to Drake. The first sergeant came to talk me into going back."

"What did you say?"

"I hadn't decided yet. He asked me if I knew what Stephenson had on Boone."

"And?" Harkins asked, hoping she'd remembered something.

"I never got a chance to answer. That's when Boone started knocking on the door, hollering 'Let me in.' Drake told me to go out the back. I came here, and Giovanna left with her son."

Harkins looked around. There was a flimsy shelf affixed to one wall. On it, a photo of a small boy in a cardboard frame. The boy looked to be about six, with big, dark eyes and straight black hair. Another photo showed a young man in an Italian Army uniform, a baby in a white christening gown, and a young woman, presumably Giovanna. The husband looked serious; Giovanna had allowed a tiny smile at the corners of her mouth.

"There's no way I'm going back now," Ronan said. "Not until Boone is arrested."

"We'll need your testimony to put Boone at the scene," Harkins said.

"Can't you arrest Boone based on what Moira already told you?" Colianno wanted to know.

"Yeah, although it's going to be tricky, arresting a senior officer, a commander, right in his own backyard," Harkins said.

"I've been thinking about Boone and Stephenson," Ronan said.

"You recall something?"

"Remember Whitman, the nurse who choked to death right after we got to Sicily? She said something once about Boone. At the time I didn't think it meant much, now I don't know."

"OK," Harkins said.

"Boone told her he'd be all set once he got back to the States. She thought he was talking about money."

"The black market?" Harkins asked.

"That's what I asked, but she didn't think so. She didn't say why."

"Was he the father of her baby?"

Ronan shrugged. "Could have been, I guess. They spent some time together; off duty, I mean. But they would have been an odd couple."

"How so?"

"Whitman was vivacious, always cheerful, and cute as a button. Boone is a sourpuss, looks like a scarecrow, and acts like he's seventy years old. Not sure it matters, anyway, because once Stephenson started paying attention to her, I don't think she talked to any other doc."

"OK, thanks," Harkins said. He left Colianno and Ronan alone and went back outside to the jeep.

Maybe Boone had been a jilted lover. Maybe Whitman had tossed him out in favor of Stephenson. It was possible, but probably not provable without testimony from the dead Whitman or a confession by Boone.

But *money*. Now, that could be a reason to kill someone.

33

4 August 1943
2130 hours

Harkins and Colianno spent the better part of the day at the crime scene and driving around Palermo making sure Ronan was safe. It was dark by the time the nurse was settled enough to stay on her own again. Colianno finally persuaded Giovanna to come back and keep the nurse company, although she left her son with friends. As the GIs left, Giovanna brought out an ancient *lupara* and laid it on the kitchen table. Colianno asked her about it.

"What did she say?" Harkins asked.

"Any more Americans show up and I'm not with them, she's going to shoot first."

They drove south on the Via Oreto, the dark hills south of the city still visible above the rooftops. A column of three U.S. Army deuce-and-a-half trucks pulled out in front of them before they cleared the city proper, forcing them to slow down. When the trucks stopped on the narrow road to let vehicles traveling in the opposite direction go by, Colianno leaned on the tinny horn.

"Come on, for chrissakes."

Harkins, sitting in the passenger seat, had a good look at the man in the passenger seat of the last jeep to pass them. It was the sergeant who'd come looking for Colianno.

"You see that?" Colianno asked. He'd seen the man, too.

"Your friend from last night," Harkins said.

When the traffic ahead of them cleared and they drove out of the city, the road went from paved to unpaved, although it was a bit wider. Harkins turned in his seat and saw the blackout lights of a vehicle following them.

"Can you see who it is?" Colianno asked. He didn't seem excited, and certainly not worried.

"No," Harkins said. "You ready to tell me what that was about last night?"

Colianno remained silent.

"Stubborn, aren't you?" Harkins said, then turned in his seat again. Behind him, he could hear the other vehicle's engine straining to close the gap, and he could tell by the sound that it was a jeep, not a truck.

"The bastard's trying to catch us," Harkins said. He turned front again and told Colianno, "Just keep driving. If that's the gang from last night, we don't have time for this shit."

When Harkins turned around again, the other jeep was gaining on them. They were doing maybe twenty miles an hour through the dark.

"Goddamn it, can't you drive faster?"

"Might be better to get this over with, Lieutenant."

"What the hell are you talking about? We have to find Kathleen and figure out where Boone is. *I'll* decide when we stop and for what."

And that's when the jeep behind clipped them, the driver using his right front bumper to bang Harkins' jeep on the left rear. It was a tactic Harkins had seen used in a police chase in Philadelphia, and it worked the same way here. Colianno turned the steering wheel against the spin, but the jeep skidded sideways into a shallow roadside ditch just deep enough to stop the tires and make the engine stall.

"What the fuck, Colianno?" Harkins yelled. "Get us the hell out of here!"

Colianno, still silent, pressed the starter. Harkins got out of the jeep and stepped from the ditch into the road just as three men approached.

One of them said, "Looks like you're having problems, there, Lieutenant."

There was enough moonlight for Harkins to see them clearly now. The short man, the one who'd done all the talking last night, was a buck sergeant, about Colianno's height but at least thirty pounds heavier.

"What the hell was that about, Sergeant?"

The two soldiers who'd been in the sergeant's jeep stepped up, one on each side of Harkins.

"Your boy there knows."

Colianno was out of the jeep, standing beside and a bit behind Harkins.

"This ain't got nothing to do with you, Lieutenant," the sergeant added.

He looked like a circus strongman, all arms and chest, skinny legs. The two guys with him were both big; the one to Harkins' left easily went two hundred pounds. The man to his right was close to that. They projected confidence, a little swagger, but moved flat-footed.

"We come for this piece of shit," the sergeant said, indicating Colianno.

"He's not leaving here with you," Harkins said.

"Says who?" the big man on Harkins' right said. Up close, Harkins could see that his face was scarred by acne. He had thick lips and breathed through his mouth.

Harkins reached down to his hip.

"You going to shoot us, Lieutenant?" the sergeant said. "'Cause we're unarmed." The three held their hands up. "Our weapons are in our jeep back there."

"It's always an option," Harkins said.

"How about you just step out of the way. Then nobody gets hurt."

Harkins looked at Colianno. Normally the skinny paratrooper was bristling for a fight, any fight, but now he just looked sad.

"It's OK, Lieutenant," Colianno said, unbuckling his pistol belt and lowering his weapon to the ground. "This won't take long."

"Who asked you?" Harkins shot back at him.

Then, to the other three, Harkins said, "I've got work to do, and this man is helping me. So you three clowns get the hell out of here and, if you're lucky, I'll forget that you ran us off the road."

"Or what?" the private on Harkins' left said.

Harkins stepped closer to the soldier. He did not want to throw the first punch, but he was ready.

The big man couldn't resist the temptation of Harkins being so close. He threw a clumsy roundhouse that Harkins easily ducked. Straightening up, he threw a quick jab, caught the GI square on his nose, which made a wet, crackling sound, an egg hitting a sidewalk. The kid went down to his knees, both hands pressed to his face, moaning.

"I got to fight this other guy, Lieutenant," Colianno said, tilting his head to the sergeant.

Harkins still had no idea what was going on, but Colianno was clear on what he wanted.

"Jesus Christ," Harkins said. "OK, then. One on one." Looked like Boone would have to wait.

The bleeding man stayed down. His partner, the other big private, was glued in place, had not even moved his feet, had not said a word.

The sergeant approached Colianno with his fists up. Colianno raised his arms in a defensive posture, like a boxer pressed back to the ropes. The sergeant hit him in the face, jabbing right through the paratrooper's hands.

Harkins had seen Colianno fight. When his blood was up, he was like a man possessed. Now he was something opposite. He did not seem afraid, just resigned.

The sergeant hit him again, and Colianno made no move to block it.

On the ground, the bleeding soldier found his voice. "Hit him, Sarge! Kill him!"

The sergeant threw two quick jabs, both of which connected.

"Don't do that," the sergeant yelled at Colianno. "Don't just stand there!"

The sergeant swung again, catching Colianno on the side of the head, then followed with a right to the body. The paratrooper doubled over and Harkins heard the wind go out of him. Still, Colianno had not thrown a punch.

Now the sergeant seemed furious, angry that Colianno would not fight back. He began hammering the paratrooper as if hitting a heavy bag. Left, right, left, right. They were not jackhammer blows, nothing meant to put Colianno down. The sergeant was punishing him, and Colianno was taking it. Willingly, even. The soldier who'd been egging on the sergeant fell silent.

The sergeant's arms were getting tired. Harkins, who'd spent years in Philadelphia gyms, knew how exhausting it was to throw punch after punch, even at an unresisting opponent.

"Fight me, you little wop bastard!" the sergeant said, on the edge of screaming, maybe crying.

Finally, Colianno, his face bloody, wrapped the sergeant with both arms in a clinch.

The sergeant freed one fist and hammered the back of Colianno's head, then his back. Colianno managed to pull his attacker to the ground.

The two men rolled in the dirt, the sergeant crying, Colianno saying something to him in a low voice.

Finally they stopped, entwined, like men who had pulled each other from a shipwreck. Colianno spoke in the same low tone. Harkins looked around. Both soldiers who had come with the sergeant were staring at their feet.

"Did he?" the sergeant asked Colianno, his voice strangled with grief. "Did he?"

Colianno let go of the other man and sat back on his haunches. The sergeant got to all fours, then stood up, wiping snot from his face with the back of a sleeve. He looked at Harkins, then at his two comrades, then at Colianno.

"Fuck it," he said. He turned and walked away, the other two men following behind.

Harkins had no idea what he had just witnessed.

He helped Colianno to his feet, then led him to the jeep, where he found a first-aid kit and started dressing the cuts on the paratrooper's face.

Colianno, his head tilted back, stared at Harkins with one eye that had not swollen shut.

"Well?" Harkins said.

Colianno waited, and to Harkins it looked as if he were weighing whether he wanted to explain anything.

"You might have heard from your brother that our drop was all screwed up."

"He said guys were scattered all over the place," Harkins said. "Just linked up with the first Americans they found."

"Yeah, that happened to me. Wandering around in the dark, every little noise making me want to piss my pants. Finally I caught on with a group. Couldn't see anybody—it was still dark—but we got in some kind of order and moved out cross-country, looking for more of our guys, I guess, and our objectives.

"We ran smack into an Italian patrol, everybody shooting at everybody. Can't see dick. No plan, no idea what we're dealing with. Finally, they pulled back, left one of their guys, a kid. He was wounded in the leg and couldn't stand. I wrapped the wound and talked to him, you know, just to calm him down. He was scared shitless.

"And when the sun came up, our guys—there were ten of us who had found each other—our guys came over one by one to look at him. He wasn't very scary when you saw him in daylight. I'd be surprised if he weighed a hundred pounds. Had this pathetic little mustache, skinny arms.

"Anyway, he finally got up the nerve to ask for a cigarette. So I gave him one and he thanked me. He was just sitting there, smoking.

"There was a sergeant in the group, name of White; he was from some other company in the regiment. I didn't know him, but he was the only noncom, so he was in command, you know? And a couple of the guys started asking him what we were going to do, when we were going to move, how we were going to find our units. We were from different companies, different battalions, even. White told me to stop talking wop gibberish to the prisoner, and I said something like, 'He ain't hurting anybody. He's just a kid, and happy the war is over for him.'

"And White said that General Patton had warned everyone not to trust the Germans and Italians, even when we took them prisoner, because they could turn on you. Shoot you in the back when you weren't paying attention, some bullshit like that. I said, 'What's he gonna shoot you with? His fucking finger?'

"And one of the other troopers, some goofy kid from Oregon or some goddamned place, said, 'Well, geez, Sarge. He don't seem so dangerous to me.'

"And White was just staring at the prisoner. Not saying anything, just watching. And finally he said, 'OK, saddle up. We're moving out.'

"And I stood up and said, 'Well, this kid can't walk. Maybe we leave him here and the guys coming over the beach will find him.'

"'We could do that,' White says. Then he walks over to the prisoner—I'm standing right next to where this kid is sitting on the ground. And White shoots him in the forehead with his rifle. Bam. No warning. Didn't even change the expression on his face. 'Now you don't have to worry so much about your little dago friend,' he says to me."

Colianno locked eyes with Harkins.

"Kid looked like one of my cousins," he said. "Shit, could easily have been a cousin."

Harkins moved slowly, poured some water from his canteen onto a bandage and handed it to Colianno, who used it to wipe blood from a split lip. They sat quietly for a few minutes. A jeep stopped; two GIs inside asked Harkins if he needed help getting out of the ditch.

"I think we got it," he told them. "Thanks anyway."

When they'd driven away, Harkins turned back to Colianno. "What'd you do?"

"Everybody was moving out, so I just started walking. I didn't really know what was happening. I mean, I had seen it with my own eyes; hell, the kid's blood splashed all over my boots. But I still had a hard time believing it, you know?"

"Yeah," Harkins said, leaning against the jeep. He had already figured out the rest of the story and wasn't sure he wanted to hear it.

"That sergeant you fought, he a friend of White's?"

"His brother," Colianno said. "He's in the Forty-Fifth Division."

Harkins looked down at his shoes. "What happened to White?"

"We took some fire from a pillbox later in the day; this is still D-Day. Not effective fire. Didn't come near hitting any of us. We crawled up on the box to throw grenades in. I was on point, and I called out in Italian for them to surrender.

"And the guys inside said they wanted to give up. Said there'd been a German noncom with them, you know, to make them fight. But they'd killed the Kraut and just wanted to surrender. There were three of them, and they were really scared.

"So I say, 'I'm taking these men prisoner,' and White comes up behind me—he's not even crawling, he's just walking up to the pillbox. He's got, maybe, four grenades in his hands, and he says, 'The hell you are.'

"He tosses one at the aperture, but it bounces off and explodes on the ground, outside the pillbox. And now the guys inside are screaming and pleading with me to save them."

Colianno had a faraway look. He was back at that pillbox on D-Day, a place, Harkins thought, he'd visit in years of nightmares.

"So you did," Harkins said. "You saved them."

Colianno nodded. "Yeah. I shot White. He kind of sat down, looking at me. Then just fell back."

Harkins looked at his driver, his face lit by a distant streetlight. Justified or not, he had just confessed to a murder, probably expected Harkins to arrest him.

I'm a lawman, Harkins had told Patrick.

Colianno had been taught to kill in the name of some cause: God, country, patriotism, good versus evil, us versus them, all of it abstract. He had killed, probably, men who'd been trying to kill him. He'd risked his life for a squad-mate he detested; had killed again to stop a further crime.

"The other guys out there, they all saw what happened, and somebody said something, I guess, because White's brother found out. Your brother, Father Pat, has been asking around. Only a matter of time before he finds out everything, too."

Harkins wondered what his brother would do when he learned that Colianno had killed another paratrooper. Patrick was far from the typical priest, had never been one to think the world was black-and-white, damned-or-saved.

Thinking about Patrick made Harkins consider his own reaction. As a cop, he'd seen life in too many shades of gray to think there was always an easy answer.

"So, you gonna turn me in?"

"I don't think so," Harkins said. "Maybe we'll wind up in adjoining cells in the stockade."

34

4 August 1943
2300 hours

Harkins and Colianno drove back up the hill to the hospital area. From a sharp turn in the road above Palermo, Harkins could see flashes on the eastern horizon.

"Artillery," Colianno said, braking, slowing to negotiate a narrow spot in the road.

Harkins looked to the east, where yellow light bounced off the underside of a few clouds, the sound reaching them later. The horizon was a tableau of backlit hills, the rugged central plateau of the island.

"Something going on," the paratrooper said above the noise of the jeep's engine. "Sustained fire like that means we're getting ready to move forward, or the Krauts are coming this way and we're trying to stop them."

"Kathleen said Patton wants to beat the Brits to Messina," Harkins said.

"That man scares me."

The jeep's blackout drive did not shine forward. The narrow strips of dim light were barely enough to warn oncoming drivers that another vehicle was approaching. The best they could do on the narrow road was a few miles an hour, and there were places where a man walking might have outpaced them.

"What's the plan when we get to the hospital?" Colianno asked.

"Check on Kathleen," Harkins said.

"That'll make her happy all over again, us hanging around."

"I'm going to arrest Boone," Harkins said, leaning forward in his seat, willing the jeep to go faster. "I wish I had my handcuffs. Nothing as satisfying as slapping the bracelets on somebody who thinks he can't be touched."

"Then what?"

"We send for Captain Adams, bring Ronan back in the morning with her story. Then, whenever the provost gets back from his meeting in Tunisia, we all march in there and present our case."

Just talking through it made Harkins' pulse quicken. The beat cop had accomplished something after all.

"We all?"

"Well, me, Adams, and Ronan. Maybe you can go back tomorrow with Captain Adams and get your witness, that old neighbor lady, to identify Boone as the guy she saw pounding on your aunt's door."

"So we get him for Drake's murder. What about Stephenson?"

"A lot of suspects, once there's a crack in their story, the whole thing gives way. I wouldn't be surprised if Boone confesses to everything."

Colianno was silent, and Harkins figured he was unconvinced. But he'd seen this before, heard detectives' stories of suspects confessing to strings of crimes, one after another, the cops taking notes as fast as they could write.

"What's going to happen to you after this is over?"

"If I don't go to jail, you mean?" Harkins said.

He'd thought about this, wondered if going back to breaking up traffic jams was going to be enough for him.

"I don't know, to tell you the truth."

"What's going to happen to me?" Colianno asked.

"Well, I think my brother is trying to arrange it so you can go back to your unit. If that doesn't work out, maybe Captain Adams and the provost will want you. You seem to have a knack for investigations."

In the dim light from dash instruments, Harkins thought he saw Colianno smile.

"What's funny?"

"Me, a copper. Be a big change for my family."

"How's that?"

"My two older brothers have both spent time in the can. Liked to boost delivery trucks. My mom says they're the reason she has the white hair."

At the entrance to the hospital compound they found themselves behind four or five ambulances jamming the road. Orderlies and nurses hurried about, red-filtered flashlights bobbing at crazy angles, light spilling from blackout curtains as dozens of hands pulled at the ambulance doors. There was a rush to get the stretcher cases out and into the surgical tents, and there were more wounded than there were people to help.

A woman stepped in front of them and pounded on the hood of their jeep with a closed fist.

"You two, give us a hand here!"

Colianno looked over at Harkins.

"Shit," Harkins said. He was about to tell the woman they had another mission—he needed to find Kathleen and pinpoint Boone—when the nurse banged on the jeep's hood again.

"I said move your asses!"

"All right," Harkins said. "Pull over."

Colianno squeezed the jeep off the main track and the two men jumped out, Colianno slinging a rifle over his shoulder. Inside the ambulances, stretchers were "racked and stacked" like triple bunk beds on either side of the vehicle's boxy rear end.

"Grab this one," the nurse told Harkins, tapping the handles on a stretcher in the middle of the right stack. He couldn't see her well in the dark, but he heard her distinct accent, New York, and she was clearly used to being obeyed.

"And don't fucking drop anyone."

Harkins took the handles and pulled, but nothing happened. Colianno jumped inside, grabbed the other end of the same stretcher, and tried to yank it free of the rack. The wounded soldier, whose entire upper torso was a cocoon of dirty bandages, groaned.

A feeble voice from a stretcher on the other side of the vehicle said, "You gotta undo the clips, one on each handle."

Harkins turned on his own flashlight, found the clips. As he slipped them off, he glanced to his left, where a waif-thin GI held a large compress to his own left ear.

"Thanks, pal," Harkins said. The kid smiled on one side of his mouth, then turned his head to look straight up at the stretcher above him, just a few inches away from his face.

"You got it?" Colianno asked.

"Yeah, come toward me."

Harkins stepped off the back running board, reaching for the ground with his right foot, bending his arms to keep the stretcher level as he descended. Colianno, still inside the cramped ambulance, bent at the waist to lower his end, but the stretcher and patient yawed to the left.

"Watch it," Harkins said.

They were a pair of inept movers, suddenly entrusted with some family's most valuable possession.

Harkins was on the ground now, straining to keep his end above his shoulders. He looked behind him, then turned back to see Colianno, and that's when the blood flowed off the stretcher and onto his face.

Harkins sputtered, spit, shook his head to clear his eyes, like a swimmer surfacing after a dive. "Jesus!"

"You drop that stretcher and Jesus won't be able to save you," New York Nurse said. "Your ass will be mine."

The GI they were carrying was a big man, not Drake-big, but bigger than either Harkins or Colianno. Harkins' palms were sweaty, slippery. He braced the handles against his leg to tighten his grip.

There was a scrum of orderlies and nurses, and now what sounded like a few docs, checking patients for what Harkins knew was triage: a grim separating of those who could be saved with immediate help from those who could wait and, finally, from those who probably could not be saved with the resources at hand. He had learned about triage in training, but had never seen it up close.

"Where do we go?" Harkins asked the crowd.

New York Nurse appeared at his elbow. "Surgical One, straight ahead."

Harkins turned; she did not come up to his shoulder. "We go right inside?"

"No, wait outside. If no one comes up to you after a minute or so, start hollering for help."

Harkins and Colianno dodged forward amid the confusion. The track leading to the surgical tents was mostly blocked by ambulances and other stretcher bearers, every team trying to move quickly. Harkins was in front, and for a few yards he was able to make his way forward by the light from one of the tent entrances as someone held the blackout curtain open. Then the curtain shut and he was back in darkness, blinking his eyes to adjust.

"You know where we're going?" Colianno said. Harkins thought he was carrying the man's feet, Colianno the head.

"I think so."

Harkins' palms slipped and he fought back, gripping the wooden handles more tightly. He felt a blister on one hand peel away, leaving a patch of raw skin the size of a silver dollar. He squeezed harder.

Then, bizarrely, an image from his childhood. He and Patrick at a church-run camp in Pennsylvania's Pocono Mountains, canoeing on a lake when a thunderstorm rolled up on them. They had turned back toward the dock—an impossibly long way across—as the sky went purple and rain battered them like thrown gravel and lightning split a tree on the bank behind them. He remembered how the hair on his arms tingled, how the air smelled like steel, how he'd nearly pissed his pants. Behind him, Patrick unable to get past the first line of a desperate prayer: "Hail Mary, full of grace; hail Mary, full of grace; hail Mary, full of grace;" and Harkins, same beat, saying instead, "Don't stop, never stop. Don't stop, never stop. Don't stop, never stop."

They made it to the door of Surgical One, but Harkins, hands full, could not open the flap. There was probably something medical people said at this point, a special "open sesame," but Harkins had no idea what might open the door.

"Help!"

Nothing. Behind him, Colianno yelled, "We need help here!"

The patient had not made a sound since they lifted him from the ambulance.

Harkins tried balancing the right handle against his leg to see if he could open the tent flap. As soon as he loosed his grip, the stretcher slipped five or six inches. Harkins felt his left shoulder pop, an old boxing injury, like someone was trying to take his arm away to use elsewhere.

Harkins was about to yell again when the blackout curtain parted, and Kathleen Donnelly motioned him in.

Thank God.

She did not look at Harkins, but only at the patient.

"He been triaged?" she asked.

"I don't know," Harkins said. "No. We brought him straight from the ambulance."

Donnelly leaned over the stretcher, was joined a second later by Wilkins. The doctor thrust his hand beneath the cocoon of dirty cotton on the boy's chest.

"Outside," he said, pivoting and hurrying back to the chaos. If Wilkins had recognized Harkins, he gave no sign.

Donnelly looked at Harkins, all business. "Outside," she repeated. "To the left. Take him off the stretcher; we have to use that again right away. Wrap him up, though."

Harkins did not move immediately. His eyes had fixed on a large metal trash can that sat against the tent wall. A bloody, amputated leg stuck out of the top.

Donnelly touched his arm, leading him back to the door.

"Go on, now," she said, gentleness in her voice. Men dying all around, Donnelly still looking to comfort. Then she turned to the operating tables, the bright lights, the bloody ballet of surgical teams, and in two quick strides was back in her element.

Outside, Harkins and Colianno found two ranks of bodies, maybe twelve men, lying on the ground, wrapped in GI blankets. They put their burden down, gently rolling him onto a blanket handed them by an orderly. When the body was faceup, Harkins folded the edges of the blanket to the man's chin.

"We supposed to do something with the dog tags?" Harkins asked the orderly, who seemed to be in charge of this growing platoon of dead.

"No," the man said. "We'll take care of that." Then, "You guys all right? You're not assigned to the hospital, are you?"

"MPs. Rolling in when the ambulances came. Just lending a hand."

"Look," Colianno said. He had pulled the man's dog tags from his shirt collar, laid them gently on the bandages around the soldier's chest. Clipped to the same chain was a silver medal.

Colianno flipped his lighter to see, fingered the medal, tucked it back inside the man's blouse. "It's the Blessed Mother," he said. "I had one just like it. Lost it in the jump on D-Day." The paratrooper ran his tongue over his swollen lip. "My mother says the rosary every day. Got a statue of Mary in the front room, practically a shrine. She says Mary listens to mothers' prayers."

Colianno pulled the blanket over the dead man's face, tucked the corners in gently behind his head. He looked up, tried a limp smile. "Hope my mom is better at praying than this guy's mom was."

Harkins thought about his mother, her unanswered prayers for her youngest, disappeared into a vast ocean. And suddenly he was choking back a sob, and his vision swam in hot tears.

The orderly was still standing there, Harkins and Colianno kneeling on the ground on either side of the corpse, Harkins with his hands pressed to his face.

Colianno lifted his hand to the neat rows.

"You get used to this?" he asked the orderly.

"God, I fucking hope not."

35

5 August 1943
0245 hours

Harkins and Colianno helped move casualties until the hysteria died down and the New York nurse sent them away.

"Go get some rest," she said. "And thanks."

The two men had not seen Boone during the rush of casualties. They looked in the surgical tents, the wards, his admin tent, and even the mess tent, where a half-dozen coffee-jangled docs and nurses had gathered to talk each other down. No one had seen Boone.

It was nearly three A.M. when they parked their jeep near the nurses' admin tent, which had become Harkins' de facto headquarters. The two men fell asleep sitting up in their respective seats, were still asleep when Captain Adams, the deputy provost, woke them just as the eastern sky showed pink.

"You two had quite the day yesterday," Adams said.

"Helluva night, too," Harkins managed before he was fully awake.

"What the hell happened to your face?" Adams asked Colianno. The paratrooper was able to open one eye fully, the swollen one only partially.

"It's a long story, sir," Colianno said.

Adams shook his head. "I'll bet," he said. Then, to Harkins, "Sergeant Sutherland briefed me on Drake's murder. Said he thought you have a suspect."

"Boone," Harkins said. "Drake found Ronan, and they were inside talking when Boone showed up and started pounding on the door. We have a witness that will put Boone there, by the way. So Drake sends Ronan out the back, and next thing you know, Drake is dead on the floor and Boone is in the wind."

"What was Ronan doing out in Palermo?"

"I stashed her at my aunt's house," Colianno said. "So she'd be safe."

"Donnelly got assaulted last night," Harkins added. "I thought the nurses were in danger."

"So why didn't you stash Donnelly, too?"

"She refused to go," Harkins said. "But I figured I could at least get Ronan out of here. Boone had started shipping nurses out, every nurse who had stood up to him."

"So Ronan is AWOL?"

"For her own protection. Boone was armed when he followed her. You ever see a doctor wearing a sidearm? I doubt very seriously he went there to shoot Drake. I think he was after Ronan."

"Jesus," Adams said. "You really think he was going to kill one of his own nurses?"

"There's something about Boone making a lot of money here in Sicily. Ronan heard something from Whitman, that nurse that maybe choked to death."

"*Maybe* choked to death?" Adams asked.

"I got some questions about that, too."

"So are we talking about the black market? Boone is selling stuff? Is that how Drake wound up dead?"

"If it's black market, I doubt Drake was involved. Besides, it looked to me like there was a struggle inside the house. Drake and Boone."

"So Ronan saw Boone?" Adams asked.

"No. She heard him through the door before she went out the back."

"So this witness who saw Boone there is also the one who saw that he was armed, that right?"

"Yes."

Harkins knew the next question, knew Adams would not be thrilled with the answer.

"So who's the witness?"

Harkins looked at Colianno, who said, "A neighbor lady of my aunt's."

"Great," Adams said. "And let me guess—just based on how this is unfolding so far—this is some old lady who doesn't speak English and has bad eyesight."

"I never said she had bad eyesight," Colianno said.

Adams sat in the passenger seat of Harkins' jeep; he looked as tired as Harkins felt.

"This is one screwed-up hospital," Adams said.

All around them, exhausted orderlies and nurses prepared for another day of treating wounded men. Harkins wondered if anyone had moved last night's dead.

"Be right back, Lieutenant," Colianno said, walking in the direction of the latrine.

When the paratrooper was out of earshot, Adams said, "Do you know your brother has heard rumors that your man there killed another paratrooper on D-Day?"

"Yeah, Pat told me," Harkins said. *And Colianno confessed,* he thought. "Any evidence?"

"Nothing concrete that I know of," Adams said. "Sounds like the paratroopers are clamming up. But right now you've got another problem. Boone isn't in the wind, he met the provost at the Palermo airfield this morning. He's coming here to talk to you."

This was not what Harkins wanted to hear.

"I wanted to talk to the provost before Boone did, but we'll at least get a chance to brief him, right?" Harkins said.

"Maybe, maybe not. But you can expect him to play by the rules."

"Meaning?"

"Colonel Meigs is an Old Army guy," Adams said. "Commanded an infantry company in the last war; does everything by the book."

"Drake was like that, a hard-ass. Not quite so old."

"Drake was a girl scout compared to Meigs. He's not just going to take your word over Boone's; he'll listen to all sides. And he's not going to like the fact that your key witness is an AWOL nurse."

"What do you think we should do?" Harkins asked.

"Talk fast and hope for the best, I guess."

36

5 August 1943
0830 hours

Wilbur Meigs was a full colonel, like Boone, but nearly old enough to be Boone's father. Harkins stood at attention in front of Boone's field table desk when the two senior officers entered, trailed by Adams. Boone had ordered Colianno to wait outside.

"Lieutenant, I'm Colonel Meigs, and this is a preliminary look at the investigation you've been running here, which, in Colonel Boone's opinion, has been slapdash and even harmful to his command."

Meigs sat, put his helmet down, lined it up exactly with the table's edge. There was a small, framed photo of a younger Boone with a woman. The woman was not pretty, and neither of them smiled. Harkins had seen class pictures with more intimacy. Meigs moved the photo carefully, then looked up. "You may stand at ease."

Harkins spread his feet shoulder-width apart, hands clasped in the small of his back.

Meigs had once been tall, but was now bent over, gnomish, almost. He still had a thick shock of white hair, brush cut. Tobacco-stained fingers turned in toward his palms. Arthritis, maybe. He walked with a cane, his right leg so stiff that Harkins wondered if it were a prosthetic. When he leaned the cane against the field table Harkins glanced down quickly: the knob was a silver lion's head.

"Have you determined who killed Captain Stephenson?" Meigs asked.

"Not yet, sir," Harkins said. "But—"

"And you are using as your driver a private from the Eighty-Second Airborne Division, is that right?"

"Yes, sir. Private first class, actually. Name's—"

"And you are aware that this private is alleged to have had a sexual relationship with one of the nurses?"

Boone, standing behind Meigs, allowed himself a tiny smile.

Meigs pulled a notebook from his breast pocket, held it at arm's length, squinted. "A Second Lieutenant Moira Ronan, I believe. Correct?"

"Allegedly, yes, sir."

"And you know that such relations between officers—even officers of relative ranks like our beloved nurses—that such relations are against regulations?"

"Yes, sir."

"Where is this Nurse Ronan?"

Boone answered. "AWOL, Colonel. In Palermo, I suspect. Hidden in a private home there by Lieutenant Harkins and Private Colianno."

"You *helped* Ronan go AWOL?" Meigs asked Harkins.

"Sir, if I can explain—"

"You'll get a chance to explain, Lieutenant. I want to establish a few facts first. Context, as it were."

"Yes, sir."

"So you helped Nurse Ronan go AWOL. I assume, then, that you did not alert Colonel Boone as to her location. Did not inform her commander."

"She was hiding from Colonel Boone, sir. And with good reason."

"Oh, and why was that?"

"Initially because Colonel Boone was going to ship her to Tunisia, so that she couldn't be part of the investigation."

"Into Stephenson's death?" Meigs asked.

"Lieutenant Ronan reported that Stephenson had raped her. That Colonel Boone has tolerated a command climate in which that kind of behavior was allowed to flourish."

"That's a serious accusation, Lieutenant," Meigs said. "A very serious accusation against a senior officer and respected surgeon."

"There's more, sir. Another nurse was assaulted, and I think it was connected."

"Who was that?"

"Nurse Donnelly, sir. Kathleen Donnelly."

"Is she OK?"

"Seems to be, mostly."

"Was Nurse Donnelly also sexually assaulted?"

"Not that I know of, sir. Knocked down. She fought back."

"And you have a theory that this was to dissuade her from—what, exactly?"

"I think it was to discourage me from investigating any further. Nurse Donnelly and I are friends, were friends back in the neighborhood where we grew up."

"So we have a nurse who was knocked down, and another who says she was sexually assaulted. Do you have any evidence of rape other than the word of this AWOL nurse?"

"Several of the nurses told me they were constantly harassed, subject to groping and unwanted advances."

"Any of them report being raped? By Doctor Stephenson or anyone else?"

"No, sir."

"But they reported, what, a not-so-great work environment?"

"That would be one way to characterize it, yes, sir."

"And you have these interviews in your notes?"

"Yes, sir."

Meigs leaned back in the folding chair, studying Harkins. He reached for his cane and absentmindedly ran his thumb back and forth across the top of the lion's head. Harkins' mouth was dry; he could feel bits of skin on his sun-chapped lips.

"Go on, Lieutenant."

"First Sergeant Drake found Nurse Ronan in Palermo, found out where she was staying."

"How did he do that?"

"He figured out which motor pool driver knew where she was."

"Whose house was this? The one where Nurse Ronan was hiding."

"It belongs to a family member of my driver, Private First Class Colianno."

"The one who had a relationship with Ronan?"

"An alleged relationship, yes, sir." Harkins was flailing; he knew it, and so did everyone else in the room. He felt like he did when another boxer pushed him to the ropes. Had to get his feet under him.

"And then what?"

"Colonel Boone showed up at the same house. Ronan was inside talking to First Sergeant Drake when Colonel Boone knocked on the door and announced himself. She left—Drake told her to leave. Next thing we have is Drake shot to death."

Meigs pulled steel-rimmed spectacles from his pocket, wiped them with a snow-white handkerchief. He settled the glasses on his face, hooked the curved pieces behind ears that sported tufts of hair as big and as white as surgical bandages.

"So you have an AWOL nurse—not the best witness, by the way—who says she was raped by a doctor who obviously cannot tell his side of the story. You have other nurses who have complained the men were paying too much attention to them, were getting too friendly.

"You have a dead first sergeant, and this same nurse claims that she heard Colonel Boone's voice outside the apartment where the shooting took place. Did she see Colonel Boone?"

"No, sir. Just heard him. But we have another witness who will be able to identify Colonel Boone as the GI knocking on that door."

This was a stretch, as Harkins had not confirmed that the old woman who'd seen the tall GI could identify Boone.

"And this witness is?"

"A neighbor. An elderly Sicilian woman."

"Did she claim to have seen the first sergeant murdered?"

"No, sir."

"But you can find her again."

"I'm sure of it, sir."

"And she won't be confused? Doesn't think all Americans in uniform look alike?"

In Harkins' few visits to courtrooms in his police work, he'd seen defense attorneys poke enormous holes in the testimony of witnesses who had otherwise seemed strong and reliable. Meigs wasn't using those kinds of blitzkrieg techniques—the old man was trying to be judicious, fair—but Harkins felt his case getting weaker by the minute.

"You want to arrest Colonel Boone on the basis of thin evidence. You can see, certainly, that his arrest would interfere with the work of this hospital? That it would be a disruption, especially given the tragic loss of the first sergeant?"

"Yes, sir. I can see where that might cause problems, but there are other considerations, such as the safety of the staff, the nurses."

"Colonel Boone has advanced another theory of what happened here,"

Meigs said. He leaned back to glance at Boone, gave him an impatient, go-ahead nod.

"Let's set aside for a moment Lieutenant Ronan's claim about Stephenson," Boone said. "She has no proof, indeed did not make a complaint until you showed up and perhaps put it into her head."

"Don't *speculate,* Colonel," Meigs interrupted. "Let's all of us try a little less speculation and a little more fact."

"Yes, sir," Boone said.

Then, to Harkins again. "Did you know your driver, Private Colianno, is rumored—excuse me—is suspected of having murdered a fellow paratrooper on D-Day?"

Boone mispronounced Colianno's name: *Cold—ee—no.* Did it deliberately, Harkins thought. Petty little bastard.

"I heard something about that, yes, sir. But as you say, it's unsubstantiated. Like Lieutenant Ronan's claim, I guess."

Boone's eyes narrowed, and his cheeks flushed, though it might have been the heat.

"Colianno is a hothead, quite capable of violence. He was in trouble for brawling and would have been in the stockade if your brother, the chaplain, hadn't taken a personal interest. Isn't that right, Lieutenant?"

Harkins did not answer, but rocked forward onto the balls of his feet, then back onto his heels. Felt the red tide of his temper rise through his chest, rode it back down again.

"Was your driver with you during the time that First Sergeant Drake was murdered?" Meigs asked.

Colianno had been on Lindner's trail, out dealing with his cousins.

"No, sir," Harkins said.

"'No, sir' what?" Meigs asked.

"He was not with me that whole afternoon."

Boone jumped in. "And you've already admitted that he was at the house where Drake was killed. Knew where the house was."

Harkins drew a slow breath, unclenched his teeth.

He wanted to say that Whitman hadn't choked to death, and that Boone had signed a phony death certificate. He wanted to question Boone about how he made money in a war zone. But he didn't have anything solid, and he couldn't expose Kathleen and her ad hoc autopsy.

"You killed Drake," Harkins said. "And I'm going to arrest you for that."

Meigs interrupted. "We're familiar with your theories, Lieutenant. But I'm not sure you appreciate what you're asking me to do.

"You want me to take the word of an AWOL nurse that she heard Colonel Boone's voice, though she never saw him. And you want me to believe a local woman, an elderly woman, who may or may not testify that Colonel Boone was outside the apartment where a murder took place. Bear in mind that neither woman claims to have seen Colonel Boone murder anyone."

"Colonel Boone is a suspect in two murders. He's got good reason to lie," Harkins said.

"Now it's two murders," Meigs said. "Anything else you want to throw in?"

"Yes, sir. There's something going on with this Kraut doctor, Lindner."

Harkins knew he was talking too much, but it pissed him off that Boone's guilt, which was so clear to him last night, seemed to be getting lost in a muddy swirl. He plunged ahead, fighting off the ropes.

"Colonel Boone has kept Lindner around long after he should have been shipped out with the other POWs."

"Colonel Boone has explained, to my satisfaction, that this prisoner is a skilled surgeon whose talents complement the staff's abilities," Meigs said.

"There was some connection between Stephenson and Lindner," Harkins said. "Some connection among the three of them, I'm willing to bet."

"You're willing to *bet*? Is that how we're conducting investigations now?"

Harkins looked at Boone, who was sweating, holding his lips pressed together tightly, then down at Meigs.

The old man shook his head, as if this were all too sad. "Son," he said to Harkins, "you are making me tired. You've got to find some solid proof, some evidence."

"Permission to speak freely, sir?"

"I think it's pretty obvious that you just say whatever comes to your mind, Lieutenant. Why stop now?"

"Stephenson was dirty. I can prove that. Lindner is dirty, and I'll be able to prove that. And I think Colonel Boone is dirty. This place is a cesspool, thanks to him, and these women have been forced to swim in it. Sir."

Boone started to speak, but Meigs cut him off. "I'll want to see your interview notes with these other nurses," he said to Harkins. He looked over his shoulder, addressing Boone. "Those nurses are your soldiers," Meigs said to the colonel. "So of course you've got to take care of them just as you would take care of one of your privates. I will get to the bottom of their complaints, Colonel.

"As for you, Lieutenant," Meigs said to Harkins, "I'm warning you about making groundless accusations against an officer of Colonel Boone's status without hard evidence."

In some still-calm part of his brain, Harkins knew that he had lost this skirmish. He brought himself back to a proper "at ease" position, hands behind his back, weight even on both feet. Counted his breaths before he dared speak again. One. Two. Three.

"Yes, sir," Harkins said.

"You have a, let's call it a relationship, with this Nurse Donnelly? The one who was assaulted?"

Harkins kept his eyes straight ahead. The hospital was a small town, just as Kathleen had said.

"Yes, sir. I knew her back in high school."

"And she is close friends with Nurse Ronan?"

Harkins was about to say that the intertwined relationships did not cloud his judgment as an investigator, but he suddenly wasn't sure he believed that.

"How much sleep have you had in the last three days, Lieutenant?" Meigs asked. His voice was calm again, like someone's grandfather.

"Not much, sir. A few hours here and there."

"I'm taking you off this case completely. You will turn over all your notes and information to Captain Adams. You are to stay out of this hospital compound and away from Colonel Boone."

Harkins wanted to speak; was afraid he'd make it worse.

"You are to find this Lieutenant Ronan and bring her back straightaway. No telling what can happen to her out in Palermo. Then I want you to get some sleep. Report back to your military police unit by eighteen hundred hours tonight.

"Captain Adams," Meigs said.

"Yes, sir?"

"Arrest this private, the lieutenant's driver. I don't want him going AWOL while you begin your investigation. I imagine you'll consider him a suspect in First Sergeant Drake's murder, but that will be up to you to figure out.

"Lieutenant Harkins will deliver the nurse to you. This is a murder investigation. Let's not get sidetracked by a bunch of he-said-she-said accusations."

"Yes, sir," Adams said.

Meigs stood, removed his glasses, and picked up his helmet and cane. He limped around the front of the table, where Harkins stood at attention, facing forward. Meigs spoke into his left ear.

"You were a patrol officer in Philadelphia, right? Not a detective?"

"That's correct, sir."

"So this is really your first case. It's understandable that you might get carried away, become a bit overzealous. Don't be too hard on yourself." Meigs patted him on the shoulder, limped out.

Boone moved behind his desk, right into Harkins' line of sight. "Get the fuck out of my hospital."

Harkins came out of Boone's tent to find an MP he didn't recognize standing by his jeep. There was no sign of Colianno.

"Captain Adams asked me to stand by to make sure you got all this stuff OK," the soldier said.

Harkins looked in the back of the jeep. Colianno's weapons were there: the pistol with the decorated holster, the M1 carbine, an M1 Garand, a .45 caliber tommy gun, a switchblade, a fighting knife with a blade as long as a man's hand—its sheath probably still attached to Colianno's boot—and a set of brass knuckles with sharp studs.

"Do you know where they took him?" Harkins asked.

"Seventh Army stockade, I think. West of the city on the way to the airfield." The MP nodded to the arsenal. "Guy liked to be ready for anything, I guess, right, Lieutenant?"

"Not sure he was ready for this," Harkins said.

37

5 August 1943
1000 hours

Harkins drove back down the hill toward Palermo. There were even more army vehicles than usual on the road: trucks loaded with crates of ammunition, fuel tankers, wreckers, bridging equipment. He saw a flatbed with a tiny airplane on the back, wings folded like an insect's; artillery of every caliber being towed east. He had been so consumed with what was happening that he'd forgotten about the war, at least until he and Colianno had carried the dead man to surgery.

"Shit," he said to himself. Then, louder, pounding the steering wheel, "Shit, shit, shit!"

He had been so confident when Ronan told him she'd heard Boone's voice outside the door. Even when Adams woke him up this morning—after his two-hour sleep—he felt like today was going to be a good day. Boone would get what he deserved, the nurses would be safe, he'd be Kathleen's hero.

"What an ass."

Instead, he'd walked right into Boone's ambush. And it wasn't just that Boone had gotten to Meigs first. Meigs, Harkins believed, was trying to do the right thing. Harkins lacked evidence and believable testimony. He did not even have a theory that made sense, while Boone had cleverly chosen Colianno as a scapegoat. A powerless private with a history as a troublemaker.

Now Colianno was in the stockade and Boone was close to getting away with his crimes.

"You're doing a great job stirring things up," Harkins told himself.

He was so tired he could not see straight. He'd had to leave the hospital compound before he had a chance to grab any breakfast. The tank was empty, and he wanted to have his wits about him when he picked up Ronan. The two of them could work on making sure her story was tight. Perhaps there were some details she had not yet mentioned, other nurses who might come forward if coaxed.

Even if Meigs had contacted the military police and told them that Harkins was no longer on special duty and would be reporting back by eighteen hundred, he still had the day. For the morning, at least, he'd be one of those GIs wandering around as if on holiday, unmoored.

He rolled to the waterfront, toward the café owned by Colianno's cousin. The shutters were closed and locked but he knocked on the door around back until a young woman opened it. She was the owner's daughter, and Harkins recognized her from the endless parade of relatives who'd come out to greet Colianno.

"Any chance I can get some breakfast?" he asked. She looked at him blankly, so he opened his mouth and mimed shoveling food in.

"Sí, sí," she said, taking his arm and pulling him inside. He had all of Colianno's weapons, plus his own pistol belt. She led him to a chair in the kitchen, took the weapons from him and stacked them in a corner, as cool as if she handled firearms every day. She filled a ceramic pitcher with water, sliced two lemons and dropped them in, then put the pitcher and a single glass on a table beside him.

Harkins touched his chest. "Eddie," he said.

She smiled, touched her own chest, and said, "Adriana."

She was a teenager, a pretty girl with olive skin and a long braid that hung over one shoulder. A plain dress crimped at her tiny waist, a clean and well-worn apron. She was barefoot, and when she walked Harkins could see that the bottoms of her feet were black with dirt.

"Dominic?" she asked.

Harkins shook his head, made sure to smile so she wouldn't think something bad had happened.

She reached under a skirted table and pulled out a wooden crate with stenciled markings. She was about to serve him stolen American chow.

Adriana smiled at him as she whipped water into a bowl of reconstituted eggs. Harkins smiled back and said, "It's true. You people can steal anything you want from right under our noses."

Since it was clear he was talking to himself, she did not respond, but worked fast at the ancient iron stove. Minutes later she handed him the eggs, even put a little green sprig on the plate as a garnish. He drank half the pitcher of water, wishing she had stolen some coffee. By the time he finished eating, she had disappeared. He leaned his head back to the wall behind him, and in seconds he was asleep.

He woke to Adriana's voice, but opened his eyes to see two of Colianno's male cousins staring at him, their faces inches from his own. When he started, they laughed and one of them applauded. They'd thought he was dead.

The three Sicilians started talking at once, their voices rising and falling like birdsong. Soon they were arguing, ignoring Harkins. When he stood, the older of the two men turned to him and unleashed a barrage of sentences, nodding as he spoke, as if this might help the Irish-American cop understand.

It was the world's most frustrating game of charades, with the two men using their hands to describe something that might have been a box. Then one of them mimed walking toward the box, looking over his shoulder as he approached, then entering a doorway on tiptoe, closing the door behind him.

What the hell were they saying?

It was Adriana who had the idea to draw the scene on paper. In a few seconds she sketched a building with four doors, two stick figures approaching it. She pointed at the second stick figure, then at the younger of the two men, who nodded vigorously.

"Fausto," she said, touching the man's chest.

"Nice to meet you, Fausto," Harkins said.

Adriana touched the older man's chest. "Michelangelo."

"Eddie," Harkins said, touching his own chest, then shaking hands all around. "Nice work on those statues."

Adriana then pointed at the lead stick figure in the drawing and said, very clearly, "Kraut."

"Holy shit," Harkins said, standing. "It's the apartment building, right? The one Lindner was headed to when he made you guys, right?"

The three Sicilians looked at each other, shared a few sentences. Then Adriana turned to him, smiled, and said again, "Kraut."

Harkins sat back down. He and Colianno had asked them to find out who lived in the apartment building and then report back. But what had they found? He was as clueless as he had been ten minutes earlier.

From the miming of the tiptoe approach, it seemed as if they'd gone into the apartment. Did they find someone or something? If they did, what did they do to that person? Were they asking for further instructions? Maybe they had a body to dump. And, by the way, had Colianno promised to pay them?

"I am so goddamned lost here," Harkins said.

The older man pointed at himself, his cousin, and Harkins, then at the sketch of the building, and said, *"Vieni. Vieni."*

"Sure, great idea," Harkins said. "Let me just tag along while we break into someone's apartment. Just what I need to round out this whole fucked-up week."

Harkins walked to the corner, started gathering his collection of weapons, then decided to take just his own pistol belt.

"Don't sell this shit while I'm gone," he said to Adriana, who smiled at him.

He put on his equipment and considered his options. He was already so far out of bounds that he couldn't count how many rules he'd broken. He'd conspired with locals who may have broken into a civilian's apartment as part of an investigation he had been ordered to stay away from. He'd helped a U.S. Army nurse go AWOL, had accused a senior officer of murder. He was responsible for Colianno's arrest, and without Colianno to translate for him, he wasn't sure if the cousins had murdered someone in the apartment, or if they were holding a captive, or if they'd just engaged in a little B and E. And of course there was still the matter of the two murders, neither of them—officially at least—solved.

"Yeah, let's go and see how much more bizarre I can make this whole thing," Harkins said.

The four of them walked to the door, where Adriana stood on tiptoe to give him a sisterly kiss on the cheek.

"Ni videmu," she said.

Harkins smiled at her. "OK, thanks," he said.

Michelangelo and Fausto followed him out and climbed into the back of his jeep, settling in like a couple of VIPs.

Before he could put the vehicle in gear, a jeep with four MPs from Harkins' old platoon rolled toward them on the narrow street.

Sergeant Desmond, whose wife had stopped writing to him, was in the passenger seat, the ranking man. He saluted when he recognized Harkins.

"Morning, Lieutenant. How's it going?"

All four of the MPs were eyeing Harkins' passengers, every one of them wanting to ask what the hell was going on. Seventh Army headquarters let everyone know that no civilians were to ride around in U.S. Army jeeps. The rule became necessary when two drunk GIs and two civilian women were killed in a rollover a few days after the Americans reached Palermo.

"Oh, pretty good. Pretty good. I'm on this murder investigation, you know."

"Yeah, we heard. You about finished?"

"Oh, I'll be finished soon, I guess. What are you up to this morning?"

"Patrolling the waterfront."

The three junior soldiers were following Desmond's lead. If he didn't say anything about the civilians, they wouldn't either.

"Anything we can help you with?" Desmond asked, lifting his eyebrows.

"I can't think of anything at the moment, thanks. I should see you in a day or so."

"Good. That'll be good, Lieutenant. They gave us a temporary guy, a lieutenant from another unit. He's one of them salutin' fiends, though. Makes the boys kind of miss you."

Two of the GIs behind Desmond nodded. The driver was still focused on Michelangelo and Fausto, as if they might jump out of Harkins' jeep, tommy guns in hand.

"Thanks," Harkins said.

Desmond touched the brim of his helmet. "Be careful out there, sir."

Harkins returned the casual salute. "Will do," he said.

When the MPs were gone, Harkins said to Fausto and Michelangelo, "If I don't wind up in the stockade after this, it'll be a miracle."

A few minutes later they were parked near the apartment building Lindner had led them to. It looked nothing like Adriana's sketch.

Fausto and Michelangelo dismounted, looked around, then signaled to Harkins that he should follow. There was a gate on the street—unlocked—and a passageway leading to a small courtyard. Four doors, with an old-fashioned water pump in the center, a couple of cats lounging in the shade.

Fausto walked to the first door on the right and walked in without knocking. Harkins followed, noticed the splintered wood where they had forced the lock, probably on their first visit.

"I hope to hell there's not a body in here," he said to Michelangelo, who stayed outside. A lookout, Harkins figured.

The apartment was spartan, the front room empty except for a skeletal wooden table and two mismatched chairs. There was an ancient cabinet, a couple of dirty dishes in a bucket, a flat tin plate piled with cigarette butts. Harkins looked: Lucky Strikes. Something else lifted, bought, or earned from the Americans.

Fausto pushed back a dirty floral curtain, revealing another room. Harkins peeked inside, still sure he was going to see a body. Instead there was a large metal box, like a footlocker. The antique lock had been battered open and hung limply from the hasp. Fausto pointed, and, since the box was too small for a corpse, Harkins lifted the lid.

The bottom of the box was lined with the other half of the floral curtain, and arranged on top of it were five golden chalices, a few patens like the one Harkins found in Stephenson's bag, and a small pile of other gold trinkets. You didn't have to be a Vatican scholar to see that all of this had been taken from a church, or from several churches.

Harkins lifted one of the heavy cups, turned it over to look for marks on the bottom, a priest's name, perhaps. On the bottom of the third one he examined, he saw that some lettering had been crudely scratched out. He held it out to Fausto to see if the Sicilian could make sense of the marks that were left.

Fausto held up his hands as if Harkins had offered him a disease.

"No, no, no!"

"A little superstitious, huh?" Harkins said. "I don't blame you. Stuff looted from a church. Probably explains why you guys didn't help yourselves before bringing me here."

Harkins closed the lid on the box, and Fausto motioned for him to come to the last room, which had a stone floor and hearth. In the hearth was a gas bottle that fed into a wire stove of some sort. On the floor were two long pairs of tongs, a thick leather glove, and some small cups. Harkins picked up one of the cups, which turned out to be made of clay. There was a short metal rack that looked like it could be used for cooling, and a rectangle made of ceramic with three indentations in it, like one of the loaf pans his mother used to make small cakes.

Someone had been melting the gold here, shaping it into tiny ingots.

"Did you find any of these bricks?" Harkins asked.

Fausto shrugged.

"Maybe you guys aren't so superstitious if the gold has been melted."

Harkins still didn't know how Stephenson and Lindner were tied to this, or even if there had been another person in the apartment. But it was clear that there was gold around, and money and murder often went together.

Harkins decided to do a thorough search. He took off his helmet and pistol belt and went back to the front door, where he started by examining the floor, worked his way up the walls and doorjambs, and even climbed onto a chair to look at the ceiling, which was planks laid over rough-cut beams. He took his time, and after a few minutes Fausto sat in one of the chairs. Minutes later, Michelangelo poked his head in and asked Fausto a question. Another shrug, some more questions. Michelangelo smiled at Harkins, who wondered if they were talking about gold.

It was hot in the apartment, but when Fausto went to open the shutters, Harkins stopped him. Anyone walking by would be able to see them.

He spent thirty minutes on the front room, down on his hands and knees and knocking each floorboard with his knuckles. By the time he got to the middle room, sweat was dripping off his nose, marking the boards he'd already checked with dark circles.

At the threshold between the middle room and the room with the stone floor, Harkins heard something. He knocked, knocked again. This floorboard sounded different. He had Colianno's switchblade in his pocket. He pulled it out, flicked the double safety, and cut his palm.

"God*damn,* that's sharp."

Colianno had told him that most paratroopers carried a small knife tucked into the placket of their jump blouse. It had to be sharp enough to free a man from his chute if things went badly; if he landed in deep water, for instance.

Harkins used the thin blade the pry up the edge of the floorboard, which did not want to come loose. When he got one end up, Fausto, who'd been watching intently, slipped one of the tongs underneath. Harkins pulled, and eventually the board gave way.

The space below the floorboard was dark, but even so Harkins knew it was shallow, that it did not reach all the way to the dirt in a crawlspace. He stuck his hand down, his fingers touching the top edge of a smooth metal box. He pulled it, but it caught on something. Using his other hand, he reached down to clear the box and found a long, coiled wire.

It was part of a wireless set, a transmitter.

"Holy shit," Harkins said to Fausto.

Harkins pulled the wireless free. It turned out that he had only the key, which the operator could use to send coded messages, tap, tap, tap. Harkins figured the larger part of the set was under the floor.

He held up the key, showed it to Fausto, whose first, confused look gave way to understanding.

"Ohhhhh," he said. Then he looked into Harkins' eyes, smiled, and said, "Kraut."

"Our Kraut might just be a goddamn spy."

38

5 August 1943
1300 hours

Harkins found Sergeant Desmond and his crew patrolling near the waterfront cemetery Santa Maria dei Rotoli, which the summer sun had beaten to a flat brown. He asked Desmond to find Kathleen Donnelly and bring her to Adriana's café. As he hoped, Desmond asked no questions. The sergeant touched the brim of his helmet in salute and told his driver, "Let's go."

Harkins then drove to the cantonment of the Eighty-Second Airborne Division near Trapani, at the far western tip of the island. The paratroopers had scored a nice rest area on a hill above the sea, but no one was taking in the view. The men were packing for the move back to North Africa, where they would train for the next invasion, and the place was all business. Harkins found Patrick talking with two other chaplains, the three men looking at something on a clipboard, when he rolled up and said, "I could use your help."

As far as he could remember, no one in Harkins' family who had ever straight-up asked for help went without. Good or bad, dangerous or fun, legal or illegal, the Harkins siblings stuck together, a fierce tribe.

Smaller by one, now, Harkins remembered.

Patrick stood up, put on his helmet, and headed for the jeep.

"Thanks," Harkins said.

"This better be good," Patrick said.

Donnelly was already at the café when the Harkins brothers arrived. Eddie Harkins thanked Sergeant Desmond for bringing her.

"Anything you need, Lieutenant."

"What the heck happened to your face?" Patrick asked Kathleen.

"I fell," she said. Then, to Harkins, "I thought you went to get Moira. Aren't you supposed to be bringing her back?"

"I'm working on it," Harkins said.

He led Donnelly and his brother to a storeroom off the kitchen, where he showed them the trunk, the stolen chalices, the wireless key that he and the cousins had brought back from the apartment. Told them about the paten—another piece of church property—that Stephenson had tried to use to pay a gambling debt.

"So you think Lindner is a spy?" Patrick asked.

"Looks that way. He was headed to the apartment where we found this stuff."

"Can't you take all this to Boone?" Donnelly asked. "Let him worry about Lindner?"

"No. I was taken off the case, thanks to Boone and the provost marshal. I'm supposed to go back to my unit; hell, I'll probably be AWOL by the end of the day. Besides, I think there's some sort of three-way connection here: Stephenson, Boone, and Lindner."

"You think *Boone* is a spy?" Patrick asked.

"No. I doubt it. I don't know. But there's more going on with Boone than we suspected, and it's connected to Stephenson, somehow."

"You better move fast," Donnelly said. "Boone told Lindner to move the POWs out of our hospital to a troopship. Sometime today, I think. Told Lindner to go with them."

Harkins looked at his watch. He had a bit more than six hours until he became an AWOL military police officer.

"You brought us here to help," Patrick said.

"Yes. I want to find out whose apartment that is, the one where we found the wireless. And for that I need Colianno and his cousins."

"Where's Colianno?" Patrick asked.

Donnelly, who'd heard hospital scuttlebutt about the arrest, shook her head. "He's in the stockade," she said. "And—let me guess—you want to bust him out of there."

Now it was Patrick's turn to shake his head.

"Eddie, for Pete's sake. You're just digging yourself a deeper hole. Pulling one stunt after another that can get you court-martialed. Now you want to bust a guy out of confinement so he can help you with an investigation you've been ordered to drop?"

"I'm not going to stop, Pat."

The big priest raised his voice, angry now. "Until what? Until *you* wind up in the stockade? If you get court-martialed, you can forget about being a cop again after the war."

"Boone is a murderer. I can't let him get away with it."

"Why can't this deputy provost, Captain Adams, take care of this?" Donnelly asked. "He came by for your notes, said he'd been put in charge of the investigation."

"He's got a lot of catching up to do. Meanwhile, Boone isn't standing still; he's covering his tracks. I'm the one closest to putting the cuffs on him."

Harkins looked at Donnelly, back at his brother. Things were moving quickly now. Soon Lindner would be gone, most likely beyond reach; Harkins would be back on patrol with his MP platoon; and there was no telling what would happen to Colianno.

"Please," Harkins said.

The three of them were silent for a moment. In the kitchen a few feet away, Adriana sang as she chopped vegetables on an ancient cutting board.

"Boone's a menace. A fucking train wreck," Donnelly said. She chewed her lip. "I'm in."

Harkins looked at Patrick. Strangely enough for a priest, Pat was not one to worry about breaking a few rules. He did worry about his little brother's reckless streak.

"I appreciate that you're worried about me, Pat," Harkins said. "I'm going to do this; it would be easier with you along."

Patrick was quiet for a long moment, and Harkins wondered if his brother was praying for guidance.

"Can you see what you're doing? How self-destructive this is? I get that you're heartbroken about what happened to Michael. But trashing your career, risking prison, none of that is going to help you feel better, not really. It's not going to bring Michael back, but it might kill Ma if you throw everything away."

"The guy who jumps out of airplanes behind enemy lines wants to lecture me about risk?"

"Don't change the subject."

"OK," Harkins said. "I'll be more careful. Right after we do this."

"Destroying yourself isn't going to change what happened."

Harkins scoffed. "I know that."

"You know it intellectually," Patrick said.

Donnelly took a quiet step out of the room.

"Shit. Since when does a Catholic priest tell somebody to stop with the guilt?"

"Ma forgives you for what you did with Michael," Patrick said. He reached up and squeezed his brother's arm.

Harkins felt a tense band behind his eyes as he tried not to choke up. His mother rarely wrote to him, angry as she was about the forged birth certificate.

"I miss her," he said.

"She misses you and worries about you. She made me promise to hear your confession."

"If I confess, will you help me?"

"Let's not bargain over a sacrament, OK?" Patrick said, but it looked to Harkins like his brother would pitch in.

"You know, you and Ma put more stock in the sacraments than I do," Harkins said, trying to make it sound like a joke, failing.

"I know, brother," the priest said. "That's why we keep praying for you."

Patrick reached into the cargo pocket of his trousers and pulled out a narrow purple stole, much more his badge of office than the uniform, the captain's bars. He draped it around his neck, put his big hands on his brother's shoulders.

Eddie Harkins crossed himself, licked a salty tear from the corner of his mouth, recited the litany he'd learned as a child.

"Bless me, Father, for I have sinned," he said. Then, right to the center of his heartbreak. "I lied when I helped Michael get a fake birth certificate, and I lied to Mom and Dad about what I'd done, and for this I am sorry."

Patrick held Harkins' face in two hands, leaned his forehead to his brother's. "I absolve you, in the name of Christ."

Donnelly was waiting in the shade outside when Harkins and his brother came out of the café. The men climbed into the MP's jeep.

"You're going to the stockade, right?" Donnelly asked, walking up to them. "Take me with you."

"I really only needed an update on what's happening at the hospital," Harkins said. "I didn't mean to take you away from there."

"Maybe I can help," she said.

Harkins looked at his brother; the priest shrugged.

"Glad for the company," Patrick said. "Hop in."

Donnelly climbed into the back and Harkins headed toward the airfield, which was west of the city and tucked against the edge of the sea. Harkins spoke over his shoulder so Donnelly could hear the conversation as he and Patrick considered ways they might talk their way into the stockade and leave with Colianno in tow.

"I could say I'm there to provide spiritual counseling. That he asked to see a chaplain. Or that my regimental commander sent me."

"I wonder how tight security is. We might be able to walk out the gate with him. That happened at our stockade in North Africa. Guy just pretended he was supposed to be leaving."

"Fake paperwork," Patrick said. "We could gin something up."

They went on like that for the twenty-five minutes it took them to clear Palermo, tossing half-baked ideas back and forth, not settling on anything that sounded plausible. Harkins, who had been embarrassed by his dressing down in front of Meigs, felt more anxious as they drew close. He needed Colianno, but was not sure he was going to succeed in getting him out of custody.

On the north coast road they encountered more traffic, most of it headed to or from the Palermo airfield, which had been taken over by the Army Air Corps. The Seventh Army stockade was on the flat top of a hill just a few yards from the main road. The constant parade of vehicles dusted the whole place with a thick layer of pale dirt, and Harkins wondered if some sadist had positioned the camp beside the road for just that reason.

There was a tiny parking area near the front gate, which was guarded by two bored-looking MPs. The soldiers stood close to each other, trying to stay in the doubtful shade thrown by a slapped-together guard shack—four slender posts with a scrap of corrugated metal on top.

"Well?" Patrick asked.

"We could shoot our way in," Harkins said.

He was surprised when Donnelly got out of the jeep and, without explaining what she was doing, walked up to the guards. After a few seconds of conversation, one of the guards motioned for her to follow, and he led her into the compound.

"What do you suppose that's about?" Patrick asked.

Harkins and his brother dismounted and squeezed in between the jeep and a rock wall that offered a bit of shade. Harkins sat down and promptly fell asleep. When Patrick woke him by kicking his foot, Harkins looked at his watch. He'd been asleep for thirty minutes. He blinked, rubbed his eyes with thumb and forefinger, blinked again.

"Is that Kathleen and Colianno walking out?" Harkins asked.

"Sure is," Patrick said. "What the heck happened to his face? Has everyone been in a fight?"

"That's a story for another time," Harkins said.

The nurse and the paratrooper were side by side. Donnelly waved at the guards, said something in a pleasant tone. Harkins and his brother got to their feet. Colianno saluted as he approached and said, "Chaplain. Lieutenant."

"Kathleen," Harkins said. "How'd you do that?"

"I got to know the stockade commander when a couple of his guys wound up in our hospital after a truck accident. His name's Riley. He used to come down to visit them every day, so we became . . . friends, I guess." She winked at Harkins. "I told them that Colianno still had some shrapnel in him and that the surgeon wanted to get it out before it got infected."

"First part of that is true, by the way," Colianno said. "I'm carrying some junk around."

"And he just let you take his prisoner?" Harkins asked.

"I promised to bring him back," Donnelly said, smiling. "What can I say? I'm persuasive."

The four of them got into the jeep, Donnelly sitting behind Harkins, who was driving. As he started the engine she leaned closer, whispered into his left ear so the others couldn't hear.

"Riley never saw the supply tent," she said. "*Wanted* to, but didn't."

39

5 August 1943
1430 hours

Back out on the coastal road, the sign for the airfield gave Harkins an idea. He dropped Donnelly and Patrick off at Patrick's bivouac; the chaplain said he'd have a driver take her back to the hospital. Colianno got into the driver's seat and said, "Where to, Lieutenant?"

"The airfield."

Over the next fifteen minutes, Harkins filled Colianno in on what had happened, what his cousins had found in the apartment.

"I never did like that Nazi doctor," he said.

"I keep getting stuck on the money," Harkins said. "Whitman told Ronan that Boone was making money. But let's suppose it wasn't cash. What if Lindner was giving gold to Boone in exchange for letting him stay at the hospital, close to his sources for information."

"That general in supply. One with the weepy dick."

"Right. Anyway, what the hell would Boone do with gold? Even if someone melted it into little bars, little ingots, it's still heavy, hard to hide, and there's no place you could put it here in the war zone where it would be safe."

"OK, I give up. What did he do with it?"

"I don't know, but I have a theory," Harkins said. "Remember that Stephenson was in charge of evacuations by air?"

"Yeah. VIP casualties and tough cases, right?"

"Well, what if his part in this was shipping stuff back to the States?"

They rolled onto the airfield, which sat on a flat section of landfill hard up against the blue water. The sun reflected off the sea, stage-lighting everything. There was a single ambulance parked next to a large tent on the water side of the strip.

"Check that out," Harkins said, and Colianno aimed the jeep in that direction.

"By the way, Lieutenant. Where's all my hardware?"

"Back at your cousin's place. I told her not to sell it."

"I hate riding around without a weapon."

"You afraid some German paratroopers are going to land on us while we're here?"

"No, but I might have to shoot a Kraut doctor. You never know."

There were two medical orderlies leaning against the shady side of the ambulance. Colianno recognized one of the men, so Harkins let him take the lead.

"You guys waiting on an evac flight?" Colianno asked.

The two GIs pulled themselves to a semblance of attention and saluted when they saw Harkins, then the taller one said, "Supposed to have been here an hour ago. No word on when it'll get here. Or if."

Harkins got out of the jeep, leaned on the hood, and said, "At ease, men," so the orderlies could lean back into the shade.

The tall man reminded Harkins of Ichabod Crane in an illustrated version of "The Legend of Sleepy Hollow." Narrow face. Long, bony hands. His Adam's apple jumped up and down when he talked. He held a lit cigarette between his fingers.

"What's your name?" Harkins asked Adam's Apple.

"Pryzbylkowski, sir. But everyone calls me Priz."

Harkins looked at the other soldier, who said, "Cook, sir."

"Doc Trennely is inside," Priz said.

The surgeon who'd stitched Harkins after Ronan had split his eyebrow.

"He's figuring out if our patients can stand the wait or if we should haul them back to the hospital and try again tomorrow."

"Who's in charge of loading the plane when it lands?"

"Well, we put the patients in, and the pilot likes to check, make sure everything's OK. But the guy who's really in charge is an Air Corps staff sergeant. Name's Trunk."

"Trunk?" Harkins asked.

"Yeah. Like a footlocker; like a steamer trunk."

"He around?"

The two orderlies looked at each other, then the taller one scanned the area. "If he was, you'd hear him, Lieutenant. Biggest goddamn loudmouth I ever met. He'll start yelling at Cook and me when he's still a hundred yards away."

Cook muttered, "Asshole."

"You guys ever work with Captain Stephenson, when he was in charge of air evac?"

"Sure," Priz said.

"Anything . . . I don't know . . . unusual about working with him?"

"He wasn't my favorite doc," Priz said. "But I guess he took good care of the patients."

Cook said something under his breath, directed at Priz, like it pained him to speak out loud. He was about twenty, dimpled chin, dark hair, and straight white teeth. Harkins thought Cook could be a movie star if he learned how to talk.

"What's that?" Colianno asked.

Cook struggled to find the words, like he was practicing a foreign language. "The crates."

Harkins looked at Priz, raised his eyebrows. "That's right!" the orderly said. "He used to ship medical equipment back to the States to get repaired. Microscopes and stuff like that. Heavy as hell."

Harkins and Colianno exchanged looks, Harkins suppressing a smile.

"Any other docs ship medical equipment back?" Harkins asked.

"So far we've only worked with Captain Stephenson and Captain Trennely, and this is only our first time with Trennely. No boxes."

"Did you ever see inside the boxes?"

"No, they was sealed up real good. I mean, they were made real nice, like little cabinets. Trunk signed for them and told us how to stow them on the airplane."

"When was that? Do you remember dates?"

"I remember the last time was the day before Stephenson got killed. He got shot in the morning. The morning before that, we were right here. Two boxes."

"You mentioned that they were heavy. Heavier than you expected?"

"We never opened them, but I've moved microscopes at the hospital. It would take a lot of microscopes to be that heavy."

A jeep passed them, trailing dust, and stopped at the door to the nearby tent. The GI who got out of the passenger seat yelled at the driver, then went inside.

"Sergeant Trunk, I presume," Harkins said.

"That's him."

Harkins and Colianno turned toward the tent entrance.

"Say, Lieutenant?" Priz said.

Harkins turned back.

"You don't mind my asking, aren't you the guy who was investigating Doc Stephenson's murder?"

"That's me."

"Oh, good. 'Cause we heard you got fired. The nurses were pretty upset. Glad to see you're still on it. I didn't like that guy, but he didn't deserve to get shot down like that."

"Yeah, thanks," Harkins said. "But don't mention our little talk here, OK?"

Priz saluted sloppily, his cigarette still pinched between the fingers of his right hand. "You got it, sir."

Harkins and Colianno walked to the tent entrance. The walls were rolled up because of the heat, the open sides protected by mosquito netting.

Harkins went inside first, spotted Trennely, the doctor, leaning over a patient. Trunk, at the other end of the tent, saw them come in and said, "Who the fuck are you fuckers? What the fuck are you doing in my tent?"

Trunk walked up to Colianno and Harkins, lifted his clipboard as if to order them out. When he saw that Harkins was a lieutenant, he said, "Sorry, Lieutenant," though he clearly didn't mean it.

"Doctor," Harkins said to Trennely, keeping the sergeant waiting.

"Oh, hello," Trennely said. "It's Harkins, right?"

"You getting ready to send a patient back to the States?"

The soldier on the cot was unconscious, his head and neck bandaged, his right arm held across his chest by a cast and some sort of wire contraption that wrapped around his midsection.

"If the plane gets here soon," Trennely said. "No one seems to know where it is at the moment, and I don't want to leave our patient overnight here."

"Shipping any other materials back? Any crates?"

Trennely shook his head. "No." Then the doctor noticed Colianno's banged-up face. "You want me to take a look at that eye, soldier?"

"No, thanks, sir," Colianno said. "Not my first black eye. It'll be OK soon enough."

Harkins turned to Trunk. "You're the loadmaster, is that right, Sergeant?"

"Yes, sir. And who are you?"

"Lieutenant Harkins, military police. I'm investigating the death of Captain Stephenson. Doctor Stephenson. I understand you two worked together."

Trunk pulled up short, glanced at Trennely, then back at Harkins. "Not exactly; no, sir. He brought the evac cases here and I made sure they got loaded safely. That's all. I'm Air Corps, not Medical Corps."

"So he never asked you to ship anything back for him? Some medical equipment to be repaired?"

"Oh, I guess so, yeah. A couple of times he showed up with a few crates. He said they were microscopes and stuff, but of course I never saw inside them."

Trennely squeezed past Harkins, moved to the other side of the patient, checked the tension on the little trapeze holding the man's arm.

"Let's take him back to the hospital," the doctor said to an orderly.

"I should help," Trunk said.

"You should stay exactly where you are, Sergeant," Harkins said. "Who was receiving the boxes Stephenson shipped?"

"I don't know," Trunk said. "I don't remember any names."

"There must have been a name and address on the crate, though, right? Somebody had to know what to do with them on the other end. Was it an Air Corps soldier who would have picked them up, or someone from the medical department?"

"I guess it was someone from the medical department," Trunk said, no confidence in his voice.

"You must have manifests, right? Names of passengers, inventories of equipment that went on board?"

"Sure, sure. I run a tight operation here."

"I'd like to see all your paperwork from the flights on August first."

"Well, that could take a while, to find it, I mean. I, uh, I don't keep everything out here on the flight line."

Normally Harkins would have said he'd wait, would have given Trunk more time to get worried, make a mistake. But he'd been days without any decent sleep. He was due back at MP headquarters in a few hours. Trunk was a bully, but a minor figure in this drama. Meanwhile, Boone was slipping away, Ronan was God knew where, and someone was going to start looking for Colianno very soon.

Harkins stepped close to Trunk, close enough to smell fear and tobacco. Without being asked, Colianno stepped close to the man's side.

"Sergeant, you just don't have the time."

Harkins wiped his face with his sleeve. Trunk was sweating much more heavily, but did not move. Harkins spoke very slowly, almost gently. "It's all coming unraveled now. Maybe you didn't know what Stephenson had in those crates, maybe you did. But he paid you for special handling."

Harkins was guessing, but he kept his eyes locked on Trunk's.

"Stephenson wound up dead because of what was in those boxes. Ended up wrapped in a mattress cover in that temporary cemetery they got down by Gela. Is that in your plan, too, Sergeant Trunk? Or were you maybe hoping to make it back to the States someday?"

Five minutes later, Harkins and Colianno were in their jeep, headed back toward Palermo. Harkins looked at his watch for the third time in fifteen minutes. He had a few hours until he was AWOL.

"So Lindner paid Boone to let him stay at the hospital instead of getting shipped back," Colianno said.

"Presumably so he could nose around headquarters while treating that general," Harkins said. "Though I'm not sure Boone knew about that part."

"And then Boone partnered up with Stephenson to get the gold shipped back to the States. That explains why Stephenson said Boone would never do anything about the shit going on with the nurses. Stephenson knew how dirty Boone is."

"Can you imagine partnering with a loose cannon like Stephenson?" Harkins said. "That's the craziest thing about this whole mess. But finally Stephenson got too out of control, and Boone felt threatened. Stephenson could blow it all up. That's certainly motivation for Boone to kill Stephenson, enough for him to want to make Lindner disappear into a POW camp in the States."

"I don't know," Colianno said. "I still think Boone is too much of a milquetoast to shoot Stephenson. My money's on the Nazi."

"Boone shot Drake," Harkins said. "And Kathleen thinks he was somehow involved in Whitman's death."

"I thought she was the one choked to death."

"Maybe. We don't have anything solid enough for charges on that. Not yet."

Colianno just nodded, like he was turning the problem over in his head. Harkins felt like he was finally getting some clarity on who'd done what and why.

"Anyway, that was quite a story you came up with back there, Lieutenant. Scared the shit out of ol' Sergeant Trunk."

Harkins looked over at Colianno. He felt like something was about to click into place, but he wasn't sure what.

"About Stephenson and the mattress cover, you mean?" Harkins said. "Yeah, I guess that was a nice touch. I even gave myself the heebie-jeebies.

"Now let's see how far we can run with it."

40

5 August 1943
1515 hours

Harkins and Colianno skirted the edge of the Riserva di Capo Gallo, the rock-strewn nature preserve on the coast north of Palermo; the hills looked like California in fire season. Harkins had spent five weeks there in the summer of 1942.

"This whole island is a giant sunburn," Harkins said.

"You should hear my parents talk about their first winters in the States," Colianno said. "Like they'd moved to the North Pole."

Thirty minutes later they were back in the city proper, where they'd left Ronan at Giovanna's place.

"After we pick her up we'll go get Captain Adams at the provost marshal headquarters," Harkins said. "He's the lead investigator now; he'll have to be in on everything. I want to bring him up to speed with what we learned at the airfield."

When they parked in front of the house where Giovanna rented some rooms, Colianno jumped out of the jeep, and Harkins followed. Best to let Colianno make the case for her coming with them.

The paratrooper went in the door without knocking, calling for his cousin and Ronan, but there was no answer.

By the time Harkins entered, Colianno had already looked in the other two rooms and was wide-eyed.

"She's not here!" Colianno said, looking at Harkins as if for an explanation.

"She was supposed to wait here," Harkins said. "I told her I'd be back for her."

"Fucking Boone!"

"I don't think so. Boone didn't know where this place is, and he was busy with the provost marshal when you and I came here. He wasn't available to follow us."

"Couldn't he have had someone else follow us?"

Harkins thought it was possible—Boone was proving a resourceful enemy—but he didn't want to say as much to Colianno.

"Where would Giovanna be if she's not here?" Harkins asked.

"There are a couple of places, a couple of people she'd go to."

"OK, let's take a look around at those places."

"Giovanna will stick with her," Colianno said. Harkins thought the paratrooper was giving himself a pep talk.

Colianno raced out to the jeep, started the engine, pulled Harkins' map from the lieutenant's musette bag.

"Shit," he said. "I keep thinking about Boone. He came to get her once."

"We'll look for her, and if we can't find her we'll get Adams and then have him pick up Boone."

Harkins was barely in his seat when Colianno jammed the accelerator, spinning gravel from under the rear tires.

They sped toward the waterfront, barely missed clipping a donkey cart, whose owner cursed at them in English. As they got closer, they heard the distinctive sound of a hand-cranked siren, which some MP vehicles mounted on the front fender. They turned a corner and were forced to stop at the intersection near the university, where an MP jeep blocked the road so that a couple of trucks could race by. A dozen or more soldiers crowded the back of each, hanging on as the drivers took the turns quickly. When they'd passed, an MP sergeant in the jeep looked at them.

"You guys better get back to your unit," he said, reaching for the hand crank of the siren.

"What's going on?" Harkins asked.

"Big Kraut attack, or counterattack, I guess. We got sent into the city to round up anybody who's on pass, especially the hospital people. That's what all the noise is about. You guys with any of the hospital units?"

"Eleventh Field Hospital," Harkins said.

"Better get up there, then. Casualties are already starting to come in, and they need everybody."

The MP sergeant tapped his driver on the shoulder and the jeep pulled out, chasing the trucks, the sergeant leaning out to turn the siren's handle.

"I'll bet that's where she went," Colianno said. "Back to the hospital. Right back to Boone."

"You're probably right," Harkins said. "She was already itching to get back to work. If she heard she was needed . . ."

Colianno put the jeep in gear and raced off after the MPs and their siren. As they moved out of the residential neighborhood it became obvious that something big was going on. Clusters of American vehicles spilled out of the city, east toward the front and south toward the hospital and supply staging areas. For the first time in weeks there was almost no military traffic headed into Palermo; it was all outbound. Everyone moved too fast, the drivers wide-eyed and leaning on their horns and accelerators. A wrecker had crashed into a sidewalk stall; a dozen or so ducks, their cages scattered around the vehicle's bumper, squawked in panic.

"Jesus," Colianno said. "You'd think the Krauts were at the gates."

From the hills above them to the south, Harkins could hear the *crump* of outgoing artillery.

The headquarters of Patton's Seventh Army had jumped forward at least a week earlier, but the provost marshal had kept a presence in the city, where most of the interaction—legal and otherwise—between GIs and civilians was likely to take place. The provost had taken over a primary school, and a dirt courtyard that was probably a playground in happier days was jammed with American jeeps and trucks. There was a fuel point—a thousand-gallon tanker set up as a gas station—that had leaked gasoline and oil onto the ground. Harkins wondered when the children would be able to return, and what they'd find.

They located Captain Adams in what had been a classroom, standing and bent over a desk, writing something on a tablet. Above his head, a crucifix hung on the wall beside a roll-down map of South America. Some GI wag had written on the map, "Wish I was here," with an arrow pointing to Rio de Janeiro.

"Captain Adams," Harkins called as he entered the room.

Adams looked up, raised a hand in greeting. He opened his mouth to speak but went silent when he saw Colianno come in behind Harkins.

"What's he doing here? He's supposed to be in the stockade."

More surprised than angry, Adams spoke directly to Colianno. "You're supposed to be in the stockade."

"He's out for a medical procedure," Harkins said.

"Don't give me that bullshit," Adams said. "Are you trying to get me fired, too? Isn't it enough that your ass is in a sling with my boss?"

Colianno started to speak, but Adams cut him off. "Wait outside."

Then, to Harkins, "This better be good."

Harkins filled him in on everything that had happened since the meeting with Colonel Meigs: his discovery of looted church gold at the apartment, Lindner's connection with someone who had a wireless set, Stephenson's shipments back to the U.S. His theory about Boone and Stephenson being partners. When Harkins finished, Adams fell back into his chair.

"Holy shit."

"Exactly," Harkins said. "Now it's time to move on Boone."

"Wait. There are a lot of loose ends here. You've seen gold in the apartment, but you never saw Lindner there. He was on his way there, right, when he spotted Colianno's cousins? Do you have any way to connect the gold directly to Lindner, or to Stephenson, or, for that matter, Boone?"

"The sergeant at the airfield, the loadmaster. He was taking payments from Stephenson to load the crates on the plane, make sure they got to the right person in the States. It's a guy at a hospital back in Chicago; I think Boone used to work there. At any rate, I'll bet the guy on the other end talks when the FBI knocks on his door."

Harkins knew what the lawyer's next question would be, and he was ready for it.

"This sergeant . . ."

"Trunk."

"Right, Trunk. He saw the gold? He opened the crates?"

Harkins did not miss a beat, but lied straight-faced. He could always go back to Patrick for another confession. "Yes."

Adams stood. "Well, this will make a great story someday. My big war novel, maybe a movie."

The captain picked up his canvas briefcase, led Harkins out of the office to where Colianno was pacing the hallway outside a row of classrooms.

"Sir, we have to make sure Moira, Nurse Ronan, is OK," Colianno said to Adams.

"We will."

Adams stopped, went back inside his office. When he came out, he'd left the briefcase behind and was buckling on a pistol belt. He unbuttoned the flap on the holster, checked the action on the .45, tucked it back in its place.

"OK, let's go get this bastard."

41

5 August 1943
1630 hours

The first waves of casualties started arriving two hours after the hospital began breaking down operations for the move forward. Sleeping tents, mess tents, supply tents already flattened and rolled by details of enlisted men, sweating in the heat and squinting against the glare. The most seriously injured patients had been moved to a general hospital being set up in Palermo, in what had been a civilian facility. Advance parties had gone ahead to scout locations closer to the front, leaving the staff shorthanded on doctors, nurses, and orderlies.

So when the ambulances and jeeps and trucks arrived with their loads of bloodied young men, the doctors and nurses of the Eleventh Field Hospital were halfway on the road, bandages and linens stored in crates, light stands folded, generators silenced, stretchers collapsed and stacked, surgical teams scattered.

Oberstleutnant Matthias Lindner watched with admiration as the Americans adjusted to the chaos. One of the surgical tents had already been broken down, but a team of nurses and orderlies yanked the operating tables from the back of a truck and set up a theater in the open air.

He watched three orderlies wrestle an X-ray machine off the back of a deuce-and-a-half and connect it to a generator that was still on board another truck so the surgeons could plan their campaign against the broken limbs, embedded shrapnel, crushed pelvises, shattered faces.

There were stretchers on the ground, wounded men being shunted to various places on the footprints of the hospital tents that had been packed up. And just as he had observed with even the most grievously wounded German soldiers, these patients waited without complaint, trying their best to keep quiet, to be stoic and strong as they waited for the teams to reach them.

"Let's go, let's go!"

An American MP was herding Lindner and the other German POWs, some of whom had been patients, some of whom had been working as medical orderlies tending to other prisoners. Colonel Boone had ordered them all away. Even if he'd wanted to try, there was no way for Lindner to get back into Palermo to pass along his information.

Most of his comrades were jaunty, healthy, and well fed on American food, happily moving away from the battle zone. Some were anxious about making the crossing to the United States on a troopship; they'd been raised on a diet of Nazi propaganda about how the Atlantic was a killing zone for the all-seeing U-boats. How would the Kriegsmarine know an American-flagged ship had German POWs aboard?

"What will they do with us when we get to America?" a sergeant named Bottcher asked Lindner. All his comrades knew Lindner had lived in the States.

"We will be prisoners there, too, of course. Though I think the conditions won't be too bad. They're not worried about us escaping to swim back across the Atlantic."

"Will we get letters, do you think? Any mail?"

Lindner studied Bottcher, who had family in Dresden. His wife drove an ambulance, and he worried constantly about Allied bombing.

"I'm sure the International Red Cross will help us communicate with our families," Lindner said, though he had no reason to think this would actually happen.

Lindner wondered if what General Glass' aide and driver said were true, that they might be shipped to someplace like Texas to work on government projects, building training camps and airfields. Lindner, who had once taken a train from New Orleans to Los Angeles, hoped to be swallowed up somewhere in the vastness of the United States. He wanted to become anonymous, just another POW. The alternative, he feared, was a firing squad.

The man who'd followed him to the apartment was a local, and could just as easily have been after the gold that his Abwehr contact had stashed there. But what if he'd been working for the Americans? What if Glass' aide, Cohen, had followed up on his suspicions? He'd made a comment about shooting spies when he thought Lindner had been looking at the papers on Glass' desk. And Glass might enjoy having Lindner shot: it would reduce the number of people who knew about his medical condition, about his predilection for whores.

"Right down there, Doc," one of the MPs told him, pointing to a line of six trucks parked on the side of the road outside the hospital gate.

The trucks were to take them south to Gela, where they would board ships for the crossing, for the opportunity to hide.

Lindner had not slept the previous night, and he imagined every set of footfalls would be that policeman, Harkins, come to drag him away. Awake, he spent the long hours on the wards, tending to patients and chatting with nurses and orderlies who were, as always, full of gossip. That's where he learned that the patrolman-turned-detective had argued with Boone. He heard about the arrest of Harkins' driver, the Italian-American paratrooper, though Lindner believed Boone had killed the big first sergeant, Drake. It was all coming apart, and, to make it worse, Boone was in a panic. If Harkins connected Boone and Stephenson to the gold, well, it would be bad for Boone.

But it was the wireless he worried about, and whether Harkins would find it. Because the wireless identified Herr Doktor Lindner as the Third Reich's most inept spy.

Lindner could see, up ahead, that the column of German POWs had reached the trucks. The orderlies who were not carrying stretchers, who were not weighed down with canvas bags full of the supplies he'd requisitioned to take care of their patients, were marching in a neat column. Good German soldiers. Disciplined.

The sergeant at the head reached the lead truck.

"Halt!"

He sounded almost happy, like they were loading for a holiday drive.

Lindner, the only officer in the group, lagged behind, staying out of the way of the sergeants. He had changed back into his own uniform, the clean but worn lightweight shirt and trousers of a lieutenant colonel in the Afrika Corps. The American uniform, the one with the tiny *P* above the breast pocket that had so infuriated the American first sergeant, Drake, was gone. Lindner no longer wanted to be easily identifiable. He wanted to be just another POW, among the thousands the Allies had captured. The truck that would move him closer to that goal was only a few yards away now.

"Doctor!"

It was Bottcher, calling him from the front of the column, where three American MPs, one of them a captain, stood with the German sergeants.

"We need your help translating," Bottcher called.

Lindner squeezed between the line of trucks and his own men, who made room for him. When he reached the little group, he tossed his duffle bag into the back of the lead truck, greeted the Americans.

"Hello, Captain. I'm Lieutenant Colonel Lindner. How can I help?"

The two enlisted MPs looked at each other, a reaction Lindner often elicited with his near-perfect English.

"I'm afraid we got a change of plans, Colonel," the American said. He was tall, at least six foot, with blond hair and blue eyes. He could have modeled for an SS recruiting poster, the Aryan supersoldier.

"There's some stuff going on at the front, and I'm supposed to hold these trucks here, see if they're needed for another mission."

Lindner tried to smile. Of course plans changed all the time, and of course these trucks were probably always in great demand. Still, he felt a flutter behind his heart.

"I see," he said. "Do you have any idea of how long we might wait?"

"Wish I did, Colonel. I've got to run back to my headquarters, see what's going on. I'll either send someone to get the trucks, or send someone to tell you guys to load up and move out."

Lindner looked around. There was an olive orchard beside the road, about two hundred meters up ahead and on the side of a low ridge.

"We'll move to the shade and wait there," Lindner said.

"Sounds good, Colonel. I'll kick some C-rations off for your guys. No telling how long you'll be here. And of course I have to leave a couple of MPs to babysit."

"Babysit?"

"Guard you. Not that I think you're going anywhere, but I gotta have a guard with you."

"Yes, of course," Lindner said. He turned to Bottcher, gave him the orders in German.

One of the enlisted MPs climbed up onto the back of the nearest truck and retrieved Lindner's duffle, handed it down to him.

"You're going to want to hang on to this, Colonel," the American said. "You might not be going anywhere after all."

"Thank you," Lindner said. "Yes, you might be right."

Colonel Walter Boone usually found surgery completely engrossing. When he opened up a human body, he lost his sense of time, frequently did not notice what was going on in the theater outside the circle of light and gloved hands that were there to help him work. He was consumed.

That was not the case today.

Boone was operating inside the only surgical tent that had not yet been broken down for the hospital's move forward. He looked up every few seconds, expecting to see Harkins and that captain, the deputy provost. He had done everything he could think of to get Harkins off his trail, to the point of shipping out nurses and even getting the hospital moving for its jump. Harkins had been taken off the case by the provost himself, should be on his way back to his own MP unit by now.

But the man didn't know when to quit.

It would take a day or so for Lindner to be off the island, and until then Boone could not rest.

A voice at his elbow was talking to him. Boone looked over, nodded.

"Ready, sir?"

The orderlies put a patient on the table and Boone looked down, saw the shrapnel wounds to the face, neck, and shoulders. He suddenly pictured Stephenson, the terrible maw of his death wound, the blood-matted hair. Boone shook his head to clear it, looked up, scanned the room once again for Harkins, then looked back at his hands. He began to probe the wounds closest to the patient's eyes.

He heard someone saying, "Doctor, Doctor, Doctor." One of the nurses was speaking to him.

"What?"

"We should check for other wounds."

"Yes. Right."

It was Donnelly, her eyes above the mask tired, deep blue. She stepped close, nudging him out of the way, then she and a nurse on the opposite side of the table reached under the patient with their hands, sweeping his torso, his legs, checking for other wounds. A patient could bleed out of a puncture in his back while a surgeon concentrated on an open chest.

"Ready," Donnelly said.

Boone scanned the other people at the table. He could identify every person on the surgical team by looking at the eyes above the mask. Everyone here was supposed to be here. No Harkins.

Boone nodded at a surgical orderly, who came closer. “Go find out if the German POWs are gone yet.”

“Yes, sir.”

A few of the people around the table exchanged looks. Why did Boone need this information at this particular moment?

“Right,” Boone said again. He looked down at the GI before him, whose breath was rapid and shallow. Boone could see a gash that started just above the man’s collarbone and stretched up and back, an angry red crescent, toward the nape of his neck. Whatever hot metal had done that had just missed the jugular.

“This one’s been lucky,” he said. “Let’s see if we can keep his streak going.”

Moira Ronan stepped up to the scrub station, sank her hands in the hot water bath, reached for the brush. On the other side of the washstand, an orderly she’d worked with for months, a Hispanic kid from Southern California, saw her and nodded. Everyone knew she’d been AWOL. Everyone probably knew about her and Colianno. In the gossip hothouse that was this small command, more than a few people probably knew that she’d accused Boone of shooting Drake, knew, even, the terrible secret she’d kept to herself. The whole mess exhausted her.

“Lieutenant,” the orderly, a corporal named Alejo, said. “Good to see you. We really need you.”

“Thanks,” Ronan said. She’d been right to come back.

She scrubbed the backs of her hands, her fingernails sore where she’d gnawed them for days. Then her wrists and forearms, her skin going red from the hot water. She’d been a surgical nurse for three years, but had never wanted so badly to be clean.

When she finished, Alejo handed her a towel.

“There’s a couple of docs operating under a tent fly we set up on the duckboards where the mess tent used to be.”

“How are we handling the rush?” Ronan asked.

“Not good,” Alejo said. “Triage is overwhelmed, I think. We’re down a couple of surgeons and nurses, and this is the most we’ve seen at one time since the beaches.”

"Where's Nurse Donnelly?"

"Assisting in Surgical One. Don't go in there. She's with the Old Man."

Boone.

Ronan pulled on her gloves, then allowed Alejo to cover her hands with another sterile towel so she could walk the dusty few yards to where a surgical team was operating. The corporal followed her.

"Have you seen . . . do you know who Lieutenant Harkins is?"

"Yes, ma'am. And no, I haven't seen him. We all thought he got chased out of here this morning. His driver even got arrested."

Ronan stopped. "What? Why?"

"Don't know. A bunch of officers went into Colonel Boone's tent, then one of them came out and, next thing you know, an MP is disarming your friend . . . I mean the lieutenant's driver. I heard they took him to Seventh Army stockade."

They walked up on a surgical team just as they were closing the patient's chest. Doctor Trennely, the sweet, homely man the nurses called Good Guy, was the lead. He looked up, saw Ronan—who was not yet wearing a mask—and wiggled his eyebrows in a Groucho Marx imitation or something like *Where the hell have you been?*

"Next patient," Trennely said, turning so that a nurse could help him change gloves. The orderlies were ready with another GI on a stretcher, this one with his head wrapped in dirty bandages, just a tiny breathing hole where his nose should be.

"You ready?" Trennely asked her.

"Ready, Doctor," she said. Back with her people, with her patients, in her element, Stephenson and Boone be damned.

"Jump in here, then."

Alice Haus, the former swimmer who daydreamed about bedding Doctor Lindner, tapped Donnelly on the shoulder.

"Triage is falling apart," Haus said. "You'd better go out and see what can be done."

"OK," Donnelly said, stepping back and allowing Haus to take her place at Boone's operating table. Then, lowering her voice and leaning close to her friend's ear, "Boone is falling apart, too. Keep an eye on him so he doesn't kill somebody."

The triage area was set up on the duckboards where the nurses' sleeping tent had stood until that morning. The patients were in the sun, and several orderlies were hurrying to set up a screen, assisted by some of the walking wounded who could wait for treatment.

A skinny kid in tanker's overalls stood holding a tent pole while two orderlies staked guy lines. The GI, who had the single stripe of a private inked onto his right sleeve, wavered a bit on his feet and smiled at Donnelly.

"Lieutenant," he said. There was something wrong with his voice. Could he be drunk? His left arm was in a sling; bandages visible at the end.

"How's the arm?" Donnelly asked.

Then she saw the morphine syrette dangling from his collar, a big numeral *1* written on his forehead in charcoal. A medic had given him an injection for pain. He was drugged, but on his feet.

"The arm?" he asked, looking down, peering inside the sling. "Shorter."

He pulled the sling back to reveal the lower part of his left arm, where his hand was missing. The stump was neatly wrapped, though not by a surgeon, and tied off with a tourniquet.

"Come with me, soldier," she said.

Donnelly walked the GI to a cluster of stretchers where two nurses, Melbourne and Savio, were checking wounds, filling out casualty tags, rebandaging. Donnelly could see right away that there was a massive backup. She sat the wounded tanker down on an empty stretcher and told him to wait.

"You're swamped," she said to her friends.

"Swamped would be an improvement," Melbourne said. "We're way past that, now. Patients are sliding back to expectant."

This meant that the flow of casualties was overwhelming what the hospital could handle. Men who could survive if they got help soon were not going to make it. "Expectant" meant expected to die.

Behind Melbourne, Donnelly saw a sergeant named Victor working to organize the efforts of the orderlies, hoping to keep the cases flowing smoothly to the operating theaters. Victor had inherited the job that would have belonged to Drake. But Drake was dead and Victor, try as he might, wasn't up to the task, and now men who might be saved would probably die within a few feet of an operating table.

"My friend here," Donnelly said, pointing at the tanker. Savio stood and walked to the man.

"I'm guessing traumatic amputation."

"I got it," Savio said. She took the young soldier by his remaining hand and led him to a wooden pallet, had him sit. The private still had a dreamy, morphine look.

Donnelly looked around. The triage area was set up in a sun-beaten rectangle of dirt created by the tents that were still standing. She did a quick inventory of the orderlies on hand: a handful of privates and not enough sergeants. Today everyone was going to have to do more.

"Morrison, Elliott, Dabner," she said, calling the three steadiest men to her. Morrison, pale and sweating, was probably fighting malaria.

"We need a bigger footprint," she said. "More space between the groups."

The three young men looked around, bone-tired and struggling to make sense of her directions.

"Move the ambulatory over there," Donnelly said, pointing.

They hesitated, and she flashed to her first mass casualty: a year out of her starched white nursing school uniform and she'd been dropped on a beach that smelled of cordite and burned flesh, men screaming around her, pain and blood and shredded limbs. She had stumbled badly, had thought about it over many long nights since.

The men looked at her, exhausted but eager to do something. She lowered her voice, though it was doubtful anyone could overhear her amid all the shouts and moans.

"Look, we're going to save as many as we can today, but that isn't going to be everyone. You're going to have to make decisions normally made by First Sergeant Drake or some more senior noncom, because we're shorthanded. They're not here, so I need you."

She paused, breathed, hands on her hips.

"Do your best, and I'll back up whatever call you make."

"Yes, ma'am," Elliott said.

"Thank you, Lieutenant," Morrison said.

Forty-five minutes after her sorry excuse for a pep talk, Donnelly and the three orderlies had gotten a handle on the flow of wounded. The men had stepped up because she'd asked them to. They were magnificent, and what she felt for them could only be described as love.

Donnelly was watching Morrison when she heard a man cry out. To her right a soldier had elbowed himself nearly upright on his stretcher, had pulled bandages off his lower abdomen, his groin. He was looking at the wound that might change his life.

"Jesus Christ! No, fuck, no!"

Donnelly stepped over two stretchers to move toward the GI, a second lieutenant. She was just about to call out when the wounded man pulled a pistol from a pile of gear beside him and put it to his head.

"Stop!"

He hesitated, just a heartbeat, his eyes clicking toward her, and Donnelly dove for him, knocked the pistol out of his hand, grabbed it from the dirt before he could pick it up again. She had landed on his lap, on the bloody bandages he'd opened.

"That fucking *hurts*!" He pushed her away with one arm.

"I'm sorry! I'm sorry!"

Donnelly scrambled to all fours, lifted herself off the man, off his wounds. She stood up, dropped the magazine from the pistol and stuck it in her front trouser pocket, cleared the chamber and jammed the weapon into her belt at the small of her back.

The GI fell back, moaning. "Why did you stop me?"

Donnelly looked down at the man. He was young, twenty or twenty-one. His trousers were gone, most of his shirt and his GI shoes had been scorched off, and his feet looked like hamburger. Donnelly figured he'd stepped on a mine.

His lower abdomen was wrapped and the bandages had bled through. Donnelly checked the stretcher; there was no pool of blood—a good sign—so the bleeding may have stopped. She knelt, lowered her voice to give the distraught soldier the only privacy he would get in this crowded circle of hell.

"May I look?"

The lieutenant was on his back, left arm over his eyes, which were closed. The grime on his face was streaked with sweat, maybe tears.

He barely whispered, "Nothing left to see."

Donnelly gently lifted the layers of bandages. She pulled surgical scissors from a pocket on her sleeve, cut from his navel toward his groin, gingerly, careful not to disturb whatever horror lay beneath. The wounded man sucked his teeth.

"What's your name?" Donnelly asked.

"Norenger. Jack Norenger."

"Have you had morphine?"

"Just one syrette. Can you get me five or six more? That should do the trick."

An orderly whose name she forgot stepped up behind her, his shadow falling on the wounded man. Donnelly turned her body to shield the lieutenant from view.

"Need help?" the orderly asked.

"I'll call you if I do, thanks."

She peeled back the bandages where she'd cut them.

A medic, probably the first to treat Norenger, had poured sulfa powder on the wound, had stuffed rolled bandages into the space between the top of his left leg and his abdomen, the place where runners pack ice when they pull a groin muscle. Donnelly lifted the roll and looked below; there was a two-inch-deep cavity there.

"Well?" Norenger asked.

The unknown medic had covered Norenger's penis and testicles with several layers of gauze.

"Is it still there?"

Donnelly looked at Norenger's face, still covered with his arm. The man had just tried to shoot himself after looking at his wound. She wasn't hopeful about what she'd find.

She gently tugged the gauze, which stuck to the dried blood. The glans penis had flowered out, was much bigger than it should be and shot through with dirt, but it was still there.

"Yes, it's still there," Donnelly said.

"But it's all fucked up."

Donnelly looked at Norenger's legs. The energy from the mine he'd tripped had shot upward, blowing the muscle and flesh away from the long bones of the leg. The blast carried with it dirt and shrapnel and God knew what bacteria, which was then covered and encased when the muscle closed back over the bone. The same upward blast had ballooned the foreskin, which was pierced in several places.

She'd learned about these effects while assisting Doctor Lindner, had seen him work for hours to clean these terrible wounds in the hopes of saving a future for—as he once put it—"some virginal teenager."

"I know who can help you," Donnelly told Norenger. "I've seen worse, and we have a doc here who can help."

Norenger dropped his arm, lifted just his head so he could look directly at her. "You're lying to me so I won't shoot myself."

"No. There's a doc here, a urologist, and I've worked with him. He's a genius. I'll go find him, but you've got to promise you won't try anything stupid. I'm taking your pistol. No more morphine."

Donnelly replaced the bandages, covering the horror that, this time yesterday, had been part of a healthy young man.

Donnelly sidled closer to the GI so that their faces were close. He smelled like a fire, like a chemical burn. "You married?" she asked.

"No," he said. "Engaged. But we've never . . . I've never even . . ."

"It's OK," she said, touching his arm, squeezing his hand. "You've got plenty to live for. You're going to come through this."

"Everything intact?"

"As good as new."

"OK," the lieutenant said, leaning back again. "I won't shoot myself. At least until you get back with this doctor."

Donnelly stood, spotted the orderly who'd offered to help her. *Reister*, she remembered.

"Hey," she called. "Reister. Over here."

The private threaded his way around some stretchers as Donnelly moved toward him.

"I want you to keep an eye on that lieutenant, the one I was just examining, OK?"

"Sure thing, Lieutenant."

"He just tried to shoot himself, but I took his gun and made him promise to wait until I got help."

"Holy shit," Reister said. "I saw all the bandages across his groin."

"Yeah. Do you know where Doctor Lindner is? Have you seen him?"

"I think I saw him with the rest of the POWs, marching out the front gate about an hour ago. They're getting sent to the States, aren't they?"

"They were on foot?"

"Maybe they were meeting some trucks outside the compound," Reister said.

"OK, OK."

Donnelly took a step toward the front gate, dodging a pile of bloody bandages. When she moved, Norenger's pistol slipped out of her waistband and fell to the ground. She picked it up, stuck it in the front of her trousers, desperado style.

"His name's Norenger. Make sure he doesn't have any other weapons."

Reister was looking at something over her shoulder, distracted. Donnelly popped him on the chest with the flat of her hand, leaned close and raised her voice. "He tried to kill himself. That's not the business we're in. Don't let it happen, you hear me?"

Reister, startled, said, "Yes, ma'am."

Donnelly turned and jogged toward the front gate, a mental picture of Norenger's shattered penis hovering before her.

"Poor bastard," she said.

42

5 August 1943
1800 hours

Herr Doktor Lindner checked his watch five times in the first hour of waiting in the olive grove. He tried to distract himself by walking around, chatting with the stretcher cases, the walking wounded. The German medics had done a superb job preparing their patients for the move. Every man was comfortable, and most even seemed to be in good spirits. There was not much for him to do but pace and worry.

The Aryan-looking MP—whose name, Lindner learned, was the Nordic-sounding Gustafson—came back after an hour and sent two of the trucks away to other duties. That left four.

Lindner stood, did a quick head count. He could get all of the stretcher cases and about half of the medics and walking wounded into four trucks. And of course he would accompany that batch.

Another thirty minutes went by before Unterfeldwebel Bottcher approached.

"I was going to let the men eat the rations the American gave us, Herr Doktor, unless you have any objection."

"No, no. Of course not. Whatever you think is best."

The sergeant passed an order to a corporal who waited nearby, and the noncommissioned officers began to distribute the canned rations the American MPs had given them. Lindner watched for a few minutes as the German soldiers, now used to American food, began to trade the cans with one another, each man looking for his favorites, or the ones he hated least.

"Bottcher," Lindner called. The sergeant approached, snapped his heels together, and stood looking straight ahead.

"The Americans are taking the trucks away one by one, you see."

"Yes, sir."

"If any trucks leave today, I shall be with the first group."

This went against Wehrmacht tradition, as officers were supposed to ensure that their men—especially wounded men—were taken care of first. It was the same tradition that had prompted Lindner, the ranking doctor in his unit, to volunteer to stay behind with the wounded Germans when their army retreated from Palermo.

Lindner knew it was wrong, and Bottcher certainly knew it, but neither the sergeant's face nor his voice registered anything amiss.

"Yes, sir."

"I'm a little worried that with all this confusion, they won't be ready for us whenever we reach the ship." Lindner sounded like the very kind of officer he detested, one who made excuses for why he should be treated differently, one who waited to be served, rather than looking to serve.

"As you wish, Herr Doktor," Bottcher said, still looking straight ahead.

Lindner was still studying Bottcher's face when an American jeep raced up to the lead truck in a cloud of dust. Inside, two GIs, both caked in white. The driver was small-framed; the passenger taller, thin.

Harkins, Lindner thought.

When the jeep stopped about fifty yards away from where Lindner waited with the statue-still Sergeant Bottcher, the dust cloud rolled forward, hiding the passengers completely.

Lindner suddenly felt bile rise in this throat, was afraid he might vomit.

I have failed, he thought. *I was ready to abandon my patients, these good men, to save my own skin.*

He thought about his brother, Albrecht, a gentle boy conscripted at eighteen and now in a Luftwaffe antiaircraft battery somewhere in Italy. Would the Abwehr really hold a private accountable for his brother's failure as a spy? Would the authorities allow his family to leave Essen, to get out from under Allied bombs?

"Herr Doktor."

It was Bottcher, still at attention, watching him now. "Are you feeling well, Colonel?"

Lindner was unable to speak for a moment as he watched the American jeep, still hidden in the roiling dust.

Without answering Bottcher, he walked toward the Americans, stepping out from under the shade of the olive trees, vaguely aware of the German soldiers getting to their feet as he passed by. He was ten yards from the road when he could finally see the men in the jeep, two Negro soldiers.

The passenger, a noncom, was talking to the driver of the lead truck, conferring over a map. The jeep's driver, seeing Lindner approach, smiled and waved.

Someone said, "Are you the doctor that's in charge?"

It was the noncom, a staff sergeant with coffee-colored skin, his blouse soaked through with sweat. He'd been wearing goggles, now pushed down to his chest, and there was a dustless stripe across his eyes.

It took Lindner a few seconds to register that the man was talking to him.

"Yes," he said, trying to swallow with a dry mouth. "Yes, I am."

The GI approached. Lindner knew how Negros were treated in the United States, had seen a man beaten by a white mob in Louisiana for speaking to a white woman. And yet here they were, fighting for their country.

"I'm Staff Sergeant Caruthers," the American said. "I'll have five trucks up here in the next few minutes. You want to get your men ready and we'll run you down to that ship you're supposed to meet."

Lindner stepped close to Caruthers, surprised the man by putting out his hand.

"Thank you," he said. "Thank you very much."

Donnelly ran to the front gate, dodging stretcher bearers, piles of rolled tents, and an ambulance that had been left in gear and was rolling forward without a driver.

Just outside the gate the road climbed a small hill, and she was soon breathing heavily, forced to slow down and unable to see over the crest. The pistol jabbed her in the stomach, so she pulled it out and carried it in her hand. She should have left it with Reister.

The road was thick with traffic, most headed to the front, a few to the rear: jeeps and ambulances and trucks, a Dodge staff car idling, its windows rolled up. In most places the track was too narrow for two vehicles to pass abreast, so as far as she could see, vehicles hung to one side or the other, drivers yelling at one another, cursing. A long file of infantry soldiers slogged along in the field left of the road, heads down, moving at a steady, slow place. The men were dusty, sweat-soaked, exhausted looking, and headed for battle. Donnelly knew that, later on, she'd see some of them again, the broken ones.

She was startled when a GI standing on the running board of a truck shouted at her. "Hey, missy, what's your hurry?"

"Keep it in your pants, Bart," another man said. "She's packing a forty-five."

Donnelly did not look left or right, but kept her eyes on the road in front of her. She wasn't even sure that Lindner and the German prisoners were still around. It had been several hours since they had moved out.

To her left a grove of olive trees climbed the same slope, and as she looked in that direction she thought she saw some men moving there, heading over the top of the ridge. Germans? A line of engineer vehicles, backhoes and road graders, blocked her view of the road in front.

A sharp pain split her side, a stitch. She stopped, leaned over, and put her hands on her thighs, sucking hot air. She was looking at the ground when a pair of GI shoes appeared. Turning her head, she looked up into the sun at the silhouette of a GI.

"You got a pistol but no canteen?" the man said, holding out his own water. "You might want to rethink your equipment list there, ma'am. No water'll kill you in this here weather."

Donnelly managed to right herself, take the canteen.

"Thanks," she said. She tilted her head back and took a pull; the water was hot enough to make tea.

When she lowered the canteen and her gaze, the trucks in front of her had cleared, and she saw the last of the German medics getting onto the back of a deuce-and-a-half, fifty or sixty yards up the road.

"Hey!" she yelled, pushing the canteen back to the helpful soldier. She pressed her hand against her ribs, where it felt as if she'd been stabbed. Tried to run.

"Wait! Stop!"

The Germans were out of earshot, and even if they'd been closer they wouldn't hear her over the noise of the struggling convoys.

Donnelly dodged left, into the olive orchard, where the only traffic was the file of heads-down infantrymen. But the ground was soft here, her big GI shoes heavier with each step. Her right foot caught on a tree root and she tumbled, felt the magazine of the pistol, in her front pocket, jab her thigh as she fell. She rose, took two more steps watching the lead truck pull away. Then she stopped, jammed the magazine into the pistol, yanked the action back, and fired two shots into the air.

Most of the infantrymen around her hit the ground, and at least four turned their rifles on her. But nobody shot her, and up ahead, the German medics turned to look.

"Hold it right there!" she yelled, pointing at the Germans.

Hand on her splitting side, she jogged forward, saw a Negro driver stick his head out of the last truck in the column. Then an American sergeant appeared.

"Hold it right there! Just wait!"

Lindner jumped when he heard the shots. He'd been thinking about firing squads.

He gripped the front edge of the bench seat, waiting for the truck to roll, to take him away from the hospital and General Glass and Palermo and the memory of Captain Stephenson. He almost allowed himself to believe he was going to make it, but the truck did not move.

Lindner was closest to the tailgate. The American sergeant in the front seat of the truck behind his got out and walked back toward the olive grove. Then he heard a woman's voice; he knew immediately that it was a nurse and why she'd come.

Kathleen Donnelly had no idea what Lindner would say to her request.

Harkins was convinced that the German was a spy, but she also knew that this was a theory, and so far his theories had not persuaded the provost. Harkins had even admitted to her that he did not have a solid connection between Lindner and the wireless set found in the apartment—he was going on the word of Colianno's platoon of cousins-for-hire. Nor had Harkins established that Lindner was paying Boone for the privilege of staying at the American hospital.

Still.

"Doctor Lindner," she called when she saw him sitting by the tailgate of the lead truck. He smiled weakly, waved at her.

"Lieutenant Donnelly," he said. Cheerful, almost.

She put her foot onto the metal loop below the tailgate, boosted herself up so that she was almost at eye level with the men in the truck.

"Who here speaks English?" she asked as pleasantly as possible. None of the other Germans raised a hand.

"Just me," Lindner said softly.

Donnelly held the sun-baked steel tailgate, hot as a broiler, and studied Lindner's handsome face, which just looked sad.

"Are there many casualties?" he asked.

"We're overwhelmed. We're losing men who could be saved if we had more hands."

"I figured as much, from all the traffic."

Donnelly saw Lindner's medical bag at his feet. He had painted over the eagle emblem of the Third Reich.

"I have a special case, a soldier who stepped on a mine. Upward blast, flowering of the leg muscles, puncture in the left groin, damage to the glans penis."

"Are you ready to do the procedures?" He smiled when he asked. Lindner was the only doctor she'd ever told about her dream of medical school. He believed she could do it.

Donnelly couldn't help grinning, too. "The U.S. Army is a long way from letting me do surgery. A long way from letting any woman do anything like that."

The sergeant who'd agreed to let Donnelly talk to Lindner appeared beside her.

"Sorry, Lieutenant, but we gotta get moving or we'll be on those god-awful roads after dark."

"Thank you, Sergeant," Donnelly said. "I'll only be a minute more."

When she turned back to Lindner, he said, "Is your friend back? Harkins?"

"No," she said. Then, after a pause, "Not yet."

Lindner looked around at the other Germans. Without looking back at her, Lindner asked, "Do you know what you're asking of me?"

Donnelly could not pretend she truly understood his burden any more than Harkins had been able to comprehend what Ronan had been through with Stephenson.

Donnelly climbed down off the tailgate. "My patient is twenty, twenty-one, tops," she said. "Engaged to a girl back home. I stopped him from killing himself. This is his pistol, in fact."

Lindner looked down at her, made no move to hand over his medical bag.

"There'll be more," she said. "More patients."

And with that, Herr Doktor Lindner bent over, pulled his medical bag and duffle from the floor of the truck, and tossed them over the tailgate. He turned to the German soldier beside him, said, *"Auf Wiedersehen,"* and climbed down.

"Where's he going?" the American sergeant asked Donnelly.

"I'm needed at the hospital," Lindner said. "I'm a surgeon."

43

5 August 1943
1830 hours

The coastal road that ran from Palermo to the front was choked with every conceivable piece of American war equipment, most of it stuck in miles-long traffic jams. Somewhere to the east, the war had kicked into high gear and was consuming men and materiel again.

Adams turned from his spot in the front seat to address Harkins, riding in back.

"Word is the big German counterattack sputtered out. Apparently while everybody was panicking because the Krauts were on the move, Patton saw an opportunity. Wants to charge ahead, get at 'em while they're overextended and vulnerable."

Harkins held on to the backs of Adams' and Colianno's seats to keep from falling backward as the paratrooper gunned the engine and shot through an opening between two fuel trucks.

"Like boxing," Harkins shouted.

"What's that?" Adams yelled over the sound of the engines all around them.

"Guy throws a jab and misses, that's an opportunity."

It had taken them nearly two hours to climb to the plateau south of the city, a run that should have lasted thirty, forty minutes. The main road leading to the hospital was a river of olive drab vehicles, all flowing north and east toward the front. Harkins and company were swimming upstream.

Harkins told Colianno to pull over, and the driver found a flat spot just off the track and above a ditch that ran beside. Harkins and Adams got out, jumped the ditch, and climbed to a rise some fifty yards away. From there they could see the long line of vehicles, some moving, some stopped, some barely rolling, an accordion of wasted effort and resources that were needed elsewhere, and in a hurry.

"Looks like Constitution Avenue on a Friday afternoon," Adams said. "Everybody trying to get out of town all at once."

Harkins and Adams walked back to the jeep; Colianno had gotten out and was pacing alongside. He had an M1 Garand slung on his shoulder.

"Where'd you get that?" Harkins asked.

Colianno cocked his head slightly.

"Never mind," Harkins said. "I don't want to know."

When the three men were in the jeep, Harkins directed Colianno to head out cross-country, parallel to the narrow road everyone else was using to get to battle. They bounced and slipped and skidded across open country for another hour, Harkins' ribs sore from sliding around the back of the jeep. He was amazed that they did not break an axle.

"Half the place is packed up," Colianno said as they rounded a curve and rolled downhill toward where the gate had been. The sign that said 11TH FIELD HOSPITAL was still in place, but there was very little behind it. An entire small town of tents was moving.

"Colonel Meigs ordered me to keep out of here," Harkins said to Adams.

"He also ordered you to deliver Ronan to me and be back at your unit by eighteen hundred hours."

Adams held up his wrist, showed Harkins his watch. "Right now you're oh for two; why not make it oh for three?"

"I think we should split up," Colianno said as he nosed the jeep around a line of ambulances.

"Sounds good to me," Adams said.

"Negative," Harkins said. "Colianno, you stick with me."

Colianno cursed under his breath. He wanted to go off on his own to find Ronan.

"If you're by yourself it looks like you escaped from the stockade. If you're with me, it's my problem to explain. We're looking for Boone and Ronan," Harkins continued, "and we want to move them, separately, out of the hospital area. But we can't interfere if they're taking care of patients, especially Boone. It won't be good if I haul him away from an operating table and some GI dies. Park the jeep and we'll meet back here in a half hour."

The three men got out of the vehicle.

"OK," Harkins said. "Let's roll."

Boone had been inside the one remaining surgical tent for nearly four hours. When a nurse told him the teams were finally getting ahead of the flow of incoming wounded, he directed another surgeon to close up the patient and he stepped outside, stripping off his mask and bloody gown.

There did seem to be some order, finally. The line of stretcher teams waiting near the surgical tables had shrunk. A nurse in triage—he thought her name was Savio—wasn't running from place to place any longer.

The nurse named Haus came out of surgery behind him, wiping her forehead with her sleeve.

"Haus," Boone said. "Since we no longer have post-surgery wards, we're going to need to move patients to the hospital in Palermo, or set up someplace they can be held and stabilized so that we can head out of here."

"We're still jumping, sir?" She looked exhausted, Boone thought, but they were all exhausted.

"Of course we're still goddamn jumping," Boone said. "Find out how many ambulances we have at our disposal."

Haus walked toward the gate, and Boone stepped around the end of the surgical tent. About twenty yards away, two operating tables were set up in the open air, each with a team huddled around a patient.

That's where he saw Lindner.

"What the *fuck*?"

The man should have been gone hours ago, should have been on a ship by now, or at least in a holding pen in Gela. Lindner was the most dangerous loose end remaining. It wouldn't matter that Stephenson and Drake were dead, that the troublesome nurses were gone, if Lindner and Boone were connected over the gold.

"Colonel Boone!"

It was the nurse, Haus, calling to him. He turned on her. "What do you want?"

She reeled back, surprised. "You asked about ambulances, sir. It looks like there's a problem with an ambulance platoon forward of here, down near the coast."

Boone only half heard the woman. Why did they have to bring every problem to him?

"Handle it," he said without taking his eyes off Lindner. Now he could see that the nurse to Lindner's right was Donnelly.

Figures, he thought. *I'd like to get rid of all of them.*

"I'm not sure what you mean, sir," Haus said.

"I said handle it!" He spun toward her. "You nurses are so indispensable around here, so sure that you know every fucking thing! You said there's a problem, so come up with a goddamned solution! Is that so fucking hard to comprehend?"

Haus stepped back, raised her right hand sharply to her eyebrow in a parade-ground salute.

"Yes, sir!"

There was something in her eye, and Boone thought she might cry, another goddamn weeper. Then he realized what he was seeing.

She hated him. They all hated him.

This was not what he had wanted when he signed up. He'd been looking for something he could be proud of, something he could throw in the faces of the doubters back home, his stick-up-the-ass colleagues from the Ivy League, with their disdain of his country-doctor beginnings. But command had been too much, too complicated, with too many people wanting stuff from him; twenty-four hours a day of relentless, whining demands. He had been weak, it turned out, easily swayed by others and just as easily tempted.

No longer. Now it was time to be hard.

Ronan spotted Haus talking to Boone, saw her salute and turn away, head toward the gate.

Ronan had been assisting in surgery for hours, oblivious to her worries. As the casualties slowed and they got ahead of the tide, she realized she had not thought any further ahead than the operating table, had not thought about what she would do once the crisis passed. Boone would certainly come for her again, even if it was just to send her to North Africa.

She ducked behind Surgical One to avoid Boone, and headed for the gate, following Haus.

"Alice," she called, catching up.

Haus stopped and turned, a smile smoothing the lines in her tired face. "Moira! I'm so glad to see you!"

The women hugged; Ronan could feel Haus's ribs and wondered for a fleeting moment if she'd also lost that much weight.

"What are you doing?" Haus asked.

"I just finished assisting. Good Guy told us to take a break, and I'm trying to avoid that ass, Boone, since I've been AWOL and I think he'll throw me in the stockade."

"I've got something I think might help," Haus said.

She took Ronan by the arm and led her to the gate, where four ambulances were parked. All had jagged holes in their boxy sides, the lead vehicle with a busted windshield and three shredded tires, some GIs hopping around, trying to get the wheels off. A staff sergeant Ronan did not recognize—he was from another command—supervised the loading of medical supplies into the three vehicles that were only a little shot up. Orderlies unpacked bandages and plasma, all of which had been crated yesterday for the move, handing the materials to medics inside the backs of the vans.

"This is Staff Sergeant Benteen," Haus said.

Benteen's right forearm was wrapped in a gauze bandage that extended from his fingers to his elbow. Blood had leaked through in several spots.

"Can you go with us?" Benteen asked Ronan. He had what looked like a shrapnel wound to his right cheek, and a chunk of flesh was missing from his blood-caked ear.

"Where you going?"

"Another ambulance section got hit by Kraut artillery, a ways up the road there. Now we got the wounded they were carrying, plus a bunch of wounded medics. I'm going back up to pull them all out. I could use a nurse, could use all the help I can get."

"I'm in," Ronan said.

"Good. Great."

Benteen bent over and yanked a large medic's field bag from a crate his men had broken open, handed it to Ronan. It was brand new.

Haus gave her a quick hug, said, "Be careful, love," and turned back to help prepare the hospital for the move.

"OK," Ronan said. She stripped off the surgical gown and cap, yanked the mask from around her neck, used the wadded cloth to wipe blood from her arms and blot sweat from her face, then threw the whole bloody ball to the ground.

"Wonder if we'll have to do one giant police call after the war," she said. "Pick up all the trash we've left around."

"What's that?" Benteen asked. He was thin, on the tall side, a cowboy drawl.

"Just talking to myself. Anybody look at your arm? Dress the wound?"

"Yes, ma'am. I did."

"Right."

Ronan climbed into the rear of the last ambulance and opened the medical bag. Because it was new, all the instruments and supplies were wrapped for shipping. She began to break things down for quick access, rearranging instruments she would need immediately.

Pinpricks of light filtered through where shrapnel had punched holes in the sides of the vehicle. Blood pooled in the center of one of the stretchers racked on the right. She flipped it upside down, secured the handles, and used the opposite side to lay out her instruments. When she stepped sideways to throw a paper wrapper out the door, she slipped on the bloody floor, went down hard on both knees and hands.

"Shit!" She wiped her palms on her trousers.

And she suddenly recalled a conversation with her mother, who could not understand why she'd leave a safe, well-paid hospital job for any number of dangers as an army nurse.

"Well," her mother had said, "at least try to stay clean."

Ronan was surprised to find she could still laugh.

Boone spotted Harkins and Colianno walking along the church wall where the nurses' admin tent used to stand. They did not see him.

"What the hell?"

Colianno was supposed to be in the stockade, and Harkins had been ordered by the provost marshal to stay clear of the hospital and away from Boone. Yet here they both were. Which either meant the provost had changed his mind, or Harkins had somehow gotten Colianno released and was here to make an arrest, ready to make a case that was so strong he could defy Colonel Meigs' orders.

Boone turned and headed back toward his own tent, staying close to two trucks being loaded by his exhausted orderlies. He was looking back over his shoulder and tripped over a pile of long stakes.

"You OK, there, Colonel?" one of the soldiers asked.

Boone didn't answer, but began jogging, dodging in and out of the line of vehicles.

There were only two tents remaining in the central part of the compound; one of them his field office and small sleeping quarters. The walls had been lowered, which meant someone had started to dismantle it. Boone let himself into the office section through a back flap, pulled it nearly shut behind him, and peered out to see if Harkins had followed. Nothing yet.

A cheery voice from behind made him jump.

"Colonel Boone, so glad to see you!"

Boone started, turned, and saw Captain Adams, the deputy provost, who must have been in the front, where Drake's desk had been.

"What do you want?"

"I'm in charge of the investigation now, remember? It seems there have been some interesting developments. Do you know an Air Corps sergeant by the name of Trunk?"

"Why would I?"

Adams chuckled. "I should have known you'd clam up," he said. "No matter. You're coming back to the provost with me, and when we find Lieutenant Ronan we'll bring her along, too. And all of Lieutenant Harkins' various witnesses. He's turned out to be quite resourceful, don't you think? I mean, I didn't expect much, him not being a detective or anything."

Boone could feel his pulse in his temples, his heart drumming his rib cage. He was suddenly very thirsty. He hadn't expected Adams, did not have a plan.

"I'm not going anywhere with you," he managed. "I have a hospital to run, and we're jumping forward. Today. Right now. Or didn't you notice everything going on around here."

"I'm sure your staff can take care of all that, sir."

Boone looked around. All of his gear had been packed up: cot, washstand and shaving mirror, field desk and file cabinet, his footlocker, with his pistol inside. There were a few scattered papers on the ground and an oak chair that he'd had an orderly carry from the wrecked church nearby.

"I got a message today from a Lieutenant Cohen. He's on General Glass' staff. G4 section."

Adams patted his shirt pockets absentmindedly. He always looked rumpled, which grated on Boone. Today the lawyer had left his helmet someplace else, but was wearing a sidearm. Playing soldier. Probably imitating Harkins, his hero.

"Must have left it in my satchel. Anyway, did you know your Doctor Lindner was treating General Glass? Cohen didn't say what for; seems very hush-hush. Cohen says that Lindner showed a great deal of interest in some maps that were on the general's desk."

A wave of nausea threatened to knock Boone down.

He had kept Lindner from being evacuated on schedule with the other prisoners because the German was a skilled surgeon. When Lindner wanted to extend his stay with the Americans he offered Boone a gift—a small gold bar; part of a stash, Lindner claimed, left behind by the retreating Wehrmacht. When Boone learned that Lindner was treating General Glass, he suspected something else was going on, but he ignored the warning signs and got Stephenson involved. After that, there was no going back.

"What does that have to do with me?" Boone said.

"I imagine you'll have to explain why Doctor Lindner was given such . . . generous privileges. Could come and go as he pleased, apparently.

"Shall we, Colonel?" Adams said politely, holding aside the curtain so that Boone could step into the front part of the tent and away to the provost's headquarters.

Boone put one foot in front of the other, ducked as if going through the door.

"Just a sec," he said.

He pivoted, grabbed the oak chair, heaved it above his shoulder and then down on Adams' head. Once. Twice.

He stood, chest heaving, looking down on what he'd done. Another line crossed. He could not see a way back to normalcy, to his role as commander, as a respected surgeon. He was reacting, making things worse.

He put his hands on either side of his face, squeezed, forced himself to breathe deeply, slowly. He took Adams' pistol and belt, opened the tent flap. Outside, the war went on relentlessly.

Boone walked outside, headed for the open-air operating theater where he'd seen Lindner. He hadn't thought about the sergeant at the airfield, Stephenson's choice, had no idea if the man knew his name. But there was another loose end back in the States—the guy who received the gold.

It would take days, maybe weeks for cops back home to get involved, get the information they needed. On this side of the ocean, the threat was more immediate. Harkins was breathing down his neck. But with Lindner gone, he could buy some time to think.

He found Lindner alone, washing his hands. Boone pressed Adams' pistol to his back, got him moving, the German in front, calm, even resigned; Boone behind him, stepping awkwardly so he could stay close and hide the pistol.

"Are you going to shoot me, Colonel?" Lindner asked. He did not sound afraid, which made Boone angrier.

"What if I do?" he asked, jabbing Lindner with the muzzle. "Other than a few nurses, no one in the whole goddamn Seventh Army would bat an eye."

The two men made their way toward the main gate, where Boone thought he could commandeer a vehicle. He didn't know where he was headed after that, but it wasn't the stockade.

Ronan had just finished repacking her medical bag when she heard Boone's voice outside.

"Where are these ambulances going?"

She froze, heard Sergeant Benteen explain the rescue mission he was preparing.

The back doors to her vehicle were open. Ronan pressed herself against the stacked stretchers and reached for the handle so she could pull them shut without being seen from outside. She jumped when an orderly stepped into the opening.

"Oh!"

"Sorry, ma'am," the private said. "Just this one more crate."

He lifted a heavy wooden box onto the rear of the ambulance. "You want these doors shut?"

"Please."

Ronan shrunk back into the somewhat darker interior, but before the door closed completely, Boone looked in and saw her. She tried to get out, but he blocked the door, yanking someone by the arm and shoving him into the ambulance. It took Ronan a second to comprehend that the other man was Lindner.

"Get in there," Boone said to her. He had Lindner by the shoulder, by the shirt. Behind the two men, the orderly who'd just loaded the crate watched them, trying to make sense of what he was seeing.

"Shut that door," Boone told the soldier.

When the two men were inside, the door closed.

"Well, Lieutenant Ronan," Boone said, wild-eyed. "Finally decided to come back to your place of duty after your liberty in Palermo."

That's when she saw the pistol, pointed at Lindner, and decided not to answer him.

Kathleen Donnelly had seen Boone and Lindner leave the gate. Lindner was in the lead, but she was pretty sure Boone shoved the German a couple of times. She followed and ran into Alice Haus, who was supervising the breakdown of a surgery suite.

"What are those ambulances doing there?" Donnelly asked, pointing to the vehicles stacked up outside the gate.

"Another section up ahead got hit by German artillery. Medics hurt, no one to take care of them or the other wounded. The sergeant in charge of those is riding to the rescue, like the cavalry."

Haus looked around, dropped her voice. "Ronan's in the last one. She volunteered to go with them."

Donnelly's breath left her. "Ohhhhh . . ."

The lead vehicle pulled around a badly damaged ambulance in the front of the line. She ran holding her side where it hurt her earlier. There would be no stopping these with a gunshot—she had gotten rid of the pistol.

The second ambulance moved before she reached the abandoned guardhouse that had marked the gate. She reached the third ambulance before it rolled and yanked open the rear door.

Inside, a strange tableau: Ronan, as far forward as she could get, sitting on a floor streaked with blood. Lindner crouched next to her and, closest to the door, Boone, holding a pistol.

Donnelly called her friend. "Moira!"

When the vehicle started to move, Donnelly jumped in.

44

5 August 1943
1920 hours

Harkins and Colianno ran up to Haus, who was watching the ambulances disappear over the hill outside the gate.

"Was that Kathleen?" Harkins asked. "Did she just get in that last ambulance?"

"Yeah," Haus said. "What's wrong?"

"We saw Colonel Boone leading that Kraut doctor out of the gate a few minutes ago," Harkins said. He bent over, put his hands on his thighs to catch his breath. He and Colianno had been on the other side of the compound, had run hundreds of yards but were unable to close the distance.

"Did you see Boone get in that ambulance?"

"No," Haus said. "I wasn't really watching for that, but . . ." She looked at Colianno. "Moira was in that last ambulance, too. I figured that's why Kathleen got in."

Colianno turned and sprinted to get their jeep.

"Where are they going?" Harkins asked.

"Up to the front somewhere. Some other ambulances got hit, and they need help with the wounded. There's a Sergeant Benteen in the lead vehicle. He's the one who knows where they're going."

Colianno was back in minutes, driving fast, leaning on the horn and scattering soldiers out of his way.

"Any sign of Adams?" Harkins asked.

"No. Let's go without him."

Harkins took Haus by the elbow. "You know that captain, the deputy provost?"

"The lawyer who threw up when he saw his first dead body?"

"Yeah. He's here somewhere. Tell him that Moira and Kathleen are on that ambulance, maybe with Boone, maybe Lindner. He should follow as soon as he can. Got it?"

"Got it."

"We're going after them."

"Bring my girls back in one piece," Haus said.

Harkins got into the jeep, touched the rim of his helmet, and grabbed the windshield to steady himself as Colianno punched the accelerator.

The roads east got narrower and more jammed with traffic as soon as they cleared the compound. In their first thirty minutes the closest they got to the ambulance was about five hundred yards, scores of vehicles between. Several times traffic came to a complete halt, and Harkins got out, thinking he could catch them on foot. But then something in the jam would give way and Colianno would catch up with him as the ambulances pulled farther ahead.

"Shall I try going cross-country?" Colianno asked.

Harkins looked at his map. The road Sergeant Benteen had chosen did not lead directly to the coast, but dropped south and headed for a long lake, Lago Rosamarina, passing through some hilly country. They couldn't jump ahead because Harkins didn't know the destination, and he wasn't sure they could get back to the road if they got off.

"No, stick to the road. Keep them in sight. Just try to get around as many of these guys as you can."

Colianno used every wide spot to swerve around whatever truck or jeep was ahead of them. Some drivers cursed, some ignored him, some laughed because he worked so hard and often wound up just one vehicle length ahead of where he'd been. A few tried to get out of his way, and Harkins waved his thanks.

Traffic thinned at the southern end of the lake, and for a moment Harkins lost sight of the ambulances.

"There," Colianno said. "Peeling off to the right."

Harkins raised his binoculars and found two of the ambulances. They'd picked up speed.

"Is that them?" Colianno asked. "I only see two."

"I don't . . ."

The rear ambulance hit a crater, springing open the back doors and giving Harkins a look inside. There were at least four people, and the man closest to the door was definitely Boone. The surgeon reached to pull the doors shut again, nearly lost his balance. Then he shifted something from right hand to left to get a better grip.

"Shit," Harkins said. "Boone's got a pistol."

"Did you see Moira and Kathleen?"

"I think so. There were definitely four people in there."

Harkins watched his driver. The paratrooper kept shifting from first to second and back again, jamming the clutch and the accelerator. When he took his hand off the gearshift he rubbed it obsessively on his leg.

"Look," Harkins said. "Lindner is the biggest threat to Boone. There's no reason for him to hurt the women."

Colianno looked over at Harkins. "He's got no play here," he said, his eyes off the road. "What's he going to do? Drive home to the States? Once we catch up he's backed into a corner. He's liable to do anything."

The jeep crashed into the bumper of the truck in front of them. There were a half-dozen GIs in the back, perched on wooden ammo crates.

"What's your hurry, Mac?" one of them yelled down at them. "Afraid there won't be any Krauts left when you get there?"

"When we catch up I can talk to him," Harkins said to Colianno. "Get him to release Kathleen and Moira, maybe Lindner. If he knows the game is up he might just surrender."

"What fucking world are you living in, Lieutenant?" Colianno said, his voice strained. "He shot his goddamn first sergeant to death! He went there to kill one of his own nurses, and she's in that ambulance with him!"

"I still think I can talk him down," Harkins said. "You got a better idea?"

The truck ahead moved, and Colianno pushed the gearshift hard.

"Yeah, I shoot him in the head as soon as I can get a bead on him."

The first round of incoming artillery exploded just off the track, and twenty yards ahead of the ambulance. Shrapnel peppered the side of the vehicle.

"Holy shit, that was close," Boone said.

Donnelly, unable to hide her disgust, said, "The close ones poke holes in the side. You might get a Purple Heart yet, Colonel."

"Nurse Donnelly," Boone yelled over the noise. "It's your precious Doctor Lindner who betrayed you, betrayed us all."

The next rounds of incoming were farther from the road; the ambulance moved again.

Donnelly waited to see where Boone was going with this. Ronan, who believed that Boone came to the house in Palermo to shoot her, not Drake, had not said a word since Boone got into the vehicle.

"He's a spy, you see," Boone said. "Not a good spy, but a spy nonetheless. Did you know he was treating a senior American officer? Probably pumping him for information. And he turned on his accomplice. Killed Stephenson to cover up what they'd been doing together."

Donnelly looked at Lindner, who appeared as defeated as any prisoner she'd ever seen. Boone was a liar, of course, but Harkins had fingered Lindner as a spy. Maybe that just made him a good German.

"And what was it that they were doing together, Colonel?" Donnelly asked. "Because it looked to me, looked to everybody at the hospital, that you were the one doing favors for Doctor Lindner. Letting him stay on while you shipped other POWs as quick as we got them patched up."

Ronan kicked her, but Donnelly was too angry to stay silent.

"You'll see," Boone said. "It will all come out in the end."

Lindner said something that was lost amid the engine noises.

"What?" Donnelly asked.

"I did not kill anyone."

Boone hit Lindner in the face with the pistol. There was a crunching sound and the German curled up on the floor of the ambulance, cursing. Donnelly helped him sit up again.

"Doctor Lindner came back to help take care of our wounded," Donnelly said.

And I talked him into coming back.

The German barrage was perfectly planned, the incoming rounds landing in a tight pattern almost exactly aligned with the road about six hundred yards ahead of them.

"Christ, that looks bad," Colianno said as the blasts silhouetted several vehicles.

"Looked like every round hit the road."

"The Krauts target highways and intersections, even if they're not sure anyone's there," Colianno said. "We do that, too."

"Does that mean they're attacking?"

Colianno shrugged, which Harkins did not find reassuring.

He couldn't tell if the ambulances—they were chasing only two now—were on the other side of where the artillery hit or had been hit themselves. Up ahead, a handful of the American vehicles pulled off, hesitant to go forward.

"Let's push," Harkins said. Colianno drove a zigzag course.

According to his map, they'd pass through a narrow valley up ahead before reaching the coast. Another choke point and a chance to catch the ambulance.

They drove around the craters left by the artillery. Two American trucks were on fire, and a handful of men were carrying wounded and dead away from the wreckage. To his right, on the other side of a roadside ditch, Harkins saw a medic holding a plasma bottle above a GI laid out on the ground, while a chaplain wearing a purple stole made the sign of the cross over the wounded man. He thought of Patrick, was sure his brother also ignored incoming fire when a soldier needed him.

Two jeeps that had rolled or driven off the road were trying to climb out of the ditch. They needed a tow.

"Hey!" a sergeant called to Harkins. "Give us a hand here!"

Harkins turned to Colianno, who said, "No way we're stopping."

He was still speeding, still careening around the wrecks, when the first tank rolled in from the left, fast, nearly clipping the front of their jeep. It was a Sherman, thirty tons of steel, hell-bent for somewhere else.

"Shit!" Colianno said as he turned sharply and their two passenger-side wheels slipped into the ditch. They skittered along for ten or fifteen yards, Harkins sure that they were going to roll, before Colianno got control and dragged them back onto the track.

That's when the second tank came up behind them.

Harkins heard the whine as the big machine downshifted, turned halfway in his seat to see the tank driver, the top of his head just visible above the coiled tow cable and white star on the front glacis plate. Nine feet above the road, his upper body sticking out of the turret, the tank commander waved at them furiously to get out of the way.

Although there was no hope of anyone, even Colianno, hearing him, Harkins yelled, "Where the hell do you want me to go?"

Colianno pulled as close to the tank ahead as he could, he and Harkins breathing in fumes from the engine grate directly in front of them. The commander of the lead tank, also standing in his turret, saw them, lifted his goggles to get a better view. He shook his head, snapped the goggles back in place, and turned to the front, his right hand resting on the big .50 caliber machine gun mounted atop the tank.

Harkins looked left and right, where the hills on either side rose to pinch the road. This was the bottleneck he'd seen on his map. The tanks were in a terrible hurry to get through. Get hit with artillery here, with no room to maneuver, they were just big targets, thick-skinned but hard to miss. Colianno and Harkins had jumped on a fast-moving train, with no place to stop, no way to get off.

They were obviously within range of enemy artillery. If a German counterattack reached them—if panzers suddenly appeared on top of the ridges, for instance—they were in a shooting gallery.

It was nearly full dark now, and Harkins could see only a few yards on either side, could just make out the tank they were following. The road curved to the left, and for a moment he thought they might be able to get off to the right, maybe pull ahead of the tanks. Then the ground to the right dropped away sharply—they were on the side of a hill now—and just as suddenly the Sherman ahead of them stopped.

Colianno stood on the brakes, their hood coming within a foot of the tank's hot grate. He backed up a few feet to get out of the exhaust, and heard the commander of the lead tank yelling at someone in the road, but nothing moved.

"I'm going up," Harkins said. "Bring the jeep up when you can."

"I want to come, too, Lieutenant," Colianno said.

"I know you do." He actually felt sorry for the kid. "I'm only stepping around this tank."

Harkins had just reached the front of the Sherman when its commander climbed out of the turret, stepped onto the deck, then jumped to the ground. Just ahead, a wrecker had attached a tow cable to a fuel truck; the fuel tanker's right wheels had slipped off the edge of the slope, and the whole rig was listing toward the drop-off.

"How long you been at this?" the tank commander asked the four GIs trying to pull the fuel truck free. Harkins could hear the strain in the man's voice.

"Half an hour," someone said.

"I can't wait around."

The tank commander was dark-skinned, with a wide face and the raccoon look of a man who wore goggles in the sun.

One of the GIs jumped in the wrecker and gunned the engine, but the fuel truck was well and truly stuck.

"Sorry, fellas," the tank commander said. "Stand back."

He climbed back on the Sherman and put on his helmet with the headset. He said something and, below him, Harkins saw the driver acknowledge the command. Then the tank rolled forward, its left track clawing at the rock face. The GIs on the wrecker jumped clear, and when the tank got close, it simply shoved the wrecker and fuel truck over the side of the hill. The mass of steel rolled over—the two vehicles still connected by the tow cable—until it reached the bottom of the ravine, a long sixty or seventy feet below.

The lead Sherman passed, and Colianno was right behind.

"Did he just shove that whole thing over the side?" Colianno asked as Harkins jumped in.

"Yeah. Let's not get in his way."

The latest rounds of German artillery exploded behind them, and as the ambulance rolled forward Boone tried to stand and look out the small windows in the rear doors, but he couldn't keep his footing.

While his back was turned, Donnelly pulled two scalpels from the medical kit, tucking one into her trouser pocket and gesturing for Ronan to do the same. Lindner was on the floor between them, his cheek swollen and eyebrow cut from where Boone had hit him with the pistol. It wasn't clear if he saw what they were doing.

Boone had just looked at his watch, asked, "How long have we been driving?" when another barrage knocked the vehicle sideways. Something tore a hole in the ceiling of the van.

The ambulance picked up speed, swerved. Donnelly felt its rear wheels slipping, and then they were airborne, the four of them thrown around as the ambulance rolled over once, twice. Someone's boot kicked Donnelly hard in the face, and she heard what might have been a bone cracking as one of the men—she thought it was Boone—grunted out a lungful of air.

Donnelly was still conscious when the vehicle stopped rolling, the ambulance on its side, rear doors flung open. Outside, the artillery continued to fall, though farther away, the flashes lighting up the dusk. Men screamed.

"Moira!" she called.

"Get out," Ronan said. Dragging her medical bag, she pushed Donnelly on the butt as the two women clambered for the opening.

Donnelly, out first, turned to pull her friend clear. Inside the ambulance they could see a tangle of arms and legs.

"Get away from the vehicle," Donnelly said.

"Lindner," Ronan said.

"Get clear first."

Another round of artillery made her point, and the women dove for the lip of the road, their feet sliding downslope. They pressed their faces into the rocks and dirt as two more rounds banged brightly nearby. There was a loud *whompf* that sucked the air from around them, then a giant, blinding fireball as the fuel tank on a nearby truck exploded.

Donnelly shielded her eyes and made out four, no five jeeps and trucks scattered like broken toys along the road. As her eyes adjusted, she saw men staggering. A figure lurched away from a flaming vehicle, a man on fire, his clothes, hair, shoes consumed, not even screaming anymore. He staggered two steps, fell to his knees, burning like he was made of straw, like he'd been marinated in gasoline. As she watched, another GI stepped close and shot the man with a pistol.

Donnelly looked away, asked Ronan, "You OK? In one piece?"

"I got a bump on my head, I think," Ronan said. "You think Lindner and Boone are dead?"

"That would make things easier, wouldn't it?"

Then Donnelly heard the call that got her moving.

"Medic!"

"Let's go," Donnelly said, grabbing the heavy medical bag by one of its handles. She scrambled to her feet, Ronan on the other handle as, stride for stride, they ran toward the wrecked vehicles and wounded men.

The artillery was close now.

"There should be an intersection up ahead," Harkins said. It was too dark to read the map, so he stuffed it into the pocket behind his seat.

"There'll be a road coming in from the left, a Y intersection. Maybe we can get past the tanks there."

"Fire up ahead," Colianno said.

An orange light reflected off the hillside above them.

The lead tank pivoted sharply to the left, and suddenly Harkins could see a column of flame, a few vehicles scattered, some GIs running, back-lit by a burning truck.

"An ambulance!" Harkins said. "On the other side of that fire."

The lead tank had turned to hug the base of the slope on the left, but the commander, probably because he could not see past the bright flames, stopped the big Sherman. Colianno swerved to the right to avoid plowing into the exhaust grate again, but he took it too sharp. There was a small berm on the side of the road; the jeep hit it, front wheels off the ground, leaned over in midair for a long second, and landed on its passenger side. Harkins pulled his legs in at the last second, narrowly avoiding getting one or both crushed.

"You OK?" Harkins asked Colianno, who landed on top of him. The jeep's wheels were still spinning, but the engine sputtered to a stop.

Colianno got to his feet, rummaged among the things flung from the jeep until he found his rifle and ammunition. He turned toward the ambulance, which was on its side some hundred yards away, its red cross insignia lit by the fire.

"You're staying here," Harkins said. "We don't know if that's the right ambulance, and I want to be ready to roll. So get the jeep right side up, then come forward."

Colianno used both hands to throw his rifle to the ground. "I hate being your fucking driver!"

Harkins went four or five steps, heard the sound of incoming artillery. Colianno reacted first, yelled, "Incoming!"

Harkins threw himself forward, jamming his chin on the ground, biting his tongue and eating dirt.

Four explosions, close together, lit the ravine below them. A spray of steel shrapnel spent its energy going up, then came down on Harkins, harmless as rain.

Harkins pulled himself upright, knee and chin throbbing, and hurried toward the ambulance. On the other side of the circle of light thrown by the fire, he could see the lead Sherman nosing forward, pushing an overturned truck. GIs on the ground were yelling at the tank commander, who screamed back.

"Get out of my way!"

Although the road was a bit wider because of the intersection, his tanks were still trapped, incoming artillery threatening to turn them into giant torches.

Harkins ran to the front of the lead Sherman, heard a man on foot yell, "Stop! We got wounded on the road!"

Harkins turned, squinted to see through the firelight, saw Donnelly and Ronan beside a wounded GI. Donnelly was on her knees, pressing straight down with both hands on the man's shoulder, maybe his chest. Ronan worked in a big satchel, a medical kit, pulling things free and talking fast.

"Kathleen," Harkins said, running to them.

Donnelly looked up at him, then back down at her patient, whose shoulder and upper torso were ripped open.

"Press on this," she told Harkins. "Right where my hands are."

Harkins thought he had a good grip, but when Donnelly pulled away a geyser of blood shot through his fingers, spraying his chin and mouth.

"Press hard, goddamn it!"

Harkins did as he was told; the bleeding subsided.

"Clamp," Ronan said.

Donnelly took something from Ronan, then slipped her hands below Harkins' fingers. "Move."

The geyser came back. Donnelly jammed the pointed end of the clamp into the pool of meat and upwelling blood. The stream stopped.

"Where else is he hit?" Donnelly asked Ronan. The two women started their head-to-toe examination of the GI. The man's right eye had been slashed; his left was open, rolled back, showing white. Harkins hoped he was unconscious.

He sat on his heels, heard a GI shout behind him, turned to see the lead Sherman moving toward them, slowly, a crawling beast. He jumped up, ran straight at the tank, and leaped for the front deck. He caught the edge of the driver's hatch and crawled up to the turret, face-to-face with the commander.

"They're trying to save a guy's life right there. You've got to stop."

"And I've got four tanks and twenty guys I'm trying to save, so get the fuck out of my way!"

Harkins pulled his .45, thought about shoving it in the commander's face. Instead he put it back in the holster and said, "Get down with me and we'll find a way around."

"You're out of your mind," the tanker said, but he pulled himself out of the hatch, tapped the driver on the head as he climbed down. "Hold right here."

Harkins and the other man jogged forward, looking for a place his platoon could squeeze past both the burning wreckage and the spot where Donnelly was trying to save a soldier's life, but the gap was too narrow. Then the tanker saw Donnelly and Ronan. In the firelight their bloody hands and arms looked black.

"How long before she can move him?" the tanker asked. He still had his goggles on; the firelight made them shine. It was like looking in a mirror.

Harkins had no idea, but he said, "Couple of minutes, tops."

The tank commander held up three fingers. "After that, I'm rolling." Then he jogged back to brief the others in his column.

Harkins hurried back to where Donnelly and Ronan worked on the wounded man. He arrived in the circle of light just as Boone, shoving Lindner ahead of him, stepped out of the darkness. Boone still had his pistol, holding it low and loose near his thigh. The side of his face was scraped, bleeding slightly. Lindner held his left arm with his right hand.

Harkins didn't even have time to think about disarming Boone before Donnelly snapped them all back to the situation.

"He's still losing blood!" She shoved a hand under the patient's lower back, moved it down toward his buttocks.

Ronan was doing the same exam from the opposite side. "I feel it. Lower right. Above the sacrum. Puncture wound."

"Pack it with gauze," Lindner said.

The German looked over his shoulder at Boone, then knelt next to the nurses. "Turn him over," he said. "Pull out rolled gauze."

He looked up at Harkins. "Lieutenant, there should be a flashlight in the medical kit," he said. Calm, like he was teaching in a classroom somewhere. "Please take it out and point it here."

Harkins found the flashlight, pointed it at the nurses' hands. His .45 was in its holster. Boone was a few feet away, pistol still low at his side, shifting his weight from foot to foot. He looked dazed. The rollover had rattled him, banged him up. Harkins wondered if he'd figured out yet that he was trapped.

The driver and noncom from the flipped ambulance were treating a couple of other injured GIs fifteen yards away; Harkins could see the soles of their shoes as they knelt beside the road. He looked over his shoulder for the tank commander, saw Colianno forcing the jeep between an abandoned truck and the lead tank.

After a few minutes, Donnelly said, "OK, I think we've stopped the major bleeding."

She stood, arching to stretch her back. When she saw Colianno, she said, "Moira, help me get a stretcher out of the ambulance and we'll load this guy onto the jeep. Get him out of here."

In the few minutes it took the women to get the stretcher, Boone came around.

"What are you doing?" he asked.

"We're loading this patient onto this jeep," Donnelly said. "Get him back to an aid station."

"Yes," Boone said. "Yes, I want you to do that. You two nurses get into the jeep and accompany that man back." He was animated now, gesturing with the pistol but not pointing it at anyone.

Behind him, Harkins heard the first Sherman start to move forward, into the circle of firelight.

"All right, people," the tank commander called down. "Let me through."

Colianno and Ronan lifted the stretcher, securing it behind the front seats. The tank approached slowly, its engine noise making it difficult to hear.

"You're going back, too," Harkins shouted at Lindner.

The German checked the patient, leaning over until his ear was on the wounded man's chest. Searching for breath.

Everything that's happening, and he's still a doctor, Harkins thought.

Ronan fashioned a sling from a green kerchief, wrapped Lindner's broken arm, and tied the ends behind his neck. She touched his cheek, then Lindner stepped close to Harkins. With the tanks close by, they still had to yell.

"You found . . . ?"

"Everything," Harkins said.

Lindner got in the front seat. Donnelly and Ronan perched in the back. Donnelly put gauze on the soldier's shattered eye, taped it in place.

Lindner said something to Harkins as the first tank rolled by just a few feet away. Harkins had to lean close.

"What?"

"I never sent a single message," Lindner yelled. "Can you believe that?"

Colianno climbed into the driver's seat, and that's when Boone stepped up to the hood of the vehicle, raised his pistol, and shot Lindner twice in the chest.

"Shit!" Harkins said.

He drew his weapon, held it in two hands, point of aim on Boone's torso. Colianno jumped out of the vehicle, pulling his Garand and taking up a standing firing position, leaning forward slightly at the hips. Donnelly and Ronan moved too, covering the patient with their bodies.

Boone spoke first. "He was a spy! He used me, used us all! He killed Stephenson when Stephenson found out."

Harkins raised his hands, arms like a cactus, pointed his pistol to the sky. "I know he was a spy. We found the wireless."

Harkins slowing everything down. He took a step away from the jeep to get Boone's weapon and attention aimed away from the nurses and their patient. On the other side of the vehicle, Colianno did the same, sliding to his left.

When the colonel looked at him, Harkins said, "We also found the gold, and the name of the guy Stephenson shipped it to. What will he say when the FBI picks him up back in the States? Is he going to know your name, Colonel?"

Boone's eyes were wide, clicking back and forth from Harkins to Colianno to the nurses. Harkins had seen the look before. A jumper he'd tried to talk off a bridge, same big eyes, openmouthed breathing right before he stepped into space.

Harkins was startled when Ronan got out of the jeep.

"Sonofa*bitch*," she said, climbing from the back of the vehicle, squaring off with Boone, who was still in front of the hood.

"That's why you didn't do anything about Stephenson, about the rape," she said. "He was right. You were never going to touch him. But he was out of control, was going to blow the lid off. So you killed him."

Donnelly got out of the jeep, came around to the passenger side, where Lindner had slumped halfway out of the vehicle. She checked the pulse on his throat, looked at Harkins, shook her head.

Boone jumped around the front of the jeep and grabbed Donnelly by the hair. She yelped, swung a fist at him. Boone hit her on the side of the face with the pistol, pulled her back a few steps, his left arm now around her throat, her heels dragging.

Harkins took two steps toward Boone, crowding him. "Hurt her and you're a dead man," he said.

From the other side of the vehicle, Colianno yelled, "I have the shot," his rifle pointed at Boone's head. But Donnelly was too close.

"No!" Harkins said. "Hold your goddamned fire."

"I didn't kill Stephenson!" Boone said.

There was a crash; Harkins thought it was Colianno's rifle. But then another, a flowering of white light and dust in the ravine below them, the German artillery back again and trying to find the road.

The lead tank was past, but the second in line gunned its engine and came on them out of the dark, a nightmare rush of black steel. Everyone hunched, except Ronan, who took a step toward Boone.

"Don't come any closer!" he said, backing. Donnelly's hands were on his forearm, trying to break his grip. When he slipped, she tried raking her fingers across his eyes.

A third tank roared up, forced them all to the edge of the road. In the ravine below them, trees crackled and burned. Another burst shell, a bit farther away, but Harkins heard something sing by his head. Shredded steel moving at a hundred miles an hour.

To his left, Colianno walked forward slowly, rifle butt tucked into his shoulder, face pressed to the stock, desperate to shoot Boone.

To his right, Ronan advancing, not willing to let Boone drag her friend into the darkness beyond the firelight.

"You got nowhere to go, Boone!" Colianno said. "Let her go and I won't shoot."

Ronan was almost beside Boone now. She'd reached the spot in the road where she and Donnelly had worked to save the soldier's life. A pile of bloody bandages, paper wrappers from the gauze, at least two steel instruments winking firelight from the dirt. Parts of the man's uniform, a pistol belt and holster.

"Careful, Moira," Harkins said. When she looked at him, he glanced down at the discarded equipment, waggled his own .45.

In a movement so smooth she might have practiced it, Ronan reached into the pile of gear, came up with the patient's pistol, and shot Boone in the leg.

Harkins jumped forward as Boone fell, kicked away the doctor's dropped weapon, then grabbed Kathleen by the arm, pulling her behind him.

Boone was on his side in the dirt, breathing hard through his mouth. Both hands were on his left leg, where blood came through his fingers.

In two quick steps Ronan was straddling Boone, pressing the muzzle of the pistol to his head, shoving his face to the road. A fourth tank charged by, impossibly loud and just a few feet away. When Harkins glanced up, he saw the commander, his torso sticking out of the hatch, wide-eyed at the scene.

"You let Stephenson get away with rape," Ronan spat. "At least until it wasn't convenient for you." She reached back and slammed the pistol on Boone's wounded leg, two sharp blows. Then she jammed the muzzle back into his cheek.

Boone grimaced, lips back over his teeth. "Oh, fuck!"

"He did awful things to us!" she said, screaming to be heard above the tanks. "To me!"

Boone looked defeated, his face suddenly wet with tears. "Go ahead and shoot me," he said. "Just kill me."

Ronan looked at Harkins, who holstered his own weapon, stepped up to her, and gently took the pistol from her hand.

After a few seconds, Ronan stood, and in a different voice said, "Dominic, hand me that medical bag, would you?"

As Colianno brought the kit to her, Ronan knelt to dress Boone's leg.

Harkins squatted next to her. "We're not going to kill you, Colonel, but I wouldn't bet against you winding up at the end of a rope."

45

8 August 1943
1030 hours

Eddie Harkins sat in the front seat of his jeep in Palermo, just outside the headquarters of the Seventh Army chaplain, waiting for his brother. He'd managed to scrounge a clean envelope from a mail clerk, and he held it on his knee as he wrote Kathleen Donnelly's name, rank, and unit on the front. He put his name and unit on the upper left and, in the upper right-hand corner, where a stamp would normally go, he wrote "Free." A small benefit of being in a war zone.

He reached under his seat and pulled out the book of poems one of his MPs had given him on the day he'd learned that his kid brother had been lost in the vast Pacific. Carl Sandburg. He found the poem he wanted and tore out the page, then wrote in the margin.

Kathleen, you asked me what I want after the war. It looks something like this.

He thought about signing it "Love, Eddie," but left it alone. He stuffed the sheet into the envelope and went back inside, handed it to the mail clerk.

A little while later Patrick came out and the two of them drove to the newly established station hospital in Palermo to visit Captain Adams, who had not yet been cleared for release. Patrick Harkins had three hours left on Sicily. Then he'd board a plane for North Africa, where his regiment was already training for the next invasion.

Harkins tried not to think about the last time he saw Michael, a cavalier, joking good-bye in front of their parents' home. *What,* he wondered, *makes for a good farewell?*

The roads were full again; it seemed every American on the island was headed east.

"Big push over there to break the line the Krauts have in front of Messina," Patrick said.

"I'll bet they're scrambling to get as many as possible off the island," Harkins added. "Right across the Strait of Messina, which means we'll have to face those same bastards if we go to the mainland from here."

"The Strait of Messina, where Odysseus sails in *The Odyssey,*" Patrick said.

Harkins looked over at his brother. "Look at you, all caught up on your classics."

They parked across a busy street from the hospital. An orderly at a makeshift desk in the lobby told them where to find Adams.

"You hear about your boy Georgie Patton?" the lawyer asked as soon as the brothers entered the hospital room. The deputy provost sat on the edge of his cot, his head still wrapped in gauze where Boone had hit him with an oak chair. He was dressed, but in his stocking feet.

"What's he up to now?" Harkins asked.

"Scuttlebutt here is that a couple of days ago he walked into a field hospital in Second Corps area, up near Nicosia," Adams said. "Found a guy whose nerves were shot. Battle fatigue, I guess. Shaking, could barely talk."

"Sounds like me on the morning after Saint Patty's Day," Harkins said.

"Yeah. Anyway, Patton slapped the guy. Hit him with his gloves."

"I heard he hit the guy with his fist," Patrick said.

"Either way, the docs weren't happy about it, since the guy was their patient. And Patton walked out yelling that there's no such thing as battle fatigue, that the guy was just yellow."

"Orderly downstairs was saying Patton threatened to shoot the guy himself," Patrick added.

"You sure are up on the gossip, brother," Harkins said.

"Gossip is like air to GIs," Patrick said. "When they get bored, even when they're not bored, it's how they entertain themselves. They make shit up."

"So he slapped a guy," Harkins said to Adams. "So what?"

"I'm not sure that'll play well with Mom and Dad back home. Nobody likes a bully."

"Hell, I'll bet poor ol' First Sergeant Drake kicked ten asses a day," Harkins said. "It'll blow over."

"Poor Drake is right," Adams said.

"He got stuck with a helluva commander, that's for sure," Harkins said. "An all-around strange guy. Know what I learned when I looked at Boone's records? He isn't married."

"He had that picture of himself and some woman, right there on his desk," Adams said. "I saw it."

"He did have a picture, even told people it was his wife. But his personnel file said he was unmarried. His pay was sent to an orphanage in Des Moines."

"He was an orphan?" Patrick asked.

"Don't know," Harkins said.

"Well, whatever else he was, he was an odd duck," Adams said.

He stood, wobbled a bit. Harkins put his hand out, braced the lawyer's arm.

"You OK?" Harkins asked.

"Just a little light-headed, that's all."

"What did the docs say about your head?"

"They say Boone hit me twice." He lifted his hand, touched himself above his left ear. "Once here, then again on the crown, up here."

"We should tack on attempted murder," Harkins said. "You went down with the first shot. The second one, he was trying to do you in. Keep you quiet for good."

Adams thought about it a moment. "We might get that to stick. It's still not a complete packet of charges."

"Is it true that he confessed to another murder?" Patrick asked.

"Yeah," Harkins said. "Once he folded, he folded big time. Turns out he killed a nurse a few weeks ago. Used morphine but signed a chart said she choked on her own vomit."

"Good Lord," Patrick said. "Why?"

"She was pregnant with his baby, and seems like she knew he was sending stolen gold back to the States."

The three men were quiet for a moment.

"I'm not finished yet either," Harkins said. "I've got at least one more conversation."

"What's going to happen to Colianno?" Patrick asked.

Adams shook his head; Harkins told his brother what he could. Colonel Meigs—from whom Harkins had kept a few details—had interceded for the paratrooper.

"Right now he's scheduled to be on the same plane you're taking to North Africa," Harkins said. "Back to the regiment."

"You sound kind of tentative," Patrick said.

"We have a couple of things to tie up." Then, to Adams, "What about you, Counselor? What happens with you after your noggin clears?"

"Colonel Meigs is moving from Seventh Army to Ike's staff," Adams said. "Wants me to go with him."

"That's good, right?"

"Yeah. Meigs is old-fashioned, but he's all for a square deal. He's predictable that way."

"My brother thinks predictable is boring," Patrick said.

"I'd like you to consider coming with me as an investigator," Adams said to Harkins.

"After the way I screwed up this one?"

"I don't know. I'm not sure many people would have been able to find everything you did."

Harkins shook his head. "I don't see it."

"You told me you were bored breaking up traffic jams and whorehouse fights," Patrick said.

"That was before I realized how easy that stuff was compared to all the other shit that goes on."

"Take some time to think about it," Adams said.

"You going to see Kathleen again?" Patrick asked his brother.

"I'd like to," Harkins said. "They already jumped, someplace closer to the front."

"Maybe you can catch up with her when they reach Messina."

"As a special investigator for the provost you'd have a lot more leeway to roam around," Adams said. "Almost as much as a chaplain."

Patrick smiled. "Just out there saving souls," he said.

"Anyway," Adams continued. "You'd certainly be more likely to see her again than if you stayed with an MP platoon."

"You bribing me, Counselor?"

"Absolutely."

"Colianno said it was bad luck, thinking too much about what happens after the war," Harkins said. "Thinking about how fast we might get home."

"Shoot," Adams said. "If I didn't think about going home, it'd free up about eight hours a day of my time."

"You and Kathleen really made a connection, huh?" Patrick asked his brother.

"I'd like to think so, but everything happens so fast, you know, with the war and all. People get married after knowing each other a few weeks, that kind of stuff."

"People having sex the first time they lay eyes on each other," Patrick said, smiling.

"You knew about that?" Harkins asked.

"Brother, everybody knew about that. Besides, I'm not blind. You had little hearts shooting out of your eyes."

"Do I have to go to confession again?"

"Absolutely," Patrick said. "But listen, you've known her a long time. And just because a relationship develops fast doesn't mean it isn't real."

Adams chuckled.

"What's funny?" Harkins asked.

"No disrespect, Father," Adams said. "But I always thought it a little strange that Catholics get marriage advice from unmarried priests."

"Unmarried and presumably celibate," Harkins said.

Patrick held his hands up in mock surrender. "Let's not go there, shall we? Anyway, it's nice to think I might see you guys at the altar someday, back in our own church."

"This whole country is full of churches," Harkins said. "Why wait?"

"Does she know you're talking like this?" Adams asked.

"No. And let's not scare her off, either, or I'll clobber you on the other side of your bald head. Sir."

Adams sat back on his cot. "Did you talk to Ronan?" he asked.

"Five times in the last three days," Harkins said. "She's not budging off her story."

"OK," Adams said. "Think about coming to work with me."

Harkins shook his hand. "I will."

"And let me know if anything changes today."

Harkins and Patrick left the hospital, walking down wide stone steps. Off to their left they could see Palermo harbor, full of Allied ships. Engineers had cleared several of the long piers of the wreckage the Germans left behind. Two new cranes were picking cargo nets from ship holds, and another crane turned slowly, a jeep suspended from its sling. A GI sat in the driver's seat of the vehicle as it swung through its arc, sixty feet in the air.

"I'm glad I got to see so much of you," Harkins said to Patrick.

"I think it helped me," Patrick said. "You know, us being together when we learned about Michael."

"I'm a little afraid to slow down, to tell you the truth. Have time to think about it."

"I've had nightmares," Patrick said. "About drowning. I can never see who it is, but I know."

They reached the parking lot, where Patrick had a jeep and driver waiting to take him to the airfield. Harkins was back to driving himself.

"Can you find another driver on your own?" Patrick asked.

"Don't do me any favors."

They turned to face each other, the priest taller, black-haired, conspicuous in his paratrooper boots.

"Will the next operation for you be a jump, also?"

"That's how we arrive," Patrick said. "So, yeah, I imagine it will. Though Ike hasn't consulted me yet."

"And the family worries about me."

"They don't know half of the stunts you pulled just in the last week."

"You planning to tell them?" Harkins asked.

"Nobody's going to hear it from me," Patrick said. "Can I at least get you to agree to not take any unnecessary risks?"

"Probably not. But Adams wants me to work for him and Meigs, the oldest colonel in the army. That guy couldn't stay up much past eight o'clock on a school night, so I'll probably be safe."

Patrick's driver got out of the jeep and saluted as the officers approached.

"Listen, Eddie. I want you to know—I want you to hear it from me—that I'm doing something I love. I'm serving where I'm needed. If anything were to happen to me . . ."

"Stop right there," Harkins said. "You know I'm superstitious."

"OK, OK."

Harkins held out his hand. Patrick took it and pulled him into an embrace. The jeep driver looked at his shoes, embarrassed.

"I love you, Eddie."

"I love you, too, Pat."

Patrick stepped back, squeezed his brother's shoulders. When he let go, Harkins saluted.

"Safe travels, Captain," he said.

"God bless you, Eddie."

Patrick got into the passenger seat and nodded to the driver. As the jeep pulled away, the priest did not look back, but raised his hand goodbye.

Harkins picked up Colianno at the provost marshal's, where Harkins had installed him while he wrapped up the investigation. The paratrooper, eager to get back to his unit, stood outside, tapping his foot like a man waiting for a late train.

Harkins moved to the passenger seat when Colianno approached. He tossed a musette bag in the back, saluted, then climbed into the driver's seat. He wore a pistol belt with a canteen and a .45.

"So you're down to just a pistol," Harkins said.

"I figured my first sergeant wouldn't like it if I showed up with a bunch of weapons I'd stolen. I'm going to have enough to explain as it is."

They drove in silence, Harkins watching the city roll by as they headed north toward the airfield.

"How did you swing this?" Colianno asked. "Me going back to my unit."

"I told Colonel Meigs that you'd been a valuable part of the investigation. That I thought you deserved another chance. He talked to your commander, Ridgway. I guess they knew each other before the war.

"And I saw Patrick just a little while ago," Harkins said. "He said he stopped asking questions about that patrol on D-Day. He found six guys who were with you that day, but none would talk about what happened. So he stopped asking."

Colianno kept his eyes on the road. If he felt any relief, it wasn't obvious to Harkins.

Thirty minutes later they pulled into the gate of the airfield. Like every other point of entry at this end of the island, it was jammed with American vehicles and GIs. Off to one side was a vast field of supplies, crates stacked under tarps, pallets lined up dress-right-dress in columns and rows. Tons of food, spare parts, ammunition.

"Look at all that stuff," Colianno said. "I'll bet everybody back home who wants a job can get one in some factory."

"Yeah, and look at us learning all kinds of skills that'll be useful when we're civilians again."

"Watch out, Lieutenant. Remember what I said: bad luck to talk too much about getting home."

"Right. Pull over here," Harkins said as they approached the flight line. At least a dozen C-47s were either parked or maneuvering around the dirt field. Engineers had covered the area with perforated steel mats, but the flying dust was wicked.

"Wonder if any of these are the same planes, the same pilots who dropped us on D-Day," Colianno said.

"Why?"

"'Cause our pilot was going too fast, was too high, and dropped us miles from our drop zone. I'd love to have a chat with him about how he screwed us over."

Harkins was about to warn Colianno against looking for another fight, but it was probably a waste of time. Instead, he pulled a canvas satchel from the back of the jeep, reached in, and extracted a sheaf of typed pages. He pulled the top two free and handed them to Colianno.

"What's this?"

"The charge sheet. This is what I drew up with Captain Adams that will go up to the court-martial authority."

Harkins looked over Colianno's shoulder as he read. The top left of the page had a single name in capital letters: BOONE, WALTER (NMI), COLONEL, MEDICAL CORPS, AUS.

Colianno ran his finger down the densely typed right-hand column, which listed the charges against Boone. The ones that stood out were the murders of Oberstleutnant Matthias Lindner, Prisoner of War; Irwin M. Drake, First Sergeant, Eleventh Field Hospital; Second Lieutenant Marilyn Whitman, Eleventh Field Hospital.

"Whitman? That nurse that choked?"

"Boone confessed," Harkins said. "I told him that someone had done an autopsy, found out she didn't choke on her own vomit. I suggested that he used morphine—I didn't have any proof—because she knew about the gold."

"She was pregnant, right?"

Harkins nodded.

"And he was the father?" Colianno asked.

"He thought so, yeah."

"So he killed her and his own baby? What a piece of shit."

The paratrooper flipped the pages to the charge sheet, where there was no mention of Captain Meyers Stephenson. Colianno did not ask why.

He finished reading, then looked out at the flight line as an inbound C-47 touched down, bounced once, taxied to a stop near the medical holding tent.

"Boone didn't confess to Stephenson," Harkins said. "And I started to wonder why that might be. What's one more murder, right?"

Colianno kept his face forward.

"Here's what I think happened," Harkins said. "Stephenson saw Ronan running for the nurses' tent when the air-raid warning sounded. Since everyone else was headed for the shelters, he thought he'd catch her alone. He followed her."

Harkins tucked the charge sheets back inside the satchel, set it on his lap.

"But she knew he was behind her. She'd crossed paths with him on purpose; the air raid just got things moving faster. She went in the door of the tent, and Stephenson thought he had her cornered.

"But she slipped out that hole the nurses cut in the wall. He was probably surprised, certainly disappointed to find the nurses' tent empty. He followed her out the same way."

Harkins studied the paratrooper.

"And you were waiting for him."

Colianno watched the ballet of taxiing planes on the cramped flight line, his eyes squinting against the glare from the sea just beyond.

"She's been through too much already," he said.

"So what's that mean? You're offering to take the fall?"

Colianno pressed both hands against the steering wheel, then dropped them to his lap. "Every day, a hundred men—a hundred *good* men—die up on the line. Why do you care so much about a scumbag rapist who was working with a fucking Nazi spy, and only got what he deserved?"

Harkins didn't answer, let the silence hang for a long moment.

"Adams and I talked about this a long time, about you. And we don't think we could make the case."

Colianno looked at him, maybe searching for something like understanding, even forgiveness.

"But if I thought we could . . ."

Colianno seemed disappointed. Looked away.

"I'm a cop," Harkins said. "You want forgiveness, talk to Father Pat. That's his business."

"And me shooting Sergeant White?" Colianno said. "You were ready to let that go?"

"Yeah, not very consistent, I admit. But I can live with it."

They sat like that for several minutes. Harkins felt the sweat bleeding through the back of his blouse.

"You talked to Moira? Tried to get her to buy that story?"

"Sure did. Bunch of times in the last few days." Harkins twisted in his seat and put the satchel in the back of the jeep. "She wasn't going for it, either."

"What makes you think you've got it all figured out?"

Harkins pointed to the tent, a few dozen yards from where they sat, where he'd bullied Staff Sergeant Trunk.

"I told Trunk that Stephenson wound up in the cemetery because of the gold. And when we got back to the jeep you said something like, 'That was quite a story you told him.' But I didn't know it was a story. Could have been true, for all I knew at the time. But you knew it was just a story, because you knew what really happened. You and Ronan knew that his getting killed wasn't about gold."

"That's a theory, I guess," Colianno said.

Across the flight line, Harkins saw his brother emerge from a tent. "Looks like that's your flight back to North Africa. Right there, with my brother."

"That's it?" Colianno asked. "I just get on the plane?"

"Like I said, unless you want to tell me the story as you see it."

"Confess?"

"Yeah."

Colianno got out of the vehicle, pulled his bag from the rear seat. "I confessed to your brother."

"What?"

"I mean he heard my confession. He told me he'd never violate the sanctity of the confessional, unless it was to stop some future crime, something really serious."

"Like murder," Harkins said. Colianno shrugged.

Harkins got out of the jeep. The paratrooper pulled himself to attention, saluted. Harkins returned the salute, but did not offer his hand.

"I'm glad to be going back," Colianno said, nodding toward the waiting plane.

"To be with your boys?" Harkins asked.

"Yeah," Colianno said, unsmiling. "And they need killers, right?"

Harkins watched the paratrooper walk into the swirling dust toward the waiting plane, watched him salute Patrick, then join a detail of enlisted men loading packages. Patrick glanced over and saw his brother. Harkins saluted, then watched the priest climb up the aluminum ladder into the side door of the aircraft.

As he got behind the wheel of the jeep he thought about the last time he, Patrick, and Michael had been together, all of them on leave in the autumn of 1942. Not even a year ago. He wondered where he'd be a year from now, and what else the war might take from him, from his family, from his grieving parents.

He put the jeep in gear and rolled away from the airfield, passing a line of four ambulances headed in the opposite direction, their closed doors hiding who knew what horrors.

Ten days earlier he'd been complaining about boredom, about being a traffic cop in an army uniform. Over the past few days he'd brought one murderer to light and, just maybe, made the hospital a little bit better place for the nurses and the soldiers who worked there. Another killer, he was sure, had escaped justice, though there was no telling what the war had in store for Dominic Colianno.

He thought about Kathleen Donnelly, her tired eyes and blood-splattered uniform, her dazzling competence and the way her mouth tasted. In his waking hours he refused to think he might not see her again, but when he slept, when his defenses were down, there was a tightness in his chest—not fear, exactly, but a recognition of just how powerless he was, how subject they both were to things they could not control. But there were ways to make a minuscule contribution to—what? Order? The law? Some idea of what was right and what was still, even amid all the hatred and destruction, wrong?

Just outside the city he stopped to let another ambulance pass. He followed it to the hospital where he'd left Captain Adams. Together they would go see the provost and learn what might be in store for him.

HAPPINESS

by Carl Sandburg

I ASKED the professors who teach the meaning of life to tell me what is happiness.
And I went to famous executives who boss the work of thousands of men.
They all shook their heads and gave me a smile as though I was trying to fool with them
And then one Sunday afternoon I wandered out along the Desplaines river
And I saw a crowd of Hungarians under the trees with their women and children and a keg of beer and an accordion.

AUTHOR'S NOTE AND ACKNOWLEDGMENTS

An online search I did a few years ago led me to the manifest from a ship that reached Ellis Island in September 1905. There among the dense columns and handwritten names of newcomers I found a bit of elegant script announcing the arrival of an unmarried twenty-two-year-old Giovanna Colonna, whose odyssey had begun in the hilltop village of Ali in eastern Sicily.

I am intrigued by the scene, though I have no facts about her day. I wonder if she stood at the rail as the ship cruised by Lady Liberty, who'd been at her post in New York Harbor for a mere nineteen years. Did she know that Liberty was there to welcome her? What did she think as she entered the immigration center's great hall, with its Tower of Babel mix of languages? Maybe she'd found friends during the passage who spoke her Sicilian dialect. Maybe she prayed to get past the uniformed officials. Maybe she hid her own fears in order to inspire some other hopeful.

Whatever else she did that day, when the customs officer called my grandmother up to present her papers, she stepped forward, propelling her as-yet-unborn family into the New World. I and my American life are the product of her bravery.

Giovanna and her future husband, Domenick Benjamin Ruggero, left their homes and families at the dawn of the last century to find something new. I am in awe of their courage—and by extension, the courage of all migrants—for picking up and leaving everything familiar to make a better life for successive generations.

It is to pay homage to these people that the principal characters of this book are the children and grandchildren of immigrants, as were millions of young Americans of the World War II generation who fought and bled and in too many cases died to defeat Fascism. I created this story in the hopes of paying some small tribute to the sacrifices of those men and women.

Historical fiction is the intersection of things that actually happened with things the author has imagined. Here are some clues for readers interested in where I've drawn that line.

The men and women of the U.S. Army Medical Corps accomplished all the heroics the fictional characters in this book do, including surgery under fire and in terrible conditions. By 1943, the time period of this story, the army had made great improvements to the medical care of wounded and injured soldiers very near the front lines. A World War II GI had a much better chance of surviving even grievous wounds than did his doughboy counterpart of the Great War a generation earlier. Thanks to the hard work of all hands, that system continued to evolve through conflicts in Korea (with its advent of the helicopter as a means for evacuation), Vietnam, and the wars in the Middle East and Afghanistan.

I have taken some liberties with the organization and movements of the real-life Eleventh Field Hospital. The actual organization, parts of which landed on Sicily on D-Day, July 10, 1943, moved farther and faster than the fictional unit depicted here and was often split into its smaller elements to provide critical care close to the fighting. Speed of evacuation really did save lives, and medical personnel did find themselves under fire.

I was surprised at some of the actual events I discovered in my research. For instance, Eddie Harkins is shocked to hear about nurses going ashore with the initial waves in the 1942 invasion of North Africa, called Operation Torch. That sounded far-fetched to him, as it did to me. However, according to authors Evelyn M. Monahan and Rosemary Neidel-Greenlee (*And If I Perish: Frontline U.S. Army Nurses in World War II*), nurses and other personnel of the Forty-Eighth Surgical Hospital did follow the assault teams, and Eisenhower did have second thoughts about that decision. The character Kathleen Donnelly would have reached North Africa when the Eleventh Field Hospital landed in Oran, Algeria, in May 1943.

Although I imagined the scene in which the paratrooper Sergeant White murders a wounded and unarmed Italian prisoner, the fictional crime is, sadly, based on actual events. In separate incidents that both took place on July 14, 1943, two American soldiers, Sergeant Horace T. West and Captain John T. Compton, both of the U.S. Forty-Fifth Division, murdered (or, in Compton's case, ordered the murders of) at least seventy-three unarmed Italian and German prisoners of war near the Biscari airfield in Sicily. Both men were tried for homicide, and both men cited in their defense remarks made by Lieutenant General George Patton, commander of U.S. ground forces in the invasion. In their separate court-martials, the defendants claimed that Patton had specifically discouraged the taking of prisoners and that, furthermore, enemy soldiers who fired on GIs and then waited until the last possible moment to surrender should be killed. Witnesses at each trial corroborated that this was the message the troops took from Patton's remarks. Sergeant West was convicted and sentenced to life in prison, though his sentence was commuted in time for him to return to action near the end of the war. He eventually received an honorable discharge. Captain Compton was acquitted only to be killed in action in November 1943. Court-martial records remained classified until 1950. [*The Army Lawyer,* March 2013. "War Crimes in Sicily: Sergeant West, Captain Compton and the Murder of Prisoners of War in 1943," page 1.]

Among the things I made up: At one point in the story, Eddie Harkins and Dominic Colianno are concerned about a major German offensive and attempt to disrupt the Allied advance in Sicily. While there were no German counterattacks that threatened the Allies on a strategic level, Wehrmacht doctrine always called for local counterattacks, at least. GIs knew this and, once they took a position or drove German defenders back, they immediately braced for an assault. For individual soldiers under fire, the difference between a local attack and a strategic offensive isn't as important as the fact that the artillery is incoming.

German medical personnel did sometimes remain behind with the most severely wounded when the Wehrmacht retreated. U.S. Army regulations dictated that these doctors and medics care for German soldiers only. Captured surgeons, such as the fictitious Oberstleutnant Matthias Lindner, were prohibited from performing any kind of surgery, even on their German comrades. Of course, many American soldiers considered regulations of any kind to be mere suggestions.

During World War II, U.S. Army nurses really did have "relative rank," as Kathleen Donnelly complains to Eddie Harkins. Most nurses were second lieutenants, so they could direct medical orderlies (who were enlisted soldiers), but the women did not rate salutes and were paid only half of what male second lieutenants were paid.

Although fetal alcohol syndrome was not named in medical literature until 1973, antipathy toward heavy drinking by pregnant women predated Prohibition, and the warnings would have been familiar to medical professionals like Nurse Donnelly.

Chaplain Patrick Harkins tells his brother a story about a Texas-born paratrooper who used a ruse to capture a crossroads that was a critical objective for the paratroopers on D-Day. The real-life Captain Edwin Sayre of Breckenridge, Texas, who commanded A Company, 505th Regimental Combat Team, Eighty-Second Airborne Division, accomplished that mission in exactly the way Patrick Harkins describes. The comment about the prisoner being an "eloquent speaker" is from a 1947 report Sayre wrote while a student at the infantry school at Fort Benning. I had the pleasure of interviewing Ed Sayre and many of his comrades while writing the nonfiction *Combat Jump: The Young Men Who Led the Assault Into Fortress Europe, July 1943.*

The scene in which Eddie Harkins learns the fate of his younger brother is based on a real incident. My father, drafted near the end of World War II, was on occupation duty in Germany at Christmas 1945. Like Eddie Harkins, he was excited when an entire packet of letters from home caught up to him. He relished the prospect of reading them in private—a holiday celebration that would make him feel closer to loved ones. As he read a few of the letters from his siblings it became clear that something terrible had happened. Finally, he opened a letter that told him his mother had died at the end of November. I suspect that each of the sixty-plus Christmases he celebrated after that had a touch of the bittersweet.

Those are the most important junctures of fact and fiction. Now I'm left with what is all true.

I am grateful to the terrific writer Mary Roach for her detailed and sensitive description of urotrauma wounds in *Grunt: The Curious Science of Humans at War.*

Thanks to Matt Bialer of Sanford J. Greenburger Associates, who patiently worked with me through the ups and downs and years. And to Kristin Sevick of Forge, for taking a chance and setting out in a new direction.

I also appreciate the generous help of Colonel (Retired) Holly Olson,

M.D.; Chief Warrant Officer 3 (Retired) Paul Russell, PA; and retired forensic pathologist Ed McDonough, M.D., who loaned their time and expertise to this effort. Any errors in the medical sections or elsewhere in the book are my responsibility alone.

Finally, and most of all, thanks to Marcia for her love, unflagging support, encouragement, and faith in me.

For more about Carl Sandburg's poetry go to www.NPS.gov/Carl.